VINTAGE WORLDS
TALES OF THE OLD SOLAR SYSTEM

VINTAGE WORLDS

TALES OF THE OLD SOLAR SYSTEM

EDITED BY
JOHN MICHAEL GREER
AND
ZENDEXOR

Vintage Worlds: Tales of the Old Solar System
Copyright © 2018 John Michael Greer

All stories are copyrighted to their
respective authors, and used here with their permission.

Published by Founders House Publishing, LLC
Cover art by Matt Forsyth
Cover and interior design © 2018 Founders House Publishing, LLC

Paperback Edition: November 2018

**ISBN-13: 978-1-945810-23-7
ISBN-10: 1-945810-23-8**

This book is licensed for your personal enjoyment only. All rights reserved. This is a work of fiction. All characters and events portrayed in this book are fictional, and any semblance to real people or incidents is purely coincidental. This book, or parts thereof, may not be reproduced in any form without permission.

**For more information please visit
www.foundershousepublishing.com**

Published in the United States of America

CONTENTS

Foreword ix
by John Michael Greer

Introduction xv
by Zendexor

PART 1: MAKING IT REAL
...validating the Old Solar System:

Out of the Chattering Planet 3
by John Michael Greer

Uranian Thule 25
by Robert Gibson

PART 2: TAKING ADVANTAGE
...frolicking/rampaging/tripping through the Old Solar System:

Incandescence 67
by Dylan T. Jeninga

The Headless Skeletons of Mercury 75
by Troy Jones III

The Lost Cosmonaut and Saucer Six 93
by Clint Spivey

The Martian Girl 139
by Christopher Henningsen

Tête-à-Tête 149
by David England

The Answer At the End of the World 161
by Arthur Vibert

Pen Pal 185
by Grant Canterbury

Perchance To Dream 221
by Peter C. Aitken

Arden Archer 243
by Damian Macrae

Methane Blue 269
by Rachel Cowan

Europa Or Bust! 283
by Shep Barnett

The Lure of the Depths 293
by Violet Bertelsen

The Dorian Grays 305
by Augustus Keden

PART 3: ZOOMING OUT
...relating to the galaxy and other dimensions

The Solar System, The Universe and Everything 347
by Al Sevcik

Death Songs of Saturn 377
by Joel B. Jones

VINTAGE WORLDS
TALES OF THE OLD SOLAR SYSTEM

FOREWORD

John Michael Greer

There was a time when the solar system was much more interesting than it is today—when swordsmen dueled along the banks of the Grand Canal beneath the hurtling moons of Mars; when strange creatures writhed in the shadows of the mighty jungles of Venus; when Mercury's Twilight Belt marked a thin band of habitable territory between the lethal heat of the sunward side and the eternal cold of the side that faced the stars; when the many moons of the Jovian and Saturnian systems, the great gas-giant worlds themselves, the tiny frozen sphere of Pluto, and even the myriad worldlets of the asteroid belt, were all crammed with living things, some of them intelligent, some of them dangerous, all of them wonderful.

Call it fiction if you will, but when Earthlings turned their eyes up past the edges of our own planet's atmosphere, those were the dreams they dreamed and the worlds they longed to visit. Professional scientists watched the color changes that seemed to mark the Martian seasons and speculated learnedly about life elsewhere in the solar system. With that as justification, the writers of science fiction's golden age flung their imaginations skyward and filled the pages of scores of lively magazines with tales of adventure on nearby worlds and the spaceways that linked them.

One of the many things that made the resulting fiction memorable was the way that each of the solar system's imagined worlds had a character all its own. The Mars of classic science fiction was ancient, dry, and desolate, scattered with the ruins of civilizations that rose and fell before humanity climbed down from the trees, a place where the clash of swords blended with the sinister hum of forgotten technologies. Venus, by contrast, was a lush jungle world, younger and more vibrantly alive than Earth. Mercury was defined by the stark polarity between its two sides, one turned forever (as scientists then thought) toward the blazing sun, the other forever facing the cold depths of outer space. Go further out from the Sun, and though the characteristic flavors of each world were not always so strongly marked, it's rare to find a story that lacks some sense of the work of previous authors or some insight into where further fictional explorations of the same world would someday go.

The phenomenon of the shared fictional universe has received a certain amount of attention from writers on literature in recent decades. The Cthulhu Mythos created by H.P. Lovecraft, Clark Ashton Smith, Robert E. Howard, and a pleiad of other authors is perhaps the most widely known example: a literary edifice bound together by common themes, and also by shared stage properties—dread devil-gods such as tentacled Cthulhu and toadlike Tsathoggua, blasphemous tomes such as the *Necronomicon* and the *Book of Eibon*, and more. Lovecraft started the Mythos as a setting for his own tales of fantastic horror, but welcomed contributions from others, and as a result the Cthulhu Mythos is alive and well today, and inspiring a new generation of authors to write their own eldritch tales.

As far as I know, however, it has not yet been recognized that what we may as well call the Old Solar System—the solar system as it was imagined in the golden age of science fiction—was also a shared fictional universe, and in fact is the grandest and most richly embroidered shared fictional universe of them all. For more than six decades, thousands of authors contributed to it, and a good half or more of the masterworks of science fiction drew inspiration from it, and fed into it in their turn.

Was it all set in a universe that doesn't exist? Of course. So is the Cthulhu Mythos. (Certainly I know of no reason to think that the authors who are busy writing new tales in the Mythos actually believe that the drowned corpse-city of R'lyeh will someday rise from the bottom of the South Pacific and release Cthulhu from his aeonian sleep!) I'm not sure why it's so shocking to point out that science fiction is, ahem, fiction, and that even if humanity does end up making the leap into space, our notions of a spacefaring future will probably have less in common with the reality than all those breathless portrayals of the year 2000 in the magazines and newspapers of 1900 had to the reality we witnessed just short of two decades ago. The most splendid shared fictional universe in the history of literature needn't be ruled off limits forever, just because a bunch of officious space probes reminded us that it was, in fact, a shared *fictional* universe.

That realization, in turn, is what has inspired this anthology.

* * *

I grew up during the last hurrah of the Old Solar System, reading science fiction set on Mars and Venus at the same time that space probes were showing us all that Mars and Venus weren't anything like the way they had been imagined. By my late teens my taste in reading had shifted in other directions, guided first by the twin stars of J.R.R. Tolkien and Hermann Hesse, and then by a range of intellectual commitments that took me far from imaginative fiction altogether.

It was in 2006 that I began to find my way back to science fiction, as a way to make sense of the difficult future bearing down on us. Out of those explorations came my novel *Star's Reach* (2014) and four anthologies under the collective title *After Oil*, which showcased what I call deindustrial SF—that is, science fiction set in the kind of future we're most likely to get at this point, in which the dream of perpetual progress slams face first into the hard limits of resource depletion and a damaged biosphere, and sends humanity tumbling back along the familiar arc of the decline and fall of civilizations.

It was in 2015, I think, that I first happened across Solar System Heritage (www.solarsystemheritage.com), the Old Solar System website hosted by my coeditor Zendexor. My first reaction was a kind of nostalgic amusement, but that gave way to more nuanced reflections as I pondered the case he made for the Old Solar System as a literary phenomenon that deserves respect in its own right. Those musings sent me back to some of the authors I'd loved best in my insufficiently misspent youth, but a little exploration also alerted me to the fact that the Old Solar System isn't completely untenanted even now.

Two anthologies edited by George R.R. Martin and Gardner Dozois, *Old Mars* (2013) and *Old Venus* (2015), have already showcased some of what today's authors are doing with the Old Solar System, and Solar System Heritage has also hosted original fiction by several of the authors whose work appears in this anthology. Since editing anthologies is familiar territory to me, the thought of an Old Solar System anthology came readily to mind; I suggested it to Zendexor, who responded with enthusiasm. We published a call for stories on both our websites, and the results are in your hands as you read this.

The stories we received cover nearly the whole expanse of the solar system, and embrace an equal diversity of styles and approaches. Some of the tales you are about to read could have been lifted from the pages of *Astounding*, *Planet Stories*, or any of the other pulp magazines that published most of the science fiction of the golden age. Others use different literary frames; our collection includes one story told in the epistolary style of the first English novels, one written in the stream-of-consciousness style made famous by the Beats, and one that takes the form of a fable. All of them, to shift metaphors, dip variously shaped ladles into the bubbling cauldron of the Old Solar System and season the resulting broth to their taste. I hope you enjoy the flavor of the banquet that results.

—John Michael Greer, May 2018

INTRODUCTION

Zendexor

This collection of tales celebrates the literary re-birth of the Old Solar System, that richly imagined adventure-playground of habitable worlds "disproved" by spoil-sport space-probes from the 1960s onwards, after which the System was a much duller place.

If you're the sort of reader who has endured too many decades without colourful Solar System pulp sf on the newsstands, if you're the sort of reader who would go into transports of delirious joy at the sight of titles such as "The Headless Skeletons of Mercury" or "Death Songs of Saturn", then this is your lucky day: one glance at the contents page will reveal that you have picked up the right book.

Nostalgic fun… sure. But *Vintage Worlds* could not achieve that effect successfully without some depth of philosophic implication. For when any so-called "counter-factual" literature achieves a measure of artistic success, it thus blasts the reductionist view that sees the growth of myth and legend as some kind of unwanted encrustation like barnacles or weeds which ought to be scraped off the surface of Truth.

Doubtless, in their own eyes, the reductionists are merely good scientists or good historians, doing their job. For instance: we now know that Mercury rotates—so forget about the Twilight Belt, and don't write about it any more. Even though it was one of the most fascinating fictional places in the System, it has been disproved, so don't write about it any more.

Let's call this the Truncator mind-set.

You find Truncators lurking in all directions; the criticism of retro sf is just one of them. Some while back I found the following statement in a history of the Wild West: "Wyatt Earp was never marshal of anywhere." And that's that—so much for the Earp legend. Fair enough, except... don't the "debunkers" and "realists" understand that there's more to Wyatt Earp than Wyatt Earp? Or to put it another way, the actual life of a legendary figure is merely one stage of his reality.

In fact in some cases the legendary person doesn't need to have existed at all. Maybe in the actual Middle Ages there never was a real Robin Hood. But that's only the first time round. In the retrospective Middle Ages, *there has been one now*. You'll meet more of this style of thought in "Uranian Thule", where legend wins decisively once and for all.

The problem with reductionism—or Truncation—is that it pretends that facts are all that matter. Facts are certainly at the root of reality. But out of such roots spring many-branched trees of legend and imagination, quite as real as fact, reaching far higher, and giving point to it all. You can see, from this view, how misguided Truncators are: they would chop down the actual trees because they only see value in the roots.

Getting back for a moment to the non-marshal of Tombstone: to a Truncator, the "real Wyatt Earp" is nothing more thanthe summation of what he did between the dates of his birth and death. Anything extra is "mere" legend, unwanted excrescences to be sawn off before we can get at the truth.

But to us more enlightened folk, the "real Wyatt Earp" had an additional side to him: namely, he was the kind of person around whom legends grow, which is why they did grow—he carried that seed-of-embellishment within him.

Similarly—and switching back to sf—the planet Mars is more than the sterile place which the space-probes show us. It has an inherent power of attracting dreamers and inspiring hopes. Those dreams and hopes would not save you from asphyxiation if you stepped out naked on the Martian surface, but they are enough to cause great stories to be written, and doesn't that qualify the Red Planet for some credit? The place isn't a lot of use for anything else.

So let's admit once and for all that roots—facts—are just the beginning, while legend is the fulfilment of history. Legend is what history is for. Bring the argument full circle: adjust the metaphor: and we can conclude, *fact is merely the larval stage of legend.*

You may ask, is this a leg-pull? No, the more I think of it, the more I'm quite serious. In fact, once legend has done its work, it's too late to undo it. In the case of the OSS, it's too late to debunk the literary characters of our neighbouring worlds. And in the case of Wyatt Earp, it's too late to insist that the Gunfight at the OK Corral be more accurately renamed the Gunfight outside the C S Fly Photographic Studio. The achievements of authors' imaginations have proved too powerful. Hence the popularity of the website, www.solarsystemheritage.com, and the appearance of this book.

"Ah but," some will say, "the flaming sword of Experience bars the way back to your innocent paradise. Wells' *The First Men in the Moon* and Lewis' *Perelandra* are great books, but if such tales were written nowadays, they would only be artificial, exercises in pastiche, sounding a false note."

This, in my view, is plain wrong. I call it the Chronist Fallacy. Critics are risking absurdity when they allege that stories which were powerful in their own time would lose their power with a different publication date on the flyleaf. You should judge a book by its text rather than by its date. Try the following thought-experiment: you enjoy a book with its title page missing; the story is set on a Mars with a breathable atmosphere, you think it's great, and you assume it's all right because it was written when people didn't know any better. Then—you find a copy with the date on it. Damn! It's modern! Anachronism; pastiche; throw it in the bin...

Allow me to emphasize again that it's too late to pretend that a story doesn't work, when it obviously does; or that it's a mere clever pastiche, when it's obviously something more.

For we are the lucky inheritors of a build-up of planetary personalities, the characters of worlds accumulated over millennia from ancient mythic gods, medieval astrology, early telescopic observation and speculation, fictional imaginings, and all the fruitful overlaps between these successive influences. (Consider for example the resonance between Neptune the sea god and the watery Neptune of "The Lure of the Depths"...)

Furthermore, who knows, it may be, or become, realer than we think. The two tales in Part 1 of this anthology suggest that one day "reality engineering" will become a real discipline, to bring what should be into line with what is, as in "Uranian Thule"; or alternatively, as in "Out of the Chattering Planet", we may find that our space probes' dismal findings were utterly deceptive after all. These stories give you the good old shivery sensation of conceptual-breakthrough sf; a wild surmise, a new view of reality.

But my guess is that most readers of this volume have picked it up with a desire for pure adventure, set against backgrounds in which the Old Solar System with all its colour and fascination is taken for granted as real – and that indeed is what you get in Part 2, with a spill-over into more cosmic contexts in Part 3. You'll find an immense variety of settings, ranged in a spectrum of verisimilitude, from the deeply fantastic Neptune story mentioned before, to "Incandescence" set on the Sun where we meet an energy life-form so far outside the range of our knowledge that no physicist could deny its possibility! And with all this freedom to hand, in most cases the contributors to this volume are happy just to move around in the OSS rather than to give reasons why it might be true. They can frolic in this way because our wondrous heritage is self-justifying. Ancient Mars with its canals, lush jungly Venus, Twilight Belt Mercury, volcanic Jupiter, habitable asteroids and moons: all are securely embedded in the literary tradition. No space-probe can invalidate this genre now that it has taken on a life of its own in our minds.

After all, our minds are just as real as anything else. In fact they're the realest things we know. *Cogito ergo sum.*

Therefore, the New Old Solar System is here to stay!

—Zendexor, April 2018

Coverage, world by world:

The Sun: *Incandescence*
Vulcan: *Tête-à-Tête*
Mercury: *The Headless Skeletons of Mercury; Methane Blue*
Venus: *The Lost Cosmonaut and Saucer Six; The Martian Girl*
Earth: *Out of the Chattering Planet; Pen Pal; The Dorian Grays*
The Moon: *Tête-à-Tête*
Mars: *Out of the Chattering Planet; The Answer At the End of the World; Perchance to Dream; The Solar System, The Universe and Everything*
The Asteroids: *Arden Archer*
The Jovian system: *Methane Blue; Europa Or Bust*
The Saturn system: *Death Songs of Saturn*
Uranus: *Uranian Thule*
Neptune: *The Lure of the Depths*
Pluto: *The Dorian Grays*

PART 1: MAKING IT REAL

...VALIDATING THE OLD SOLAR SYSTEM:

Born in the brawling Navy town of Bremerton, Washington, and raised in an assortment of Seattle suburbs, John Michael Greer began writing stories as soon as he could hold a pencil. The author of more than fifty books on a dizzying assortment of subjects and of a widely read weekly blog at www.ecosophia.net, he has previously edited five anthologies of original science fiction stories for Founders House Publishing. His published fiction credits include the science fiction novels The Fires of Shalsha *and* Star's Reach; Twilight's Last Gleaming, *a near-future political thriller;* Retrotopia, *a utopian romance; and the first two volumes of a seven-volume epic fantasy with tentacles,* The Weird of Hali: Innsmouth *and* The Weird of Hali: Kingsport. *He lives with his wife Sara in Rhode Island.*

More than once in the past, science has jumped to conclusions on the basis of inadequate or misleading evidence. In "Out of the Chattering Planet," Greer presents a classic what-if science fiction tale, exploring the possibility that our knowledge of the solar system may be much less accurate than we dream...

OUT OF THE CHATTERING PLANET

John Michael Greer

THE FOLDER LAY flat under the lowest drawer of the desk, and Tegwyn Jones would never have found it if she hadn't given the stuck bottom drawer so hard and sudden a yank. As it was, the drawer lurched right out of the desk, and Tegwyn fell. Instinct took over; she landed on her side, striking the Persian carpet with one hand as though it was a mat in the old judo dojo downtown. In the instant after she hit the carpet, she spotted the yellowed folder, just visible in the shadowy recesses of the desk.

All around her, the bric-a-brac of Great-Uncle Meredith's study caught pallid light from the windows. A thin layer of dust spread over everything, for the old man had been gone six months and no one but the attorney had been by. It was all painfully familiar. Four tall filing cabinets, each drawer marked with a typed paper label in the frame above the handle, flanked two tall bookshelves full of hardbacks from scholarly presses. A rack of fencing foils and sabers hung on the wall, for the old man had been a great aficionado of the sword, one of many interests they shared. The great wooden desk with its serried ranks of drawers was freighted with memories, but the folder she glimpsed wasn't one of them. It sat in the shadows, an unexpected guest in the room.

Tegwyn rolled to a kneeling position, reached in and extracted the folder. A cryptic notation on the tab in her great-uncle's unruly handwriting read Em. 223 1947 & 1953 comp. Inside were stiff old-fashioned photographic prints, eight inches by ten, each in its own numbered paper sleeve, and a few sheets of onionskin typing paper with faded gray lettering on it from a manual typewriter. Curious, she pulled the first of the prints out of its sleeve.

It looked like a black and white photo of the planet Mars, taken through a telescope. The disk tipped with white at top and bottom was unmistakable. The one difficulty was the clarity of the image. Tegwyn had seen plenty of photos of Mars taken from Earth, most of them in that same house—Great-Uncle Meredith had a great collection of books on nature, science, and history in the library downstairs, where Tegwyn had spent the most bearable hours of an unhappy childhood—and all of them showed, at most, vague light and dark blurs. The photo in her hands was still blurred, but much less so; sharp gradations between paler and darker regions stood out clearly, and so did straight dark lines she didn't recognize at all, running from the polar ice caps to the dark areas or between one dark area and another. Something about the lines stirred a faint trace of memory, but whatever it was would not surface.

Intriguing as it was, she had work to do. She stood up, returned the photo to its sleeve, set it on the desk, and started sorting through the files in the bottom drawer.

THE EMAIL HAD reached her when she'd gotten back to Gao, after months in the dusty little camp deep in the Sahara in the southern reaches of the Tanezrouft. Drowned in the ocean off Virginia Beach, it said, and that made no sense at all: the old man had friends at Virginia Beach and vacationed there now and again, but he'd always hated swimming, and avoided watercraft of any kind since he'd left the troopship that brought him home from the Korean War.

The three days she'd had to cool her heels in Gao, though, had been long enough for her to send an email back and get the response, and find Great-Uncle Meredith's obituary on the website of the local paper back home. That settled the matter. She'd been looking for a reason to leave anyway, between the ugly academic politics that surrounded the project and the CIA's all too blatant involvement in it, and minutes after the Land Rover got her back from Gao to the camp she was in Dr. Edelbrock's tent giving him her resignation.

It took another month, though, for a replacement to fly out and get up to speed on the various parts of the dig, the chores that had to be done, the ongoing and always delicate negotiations with the proud Tuareg tribespeople whose permission had to be gained for each expansion of the archeological site. Then a truck packed with people and goats took her south across the border to Niamey, a rattletrap plane that had seen many better decades flew her from there to Lagos, two less uncertain flights landed her in Pittsburgh. All the while, questions she couldn't answer circled in her head, and the blaring televisions and constant chatter on all sides set her nerves on edge after the vast silences of the desert.

In Pittsburgh she'd rented a car and headed east, following the old state highway through the rumpled green Alleghenies into the mining country of her childhood, past one dilapidated little town after another, until Welsh place names started to pop up on the signs: Llantwit Road, Aberdare Road, Pontypool Baptist Church, relics of the mining families who'd fled poverty in their native mountains to find it waiting patiently for their arrival on the far side of the Atlantic. Then, sudden enough that it made her grip the wheel hard, the oh-so-familiar curve between two ragged hills dotted with oaks, and beyond it the gray huddled roofs of Carmarthen, Pennsylvania.

Memories boiled up as she drove down Center Street and turned up North Mountain Road, past the old judo dojo where she'd earned her black belt while still in high school, past the grim brick mass of the high school itself, and then up the slope past a once-prosperous neighborhood where every third house was abandoned and every third corner had an off-brand church on it. The houses gave way to overgrown farms, the farms to ragged oaks, and then the road curved one way and a gravel driveway curved the other, up through a dozen acres of overgrown woodlot to Great-Uncle Meredith's sprawling gambrel-roofed farmhouse.

His blue Buick was gone. The stray cats that always lurked around the door, waiting for the old man to put out a pie plate of kibble and address each of them with some improbably ornate name, were gone too, and the light he always kept burning above the door had gone black. That was when it sank in that the old man really was dead, and she sat there in the rental car for a long moment, fists clenched, eyes shut, until she'd regained enough composure to get out of the car, pull the spare key out of her purse, cross the gravel driveway to the silent door.

She knew where he kept his will, and though she didn't know the number of his attorney in Carmarthen, she knew the name and found the other details quickly enough in the phone book he kept in the kitchen next to the Old Farmer's Almanac. The phone call, the drive down to the attorney's office to sign papers, a trip to the mini-mart that was the only grocery in town now that a Saturday-only flea market occupied the hulk of the the grand old XL-Ephant Foods on Mona Street: all those kept her mind full of things that didn't matter, gave her something to do besides think about the hole the old man's death had torn in her life.

When those ran out, the desk drawers offered a welcome distraction. The will gave the house and most of his money to Tegwyn, but there were bequests to local charities, family records and photos that had to go to her younger cousins in

Johnstown, papers to forward to scholarly colleagues or the midwestern university where he'd taught for twenty years. That was what sent her to the stuck bottom drawer, and to the strange photos of a Mars with dark lines on it, lines she was sure she'd seen somewhere before.

SHE WAS IN the kitchen, getting a saucepan of mac and cheese going for dinner and trying not to think about all those other dinners she'd had in the same place, when the memory finally surfaced. Once the macaroni was cooking, she headed for the library, knelt, and pulled a big book out of its place next to three other children's books on astronomy.

It took three tries to find the right page, but there it was: a Chesley Bonestell painting of Mars, dating from the nineteen-fifties. Across the pale rust-red of the planet's surface, a spiderweb of dark green lines spread down from the poles. The next page had another Bonestell painting of a long straight watercourse stretching into the distance, dark green vegetation stretching a short distance out from it to both sides, rust-colored desert beyond that.

The canals of Mars. Tegwyn closed the book, got up, carried it back with her into the kitchen, leafed through it meditatively as the macaroni sputtered on the big white-enameled stove and the kitchen clock sounded its familiar tick-clunk, tick-clunk on the far wall. She'd read the book often enough in childhood that it all came back to her promptly: how Schiaparelli thought he'd seen canali, "channels," on the Martian surface; how newspapers in England and America turned that word into "canals;" how dreams of life on a nearby world clustered around that mistranslation, populating the deserts of a dying Mars with an ancient, wise, fading race whose last great engineering project brought water down from the polar ice caps to keep a fingernail grip on survival—and how space probes beginning in the 1960s had shattered the whole gorgeous dream and left the solar system lessened by its absence.

The sudden chime of the stove timer roused her from her reverie, and she set the book aside and busied herself with the mac and cheese. After dinner, though, she climbed the stair to the old man's study again, sat at the desk, and looked at the photos she'd found, one at a time.

There were eighteen of them in all, big old-fashioned glossy prints that looked as though they'd been developed by hand. Eleven of them showed the dark lines stretching across the planet, for all the world like the Bonestell painting; the others showed the same world, but with no dark lines. She frowned, then picked up the onionskin paper. One of the two sheets had a complicated chemical recipe involving half a dozen unusual metallic salts. The other had the following words on it in Great-Uncle Meredith's familiar scrawl:

Photos taken with Leica large format camera through 12-inch Newtonian telescope using high speed emulsion 223. Photos 1-4 taken March 11th, 1947; photos 5-11 taken November 9th, 1947; photos 12-18 taken December 29th, 1953. All three nights were very clear, and the emulsion was identical and worked well on other subjects. Why the difference? Tegwyn set two of the pictures side by side, considered them. The dark areas and the ice caps were equally clear, but the lines were present in one and absent in the other. After a few moments she shrugged, pushed the chair back and got up. The long day weighed on her, and the spare bedroom still needed dusting and fresh linens before she could sleep.

She woke up with a sudden cry. The dream had been painfully vivid: Great-Uncle Meredith was perched on the desk chair in his study, where he'd sat so many times to read her stories in her childhood, where he'd sat so many times again to talk her through her hurt the summer after her parents got divorced. He'd leaned forward as he always did, the desk lamp gleaming off his round glasses, as though he wanted to tell her something, and in the dream she'd known it was something she needed to hear.

Waking, the cold gray emptiness of the room confronted her. Tears pooled in her eyes; she fought her way back to composure, hauled herself out of bed.

She showered and dressed, fried eggs in a cast iron skillet easily three times as old as she was, picked at breakfast while trying to figure out her next step. The courts were overloaded with bankruptcies and drug cases, the attorney had warned her, so it would be months before the estate was settled.

Lacking anything else to do, she returned to his study and started sorting through the contents of the file cabinets, looking for the family records and scholarly papers mentioned in the will. It took nearly the whole day to find them, and in the process she found something else: a drawer full of documents and photographs from Great-Uncle Meredith's teen years, chronicling a youthful fascination with amateur astronomy she'd never known about. A clipping from the Carmarthen Chronicle showed a teenage Meredith with black horn-rimmed glasses and jug ears. He was standing next to a telescope taller than he was, with a boxy camera mounted on one side to take pictures of the stars and planets. Further back in the same drawer she found folder after folder of brilliantly clear pictures—Saturn with its rings, Jupiter's red spot like a bruise, the Andromeda galaxy, much more. Further back still were pages and pages of chemical formulae, receipts for chemical purchases from Price-Hughes Photo Supply down in Carmarthen, and torn-out copies of old Popular Mechanics articles on astronomical photography.

Curious, she read one of the articles, glanced through several others. The main problem astronomers faced in those days, she gathered, was that photographic emulsions were much less sensitive than the human eye, and observers spotted any number of features no film could record fast enough to keep the air's turbulence from turning them into meaningless blurs. Meredith had marked phrase after phrase in one article, ending with a sentence full of underlining:

The great limiting factor in astronomy today is the sensitivity of existing emulsions to faint light.

Tegwyn began nodding after a moment. The Meredith she'd known would have seen that as a challenge that begged to be taken up. As she paged further through the files, that guess turned out to be spot on; he'd plunged into experimentation, looking for a photographic emulsion that could catch images as quickly as the human eye, or more quickly still. Page after page of notes chronicled his failures and frustrations—and then there was emulsion #223.

He'd tried it in desperation, mixing together a dog's breakfast of photosensitive salts, and only discovered its astonishing properties by accident. It was so unstable that he had to keep the plates on dry ice until the moment they went into the camera, and even then half of them turned out spoiled, but some quirk of chemistry gave the plates that didn't spoil unparalleled sensitivity to light. Night after clear night he'd gone up the back side of Stroud Mountain, where the slopes blocked Carmarthen's lights and rose high above the coal smoke, and snapped image after astonishingly clear image; he'd written letters to Eastman Kodak and half a dozen astronomical observatories, trying to interest them in his discovery; and then the Korean War broke out and his draft number came up, and telescope, camera, and test tubes sat in the basement for four long years while he carried a rifle up and down the Korean peninsula and tried to stay alive.

It took Tegwyn most of an hour to find out what happened after that, because the relevant letters had been tucked into a different drawer: three of them, one from Eastman Kodak and two from observatories, expressing polite disinterest. Meredith had taken a few photos after that, but when his GI Bill benefits took him to the University of Pennsylvania he'd gone into historical linguistics instead of chemistry or astronomy, and that was that.

Except for the photos he'd taken before the war, that is: the photos that Tegwyn laid on the desk, that showed, however impossibly, canals spread across the face of Mars. Oddly, though his notes suggested that he'd taken more than two hundred photos of Mars using Emulsion 223, the only prints she could find were the ones that had slipped under the drawer.

LATE THAT AFTERNOON she got a phone call from the attorney in town, made an appointment to sign papers the next morning, tried to make herself go back up to the study and continue sorting papers, and failed. For a while she sat on the big green sofa in the living room staring at nothing, listening to rain pattering against the windows and feeling empty and lost. When that became unbearable, she dragged herself off the couch and headed into the library.

Maybe it was the photos, maybe not, but she wandered over to the shelves where the old man had his collection of classic science fiction: reams of it, all those bright romantic dreams of adventure in a solar system much less bleak than the one humanity turned out to inhabit. Words on the spine of a novel by C.S. Lewis made her smile, remembering one of her great-uncle's jokes. "Out of the Silent Planet my Aunt Fanny," he'd say now and then, when they'd had to put up with the nonstop babbling of some visiting relative or the squalling of a radio in the next car over at a traffic light. "It should have been called Out of the Chattering Planet." She finally pulled down a Leigh Brackett novel with a gaudy cover, curled up in the armchair where she'd read it the first time all those years before, and fled into the story for refuge.

She was most of the way through a rousing tale of derring-do along the canals of Mars when a sudden thought made her stop, set the book down for a moment, and stare at nothing in particular for a while. The Martian deserts of the story had reminded her all too forcefully of the real deserts of the Tanezrouft—or was it the other way around? All at once it occurred to her that when she got her black belt in judo and followed it up with fencing lessons at college, when she clawed her way through the academic jungle to a Ph.D. in archeology, when she cut her teeth excavating Hohokam ruins in Arizona and then headed to the first of three digs in the southern reaches of the Sahara, she'd been looking for Mars—not the bleak planetscapes revealed by the space probes, but Mars as Leigh Brackett, Edgar Rice Burroughs, and a hundred other authors had imagined it.

She tried to drag her attention back to the novel, but the glory had gone out of it. All she could think of was an image some lander from Earth had beamed back, a rock-strewn desert that looked like nothing so much as an unusually dull corner of northern Nevada. After a while, she closed the book, turned to go.

That was when she noticed the sword. It was resting atop one of the bookshelves, as though set there to be found. Puzzled, she went over and picked it up. Great-Uncle Meredith had owned a dozen actual swords alongside the foils and sabers he'd used to fence with, but this wasn't one she recognized, nor was it of a type she'd ever seen before.

The blade ran straight for most of its length and then widened slightly and curved to a lethal point; the hilt was oddly shaped, with spidery bars splayed out to protect the hand. She tried a few cuts and thrusts with it, found it light and wickedly fast. Her great-uncle would have adored such a thing, she knew—but why had he never written to her about it?

AN HOUR AT the attorney's office the next morning listening to endless legal babble left Tegwyn bored and irritable, and it didn't help that while she was there, two cars plowed into each other headfirst on North Mountain and forced her to go back to Great-Uncle Meredith's house the long way around. On the way, though, she spotted a sign above a little storefront: PRICE-HUGHES PHOTO SUPPLY. For an instant she wondered why the name seemed familiar, then remembered the receipts she'd found in the old man's files. An instant later she nosed the rental car into the parking lot. It seemed utterly improbable that anyone there would remember a man named Meredith Jones, much less recall the experiments he'd made so many decades before, but it was that or go straight back to the old house with its burden of memories.

Inside the shop, a bent old man with flyaway white hair looked up from a computer screen and came up to the counter. "Can I help you?"

"I'm honestly not sure," said Tegwyn, and introduced herself. The man gave her a little smile and said, "Welcome back to Carmarthen. I'm sure you don't know me from Adam's off ox, but I knew your great-uncle; I'm Elwood Price, in case he ever mentioned me. Damn shame that he's gone. Let's see, didn't he say you were doing something somewhere in Africa?"

"In the Sahara Desert," said Tegwyn.

"No kidding. Me, I wouldn't go there for anything. Summers here are bad enough. But yeah, Merry and me, we met when we were back in high school. Back then he and a couple of his friends were always coming over to the old store on Merritt Street to talk to my granddad about photography. You ever see any of the pictures he took with his telescope?"

"Actually, yes," Tegwyn admitted. "I found some photos of Mars he made when he was still in high school."

"Pretty good, huh?" He went on without giving her a chance to answer, reminiscing about the high school photography club they'd both joined, the girls they'd dated, the way they'd drunk each other under the table to celebrate getting home alive from Korea and the far more sedate celebration they'd had when Meredith moved back to Carmarthen after his retirement. Tegwyn managed to slip in questions at intervals, enough of them to make sure that Elwood Price didn't know anything about Emulsion #223 or dark lines crossing the face of Mars.

When she finally extracted herself from the shop, she

climbed into the rental car and managed a wan little laugh as she drove away. Out of the Chattering Planet, she thought.

After the lawyer's office and the photo supply shop, the big gambrel-roofed house off North Mountain Road seemed blessedly quiet. Tegwyn got settled in the library, with the same Leigh Brackett novel in her lap, but just then the phone rang in the kitchen. She threw an unsanitary look toward it, but got up, left the library, picked up on the third ring. "Hello?"

"I'd like to speak to Tegwyn Jones, if I may," said the voice on the other end: a man's voice, elderly and precise, with a hint of an accent Tegwyn couldn't place.

"That's me," she answered.

"Delightful. My name is Hythloday—Gabriel Hythloday—and I was a friend of poor Meredith. Could you spare a few minutes? I'm sure you're very busy."

"Go ahead," said Tegwyn. "I'm curious where you got my name."

"Meredith talked about you quite often, of course, and another friend just called to tell me you were in town. I'm sure you know how quickly news gets around here, Ms. Jones."

That stirred up bitter memories from her childhood, but she let it pass. "Go ahead."

"Thank you very much. The matter's simple enough. Meredith and I shared an interest in astronomy when we were both in high school, and he made a most interesting discovery. A short time before he left for Virginia Beach, we spoke about those days, and about a certain theory he'd come up with to explain what he'd found. Since the news came it's occurred to me more than once that getting proper recognition for his discovery, and proper attention to his theory, might be a fitting memorial for him."

"Thank you," Tegwyn said, touched. "That's very kind of you." Then, guessing: "This discovery of his—are you talking about his Emulsion 223?"

After a momentary pause, Hythloday said, "Why, yes.

Did he tell you about that?"

"No." She hadn't meant to say more, but the old man on the other end of the phone was so obviously sympathetic that she found herself going on: "I found some old photos of Mars he took in high school. They're very odd—they seem to show the canals, if you know about those."

The pause this time was even more definite. "I do indeed," said the old man. "And yes, I remember his Mars photos very well." He paused again for a moment. "Do you think I could trouble you to come out to my home tomorrow evening, say? I'm getting on in years and it isn't quite as easy for me to get out as it once was."

Tegwyn agreed to that, and the old man went on. "Thank you, my dear. I live on North Mountain Road just past the intersection with old Route 11—you know the place? Excellent." He gave her the address, went on. "Perhaps you could bring the photos you found with you. Oh—and did you by any chance find an unusual sword in the house? Single-edged, curved toward the tip, something of an odd hilt?"

"Yes," said Tegwyn, "and I've been wondering about it since it turned up. Is it yours?"

"Not precisely," Hythloday said, "but I lent it to Meredith a year ago. He was hoping to trace down its provenance. Quite an oddity—I don't know of another one like it anywhere on earth. If you could also bring that, I'd be most grateful."

ANOTHER EMPTY DAY slipped past, and as the sun slid down behind Stroud Mountain, Tegwyn left Great-Uncle Meredith's house with a sword in one hand and a packet of photos in the other. It amused her to imagine Leigh Brackett describing some such scene in one of her stories, though a hovercar would be more suitable for any such scene than the cheap rental compact she'd picked up at the Pittsburgh airport. She climbed in anyway, tucked the sword and the photos in convenient places, headed down the driveway to North Mountain Road.

Six miles further up the road, she passed the intersection

with old Route 11. That whole end of the county was practically abandoned these days, now that the mines were played out and the last jobs shipped overseas, so it wasn't a surprise to pass one empty house after another, most of them well on their way to losing their final battle with age and the harsh mountain weather. What was a surprise was the shape that rose from among the trees at the address the old man had given her: a perfect off-white hemisphere pierced with windows at odd intervals. She blinked, then remembered the fad for dome houses back in the 1970s. There weren't too many of them still around, she thought, and wondered for an amused moment whether Gabriel Hythloday would turn up wearing tie-dyed garments and leather sandals.

To her disappointment, the figure who came to the door to meet her was dressed in an utterly ordinary sweater and slacks. Gabriel Hythloday turned out to be tall and spare, with bronze skin and a fringe of neatly trimmed white hair around a bald skull. Smiling broadly, he shook the hand of Tegwyn's that wasn't holding a sword—she had the envelope with the photos tucked into a convenient shoulderbag—and led the way in. The house was as odd inside as out, Tegwyn thought; from the entry, a door opened onto a long narrow corridor, with another door beyond that, and then a pleasant circular living space with big comfortable chairs around a coffee table, a spiral stair to one side leading up and down, and no windows at all.

"So," said Hythloday, waving her to one of the chairs. "Please make yourself comfortable. May I offer you something to drink? I recall Meredith mentioning a certain fondness on your part for well-hopped IPAs, and I think I have something suitable."

That got an unwilling smile out of Tegwyn. "Please." She set the sword on the table, settled into the chair, pulled out the envelope of improbable photos and glanced again over the canals of Mars.

He came back a few moments later with a pair of glasses,

handed her one, waved aside her thanks. "It's the least I can do for my old friend's favorite grandniece. Ah, you have the photos. May I?"

Tegwyn handed them to him, and he went through them one at a time. "Yes, these bring back memories. Were there any others, do you think?"

"Not that I could find." She sipped the beer, let the sharp edge of the hops clear her mind. "These ones fell back behind a drawer in his desk."

"Ah," he said, as though she'd answered an unspoken question. "Now you know about his discovery, the remarkable Emulsion #223, and the pictures he took with it. Most of them were impressively clear, but in no other way out of the ordinary. But these—" He gestured with one of the Mars photos. "These showed things that many people had seen before that time but nobody had been able to photograph. Things, I might add, that no one has seen since."

Tegwyn gave him a puzzled look. "You're suggesting that the canals were real."

"Oh, yes." He sipped his beer. "Astronomers saw them and mapped them all through the second half of the nineteenth century and the first half of the twentieth. After that? Nobody saw them any more. The conventional wisdom holds that they were never there in the first place, but your great-uncle came to believe that the conventional wisdom is wrong."

He pulled two of the photos out of the stack, handed them to Tegwyn. "These are views of the same side of Mars, more or less, taken most of a year apart. Do you see the difference?"

A quick glance revealed it. "Three of the lines are gone."

Hythloday nodded. "Gone—or hidden."

She gave him a long wary look.

"I'd like you to imagine," the old man said then, "just for the moment, that the old notions about Mars were real. That it was inhabited by intelligent beings long before humanity's first ancestors came down from the trees, that it passed through its own era of technological discovery millions of years ago, rode countless cycles of expansion and decline thereafter—"

A slight jolt shook the floor, and Hythloday rolled his eyes. "That's the furnace," he said. "I really do need to have that seen to before winter. But where was I? Ah, yes. Imagine that these ancient and technologically advanced beings took note of the inhabitants of the third planet from the sun—young, brash, violent, and given to dreams of expansion. Perhaps they even learned a little about how the European nations treated the ancient cultures of Asia or the native peoples of this continent. In any case, once it became clear to them that humanity was working on technologies that could cross interplanetary space, they would have had every reason to conceal themselves from their brash and youthful neighbors, and to make their world look far less inviting than it actually is."

Tegwyn was staring at him now. "You're saying that my great-uncle believed this?"

"In a manner of speaking," Hythloday replied with a smile.

"You're forgetting something," she said. "Space probes."

"Yes, I was getting to that. It's quite true, of course, that humanity has sent quite a few space probes to Mars. Do you happen to know how many of them got to their destination?"

"No." Then: "I know there were a lot of failures."

"Quite a remarkable number of failures," the old man agreed. "Close to half the total number of probes launched. When I was younger, NASA scientists used to joke about a Great Galactic Ghoul that hovered in space somewhere near Mars and ate space probes for dinner. Do you recall what Meredith used to say about coincidence?"

That got an uneasy laugh from her. "Yes. Once is chance, twice is coincidence, three times is enemy action."

"Exactly—a saying from his military days, I believe. Of course we are talking about a great many more than three times. But let us return to our hypothetical Martians. If they wanted to keep humans at bay in an age of space probes, they would have every reason to destroy a certain number of probes—or more precisely, to collect them, and reverse engineer them."

"Why?"

"Humanity's knowledge of Mars doesn't come from the probes themselves, you know. It comes from radio signals purporting to issue from the probes—radio signals that quite reliably report that Mars is far more hostile to life than anyone on Earth had any reason to think before the canals disappeared."

Tegwyn opened her mouth to object, closed it, noticed the beer in her hand, and downed a good swallow of it. In the silence, a curious vibration seemed to come up through the floor.

"That was my great-uncle's theory?" Tegwyn asked then. When Hythloday nodded: "That's a lot of wild speculation to pile on top of a few old photos."

"There were rather more than a few photos of Mars that showed the canals, you know. If I understand correctly, Meredith took well over two hundred of them."

"Do you know where the others are?"

"That's a somewhat complicated matter." He sipped at his beer, imperturbable. "Hiding the canals through a suitably grand engineering project, sending falsified images and sensor data back to Earth from hijacked probes—that might be enough, but our hypothetical Martians would need to be certain. We can even suppose that information might have been leaked early on, and combined with the data from the astronomers to give the old science fiction writers a far better idea of conditions on Mars than they had any right to have. Given the necessary technology to travel across space and evade the relatively primitive means of detection humanity uses to spot objects in space, it would be a simple thing to place agents on Earth. The agents could have any number of special duties, as I'm sure you can imagine, but the most important would be to see to it that any evidence that might reveal the great deception was put safely out of reach."

That was when Tegwyn decided she was listening to a madman. She set the beer aside and stood up, saying, "I'm sorry, but that's just plain crazy. I think I need to leave."

"That won't be possible," said Gabriel Hythloday.

Quick as a cat, she stooped, took the sword by its oddly shaped hilt, brought it to a middle guard as she straightened. Hythloday, eyes suddenly gone wide, flattened himself into his chair and said, "My dear, please don't do anything rash! I mean you no harm whatsoever—quite the contrary, in fact."

Her eyes narrowed. She watched him, said nothing.

"Do I have your permission to touch a certain portion of the arm of this chair? That will make it ever so much easier to explain."

Baffled and wary, she considered him. "Go ahead."

He moved his hand with exaggerated slowness, pressed what must have been a concealed button under the upholstery. An instant later, the floor, walls, and ceiling of the room changed to infinite black—

Spangled with stars.

For a few moments it reminded her of planetariums Great-Uncle Meredith had taken her to see during her childhood, but no planetarium on Earth could achieve the perfect clarity of the imagery that surrounded her. The constellations she recognized lay drowned in an ocean of cold and silent stars.

"If you'll glance to your left," Hythloday said then, "you may understand our current position a little better."

She spared a quick glance that way, then turned and stared, forgetful of the sword in her hand and the old man in the chair facing her. Vast and dark, the nightside of Earth spread before her; off to the west, an illuminated crescent blazed blue, and the sun stood above the planet's rim. Elsewhere, a spiderweb of lights sprawled across eastern North America. She could just make out the little glowing spot that was Carmarthen, south of the luminous threads connecting the great hubs of Pittsburgh and Philadelphia.

"That—" Her voice caught in a throat gone suddenly dry. "That's got to be fake."

"I assure you it isn't."

She turned, stared at him. "We'd be in freefall."

A dry chuckle punctuated the darkness. "Yes, I know. The scientists of your planet still haven't worked out artificial gravity, have they?"

Your planet? She pushed the thought aside. "If—if that's true—you're kidnapping me."

"In a manner of speaking." She could barely see his face in the Earthlit darkness. "Tell me this, my dear. Do you really want to go back down there?"

She could not answer him. "Where are you taking me?" she asked instead.

She knew the answer already, but Hythloday's words still came as a shock. "To the world you know as Mars, of course. It has other names which you'll learn in due time—words in the native language, and words in the languages of the humans who live there. Oh, yes, there have been humans on Mars for well over ten thousand of your years—brought over by the Iru, the native species of the planet—and we have no more desire than the Iru to see your people invade our world." A soft laugh stirred the darkness. "Though exceptions can be made for individuals."

A sudden improbable hope stirred in her. "Yes," Hythloday said, as though she'd spoken it aloud. "We found out about your great-uncle's inquiries some years ago—it doesn't matter how—and the relevant authorities decided the best way to deal with that was to offer him the opportunity to come to our world. Very often that's the best way to do things, as our world is far from overcrowded these days. He accepted with quite some enthusiasm, on one condition—that you be permitted to come as well. After appropriate investigation, that was also granted."

Slowly, she lowered the sword. "People are going to ask questions."

"Not at all. Your rental car is already sitting on Prott Road next to the river, and everyone will come to the quite reasonable conclusion that you drowned yourself out of grief. Since no one but you ever saw a curiously shaped house on North Mountain Road just past old Route 11, what other conclusion could they come to?"

After a moment, she put the sword back on the table, sat down again. "Excellent," said Hythloday. "We have a somewhat lengthy voyage ahead of us—some six months as you count time—but you'll find a suitable room awaiting you, and there are devices aboard this ship that can synthesize clothing, food—" He gestured with his glass. "And quite adequate beer. Also recordings and texts, to help you learn what you need to know: languages, history, culture." He drained the beer. "And when the voyage is over, your great-uncle will be waiting to greet you beside the Grand Canal."

She considered that, and after a moment picked up her glass and finished the beer. The blue glow of Earthlight reflected off the blade in front of her, and she asked, "And the sword?"

Hythloday chuckled again. "A thought of your great-uncle's. Yes, it's an Iru blade—and you may have some use for it after we arrive. You'll find our societies are highly traditional, in certain senses."

He sat back, said no more. Tegwyn turned in her seat to look at the Earth, already visibly further away. *The Chattering Planet*, she thought. *And I'm out of it.* She sat back in her chair, the way she'd done so many times on summer nights from the lawn behind Great-Uncle Meredith's house, and looked upwards, welcoming the tremendous silence of the stars.

Born in London in 1954, of mixed Scottish and Belgian extraction, Robert Gibson works from home as a private tutor. He lives close to the sea in Heysham, Lancashire. He writes:

"For most of my life I suffered from terrific writer's block, very frustrating. Then in my late fifties I underwent a dazzling conversion experience, consisting of the revelation that it would be a good idea to show some consideration for the reader, i.e. write stuff that a fellow creature might conceivably wish to read.

"Since that mental breakthrough I have never looked back.

My published works are the Old Solar System novel Valeddom *(2013) and the novella collection* Uranian Gleams *(2015), the alternate-Earth Kroth trilogy (*The Slant, The Drop *and* The Rise, *2013-15), and the previous-universe novel* Man of the World *(2016). I am currently working on a Uranian novel.*

"I am married to Mary, who proofreads most of my writing, thank goodness. I lack binocular vision and so, being also a member of UKIP, am appropriately swivel-eyed. My favourite poet is Dante, who got me into Italian literature. From the age of six I was fascinated by astronomy—the bit in Valeddom about the encyclopaedia is autobiographical."

Like the previous story, "Uranian Thule" refuses to consign the Old Solar System to history's dustbin. Unlike "Out of the Chattering Planet," however, Gibson's tale bases itself not on the weakness of humanity's technologies but on its potential for future strength. The Old Solar System may be so tantalizing a prospect that sufficiently advanced technology might be deployed to make it real...

URANIAN THULE

Robert Gibson

prologue

WE HAVE ALWAYS been careful how we tell our tales to you Terrans. To convey their gist, to preserve their pace and colour, we have ensured up till now that our narratives rollick along without getting tangled in a log-jam of pedantic notes or provisos. Of course this smoothness has been bought with a sacrifice of accuracy, as when for example we resort to the use of Terran terms which are not truly appropriate to Uranian conditions. However, our Earthly readership likes it that way; all you desire is an effortless plunge into our trove of story.

At least, that's what we thought until recently. Then, what do we hear? Rising clamour from your world, demanding the 'unvarnished truth'!

Well, actually, that suits us. In fact the days are coming when, whether you like it or not, we shall 'give it to you straight'.

Already we are making moves to wipe away the 'varnish' in our translations. For example in the story that follows you may note that although we introduce Noav Neen as a 'daydreaming youth', we soon amend that portrayal to give sharper focus to his so-called 'dreams'.

On the other hand we won't push realism down your throats.

Really, you have our assurance.

Consider how flourishing is the ether-commerce between the third and seventh planets: surely, neither party wants to spoil this happy situation, which has persisted for several lifetimes. During this expanse of time you and we have never met face to face; this has precluded all conflict between us, while our storytellers and yours engage in friendly rivalry. You eagerly accept all our transmissions, while we in turn happily open our ears to the fascinating adolescent cultures of the Inner Solar System. What a pity it would be, to disrupt such an entertaining relationship.

History, however, is about to enter a new phase.

It had to happen: nothing could have stopped our aeonian count-down, which has finally reached Year Zero.

We repeat, do not be alarmed. Change need not mean loss. You say you love our fictions: well, let your trust remain constant in the new era in which you will learn that those fictions are true.

Then you will see that we have not invented, and do not need to invent, any of our tales, since the truth on Ooranye *is* one interconnected saga, bearing the message that the future belongs to us.

1: the backgrounder

NOAV NEEN SKIMMED across the plain on his pre-dawn round. All was quiet except for the flap of his cloak in the breeze which whickered around him as he moved efficiently from installation to installation among the outlying fields of the village of Hazz. The air was dim, the microscopic *throom* suspended throughout the atmosphere still in the faint half of their thirty-hour cycle which defines the Uranian night, yet because the fields were bright with their own luminescence it was easy to spot the farm machinery outlined against the glowing stalks of vheic. The routine was familiar. Each time Noav Neen came to a compressor he would inspect the gaunt metal tubing, shine a torch through the intake at chin height, and where necessary clean it of wind-blown chaff. Then after he had tested the operation with some vheic plucked from the adjoining field, and had obtained a satisfactory glow from the output chamber, he would re-mount his skimmer and speed for a mile to the next farm... Simple work, this, but satisfyingly important. Vital preparation for the midmorning harvest, the check-out round was well suited to a hale, unambitious, day-dreaming youth.

Aware that his days stretched before him, he could complacently enjoy the never-ending rapture of sight, the breathing awe and natural richness that soaked into him from the land and sky-scape around and above him. Personal ambition drowned without trace in such oceanic wonder; the endless plains, mostly bare but never monotonous, brooded with potential, their brown and liverish corklike granules—the surface *gralm*—randomly producing occasional seeds, leading to the growth of isolated groves, mini-ecologies, each almost a world in itself, while on a more rapid timescale the sentient clouds of the upper air, with their predatory fighting formations, contorted in their endless variety.

Perhaps most powerfully of all, the faint Sun, unrelated to this world's cycle of day and night, shone from its fixed, suggestive position as the pole star of the giant planet. This unwinking solar eye ceaselessly reminded Noav Neen, humble villager of isolated Hazz, of the precise direction in which he must skim if he were ever to visit the sunward polar metropolis, Skyyon.

"Just follow the Sun, to reach the magnificent city." What simple advice, if and when that day came!

He had never yet made the trip. But from that one navigational datum his imagination bled naturally into diffuse contemplation of great men and women and great events. This halation of ordinary life, whereby the small bleeds out into the great, is what sustains backgrounders. One humdrum task will shine fuzzily round its edges, to mingle its light with neighbour lights, and so on via a chain of glows to take a lonely rural Nenn all the way from his remote village, via daydream, to the hub of civilization, putting the rural backgrounder in touch with the great world, including him in a sense of belonging. Thus on Ooranye the distinction between potential and actual is not as sharp as on Earth; wishing to do a thing is more like really doing it, here.

Noav Neen thus contentedly visualized the Sunnoad's palace, airship fleets docked around the summit towers of Skyyon and of other great cities, temples of knowledge, arenas of decision, councils for adventurous designs. At this very moment—according to news which filtered via traders and radio relays across the plains—the Sunnoad himself was assembling a skyfleet large enough to penetrate deep into the unknown wilds of Fyaym. Although folk could only speculate on what his aim might be, the secrecy suggested some weighty plan to thwart the lurking Fyayman powers. All guesswork, of course... and skyfleets were no novelty in Uranian history. But people of this generation had acquired the habit of expecting some doom or marvel which must presently shake the world, now that the count of years had reached zero.

(Terran readers, you need to remember that one of our years is eighty-four of yours, a longish human lifetime, and consider also that, since the first of our people emerged from the Lake of Dmara, thousands of these lifetime-years have ticked by, counted not forwards but backwards, from the initial 14,286—determined by instinct—backwards ever since then in a stupendous count-down to this zero end.)

Noav Neen therefore, like all contemporary Uranians, lived with a sense of high privilege—extending alike to the great and the obscure—that he would live to see the meaning of it all. He did not need to formulate the thought, "That same Sun which stares down on me here at Hazz, shines on the Sunnoad's gathering fleet at Skyyon." To be any person, anyone at all, from Sunnoad to farm worker, was to share in all being. And therefore the contented young field-hand was not even sure that he need ever actually make the trip to the polar metropolis.

Noav Neen, in short, was a *backgrounder*.

We never risk using that word in polite conversation. To utter it would be far too great a risk. All of us know, deep in our minds, that if the distinction between *foregrounders* and *backgrounders* were ever brought into the open, our culture might be torn apart. Anguished jealousy, let loose, could destroy the current peaceful acceptance that some people are spot-lit by destiny, and others not; that some life-stories get into the history books, while others do not. As things are, all egos, quietly aware of their lit or unlit status, accept it as part of their identity.

Even if the silence which prevails on this issue could be broken without mayhem, it would be in the worst of taste to indulge a frankness which could only embarrass us all and benefit no one.

Therefore, only in the tales which we tell to you Terrans can we Bards be explicit and say, for example, "Noav Neen was a backgrounder".

Noav Neen, backgrounder, went about his farm duties in the hour before morningshine, on what was due to count as Day 11,176,885 of the Actinium Era. He was scheduled, after he had finished his early round, to perform a task in the centre of the village. Somebody, when the air had brightened, must climb the central tower of Hazz and change the day-number underneath the clock. The Day/Era count is our forward, practical dating system (unlike the long mystic backward count of U-years to which it bears no relation), and so the Day-number needs to be updated every morning. Today his name was on the rota. Thus he expected shortly to climb and unhook one digit and replace it with another, augmenting yesterday's 11,176,884 by 1. He confidently expected to finish his inspection round in plenty of time for that clock-tower duty.

Meanwhile as he approached the last farm the scene appeared quite normally deserted. He did not expect to meet anybody at this early hour. The bright golden fields were on his right, the dim plains on his left, on his approach to the gaunt structure which he was due to inspect. The eternal breezes flapped their invisible wings around his ears—

"Noav… Neen," drawled a young woman's voice.

The playful tone, which mockingly separated the two words of his name, sounded half-familiar. At the same time a white smudge glided into view from behind the compressor. Clad in a billowing white furry cloak, she hovered and dazzled like a rogue cloud who swoops to graze the surface.

She brought her skimmer to a stop a couple of yards from Noav Neen.

His eyes adjusted to recognize the daughter of Paov, the man who owned this farm.

"Reyazz," he acknowledged, his wry smile concealed in the dimness. Here was a girl whom he *had* admired in the past. "Looks as if you were waiting for me," he added, to show that he, too, could tease.

Ignoring that, she hugged her furs more closely about her and gazed around the sky. "I'm waiting for *refelc*—my favourite hour. Don't let me interrupt your work, Two-Names."

"Almost finished. This is my last one for today." He poked at the compressor, while considering her dig at his double name, *Noav… Neen*. Naturally his mind did not dredge up into full view the dangerous idea, *foregrounders have two names, backgrounders one*. That fuse could stay unlit; the rule was not hard-and-fast, and therefore one's blurry awareness of it was all the more easily suppressed. "And by the way, so what if my name is written with a space between the syllables…?"

"You work it out," she chuckled, but it was an evasive chuckle—she, too, shrank from the brink of conscious admission that some are spot-lit, others not.

"Nothing to work out. For that matter, you could just as well be a Two-Names yourself: 'Rey...Azz'."

"Huh," she shrugged.

She was right to scorn his reply, he realized. His name and hers *were* differently structured. One's name is derived from the sounds one makes with one's first breath. His and hers had each been noted carefully by those who'd listened at their births. *His* listeners must have heard a pair of noises with a distinct pause between them; hence his two names; whereas the new-born "Reyazz" had uttered syllables so close together, that they had to count as one word. The matter was decided.

Aware of having been worsted in argument, he toiled in glum silence, attacking the last bit of chaff wedged among the pipes.

She, however, had more to say.

"I'm quite happy as I am, but as for *you*, I reckon you could make more of your life."

The riposte was out before he could suppress it: "And *you*, I rather think, could make less of yours." At first he grinned at his own outspokenness, and then he felt dismay.

Reyazz, however, threw back her head and laughed at his reference to the over-colourful swathe which her love affairs had cut through village society. Her mirth set his mind at rest. She was far from angry. He, for his part, felt reluctant admiration for her splendid disregard of public opinion.

She remarked, "You're not too slow at times, Noav, I'll give you that."

"You sound like my grandmother," he replied.

"Come, let's call a truce," she suggested, "and wait for *refelc*."

Companionably, he and the girl then aligned their skimmers and hovered side by side while they awaited those spectacular moments when night turns into day.

From her closeness to him, a complex of irrelevant feelings, woven from her slim height, unusual blonde hair and wilful concentration caused his thoughts to meander. From his *you sound like my grandmother* his memory skipped back to words he'd had, with that same grandmother, quite recently.

Doa Trool, Elder of Hazz, had said:

"Don't be too hard on her, Noav. A girl has a right to change her mind."

"A girl doesn't have the right to be taken seriously, if she first makes a pretty speech announcing her engagement to Jovald Brenn, saying he's her ultimate man, then makes another pretty speech fifty days later after ditching him in favour of Gengr Hroll, now saying *he's* her ultimate man, and then, after discovering that *that* ultimate man isn't good enough for either, ditches him and—"

"Reyazz wouldn't agree."

"Facts are facts. The whole village knows."

"I mean, she wouldn't agree that she *needs* to be taken seriously—yet."

"How do you make that out, Grandmother?"

"It's not any old ultimate, it's only the *ultimate* ultimate that counts. You know the old saying, 'The love that comes last / Redecorates the past.'"

Oh well, it was perhaps too much to expect that he might win an argument against Doa Trool, or for that matter against Reyazz. Never mind: he was competent in his own sphere. His glance flicked across the fields. As the seconds ticked by towards the moment of *refelc*, the vheic plants glowed golden, rustling as if in a whisper of anticipation for the Uranian equivalent of "dawn". *Glory,* whispered the plants; *we're the glory of your culture.*

His thought-stream answered... *Indeed, without the glowing energy of the vheic, where would we be?* Without it there would be no fuel-phials to power skimmers or factories... yet the supply was not excessive. A natural, grounded boon, it sustained the civilization of the Nenns, the Uranian human race, without allowing them to disturb the eco-balance of their world.

Limited in effect, the compressed vheic-phials did not yield their energy more than six yards above the world's surface. That in turn meant that warships, which flew much higher than skimmers, required a different power-source, rarer, more expensive. ...*So, humans, your wars cannot destroy too much, and moreover you cannot get off the planet...*

It wasn't actually the plants whispering, it was Noav Neen musing—unless you believe, as do some Uranians, that our World Spirit really does sometimes speak through the vheic; and no Terran reader could believe that.

A flicker—his breath caught—

The dome of sky abruptly sparkled.

Thousands of bright pinpoints!

It had begun: the breath-taking, twice-daily stellar show. The upper cloud layer of Ooranye had become transparent and would remain so for three wonderful minutes. During *refelc*—as in the similar *pmetn* every evening—the lamps of the cosmos shine upon the admiring faces of Uranians.

Refelc and *pmetn* occur because, regular as clockwork, twice a day the rotation of the stratospheric planar *throom* must turn all those tiny polarized motes briefly edge-on, thus allowing starlight to pass through. At all other hours, our firmament is limited to the Sun and the five Uranian moons. Only during *pmetn* and *refelc* is the cosmos revealed as incomparably more gigantic. Predictable yet marvellous, these are the minutes of extra romance. So, inevitably, Noav Neen and Reyazz swapped glances. She saw in the blur of his face the nondescript handsome grey of a backgrounder; he similarly saw, in her beauty and poise, a like common richness, a wholesome mediocrity—though one which knocked a bit harder against that ceiling of achievement under which backgrounders are confined by fate.

The three minutes slipped by. Then with a second flickery snap the upper layer of atmosphere re-clouded. The stars disappeared. *Refelc* was over.

The pair of watchers let out their breaths.

"Well, that was nice," sighed Reyazz. "Now I have work to do."

She touched the controls of her skimmer, and the hovering vehicle began to turn. Noav, wanting to keep her for a few more moments, sought for something to say. "Fifteen hours till we again see the stars. A pity it's so long."

Her mouth twisted, "Oh, just lose yourself in your work, Two-Names! The absorbing tasks of your day—fifteen hours will be over before you know it." Her skimmer's motor hummed and she began to slide away, and then the most fantastic of circumstances came to his aid.

Unbelievably, the stars appeared again.

Reyazz shouted and smote her skimmer's controls. Its motor shut off; she swayed back in her seat. Noav Neen rode his own skimmer back to her side. He unthinkingly put his arm round her. He stared askance at the glitter which had so astoundingly returned to the sky.

He had to believe it. An *eomasp*. A once-in-hundreds-of-lifetimes event. Caused by the sensitivity of upper-air *throom* to emotional waves. Some mass outbreak of human excitement must have spread as news to major centres of population. Some crisis or discovery strong enough to disrupt the rhythm of night and day and mark the close of one historical era and the opening of the next.

He gasped, "What big thing...?" He drew breath. "No more Actinium Era," he marvelled aloud. "No more Era 89." The chemical names and numbers, from the periodic table so 'hard-wired' into our brains that we never have to learn it as you Terrans must, gabbled in Noav Neen's mind. "Era 90 now," he tried out the words, "the Thorium from now on... so so amazing... but maybe..."

A throaty murmur at his side: "Guessing?"

He whispered, "Unfinished business. From way back."

Reyazz hunched forward and muttered, "Makes sense... The Sunnoad... must have given the order."

"To succeed where Fiarr Fosn failed, so long ago."

She nodded. "I think. I hope."

They pondered the age-old dream to send a fleet all the way to the Starlit Pole... the antipodes of Skyyon. Thus traversing our giant globe.

"That must be it," murmured Reyazz. "What else could have caused the *eomasp* now? A new beginning..." Her eyes then blazed directly into his. "Will you still glory in your humdrum tasks, Two-Names, at a time like *this*?"

"Shh," he admonished, gazing at the stars. But it was he who uttered the next sound; "Hey—"

"What?" But she had seen it too: *another flicker*. Not the end of this unscheduled *refelc*, but something nested inside the main disturbance. "Don't like that," she opined. "Noav, what do you reckon—that twitchy extra whatsit—"

"Can't say." All he knew for sure was that his wonderment, like hers, had become tinged with unease. "Like an add-on, a lesser *eomasp*," he suggested, "having its little flutter inside the main one." He was in some apprehension lest she retort, "What makes *you* an authority?" Fortunately she did not say any such thing.

Instead they were peaceably recalled to the marvel of being alive on the first morning of a new era, as the unscheduled minutes of extra starlight came to a proper end, in the glow of regular morningshine.

Their gaze swept the land and then each other. Their mutual smiles brimmed with a sense of joyous life, with the privilege of knowing a Day One.

But—Day One of *which* era? Had they just experienced a double *eomasp*?

On rare occasions in the planet's immense past there had occurred 'staccato' *eomasps* with a string of miniature eras lasting while the multiple emotional gales blew themselves out and ending when the *throom's* rhythm stabilized. Necessarily, these convulsions in nature's rhythm signified dire cruxes in Uranian history. Today's two *refelcs* within minutes of each other, with a possible third nested inside the second, must already inspire terrifying speculation in Hazz and other remote areas where news was outpaced by rumour. If, now, there came yet another untimely daybreak... well, joy and wonder and disaster had been known to arrive wrapped in one parcel.

Reyazz said simply, "Back to the village." She shot away and Noav Neen in grim agreement set his skimmer in her wake; they curved between the fields, past the farm buildings that still shone their night lamps, till they reached the central octagon into which the other settlers had begun to stream. On the periphery of the gathering crowd they halted. Quickly the general mood reassured them. The excitement was cheerful; the scene lacked the smell of fear.

Reyazz murmured, "Somebody's doing your job."

Noav Neen took a spyglass from the inner pouch of his cloak and trained it on the village centre.

First his 'scope lingered upon the stone platform from which the Date Spike soared. Standing on its edge, a woman, her hood down, her white hair frizzled by the morning breeze, gave focus to the gathering. The people were probably reassured, thought Noav Neen, by his grandmother's *not* making a speech. She was merely granting a few quiet words to those individuals who pressed towards her; gentle words that did not carry far but doubtless confirmed to late risers the bare momentous fact, that the stars had shone outside their due hour. Meanwhile, despite the ripply oddness of the *eomasp* that had marked the change of epoch, wonder was outsting fear during every minute that passed without another *refelc*; apprehension ceded to the marvel of a new age.

Satisfied that Doa Trool could handle this situation, Noav Neen could give attention to what Reyazz had just said. *Somebody doing my job, eh?*

He aimed his 'scope higher.

Yes, a figure was climbing the Spike from rung to rung, towards the big board that displayed yesterday's date.

"Who is it?" asked Reyazz.

With the 'scope Noav Neen was able to identify the agile villager who must have been assigned the update extra early. "It's Gherruk. Let's get closer." They dismounted, tethered their skimmers to posts at the edge of the Octagon and began to stroll forward among folk whose eyes were likewise on the date-board.

Cheers broke out when Gherruk attained the summit platform of the Spike and reached out to unhook, first of all, the old Era-Sign, the symbol for Actinium—element and Era 89. (Terran readers may as well visualize it as 'Ac'.)

Reyazz whispered, "What an honour! Such a pity you weren't there in time."

"I suppose I do envy him," Noav Neen admitted good-naturedly. Her insistence could not annoy him. A great era, hundreds of lifetimes long, had reached its close and a new one must begin. On such an occasion, who could stoop to pettiness?—though his mien did show a wistful tinge at the moment when the fellow who was the focus of all eyes dropped the old era-sign into the hung bin.

More wooden squares must drop into that bin in the next few minutes. Gherruk was reaching for the digit '4', at the right-hand end of the '11,176,884' day-count of the late era. Plonk! - that, too, dropped away, followed, from right to left, by an '8', another '8', a '6' and so on...

Reyazz whispered, "Go on—it's not too late. You could go to help him, Noav. Volunteer!"

At last he showed some irritation. "What's the matter with you?" he hissed at her. "If you're so hungry for the limelight why don't *you* go ahead and butt in?"

She retorted, "What do you take me for, some sort of *flunnd?*"

Shocked by her language, he replied coolly:

"If you're not, then neither am I. Look, why are we having this conversation?"

"You were *given* that job. It's *yours*."

Suddenly he understood. Reyazz was not exactly a flunnd—a "backgrounder who adopts the airs of a foregrounder"—though she would have deserved such an epithet if she herself had taken the attention-seeking action which she urged instead upon Noav Neen. As things were—

Reyazz was a—um, well, a sort of vicarious *flunnd*.

She egged others on. She couldn't stand the thought of missing an opportunity, even indirectly, to make a splash.

However, this morning of all mornings must not, would not be spoiled. No need to bicker, or to worry if they nevertheless *did* bicker. Small stuff had no chance today.

She shook him by the arm. "Did you hear me?"

He calmly nodded forward. "Watch him go down now."

"But he hasn't finished."

"Yes he has."

Gherruk had reached the end of the un-hookings although one digit remained. He did not touch the left-most number, the '1', because that could stay nicely where it was, since its new job was now to denote Day 1 of the new era. And then, as Noav Neen had predicted, the man started on his way down.

"Already? But he hasn't finished, hasn't hung out the new era-sign!" cried Reyazz while from other spectators words flew around: "Thorium!" "It's 'Day 1, Thorium'!" "Put up the Thorium sign!" and from somewhere in the crowd a lout yelled, "Go back, yer great *yollop*! Finish the job!"

Noav Neen winced—a *yollop* in stories is a character who acts as crass foil to the hero; in real life, Fate similarly assigns to *yollops* the unappetising role of vicious contrast to the virtues of others. Not the kind of thing to mention in polite company: perilously close to the duality of foregrounder/backgrounder.

Elder Doa Trool's voice rang out:

"Pipe down, Haub! Gherruk is not a *yollop*. He's obeying my instructions."

Noav Neen, having winced again at that word on the lips of a lady, nevertheless saw the effectiveness of his grandmother's technique in controlling the crowd: something in the voice, he supposed; she'd always had that sort of tonal power. The lout, Haub, who had hurled the epithet—and who was obviously a *yollop* himself—gave no more trouble.

Doa Trool at last made her speech.

"Nenns of Hazz, it is Day One!" Wholehearted cheers—she had them back on track from that moment: the magic phrase *Day One* nuanced with the resonant term *Nenns* (Uranian humans), more portentous than 'people'. "Yes, Day One—that much we know; and as for the new era-sign: we'll hang that up just as soon as we are sure which sign it must be. It is not for us few to decide whether what happened was a single or a double *eomasp*. The big cities, the observatories, the Ghepions will know. We shall just have to wait a few days for word to reach us. So go back to your tasks, Nenns of Hazz, and wait for news from Syoom."

That was the right word on which to end the speech: Syoom—the name shining in a myriad contexts, from the qualitative 'civilization' to the merely statistical 'land in which a lone wayfarer has a more than fifty per cent probability of surviving a thousand-mile journey'. Either way it means the arena of most human history upon Ooranye; around four hundred million square miles, a fifth of our giant planet's surface. The village of Hazz was, in that sense, well inside Syoom. Yet in Doa Trool's words, "news from Syoom" meant news from the main urban centres—a usage understood by her audience, who could comfortably have it both ways: they, though in Syoom, could await "news from Syoom".

The crowd dispersed to their daily routines, as did Noav Neen and Reyazz. For the rest of that day, and for a few days more, familiar activities and scenes continued, but with an overlay of expectancy and wonder. This unforgettable transition period, uniquely combining the suspenseful and the idyllic, was ever afterwards remembered as 'the tingling days'.

In a practical sense life went on as normal except that

those who kept journals or composed letters had to continue a doubtful dating sequence, in accordance with distant precedent: for this was how, on occasions in the ancient past, folk had dealt with uncertainty as to the era-name—namely by a temporary continuation of the old sequence, by adding the new numbers on the board to the old era's total. Thus collectors can quite often find, tucked away in drawers or cabinets all over Syoom, documents dated (for example) "11,176,885 Ac" and for a few numbers more, up to and including "11,176,893 Ac", which in reality was Day 9 of the new era.

Those last are the rarest examples—for Day 9 was cut off short of noon.

Noav Neen, on that day, glimpsed the new eomasp out of the corner of his eye as he was strolling across the Octagon towards one of the village shops. He had been about to purchase a laser charge-unit for his *sponnd* (even in the most peaceable eras no Uranian feels right without a charged weapon), but when he glimpsed the mid-day stars, he forgot all else. He spun round and ran, thanking those stars that they had appeared when he was just a few yards from the clock-tower. Other villagers had begun to stream into the Octagon, but he could reach its central Spike before anyone else.

Reyazz's promptings, days before, now came to fruition in his heart. This time he *would* act. While the rest of the folk of Hazz were dazed by the wonder of the new eomasp, he began to climb, visible to all, unquestioned by all. He had worked out what must have happened, and so, he guessed, had most of them; during the past eight days the climate of opinion had veered towards the idea that the quivery refelc *had* been a double eomasp. Therefore the world had leaped past era 90, the Thorium, to Era 91, the Protactinium; which in turn meant that *today*—

Noav Neen reached the platform and put his hand into the era-sign bin. With an intoxicating sense of destiny he drew out the sign for… Uranium.

At long last, at long last—Era 92!

He held the painted wooden square aloft and gazed down at a pool of faces. In them he saw, mirrored, his own cross-currents of subdued exultation and incredulous belief. Never again would there be a moment like this. Necessarily ultimate, Era 92 must culminate all.

He placed a "1" alongside the Uranium sign. Day One again—but the last Day One there ever would be.

Then he shifted his hold on the Spike. He grasped the rungs again and made as if to descend.

"Freeze!" came an authoritative shout from down below, that cut the air with a suddenness which enforced its own command.

Halting his limbs, he silently obeyed.

"Right—now turn around!"

Noav Neen continued to obey as if in a dream beyond surprise or doubt. Turned about, he stood on a rung, his arms grasped a higher rung behind his back, his body swayed forward in a posture of respectful attention.

The Elder boomed again, "Now tell us—what made you so sure?"

Not rhetorical, that. With a pacific inward smile Noav Neen understood. Far from being reprimanded he was being invited to take part in a useful double act.

To have hung the final era's first date-sign on the board at Hazz, was a great enough memory for any villager to treasure for the rest of his life, but *this*—to be appointed to explain the reason—was an honour greater by far.

He was even more content to catch sight of Reyazz standing a few rows back from the Elder; the girl looked tense as she tossed her breeze-blown tresses while leaning forward as if anxious not to miss a single syllable of Noav's response.

This was his moment to donate to the history of Hazz.

"Those of us who guessed," he began, "eight-and-a-bit days ago, that the Sunnoad must have given the order to sail the Fleet to the Starlit Pole, are vindicated, because that number of days is a plausible duration for the journey! What else could have caused this new eomasp? What other source of etheric disturbance could prove to be as great as the giving of the order? None other than its success! *The Sunnoad must have triumphed in his mission!*"

Fragmentary shouts... broken-off cheers... they weren't sure whether to believe him.

"Disaster," suggested Doa Trool, "is an alternative to your answer. Cataclysmic failure like that of Sunnoad Fiarr Fosn at the end of the Phosphorus Era. *That* could equally cause an eomasp. Like it did, way back then."

Heads bobbed in a reflex of anxiety. Villagers craned their necks as if a nemesis from the Fyayman wilderness could already be discerned on the horizon. How the Elder trusted him! How firmly she believed that he was poised to give out more words both immediate and good!

"This," proclaimed Noav Neen, "is where we must bear in mind the flickery nature of Era 89's end. A double eomasp—so that for the past few days we have been living not in era 90 but in era 91. And therefore *now* we have moved on still further, into Number 92, the Final Era, the fulfilment of our history! No disaster could introduce *that*."

"Thank you, Noav Neen."

She motioned to him to descend from the Spike, and then she herself stepped up onto its platform and called out to the crowd, "Cancel your rotas for today! Let's celebrate the last ever Day One for Nenns!" Uproar of delight—

Noav Neen meanwhile descended the last rung.

His grandmother touched his elbow and murmured: "I hope you're right."

"I must be right."

"In that case we're left to wonder, how Sunnoad Iyen Noom can have managed to find a way to succeed where Fiarr Fosn, his ancient object lesson, failed."

"That'll be where our double eomasp came in," hazarded Noav Neen.

The Elder appraised him. "So it comes down to that.

To precisely how our Actinium Era ended. But will we ever know?"

2: the foregrounder

IN THE TRANSPARENT blister underneath the flagship *Vaneng's* ovoid bulk, from a swivel chair at the centre of the control room, Sunnoad Iyen Noom 80525 faced the semi-circle of viewscreens on which his eight fleet admirals had appeared in answer to his summons. Another part of his attention swept past those televisual images and lit upon the bare and distant horizons which his 240 airships might cross within hours, if and when he gave the order. He could also see down, through the window-like floor, the plain a mile below, dim in the pre-dawn greyness of *pallyne*, the prelude to morningshine of Day 11,176,885 Ac.

With the heightened situational perception enjoyed by the world's one and only Noad of Noads or "focus of foci", Iyen Noom, 80,525th wearer of the golden cloak, could spot the crouch of imminent history upon those murky plains and in that expectant arc of forward horizon, all scribbled with potentialities and warnings. It was an unwritten requirement of the office he held, that his mind must work like a weather-map of destiny, overlaying his physical eyesight with the currents of fate almost as clearly as isobars are traced upon charts of atmospheric pressure. The analogy could be taken further: weather prediction can be useful for decision-making... but there is no guarantee.

An amber light winked from the third screen: Tyarwa Zade aboard the *Zintyon* was buzzing for permission to open the conference.

"Go ahead, Admiral T-Z," said the Sunnoad with impeccable courtesy, expecting a sharp analysis from that imperious beauty with violet eyes, for he knew that her spectacular appearance was matched by acuity of mind. In addition, Tyarwa Zade possessed one particular fund of experience which the Sunnoad himself lacked. She was a second-lifer. That is, she belonged to that sixth of Uranian humanity who have already lived in a previous incarnation on this world. The proportion is increasing, but only slowly; almost every Nenn can expect to live twice, but the two lives in our binary span tend to be set far apart. Unusually, however, Tyarwa's first existence had been relatively recent: she happened to have lived a mere four reigns ago as the daughter of one of the current Sunnoad's close predecessors, Miokk Monray 80521. That suggested a likely modernity of outlook combined with (to employ a Terran phrase) "an old head on young shoulders".

Hence, Iyen Noom expected bold though responsible advice. And yet—

"Your call, Sunnoad I-N," was all she said.

The Sunnoad's majestic lower jaw moved slightly askew to convey wry appreciation of this almost wordless report. "I take your meaning," he replied. That she could say so little, indicated strongly that her sector of Syoom was quiet, unusually quiet. Therefore, to say "Your call" was tantamount to saying, "Go ahead… but on *your* authority alone."

Might she have gone queasy?

His gaze panned across the row of screens.

Ah, another second-lifer's lips were shaping to speak. The relative forwardness of such people was to be expected; it was no surprise that although they were one in six of the population at large, they accounted for three out of his eight Admirals.

Capfaym Duuv, the lean-faced, psi-sensitive hero of the end of the Thallium Era, who looked as pale and intense now as he had then, phrased his words as if he, too, wished to be commanded:

"Here aboard the *Lwon*," he said, the fingers of his left hand tapping the console in front of him, "our readiness has reached its peak." His right hand closed about the strands of his scarf, as though in shivery reaction to a first-life memory. The Sunnoad, watching him, then saw the hand release the scarf, and guessed: *The old Thallium Crisis has, on reflection, in-*

spired him with courage. But if he's thinking, "Nothing can be as bad as that epoch", he's wrong.

"So you, too, imply that this is a good moment," remarked Iyen Noom. "And you know about moments." He paused then. Reincarnation was all very well, but, by all accounts, the previous life was only remembered dreamily, like earliest childhood. It could bequeath wisdom, but little exactitude, and comparisons could be quite misleading...

The third second-lifer now spoke.

This was Vyada Ledwa, the admiral on board the *Xemmb*, on the fleet's right flank. She was short and plumpish as Uranian women go, though still beautiful by your Terran standards. Her first life was unexceptional as far as anyone knew; still, a life is a life, and is apt to help one's chances in the next one.

"You could *procrastinate*," she said cleverly.

Iyen Noom smiled at the long Terran word. During the past few lifetimes the orbiting observers from the third planet had superficially affected the culture of Ooranye, adding a veneer of amusing vocabulary and quaint idioms to native Uranian speech. He himself could play that game as well as anyone, for it so happened that he was one of the most accomplished linguists ever to wear the golden cloak; he could speak fluent Terran and had done so on several occasions in radio communication with the curious alien humanoids.

Seconds ticked by while his intentions veered towards an irrevocable decision. Yes, *he* would use a Terran catch-phrase, and his admirals would hear him say it just before he gave them the order to advance... Like new rivers on a flood-plain the currents of fate were now pouring across the Sunnoad's field of view; his lofty brow puckered, his mind's eye strained, and with perfect timing he gave tongue:

"We have reached our understanding, you and I."

The timing was perfect because, at that most appropriate instant, the natural event of *refelc* occurred: above all points on the horizon the skies turned suddenly clear and twinkling as the stars popped into view—the symbolically ideal moment at which to resolve upon great adventure.

Holding his audience spooked and enthralled, the Sunnoad continued:

"We've reached it at a run, haven't we? While your thoughts, like mine, energetically pursue the open question, whether this is a mere fleet exercise or the real thing, a shyer question squirms within, namely, *what* real thing? The public knows we've loaded each of our ships with a *tetrak*: a device which should enable us to interpenetrate the molecules of solid matter and explore the depths of our planet in the manner of the Bismuth Era voyages twenty million days ago. A great enough idea; but rumours abound, that it is a blind; that an even greater mission is 'on the cards'. You, and some others, correctly believe that the real aim of our muster is the ultimate overland assault on Arclour."

He paused with a slow nod, as if to say, don't deny it. The hush was absolute; and so he went on:

"Arclour. A rarely spoken name, yet never forgotten; what citizen of Syoom has not at some time thought about reaching the Starlit Polar land? 'Onward to Arclour' was the watchword for my ancient ill-fated predecessor, the 723rd Sunnoad, and we all know what happened to him, and to his vast fleet, yet we also always knew that we Nenns could not remain intimidated forever." With a new bite of formality, his speech slowed. "I have pressed the crystal button, I am speaking etched words, every syllable graven as record, as I now say that we, today, will begin the second serious attempt upon that antipodeal Pole."

At that moment *refelc* came to an end. The spellbound admirals had ignored the usual solemn watch during the three-minute appearance of the stars, for the beauty of the heavens could not compete with the Sunnoad's portentous words. But as the Noad of Noads paused after his phrase *antipodeal Pole*, and the moment of brightening occurred whereby the stars disappeared, the sky went from black to deep blue, and morning-shine began all over Ooranye, his eight key subordinates gazed at each other in the light of a new day and their eyes and teeth flashed in an instant of ecstatic pain—for to be alive at such a moment is to writhe in the clamp of history. The next instant, recovered from the nigh unbearable spasm of context-awareness, more calmly and joyously they sensed their new freedom: for whereas the Sunnoad had taken all the responsibility upon himself, the glory of success must be shared around!

Iyen Noom continued with remarks calculated to reassure as he built up to the formal and irrevocable command:

"We can do it. We have 240 ships whereas Fiarr Fosn had 1500; but we have what he did not—the lessons of disaster. If we move this very hour, I predict that we shall, within days, stand on the very point antipodeal to Syoom's Sunward capital. How do I know that this is the best time? I do not know; no one can be sure; no one can see into the future to gain hindsight of the best. But as the Terrans say, *How long is a piece of string?* We procrastinate no longer. Plan UTHU2—execute!"

The grey complexion of Uranian skin is rarely affected by the emotions within, but at those last words the eight admirals coloured a visible tinge of mauve, as in a flurry of elation they relayed the order to their captains; infected by the same enthusiasm, captains passed the tidings to crews; diffusing more widely still, the radio messages were overheard at scattered encampments of gathered watchers across the plains, both friendly and hostile, who had been drawn by curiosity to keep an eye on developments, and who now saw 240 lofty ovoids begin to hum away in the direction of the Fyayman border.

In a tidal wave of exultant awe the news of the mission roared through the ether across all the main population centres of Syoom: *the Sunnoad has given the order; the Fleet is headed for the Starlit Pole, the conquest of Arclour!*

From millions of human minds, emotions poured into the atmosphere. Consequently the microscopic *throom* quivered into renewed alignment like suddenly magnetised iron filings. Net result: an *eomasp*, the unscheduled re-appearance of the stars, mere minutes—instead of the normal fifteen hours—after their last show.

All who had heard the news about the Expedition could immediately understand why the eomasp had occurred now, and why, therefore, the long Actinium Era had reached its close. The huge collective excitement was at once the cause, the justification and the announcement of a re-set of the calendar, and today must count as a Day One.

Hail the outset of the Thorium Era!

Only—doubts arose during the rapturous communion under the unscheduled stars. While crowds of faces recognized their own wild thrill in others' eyes, there occurred the strange supplementary quiver, the peculiar flicker which might or might not count as a subsidiary, "nested" eomasp.

On the ground, among the population at large, the new uncertainty did no more than cast some temporary doubt upon the count of eras. But up in the Sunnoad's fleet there was consternation among the admirals. Linked by televisor to the flagship control room, they were in a position to note that one face alone appeared significantly relaxed.

Sunnoad Iyen Noom 80525, to judge from his expression, knew what was going on.

Must they simply trust his fatalistic understanding?

They were underway, they were committed, but still, to be effective, they had to be more "in the know".

After some conference with his peers, Admiral Capfaym Duuv was appointed spokesman. His youngish face more gauntly drawn than usual, he turned back to the screen image of the man in the golden cloak.

It was an awkward moment. One does not lightly interrogate the Sunnoad.

The admiral had, however, thought of a tactful opening.

He said, "Sunnoad I-N, *have* we begun the Thorium Era, or—have we leaped over it?"

Iyen Noom replied, "You refer to the quiver in the air. That was the 'leap'. Yes, we are now in Day One of the following, Protactinium Era."

"Then what happened to the Thorium? Why was it stillborn? Some huge event must have occurred, to make the eomasp double; yet what could equal this expedition-launch?"

"Well put, Capfaym," said Iyen Noom. "You did right to ask me." Drawing a deep breath, like one who has decided (as you Terrans put it) to "come clean", he continued: "We need to remember certain exceptions in our history. Eomasps are associated with mass emotion, but we need to ask ourselves, 'emotion' felt by whom? Or by what, where?" He smiled a trifle regretfully, and remarked, "I can see you are thinking that I am about to claim that I alone, by virtue of my position, was able to cause the 'nested' disturbance. Well, I did feel that extra eomasp answer to something within me. It made immediate sense in view of a decision I had reached, purely in my own mind. You wonder at this. Can any one human mind, you ask yourselves, be powerful enough to alter the rhythm of daylight? No, but—*one can choose a path which leads that way.*"

"And what path is that, Sunnoad I-N?" asked Capfaym amid the eerie suspense.

"The path of avoidance," replied Iyen Noom. "Avoidance of the disaster which befell Fiarr Fosn 723 and the First Fleet. I can tell you now what I could not tell you before, that we are headed for *success.*"

They had never seen the Sunnoad look so grim. It was as if the idea of 'success' in an enterprise of this magnitude entailed a new kind of fear.

He went on, "Our penetration into Fyaym will doubtless arouse some powers against us. At the first sign of their appearance, our revised Plan UTHU2 dictates evasive action by an alteration of route. Instead of trying to fight our way past a Fyayman enemy, each of our ships will use its *tetrak* to disappear into the body of the planet, follow a transect within its curvature and re-emerge at close proximity to Arclour. An option that certainly wasn't available to Fiarr Fosn."

Would they accept such strategy? In their heart of hearts?

"But," mused Tyarwa Zade, "even if Fiarr Fosn had possessed tetraks, would he have used them, thus leaving all his enemies between him and Syoom?"

"Fiarr Fosn," said Iyen Noom, "committed fifteen hundred ships to his enterprise and advanced along a Syoom-wide front, rousing all Fyaym against him. I by contrast shall lead less than one sixth of that number, in compact formation. We're not leaving Syoom denuded of defence and we'll cause less of a stir. Discoverers, not conquerors, is what we aim to be. Still taking a risk—but a different sort of risk."

"The risk of success," nodded Tyarwa Zade.

"That's it," smiled the Sunnoad. "And the instant I made my decision, this entire probability-line of success became the main one, and the other split off. Hence the eomasp-within-an-eomasp: a troublous ripple in the ether, signalling a fork in destiny."

"So—no Thorium Era for us," said Capfaym Duuv.

"Not on this time-line, no. The aborted Thorium Era was the one in which we undertook to fight our way to Arclour; a line cancelled, rejected, wiped out as far as we're concerned." The voice of Iyen Noom 80525 sank to an elegiac murmur. "And so the wail of the unborn Thorium becomes a whisper and then a fading memory, a tremor, a crunch of gears, a parcelled *eomasp* unopened, while we sail on into the Protactinium."

His string of mixed metaphors flailed them into silence, except for one question from the admiral with the sharpest tongue:

"But why decide just then?" wondered Tyarwa Zade.

The Sunnoad brightly quoted again: "'How long is a piece of string?'" He added, "We're passing into Fyaym now. We'll end this conference. You'll want to supervise your captains."

Indeed the fleet had just that instant crossed the invisible boundary, "sfy-50", which separates Syoom, the civilized world, from its antithesis, *Fyaym*—the land described statistically as that area in which a lone wayfarer has a *less*-than-fifty-per-cent probability of surviving a thousand-mile journey.

That's the dry definition; but when the rains of emotion flood into the scene, they give forth baleful growths.

You don't have to be the Sunnoad to see the Fyayman plains as a different "colour" from those of Syoom. Literally, of course, there may be no difference; but just as you Terrans have a saying about viewing life through "rose-tinted spectacles", so the Uranian venturer into Fyaym may see the land through a "liver-tinted" glass of justified dread. Not that this stops the hardy wayfarer—it may act as an inspiration. Besides, there are degrees of Fyaym; in some areas just across the border there lies a "continental shelf" of relatively mild perils, whereas in other sections the chances of individual survival drop steeply as you probe into the wilderness. Of course if instead of going alone you travel as part of a company, your prospects are usually brighter, though in such a case the calculation becomes so complex that statisticians are apt to throw up their hands in despair, because one then needs to factor in the likelihood of attracting attention from higher Fyayman powers.

You don't have to be the Sunnoad to see all this; but if by chance you are the Sunnoad, your faculties can scribble their visionary notes across your eyeballs in peculiar encouragements or warnings scarcely imaginable to other folk. The closest advisors to Iyen Noom 80525 have testified, however, that he remained confident as the fleet plunged deeper into the unknown.

This confidence roused equal hope and dismay in the mind of Chy Nexepp, flagship Navigator and would-be Corrector.

His fingernails bit into his palms as he whispered to himself, *my chance, my chance*. All his life he had known what he wanted to be: the man who proved himself right and the Sunnoad wrong.

The clash occurred early on day four.

The fleet had had a "clear run" until near the end of day three of the voyage, and of the Protactinium Era. Then lookouts spotted signs of serious opposition to the passage of the ships through the skies of Fyaym. The ovoid hulls of the Syoomean airship had been grazing the peaks of a range of saw-toothed mauve mountains banded with pink and white clouds, when suddenly a vast tentacle of grey mist squirmed out of a canyon ahead of them, accompanied by a dusting of flyer-motes, and Iyen Noom at once read the presence of an alliance between nebular and ground-based powers. "We'll look into this—but not now," he declared to the officers in the control room, and forthwith gave the order for each ship in the fleet to use its *tetrak*. The duty technician who had spent days waiting for this moment pressed a stud and everyone on board experienced a queasy moment; the view through the screens and floor blurred as though the solid world had turned into pale vapour. The only hard shapes still visible were the other ships of the fleet, who likewise had phased into "between" mode; they and the flagship were still solid to each other. "Descend," the Sunnoad commanded his Navigator, "on the UTHU2 bearing." Chy Nexepp obeyed; the floor tilted; the chairs swung to adjust as *Vaneng* followed by the other ships aimed its prow down into the vaporous fuzz that was Ooranye. The transect began.

Nobody had done anything like this since the Bismuth Era, but no doubts were expressed.

A few hours later Chy Nexepp, dourly determined, thumbed open the door of the Sunnoad's cabin and shut it behind him. He opened his mouth but Iyen Noom beat him to it. "You want to know," the Sunnoad said, "how much I am considering the possibility, that the conspiracy theories might be true: that there is a Terran base somewhere on Ooranye and that the most logical place for it is Arclour—the conveniently remote land which we Nenns have never reached. Well, you can have my answer, which is—I wouldn't be surprised."

Chy Nexepp's mouth gaped in mingled triumph and panic. He'd yearned for an issue on which he might challenge the Sunnoad and thus go down in history as a Corrector. And now he'd got it he was terrified. "But then—for skies' sake!

we shouldn't be doing this!" A muscle in his glistening cheek twitched...

"So," said Iyen Noom drily, "you've just worked it out, Chy. Left it a bit late, haven't you?"

"It's hearing you admit it so coolly," husked the Navigator. "It's hearing how you admit all and yet seem not to understand." He had just put it more strongly than anyone should, except one who aspired to be a Corrector, but he saw, with a pang, that the Sunnoad looked merely amused.

"State your case."

Chy collected himself. "If the Terrans have landed on our world, it would be a big mistake to find out." Silence. Another try: "Sunnoad, we could be headed for a calamity that would make the end of Fiarr Fosn's expedition look like a picnic. At least *he* was beaten by native Uranian forces..."

Iyen Noom gave a nod, merely courteous, not impressed.

"Is ignorance bliss, then?" he relaxedly asked.

"At the moment, yes! At the moment the Terrans' influence is manageable! After all, we're influencing them too; from what they tell us, our tales are 'all the rage' there. But if we find a colony of them lurking actually on our world... it might mean war."

"And might they win?"

"Who knows? Their world is tiny compared with ours, but—size isn't everything. They are the ones with space travel."

The Sunnoad stooped by a desk, toyed with a pen and then looked up. Chy Nexepp saw in his leader's eyes that the argument was over.

"Chy, you have not stated openly the source of your fear. Deep down you dread encountering the Terrans because you find the idea *spooky*. You sense, as we all do, that between our species there is a huger divide than any of us have so far put into words. We're happy to talk to them over the ether, but the prospect of a face-to-face meeting with them would seem, to you or me or any Nenn, uncanny. And what I'm counting on is—*that they feel the same way about us*. Think: whether they have a secret base or not, they have never dared to land openly on our world."

Chy Nexepp departed the room in a mood of defeat. The conversation had not found any usable outlet for a would-be Corrector. Thus, the voyage continued without political upheaval. Nobody else dared to suggest that this Second Fleet might suffer a fate more disastrous than that of the ancient First.

Near the end of Day Eight, the airships returned to their natural element as they slanted up into the air of Ooranye and phased back from intermolecular to normal solid mode. Whoops erupted from normally dignified crewmen at the completion of the subsurface transect. The fantastic achievement of the ages would shortly be theirs! They had almost reached the very borders of fabled Arclour with its legendary starry skies, confirmed theoretically by scientists who predicted a "polar hole" in the upper atmospheric *throom* layer, and sure enough, through the upper ports of each vessel the stars indeed already shone! On the last hour of its voyage the sky-fleet, thus arrayed in stellar gleams, sailed under the glory of the Milky Way towards its final destiny. Every minute or so someone would utter a comment of wonder, make a gesture of triumph, or let out a cheer. Presently these high spirits died down, as up ahead a disquieting shape began to loom. The fleet came to a hovering halt.

Juf Nootarl, chief gunner at his post in the blister under *Vaneng*, became professionally wary as he viewed the peculiar wall which stretched across the forward horizon. He muttered a rare, mythical word, "Cuvv", while hurriedly he re-checked the sighting-controls of his weapon systems. Magnified further in those 'scopes the "wall" became a twisted fabric of writhing and pulsing cloud, like a brown matting of slow-motion tornadoes hung from some invisible curtain-rail which doubtless extended all around the Pole. This indeed looked like the legendary "Cuvv", the barrier which some traditions suggested must surround Arclour. The gunner could only gaze at it for a minute or so before a horror crept upon his brain and he had to avert his eyes. He preferred to look at the face of the Sunnoad. Who knew what patterns that man was seeing? They seemed to elate him; had he been expecting something worse? Things looked sufficiently bad to Juf. The wall, the Cuvv, seemed uncanny, and the worst was not knowing why.

Then he froze in further shock: the Sunnoad's eyes met his.

"I'm going out," Juf heard the Noad of Noads say. "And you, gunner, carrying your remote control box, will follow me, to the Wall. The rest of the Fleet stays where it is."

A hiss of indrawn breath from Navigator Chy Nexepp—but no protest. Insanely audacious though it appeared, the move could be justified. Relay-formations were a part of Syoomean strategy. The Fleet itself had shed one ship every five hundred miles to form a chain of relays stretching back along its route from Syoom, most of them still in intermolecular mode as they hovered inside the planet, so that the expedition's total strength in vessels at Arclour had been reduced to a mere two hundred. Iyen Noom was now adapting the relay principle to personal reconnaissance, and the big question in the would-be Corrector's mind was, *is this my chance? Has he played into my hands? Or is this his final victory? Damn it, flunnd it, I cannot tell which.*

From the two hundred ships all eyes watched two men dwindle across the plain against the backdrop of the Wall: the Sunnoad skimming ahead, the gunner following half a mile behind. No one yet knew whether they were witnessing heroism or madness. But they all accepted the principle which allocates the tallest plumes of risk to the top rankers, who from their heights of achievement are likely to see furthest.

Iyen Noom 80525 came to a halt about fifty yards from the oppressive cloud-wall. Half dreamily he reflected, *I have nowhere to go but through.* Indeed his next move, as you are likely to have read in previous versions of this story, was to open the throttle of his skimmer one more time and, in a surge of heroic daring, penetrate the barrier. Or rather—let us narrate the episode at a higher level of precision-he physically stayed where he was, but by the use of his unique faculties he saw through the barrier.

The situational vision, or context-awareness, of Sunnoad Iyen Noom, employed at full power, abruptly removed the Cuvv—wiped it from his field of view. This did not mean that it was an illusion, or that it had ceased to exist. But all objects now brought to his attention were visible to him *only according to their importance*.

We, the Bards, can invent what we like here. The tale is a complete fiction, after all, and has always been so, although (to use the convoluted plu-pluperfect verb tense necessary with reality-engineering) once upon a time it *had had* once been true…

So let us say that the Sunnoad looked upon a province of shimmering energies, of violet horizontal fields and spiral verticalities, of observation towers where suited figures worked upon platforms, some of them close to where he hovered—

The limitations of language will not, unfortunately, allow us to portray the relational *kind* of existence which he was able to smell out in front of him. Never mind; let us concentrate upon what happened next.

He had only glimpsed the Terrans for a minute or so when he noticed that the tempo of their movements had changed. *They were packing away!*

We, at our leisure, understand what Iyen Noom read instantaneously from patterns and motions: namely that the Terrans, noticing his gaze, knew that "the game was up". They could only hope that they had done their work uninterruptedly for long enough, to establish that the grafted past of Uranus-as-Ooranye would stay grafted, all the way back in retrospective reality, to give the formerly lifeless gas-giant planet its identity as the habitable world which (now) always has been thus—

You might say their "piece of string" turned out to be long enough.

A sense of this accomplishment came to the Sunnoad as

he saw the border of the shimmering Terran colony begin to recede. The area governed by the aliens shrank as he watched. Now he himself did move physically forward. He radioed an instruction to the gunner, Juf Nootarl, to follow him at a constant distance; the fleet, he knew, would follow Juf. Having made these arrangements Sunnoad Iyen Noom skimmed in wordless pursuit of the diminishing alien power until, a couple of hours later, its shrunken circle drained into a final vortex of non-existence. He was left alone above a field of crunchy curl-leaved vegetation called *spruth* at the very Starlit Pole of Ooranye. He dismounted and trod that ground, the first Nenn ever to do so.

His fleet arrived minutes later, and hovered at a few hundred yards' respectful distance, seeing him bowed in thought down on the plain. They left him in peace to commune, while they, aboard the ships, revelled joyously in this historic moment and relayed emotional messages back to Syoom, causing the eomasp of that day, and the start of the Final Era. The fearsome Cuvv was forgotten as if it had never been, by all save Iyen Noom. And that was *because* it had never been. Cuvv? What Cuvv? Only the most slender tradition, a now-always-fictitious tradition, allows us to mention that fearsome cylindrical Wall, a fence of pressured gas-giant atmosphere, a relic of what now never was, in our tale. The admirals, captains and crews were joyously un-bothered. They had no awareness of what "had had been" the truth.

Presently the Sunnoad walked to stand under his flagship's hull. Seeing he had finished his meditations the duty officer pressed a button and an *ayash* air-tube whisked him up into the hold of *Vaneng*. Everybody thought they understood the abstracted mien with which he received their congratulations as he strode to the control room, for they, too, were dazed by what they had done, though unlike Iyen Noom they had no idea how *much* they had done. He broadcast a dignified speech, in suitably fine words to celebrate a new era, and then informed them all that he intended to remain in this region for some few hundreds of days, to establish the first colony of Nenns in Arclour.

During that pioneering epoch adventurers and sightseers flocked all the way from Syoom to the polar starlit plains. The risks of the journey remained formidable even for large fleets, and were all the greater for smaller parties, but nothing could abate the enthusiasm of the Syoomeans during the great dawn-days of Era 92. The known presence of the Sunnoad as well as the tales of excited travellers encouraged emigration to Bvozzik, the town that grew within sight of the Pole. Cultivation of the *spruth* yielded an energy bonanza, for the plants provide far more raw power than do the vheic. Iyen Noom mingled with the enterprising throngs, honouring them, encouraging them, but also causing some disquiet by his melancholy. They had plenty of opportunity to guess that some revelation had deeply disturbed him. With every day that passed more people began to wonder what the man had seen, and what awful thing he had learned.

Surely, a Sunnoad would either tell without being asked, or would think it best not to tell. Therefore, for a while, nobody ventured to tackle him with any such direct question, until at last on Day 25 of the Uranium Era he was approached by Flonor Gohuz, one of the so-called "silent admirals", a first-lifer like the Sunnoad himself, who had followed him in quiet obedience on his great voyage. Daring to waylay the Noad of Noads during one of the latter's times of solitude on the summit of a low hill on the outskirts of Bvozzik, the admiral made a shrewd offer:

"Whatever has distressed you, Sunnoad I-N, must be too uncanny for the public to accept. So, why not tell it to me in confidence, that I may then take it to the Bards, and that they then make a fiction out of it?"

"It is fiction now," replied Iyen Noom, and then, noting the Admiral's puzzlement, added drily, "I'll do as you suggest."

He proceeded to narrate the far-fetched history which you are reading.

Flonor Gohuz departed from the Sunnoad's presence in the belief that he had helped. He had not. The deep-rooted personal problem remained for Iyen Noom 80525, who alone had perceived the ex-truth before it had forever ceased to have ever been true. And now, thanks to his cursed faculty of context-awareness, which seemed immune to cause-and-effect, he remained the sole remaining plague-spot of awareness that once things *had had been* different; so that, while he lived, the integrity of the entire planet Ooranye remained tainted to that extent, by that one plu-plu-perfect drip, the leakage from the expunged reality.

The cure must be that he disappear. He must get lost and die. Then, the last link with what *had had* been would be gone like the last lingering dot in a switched-off vidscreen. Thenceforth, only pure fiction would remain to tell of the Terran hand in Ooranye's origin, and who cares about harmless fabrications?

Yes, *he* was the only spoiler. With him gone, and the world untroubled by doubts, and the economy furnished with the powerful new *spruth*-fuel (which experiments showed was not altitude-dependent like vheic), Nenns could achieve space-travel at last, and enter upon their natural primacy.

3: both

NOAV NEEN LAY propped on one elbow. Munching rations, he kept a keen eye upon the swale below the ridge. He had stalked his quarry on foot; his skimmer, with its betraying hum, lay grounded a half mile away, in this scene empty of humanity, over a hundred and fifty miles from Bvozzik and deep in the wilds of peripheral Arclour. Hunters must be scattered thinly out here, nor could he spot his prey, the tri-zdeel. It had bounced behind another ridge and by this time might be prepared to come at him from any direction. The mutual gamble, whereby Noav Neen was quarry as well as pursuer, plus the tri-zdeel's unprovoked attacks upon farmsteads, allowed him to hunt it with a clear conscience.

Noav Neen was part of the second wave of immigrants to Arclour in these delirious early days of Era 92. If he survived to return to his native Syoomean village of Hazz, he'd take back a fund of glorious tales to last him the rest of his life, as well as some material wealth. The new settlement, Bvozzik, after a initial flourishing spurt, was besieged from all sides by malevolent creatures, hazardous clouds, various predictably unforeseeable Fyayman forces; this was the expected Time of Troubles, an ideal period for Noav and the other adventurous spirits who had crossed the world to seek their fortunes where life was cheap yet vivid. If he were killed, he'd surely begin his second life with a satisfying soul-rootedness in the era's heroic dawn. A good bargain for a backgrounder, who accepts life as a backgrounder does, in obscurity redeemed by the halation of glory which surrounds everyday things.

His grip tightened on his drawn laser: the tri-zdeel, twice man-high, had rolled into view below, fifty yards off, from behind some boulders on the right of the slope.

A ball furrowed by three grooves, the nightmarish creature bulged this way and that as if pummelled from within. Noav Neen tried to judge the distance and the terrain, to determine whether to risk a flank attack. Then, to his shock, a man appeared, following the zdeel at a distance of a mere twenty yards. The hunter loped forward, apparently intent upon giving battle; the zdeel sensed his presence, turned, split...

Noav Neen made ready to spring but the other man, who looked rather old for this game, was acquitting himself well, wielding his laser sponnd expertly to bisect one of the monster's components before the others could complete its surrounding manoeuvre, and then fencing with his back to a boulder. The remainder of the zdeel whizzed and slashed with steel-tipped tentacles; the man seemed to be a match for them but he would tire... Noav decided to intervene. He strode down-slope to hit the monster in flank. Within thirty seconds the job was done; segments of zdeel lay twitching as their blood oozed into the soil.

Turning to greet the stranger, Noav was at first prepared to receive some mild reproach for having robbed him of the sole credit for the kill, but in the fellow's demeanour there was such lofty ease and dignity as to rule that out. Only the slightest hint of wry disappointment showed in the olster's smile as he sighed, "Thank you, sponndar."

"Thank *you*, sponndar," reciprocated Noav, realizing that the other did not want to give his name.

Whoever he was, a sort of intangible costume, a pleated aura of tremendous responsibility, hung about him as they conversed, though the man was quite affable, sitting on a boulder and sharing reminiscences like any chance-met stranger. Partway through their chat, a meteor of an idea streaked through Noav's mind.

Sure it was, he'd heard some rumour... the Sunnoad had not been seen in many days... but no, it was too fantastic... the notion faded in the light of common sense.

Noav presently said, "Look, sponndar, I feel obliged to warn you, as one hunter to another, your technique is going to get you killed quite soon. You need to learn a reasonable amount of caution..."

The man appeared to consider this. A smile quirked: "What price reason? Why are you here? To impress some girl back home, I'll bet."

Noav Neen opened his mouth and could not find a word.

"Ha!" the stranger grinned, "I have, as the Terrans would say, hit a bull's eye—whatever a bull may be."

It was as impossible to resent the good humour of this statement, as it was to deny its accuracy. Before long the youngster was confiding in the elder, recounting various puzzlements in his chequered relationship with Reyazz. Trying to be scrupulously fair, Noav included the admission, "I was wrong to judge Reyazz. As my grandmother says: *The love that comes last*

/ Redecorates the past..."

He went on talking for a while without noticing that the older man had straightened, with a new brightness in his eyes, like one who hears a thunderous victory-charge that puts to flight his former reason to die.

"Hmm... er... I must be getting back to work," mumbled the stranger, almost stammering as his former weary sagacity was curdled by hope. "Thank you very much indeed for all your help—and advice."

Noav, seeing the transformation of the other's expression, responded, politely but mystified, "Glad to be of assistance." *Skies! What did I say?* He added, "I don't know who you are but my guess is, you've got something better to do than hunt tri-zdeels."

"And when you get back to your Reyazz," smiled the other, "you'll be able to tell her that you did something more than hunt, today." And he took his leave.

Cryptic to the last, thought Noav as the other receded from view. But after all, such was pioneer life: a scrawl of paths, loosely scattered, randomly intersecting.

Anyhow, it might make another good tale to tell Reyazz, if I can but do three more things: one, survive this hunting stint; two, chance to learn to whom I talked just now; and three, return safe to Syoom.

As a matter of fact these extra things eventually were achieved by that paradoxically renowned backgrounder, known in after days as Corrector Noav Neen.

PART 2: TAKING ADVANTAGE

…FROLICKING/RAMPAGING/TRIPPING THROUGH THE OLD SOLAR SYSTEM:

Dylan T. Jeninga is an enthusiast of the fantastic yet (perhaps marginally) credible, and it was this interest that drew him to science fiction when he was a young boy, and more recently to the classic tales of our Solar System as it ought to have been. Born near the Wisconsin/Illinois border on the last day of 1993, he now lives in Chicago with his soon-to-be-wife (who, the reader may be sure, has a hand in shaping everything he creates). He works as an improvisational actor/hopefully temporary shop clerk, and he writes everything from realistic adventures among the planets to sojourns to the distant stars.

In "Incandescence," Jeninga takes us to a more familiar ball of fusing gas. This chronicle of adventure on the Sun reminds us that even amid the wonders of the Old Solar System, there may be more to the universe than we anticipate...

INCANDESCENCE

Dylan T. Jeninga

Solar Resources, INC.
Meri Solar Orbital Station Report
Date: 9.16.2732
Subject: Account of the incident involving Neutron Collection Rig #1313 given by Neutron Rig Operator 115386

I'M NOT CRAZY.
I know how intense it is, I've been a neutron miner for six years. The surface where we work is nearly six thousand Kelvin and the gravity is twenty-eight times Earth normal. Nothing could survive in that. I'm a Jovian kid and even I think that's too much.

But I know what I saw.

It was near the end of my rotation, and I was getting ready for three months on Venus with the family—we've been saving up, and I couldn't wait to get away from the sharp edges of the Rig for some tropical beaches. I had already started cleaning up for Alejandra, my alternate, since she always leaves the place tidy and I like to return the favor. After all, our rig is our home for half the year.

I was in the nest—the bridge. I get pretty cozy in there, with snacks and pillows and the last season of whatever show

I'm watching. I can never get the current season, solar interference makes radio and laser communication a lost cause, and it's not like corporate'll let me dispatch a courier droid to pick up the latest episode of Far Horizons.

I was keeping an eye on the systems when I noticed the temperature on A deck was way up. That's the observation deck. I didn't bother to check the readings from the heat funnels in question, they konk out sometimes and it's a pretty quick fix. If I had, I might have suspected something was up.

I threw on my sunsuit and grabbed my tools. I always wear my suit when I'm working on a technical issue in case of unexpected accidents. They'll save you from getting fried, though not everybody likes 'em because they're cumbersome to work in. I know one guy who just prefers to go naked unless it's an EVA.

I was heading up the stairs when I got an alert on my Heads Up Display. The photonic force shield was triggering on A deck. Unusual, but not unheard of, the shield mostly keeps us floating on the photosphere, but occasionally a solar flare comes down on top of us. In fact, I thought, that explained the heat spike. It didn't strike me then that with a flare, the shield is triggered first, and the spike follows after.

So I got to A deck and checked the thermometer beside the door. The temperature inside had gone up since I left the nest by almost four hundred Kelvin. No going naked then even if I'd wanted to, it was at a sunsuit-mandatory level; something was dangerously wrong with the funnel in there. I grabbed the handle. It was warm to the touch despite my insulated gauntlet. I pulled the door open...

And damn near went blind. The visor on my helmet adjusted as quickly as it could, and the wide duraglass windows struggled to compensate as well, but they couldn't dim it completely. There was this incandescent... thing blazing right outside. It floated by the window, flickering brilliantly like a nuclear candle, and It moved, pushing against the shields and making them ripple. Even through my clamped eyelids,

I saw it flit luminously back and forth, reaching out with tendrils like it was trying to get in. And the heat—it hit me like a wave!

I slammed the door. I'm not ashamed to admit, I was sweating, and from more than just the heat. I stood there staring straight ahead, watching the afterimage dance before my eyes, taking deep breaths and trying to get a grip.

There isn't any life on the Sun, I know. How can there be? But I saw something, some kind of... being, and there really was a temperature jump. You can check the system alerts on my suit.

I ran back up to the nest and threw myself into my chair, praying under my breath the whole way. For an hour I stared at the thermometers, shields and funnel readings, not even taking off my suit. When nothing happened, I began to scold myself. An experienced neutron miner like me, getting jumpy at what was probably a coronal mass ejection? I wondered if maybe the solitude was finally getting to me. That was when I sent the first courier, the one asking for a few days early leave on psychological grounds, just in case.

But then it happened again. A heat spike on B deck, just one deck down from the first - recreation - and then a hit to the shields.

The funnels were working full bore, trying to keep up, but the temperature was climbing steadily. Part of me was reluctant to leave the relative security of the nest, but I had to find out if I had really seen what I thought I had. I went down to G deck first and grabbed the biggest, heaviest wrench in the workshop. Never mind that it would probably be useless, it made me feel safer, holding it like a club.

When I got up to B deck, perspiration was already collecting inside my visor. The thermal readings on my HUD told me it was hotter up here than last time, by several hundred degrees, and there was a smoke alert inside the rec room. The handle of the door was scorching when I touched it.

Everything within was burning or melting, the workout

benches, the pool table, the gaming station. The walls, ceiling and floor glowed a dull red. The small viewports were beginning to warp, but nonetheless it was unmistakable - the ephemeral light of the thing I had seen before, right outside.

I slammed the door shut and hurried back to the nest, hindered by my clumsy suit, and focused the shield around B deck. The temperature dipped slightly, and when I drained the air from the room to put the fires out the heat funnels were able to really cool things off. But of course, focusing the shield on one spot weakened them everywhere else.

There was a spike and a hit on C deck, habitation. In a panic I refocused the shield again. There was another spike on D, and then K, I, F—the thing was jumping around, and I swear it was testing my defenses. I strengthened the shields wherever they took a hit, but I was playing catch up, and the unwieldy gloves meant I was hardly agile. I don't know how long that went on, time became lost to me, but I knew a slip up was inevitable.

Suddenly, there was a blow to the shields like nothing that had come before on J deck, neutron storage and fuel processing. Now, the shields around that deck are normally thinner, that's where the magnetic sifters are, and they need to be able to pull neutrons through from the photosphere. It wouldn't take much to penetrate them.

You hear about accidents in space, a spaceship vaporized because a few grams of neutron fuel weren't contained properly. I was sitting on thousands of tons of the stuff, and that thing was doing damage from outside, even if it never got in.

I didn't think, I just pulled the bulk of the shields there, cocooned J deck so totally that it would have taken all the guns of Solfleet to get through them. I don't know how it knew I would do that, maybe it didn't. But it left me wide open.

My monitor went red. There was a breach on D, life support. Evacuate. That was when I sent the second courier, letting you know I was abandoning my post.

I stumbled to my feet, clutching my wrench, and stepped onto the stairwell. The searing heat practically bowled me over, and I staggered back into the nest. The thing was a few decks below me, but the rig felt like the mouth of a volcano. The thermometer on my HUD read thousands of Kelvin, near the limits of my protection.

The lights flickered and died, and the red emergency lights shown through the smoke. Tentatively, I stepped back out onto the stairs. Out of the darkness below, there was an infernal glow, like the devil rising out of hell. It was getting closer. It was coming for me.

I ran so hard, I didn't even notice the sunsuit.

I realize now that if the gravity filters had cut out, or the shields had shut down, or the heat funnels had all malfunctioned, I would have been dead in a second; boiled in my suit or crushed by the pull of the Sun. None of that occured to me at the time, but I'm surprised it didn't happen before I got out. The fury of Sol had got inside and it wouldn't be long before the rig collapsed like it was made of wax.

The station interior was a furnace, the angry orange glow of the steel walls illuminating a thick smoke that shrouded everything. If I didn't know the layout so well, I never would have made it to the escape pod.

I wasn't fast enough. I only remember getting inside the pod and looking out of the unclosed hatch, seeing it come up the stairs. It was like Moses seeing the face of Jehovah. I only caught a glimpse of it before I lost my vision, burned out my retinas, the doctors say. But for a moment, I stared into that god of searing fire, and I think it saw me too.

I guess I got away. Someone picked me up in orbit and brought me to Meri Station. I don't really remember any of that.

You corporate suits won't believe me. Mental stress, you'll say, or I just got lazy and let a flare trash my rig. I don't think that much neutron fuel has ever gone up at once, they could probably see the flash from Pluto. Trillions of dollars lost,

I'm fired of course. I'll probably go to jail for criminal neglect of company property, or else you'll sue me into oblivion.

But the surface area of the Sun is more than six billion kilometers squared, more than enough room for there to be things that we, who have conquered the Solar System, have never seen.

There are other rigs out on the photosphere. It was real. You'll see.

Troy Jones III has had stories published in the After Oil *anthologies volumes 3 and 4, and (most recently) in* Merigan Tales: Stories from the World of Star's Reach. *He lives in Huntsville, Alabama.*

Mercury is one of the classic settings of Old Solar System fiction, and the tale of unexpected contact with dangerous extraterrestrial life was a standard theme of science fiction's Golden Age. "The Headless Skeletons of Mercury" is a title that could easily have graced a story in one of the great pulp magazines of that period, and Jones' story follows suit in a rousing contribution to the genre of interplanetary adventure...

THE HEADLESS SKELETONS OF MERCURY

Troy Jones III

It WOULD BE an understatement to say my brief sojourn on Mercury has been exciting—crazy, even. My arrival had been disaster enough, my rocket nearly crashing, and not two weeks later I found that Mercury had, in fact, *not yet begun to crazy*, as the kids say.

But first, before I can get to the exciting stuff, a staff meeting. (If I had to suffer through it then so do you now.) Director Sung paged everyone for an "all hands" emergency staff meeting. Nothing good ever comes of a staff meeting, I've found, emergency staff meetings doubly so. Sung actually even said "emergency all hands," like something out of a second-rate adventure tri-vid.

The reality of an all-hands staff meeting is, of course, considerably less exciting than a second-rate adventure tri-vid, emergency or no. (Little did I know, I'd soon have all the excitement I could handle.)

I was first to arrive in the conference room aside from Mister Sung himself. He does not like repeating himself, so Sung wouldn't say what was up until the full complement of staff—all sixteen of us—piled into the conference room. The unfortunates who'd been off-duty when the call went out were the last to arrive, wiping the sleep from their eyes as they stumbled into the meeting.

The very last into the conference room was Doctor Packard, one of the few people whose named I recalled (I am bad with names). She made her displeasure at being woken up known immediately.

"The Sun better be going supernova, brother," she drawled at Sung. (For some reason Doctor Packard calls everyone *brother* or *sister*, as appropriate.) "Otherwise, I'm headed back to bed."

I couldn't resist. "Just a regular nova," I said, smirking at my own wittiness. "Nothing worth waking up for."

Packard scoffed, but Director Sung held up a hand to forestall whatever witty rejoinder she may have had planned.

"Let's begin," he began. He pulled out a tablet and gave it a few taps. "First, you may notice we have a new face at the table. Everyone welcome DeJanay Jespers, our new life-support engineer." He gestured at me.

Everyone grumbled welcoming-ish noises. Some more welcoming-ish than others.

"D.J.," I said automatically. I gave an awkward little wave at everyone.

Sung tapped his tablet again, I presume making note of my nickname. "I'm sure she'll be a fine addition to the team. But that isn't why I've called you all here, of course. Scott, are you still there?"

"Yes," said a disembodied voice. I presumed (correctly, as it turned out) that Scott the Disembodied Voice was teleconferenced from Dayspring into the meeting.

(There are only two installations on Mercury, in case you don't know: Eventide Research Station, where we were, on the edge of tidally-locked Mercury's eternal night, and Dayspring Solar Observatory, which has a view of a tiny corner of the Sun from Mercury's eternal dawn.)

"Are you still receiving the transmissions?" Sung asked the voice.

"Yes."

Sung sighed irritably. "We're receiving another distress call," he announced to the meeting. "Sunside this time."

Heads swiveled to look at me. I put up my hands. "Not me this time," I clarified unnecessarily.

(The rocket that brought me here from Mars had made an unplanned emergency landing—don't say "crash"—during final approach less than two weeks ago, fortunately with no loss of life. Still, not a very auspicious start to my Mercury tour. I'm sad to think my own arrival may have occasioned an all-hands emergency staff meeting similar to this, and hope my co-workers do not resent me for it if it did.)

"Can you see the crash site from Dayspring?" Sung asked Scott.

"Kind of. It isn't over the horizon from me, but it's backlit by the sun. There's something there, but I can't get a clear visual on it."

"Have you been able to raise them by radio?"

"No. It's an automated emergency signal from a downed craft's black box. Or so it seems."

"So it seems?"

"Well, it *purports* to be an automated black-box signal. But the transponder UID and telemetry data are all gibberish. Can't extract a flight number, manifest, or even the name of the craft. Very strange."

Someone I didn't know volunteered a theory. "Maybe the black box is damaged?"

Director Sung raised his eyebrows at Cat, the senior communications tech (whom I knew because she was my bunkmate).

She was skeptical. "Possible? But that would be a very weirdly specific malfunction. Black boxes are designed to survive a crash, and are multiply redundant to prevent other failure modes. Of course, nothing is 100% crash-proof or

100% malfunction-proof, but a critically damaged black box will usually just stop transmitting. I've never heard of a black box damaged such that it will transmit gibberish," she said and scratched her head. She has enviably glossy black hair. "Black boxes are also very hard to deliberately tamper with, if anyone is thinking anything along those lines, although, again, nothing is 100% fool-proof. You can never underestimate people's ability to invent new forms of foolery."

"It's the skeletons," someone else whispered. Sung either didn't hear, or chose not to dignify that with a response.

I spoke up. "Military? Classified, maybe?"

Scott the Voice answered. "Ehh. That seems like the most reasonable hypothesis. The Agency has no record of any civilian craft passing by Mercury within the right timeframe, and no craft are reported missing anywhere in the solar system at the moment. It may be a classified craft with some kind of encrypted black box. It would have to be stealth, too; we didn't see it go down on radar. That doesn't really sit right with me either, though. No reason I can think of for the military to be out there Sunside. The whole thing makes no sense."

Director Sung waved away Scott's concern. "We are required by law to respond with all reasonable ability and haste to any distress signal. But we can't send a rocket because the rocket we should have had available crashed two weeks ago and isn't yet ready to return to service." He frowned at me, as if blaming me for that mishap. I wasn't even piloting the thing!

"It will be at least another week before we have a rocket," he continued. "So we'll have to send a rover. The problem is that the crash site is Sunside, deeper Sunside than our rovers are able to go safely. Scott, do you think you can modify a rover to go Sunside?"

"Ehh. I have a few ideas."

That answer didn't exactly inspire me with confidence, but it wasn't my place to criticize, so I held my peace.

Sung made more notes on his tablet. After a few moments he looked up at Doctor Packard. "Lynn," he said, "I'll need you to go. There may be casualties."

"What? Y'all can't send me Sunside! Do you see this red hair?" She pointed at her hair. "Do you see this pasty skin, brother? I will *burst into flames!*"

She was being facetious, of course. I grinned. I intuited (correctly, it turns out), that Doctor P. was someone I'd get along great with.

Sung ignored her objection and consulted his tablet again. "D.J.," he said—and I am 99% sure he had to read my name off his tablet—"I'm sending you too."

The grin fled from my face. "Me? I'm an enviro tech. I don't know anything about pulling injured people out of crashed rockets. I know about recycling your air and water."

Sung shook his head. "We're *all* scientists and technicians here, and a few medical personnel. No one who pulls people out of crashed rockets professionally. But we have to make do. It's the law. And since you're the new guy, you get to go. Plus, you have recent experience with crashed rockets, yes?"

"To tell the truth, it was more of an emergency landing than a crash, per se."

"Perhaps that's what this is, too."

So unfair! But he's the boss, so I nodded my acquiescence.

"While we're here," said Sung. "Let's go around the room and give updates on the projects we are working on."

The worst part of any staff meeting. But Doctor Packard took my arm and pulled me to my feet. "Come on, sister. Let's blow this taco stand."

Sung had not formally dismissed us, but neither did he make any move to stop us from leaving the meeting early. Whether that was because he recognized that time was of the essence in our rescue mission and there was no need to hold us in a meeting listening to TPS reports, or whether it was because Doctor Packard simply does whatever she wants, asking forgiveness afterwards instead of permission beforehand, I couldn't say.

(Lest anyone accuse me of needing a photographic memory to reconstruct these conversations, I would like to add here that all Agency meetings are transcribed electronically. I don't need to rely on my own memory to accurately relay what was said.)

In any event, Doctor Packard and I retrieved our spacesuits and boarded the train to Dayspring.

(Eventide and Dayspring are at opposite ends of the so-called Twilight Belt, the relatively least uninhabitable part of Mercury, bathed only in light from the Sun's corona. Eventide is on the edge of Mercury's deep-frozen eternal night, Dayspring on the edge of Mercury's deadly dawn. The two facilities are connected by a maglev monorail.)

On the way, Doctor Packard insisted I start calling her Lynn; since we would be spending several hours together in a rover cockpit, we might as well be BFFs (as she put it). The ride was mostly uneventful, though the view was amazing. Mercury in the ghostly light of the Sun's corona is so much cooler-looking than you might think—a literal Twilight Zone. Lynn and I were the only passengers on the train. Anyway, the train from Eventide to Dayspring runs *really* fast due to the lack of wind resistance. We were at Dayspring in what seemed like no time flat.

The rover was waiting for us amid a forest of solar panels. (Dayspring, in addition to the solar research observatory, also has a vast array of solar panels pointed toward the tiny corner of the Sun peaking over the horizon. It provides power for both itself and Eventide.) The rover's body was the size of a small bus, held a good four meters above the ground by six enormous knobbed tires and a complicated suspension system. *At least we won't have to worry about bottoming out*, I thought as I studied the vehicle through the train's window. A utility walker—looks like a five-meter-tall robot but has a person inside driving it—appeared to be welding spindly metal struts to the roof of the rover.

Scott's disembodied voice crackled over the train's PA system as soon as it stopped. "No time for pleasantries. Go ahead and suit up, if you haven't already, and EVA to the rover. I will let down the ladder for you. You can take off your helmets once you're inside."

The rover's hatch opened and a ladder descended. We suited up. I smushed my afro into the goldfish-bowl-like suit helmet and sealed it to my spacesuit's collar. Lynn and I double-checked each others' suits, per SOP. We left the train and clambered aboard the rover.

The utility walker, piloted by Scott, finished welding the metal struts to the roof of the rover and draped a highly reflective metallic cloth over it. (I presume the cloth was salvaged from a solar panel or something.) The metal arms he'd welded to the roof held the cloth in place, away from the body of the rover.

"That will have to do," came Scott's voice by way of the rover's transceiver. "I wouldn't want to attempt a Sunside crossing like this, but it should get us to the crash site and back. Our makeshift umbrella will reflect the worst of the light and radiation. Hopefully."

"Radiation?" Lynn asked.

"A few hours out there should be equivalent to smoking a few dozen packs of cigarettes, assuming we stay under the umbrella. Not something you'd want to do routinely, but a one-time trip should be all right."

I had a major concern. "How will we see to get there? This cloth completely blocks the windshield?"

"No way around that. We're driving directly into the Sun, and even with the best filters, we wouldn't make it very far with the Sun shining through the windshield, given that this is Mercury. We'll have to drive by instruments. Fortunately, it's mostly a straight shot. Just drive straight toward the radio signal and roll over any rocks and craters. There are no cliffs or major obstacles between here and there. That part should be easy enough."

"I will warn you though," he continued, "it's going to get hot even so. And not so much because of the Sun—at least not directly." I could feel a mansplaining coming on. "Mercury has no atmosphere worthy of the term. That's both good *and* bad from our perspective. Good, because we don't have to worry about being baked in the non-existent superhot air. Bad, because air-conditioning works by heat-exchange. But there's no air outside the rover to which we can exchange the heat building up inside-"

I cut him off. "I'm an engineer. I know how AC works."

"Ah right, sorry. Anyway, it will get hot, even with the umbrella. I don't know how long we can safely stay out there. Hours, probably, but how many hours I couldn't begin to guess."

"Scott," I asked. "Do you think there are any survivors out there?"

"No."

Lynn snorted. "Knew I shoulda stayed in bed."

"Sorry to be blunt, but no. If there are, then they've already broken the record for time spent Sunside on the surface, and it will be at least a couple of hours before we get there. But like Sung says, we have to check it out."

"You keep saying 'we'," Doctor Packard pointed out. "You're coming with? If so, ditch that walking tin can and get in here already. The sooner we get this over with, the sooner I can get back to my beauty sleep. And Heaven knows, I need all the help I can get in *that* department."

I grinned and held up a hand. Lynn gave me five.

"Not ditching the tin can. Old Sparky may come in handy out there. Sparky and I will ride on top of the rover. Once I'm finished out here, we'll be on our way."

He'd draped the reflective cloth such that there was a seam in the back that Old Sparky the Walker could duck through. And so the walker ducked under the "umbrella" and climbed back onto the rover, and we drove off into the everlasting sunset. (Or I guess it would be more of an everlasting sun*rise* since we were driving toward it.)

DRIVING AROUND SUNSIDE on Mercury with only a makeshift umbrella for protection sounds like it would be fun and exciting, but the reality of the drive to the presumptive crash site could only be described as tedious. The umbrella blocked our view of everything. We initially had the idea that I would drive while the good doctor caught a nap on the way, but the ride was way too rough for napping. I'm pretty sure we jounced and bounced over every single rock and crater on the whole of Mercury. (I think the rocks all secretly moved into our path when we weren't looking, just to mess with us, and brought all their cousins from Mars and the Moon. I am 99% sure that happened.) Imagine, if you will, driving a four-wheeler over the roughest rocky ground imaginable, at max throttle because there was a remote chance that there might be someone still alive waiting to be rescued... for hours. It was like that, but worse: low gravity gives the teeth-rattling, whiplash-causing bounces and bumps extra height. My job was to hold the control stick steady and keep the one blip on the instrument panel lined up with the other blip. Fun times.

We did get stuck once and Scott had to pull us free, so there was that bit of excitement on the way. One of Old Sparky's "hands" was a claw-like clamp at the end of a winch, which allowed him to "single-handedly" pull the rover back out of a pit of fine, sand-like particulate matter while the rover's prehensile "feet" clenched the rocky ground to provide an anchor. Once we were free, we drove around the quicksand pit.

Since Lynn couldn't take a nap, we chatted—where we were from, where we went to school, stuff like that. I mostly listened since I was focused on driving. Lynn shared funny doctor stories. Scott talked about piloting a battle-walker in the war. Regular conversation stuff.

At some point the conversation somehow moved to the possibility of discovering life on Mercury. I'd been under the impression that it'd been comprehensively proven impossible. Scott begged to differ.

"Anywhere energy is continuously pouring into an open

system," Scott was mansplaining again over the radio, "life can *and does* find a way to organize that energy flow into more life, and more complex life. The specific local conditions almost don't matter. Too hot? Life can adapt. Gravity too high, too low, too wildly variable? Life can adapt. Too much hard radiation? Life can adapt to that, too—to use it and depend on it, even. Just look at all the people who said life couldn't exist on Mars, or Venus, or Jupiter, or Titan. It doesn't just exist in those places, it flourishes. Where there's free energy flow, life is not just possible, but inevitable."

Lynn snorted derisively. "Scott believes in the *skeletons*."

Just then a particularly obnoxious rock bounced us clean into the air. Not the air—there is no air. Bounced us off the ground. I struggled to keep the rover on track as it slammed back down onto the surface.

"Skeletons?" I prompted.

I hadn't heard of the "skeletons," so they filled me in on the local legend. Occasionally, explorers and daredevils making Sunside forays would claim to have seen headless human skeletons, or sometimes headless animal skeletons, dancing in the distance—the dancing is apparently a pretty consistent feature of this particular legend—and swore up and down that their brains weren't addled by alcohol, or headpepper, or heatstroke. So far, no one had produced any incontrovertible photographic evidence of these dancing skeletons, of course. The excuse was that the hard light and harder radiation made cameras unreliable past a certain point Sunside, and the skeletons—naturally—lived beyond that point. No satellite had ever seen them either; if the things existed at all, they mostly stayed underground, apparently.

"I don't know about skeletons, but I'm sure there's life of some kind out there Sunside," said Scott. "Maybe just microbes or something. But definitely something."

I didn't care to let the conversation be steered toward microbes. "Maybe the skeletons only come out to taunt people attempting Sunside crossings."

"If we're lucky, they'll come out and taunt us!" said Lynn.

Scott didn't have anything to say to that. We bounced and flounced our way on across the sun-beaten wastes.

At some point, I looked for the "mute" button on the console, found it, and pushed it.

"What do you think of Scott?" I asked Lynn. "He seems like a fairly level-headed guy. Aside from believing in the skeletons or whatever."

"Scott?" the good Doctor shrugged. "He's a good kid."

"I don't even know what he looks like. Is he single?"

Lynn laughed heartily. "Sister, if you came to Mercury looking to hook up, you're on the wrong planet. This is the Twilight Zone in more ways than one. And, he looks about like someone who would be named 'Scott'. But, you'll get a chance to see him when we get back to Dayspring and you can judge for yourself."

A thought occurred to me and I uttered an impolite word. "I was planning to do my eyebrows today, but didn't get the chance. I will have to face him with my overgrown unibrow."

That got another laugh. "Guys don't care about eyebrows, sister. Trust me, I know."

"Yeah, but I feel more confident when I look like a normal person."

We continued chatting and laughing as the rover rattled along. Private girl stuff, you know.

Eventually I remembered to take Scott off mute.

The radio immediately crackled to life. "Okay, so, weird thing about the rover's radio," said Scott. "The transmitter and receiver have separate mute buttons. You muted me from being able to talk to you, but I've been able to hear you all this time."

I looked down at the console. It was true: two mute buttons. Dang it!

Lynn laughed. "So, like a true gentleman, you muted us on *your* end, right?"

Scott was quiet a moment. "I... ehh. I neither confirm nor deny that version of events," he said at last.

Lynn evidently thought that was hilarious and gave it a great belly laugh, but I was genuinely annoyed. I focused on driving, saying nothing.

After an awkward silence, Scott spoke up again. "You know, in ancient Greece and Rome, unibrows were considered beautiful, for both men and women. And anyone unfortunate enough to not have a natural unibrow drew a fake one on their face with charcoal."

"You're making that up," I accused.

"It's true! I read it somewhere."

"*Where?* Where would you read something like that?"

"I don't remember. Anyway, we should be arriving at the crash site soon."

"A very smooth change of subject. Don't think we won't talk about this later," I warned.

We continued in awkward silence. It was starting to get noticeably warm inside the rover, and not entirely as a result of my embarrassment.

We arrived. The umbrella still blocked our view, but we'd made it, at least.

"Drive around the site to put it in shadow," said Scott. (Referring to the rover's shadow, of course. Since the Sun was still on the horizon, less than half risen from our vantage point, its light was still coming at us from a mostly horizontal direction. The rover and its umbrella cast a long shadow.) "I'll step out from under the umbrella and see what we've got. Don't move the rover while I'm out there; without the shadow I'll fry in a matter of minutes."

He stepped out from under the umbrella and patched Old Sparky's camera through to the rover's console so we could see what he saw.

He wasn't looking at a crashed rocket.

"Is it an antenna?" I asked. Because that's what it looked like, kinda. It was a slender, yellowish-white, many branched... thing. I don't know how to describe it exactly. Like a leafless tree where all the branches have smaller branches, and the smaller branches have tiny branches which in turn have miniscule branches and so on down as far as you can see. The whole structure was about the size of a mature tree, too.

Lynn snorted. "If this is a prank, a beacon dropped here by some college kids for a laugh, someone's going to jail. *Me*, if I ever get a hold of 'em."

Scott's voice crackled over the radio. "I don't think it's a prank. I don't know if you can see on the console, but this thing looks like it's made of *crystal*. Silicon, maybe. It doesn't look like any kind of antenna I've ever seen, but it's definitely the source of the distress signal. No idea where it came from. Alien?"

We sat in silence a moment, trying to wrap our brains around it.

"I don't know," Scott said again after a while. "But we can't stay long. I'm gonna try to break off a sample and then we'll head back."

I looked at the thing, entranced. Whatever it was, alien tree or antenna or something else entirely, it was really pretty. I realized that the tree appeared to be subtly swaying in the breeze, like a concert-goer swept up in the romantic music.

But then I remembered that there was no breeze on Mercury.

"Scott, wait!" I said. "I don't think that's a good-"

Too late. Scott snapped a small branch off the crystalline tree.

As if on cue, more crystalline antenna-like things pushed up from the ground, all around us. And what emerged... well, I could see why earlier sightings had called them "skeletons". Up close, they looked less like human skeletons and more like walking snowflakes (if I were forced to find something to compare them to): intricately complex beings of branching crystal with many multiply-jointed limbs that articulated in all kinds of crazy directions.

Each "skeleton" had its own unique structure, no two individuals exactly alike. Some stood on four "legs", some two, some six, some just one. They had enormous variation in size as well, ranging from the size of a housecat to the size of Old Sparky, and everything in between. The way the creatures moved—how should I describe it? Smooth and precise and "ripply", if that's a word—like dancers, I could definitely see that part of the legend—yet utterly inhuman with their crazy numbers of limbs and joints, and no obvious heads or sensory organs.

The "tree" that had been broadcasting the distress signal pushed its way out of the ground as well. Fully emerged, it stood on three legs and was well over twice the height of the rover. It was, by far, the biggest of the skeletons.

"They're beautiful," I whispered, taking it all in. (Not sure why I felt the need to whisper, but I did.)

Then the creatures attacked.

Mostly they swarmed Scott, I presume because he'd broken off their ancient elder chieftain's "finger". (I am, of course, assuming that bigger equals older.) They attempted to drag the walker into the light—I believe knowing the effect it would have on its pilot (though I have no way to prove that).

The utility walker seemed much stronger than any individual skeleton, but there were many of them working together and only one walker. Scott was punching and kicking at his attackers, but it was hard to tell how much damage he was doing, even when he connected and broke off a piece of a skeleton here and there. Inch by inch, the mass of skeletons shifted Old Sparky toward the edge of the shadow.

One of the creatures slipped through the umbrella seam and climbed onto the back of the rover.

"One on us," I reported to Scott over the radio.

I wasn't sure what I expected him to do about that—he had his hands full with his own fight for survival—but Scott pulled an arm free and tossed his claw/winch/hand thing—sorry, I still don't know what the right word for it is—and it clamped around the "spine" of the skeleton crawling on the back of the rover. He pulled the winch cable taut, then twisted the walker's torso hard. The creature was jerked off the rover, through the umbrella seam, and launched across the barren landscape as if shot from a trebuchet. It broke into pieces from the force of the throw.

(Turns out utility walkers can generate crazy amounts of torque.)

"D.J., go! Before any more get under the umbrella!" Scott shouted over the radio.

"No! You'll die if we take our shadow off you!"

He was quiet a moment. "I'm sorry I never got to see your eyebrows," he said. "I'm sure they're amazing. Now get out of here."

I gritted my teeth. "No heroism today, Mister," I said. "Lay down."

I put the rover into reverse, and the console screen automatically switched to the back-up camera. I turned the rover so that the seam of the umbrella was lined up with Scott. He was struggling to force the walker to the ground.

I backed up. Scott got prone just as a massive tire rolled over him and the aliens. The skeletons swarming him were shattered and scattered. (Turns out they were as delicate as they looked.) The walker was unharmed. We stopped and Scott used his claw hand to climb onto the rover.

I drove toward the "ancient chieftain"—the tall skeleton—but it stepped out of the way rather than let one of its legs be run over. (Which was fortunate, since—now that I think about it—a collision with it might well have damaged or torn off our umbrella, as big as it was. In the heat of "battle" though I wasn't thinking about that.)

The rover's reverse top speed is the same as its forward top speed (which, truth be told, is not all that fast to begin with), so we just reversed the whole way back to Dayspring instead of turning the rover around. Turning around would have required rearranging the umbrella so that the seam would not be facing the sun anyway, and we didn't want to give the skeletons another chance to ambush us.

We bounced and flounced back across the sun-beaten wastes, in reverse this time, all the way back to Dayspring. The creatures did not pursue us. Scott had noted the coordinates of the quicksand pit, so we were able to avoid it.

We were all suffering from heat exhaustion by the time we got back. The umbrella worked well in keeping the Sun's heat off us, but there was still waste heat building up inside the rover, not to mention radiant heat from the ground. (Rock is a poor conductor of heat, which is why it's possible to walk across hot coals on your bare feet, but the hard-baked ground of Sunside Mercury is *really hot*, so heat from the ground couldn't be ignored entirely).

Regardless, we all made it back.

(And as with the recorded meeting, the rover's black-box recorded all conversation between me and the others, which I was able to refer to when making this account.)

Anyway, that's the story of how humanity's first contact with the Mercurians turned into a "massacre", as the media put it later. We still don't know for sure what the skeletons' intentions were with the fake distress call and all that, but I was there and I believe they were acting malevolently. Some have speculated that they were just trying to communicate with us by imitating a signal they had earlier detected (i.e., the distress signal from the emergency landing two weeks prior). That's an interesting theory, but why did they not alter their signal in response when we tried to raise them by radio? Others theorize that the skeletons' motivations and actions were and are "utterly alien", and that it would be fruitless to try and understand them in human terms. That's just a cop-out, if you ask me. An ambush is an ambush.

We are not murderers; we acted in self-defense. This I affirm unreservedly. And that is the end of the story.

Clint Spivey spent eight years as a meteorologist in Europe and Asia. He now teaches English as a foreign language to university students. He is fortunate enough to be able to work on a rice farm during the spring and fall. His fiction has appeared in Into the Ruins, The Moon Magazine, SQ Mag *and* Perihelion.

An elegant homage to the interplanetary science fiction of the Golden Age, "The Lost Cosmonaut and Saucer Six" explores the classic scenario of contact between a human space traveler and an advanced civilization on another world. This time, though, the space traveler is from the Soviet Union, and the story takes off from there on a journey of its own...

THE LOST COSMONAUT AND SAUCER SIX

Clint Spivey

THE CREATURE'S CRIES, though unintelligible to the Silaster saucer crew, were clearly ones of terror. Fluffy white clouds lingered above glittering turquoise seas as the creature's tiny capsule drifted further from its world's embrace.

"Translation almost complete," said the navigator from her station.

Commander Kelniss was as curious as the rest to hear the creature's words, but knew it mattered little. They were posted to observe the inhabitants of the blue world below, but forbidden to interfere. They'd been content watching the foraging primates rise to agriculture and cities from afar through telescopes and probes. But when Frespar begun detonating nuclear devices over cities, Kelniss' people realized more robust monitoring was required. Thus, the presence of Saucer Six as witness to the dying native's cries.

"Translation complete," Lienlin, the navigator said.

"Play it," Kelniss ordered.

"Why won't you answer me?" the native shrieked over the comm. "I know you're there. Speak to me!"

"Is it calling to us?" Kelniss asked?

"The signal is directed back to the planet below," Lienlin said, her twelve spindly fingers dancing about her control panel. "I think she is speaking to her people on Frespar."

"She?"

"Comparisons of their broadcasts indicates a female."

Her translated cries became more desperate, degenerating, finally, to cursing her superiors safely on the surface. All the while, her capsule tumbled further away into the scorching radiation of the solar wind.

Kelniss knew she wouldn't last long in such a primitive craft. Frespar's inhabitants were no less fragile than his own people, the Selastrii. And while the massive disc-shaped ship shielded them from the sun's punishing radiation, the alien would soon be a cinder within hers.

Despite every rule and regulation against such an order, Kelniss commanded his crew to bring her aboard.

Lieutenant-Colonel Natasha Laranova was burning. Had Laranova's fury abated long enough for tears, they'd likely steam away from her dying face within the searing Vostok capsule.

She knew the risk of space. All in the space program did. They'd all mourned their fallen comrades. Some burned to unrecognizable piles of ash in launch fires, others upon failed reentries. It was part of the mission that they all accepted.

What infuriated her, was to spend her final moments ignored. A forgotten failure. Her very memory an intolerable blemish to the Soviet regime. Her name and photos scrubbed from history books.

She'd just keyed the comm for a final stinging rebuke when she was pulled into her seat. The sudden force shoving her backward froze Laranova. Was she tumbling back to Earth? Her crude instruments didn't seem to indicate such.

As if in answer to her confusion, she felt the capsule turn, a strange energy buzzing through the craft. When she saw the massive silver disc pulling her toward it, Natasha Laranova *did* shed a tear.

THE FRESPAREM WOMAN faced them from the rear of her cell. Her bulbous helmet at her feet, the woman trembled with balled fists but did not look away. Kelniss stepped toward the clear wall separating them.

"Can you understand me?" he asked.

She started at this, looking around before nodding her head.

"Seems the translation software works," said Lienlin. "I think she's indicating assent."

Kelniss stepped forward, the door spiraling open from the center.

"We will not harm you," he said. He towered a good head above her. Few Selastrii had seen a Fresparem so close. Their primate heritage was quite evident in the abundant hair on their bodies as well as their build. They had only five stubby fingers to the Silastrii six. Tiny ears compared to the massive round ones his own people had atop their heads. Her eyes, while tiny, boasted much more color than the solid Silastrii green.

Kelniss stepped close. "Can you speak?"

"Yes," she said.

NATASHA HAD BEGUN wondering if heaven and hell were real things, and perhaps their denizens were stranger than any ancient text had depicted. But once they led her from her cell, and she saw more of the ship, she knew something even more impossible had occurred.

"You harbored surprisingly few pathogens from your world," Lienlin said while walking beside her. "Decontamination was far faster than anticipated."

Natasha hurried her step to keep pace with the lanky... aliens, no easy task in her bulky space suit. She still had trouble processing the word in her head. Somehow, devils of her own madness seemed preferable to admitting the truth. The six-fingered, orange-skinned creatures boasted only wisps of hair between the round, mouse-like ears hair atop their heads. Their bulbous green eyes lacked a discernible iris. Only a darker shade indicated any pupil, always constricting whenever they looked her way. They wore high collared tunics with trousers, black trimmed with silver above black boots.

"We enter quarantine before launch," Natasha said.

"A prudent step," the alien said.

"You must understand," the leader, Kelniss looked toward her. "We have monitored your world for many lifetimes, but never once made contact. Never once spoken with a member of your species. Such is forbidden."

The conversation was a mere afterthought. The pristine golden corridors were an easy four meters high. Far from cluttered human design, such as battleships back home with piping crowding every cramped corner, this place was seamless perfection.

"Then why save me?"

The two aliens shared a long look at one another before answering.

"Because," Kelniss said, gesturing forward as a round door opened before him, revealing a massive window looking upon a greenish-gold world. "The Selastrii are not one to leave anyone to suffer."

The bridge was hushed as the ship descended into the clouds. Such was the majesty of the towering cumulus, billowing white clouds resembling skyscrapers and mountain ranges set adrift in the upper-air winds, that Natasha suspected even the aliens appreciated the outside splendor. Earths nearest neighbor in size and composition. The brightest star in the night sky.

"Venus," Natasha finally whispered. Her companions seemed confused by this, indicating, perhaps, a limit to their translation capabilities.

"Silaster," Kelniss said, returning his gaze to the screen.

They were within what she assumed was the command center. A great spherical room towered nearly two-stories above them. Others minded stations and panels at various points about the sphere's interior, but nearly half-a-hemisphere was dedicated to the wondrous vista outside.

"What do you call this ship?" Natasha asked.

The question seemed to puzzle the aliens.

"This is the sixth ship built," Lienlin answered. There were some garbled noises as the translator struggled with a word. "Saucer, I believe you would call it. This is Saucer Six."

"You're being taken to Pinnacle, our chief city," Kelniss said. "From there, our leaders will decide your fate. I'm sorry to say, you may never set forth on Frespar again."

Natasha could only nod, memories of life within Russia the furthest thing from her thoughts. Entire cities floated among the clouds, crowded with soaring towers and sprawling plazas beneath translucent domes. Each city tethered by impossibly thin strands vanishing into the clouds toward the surface. Zeppelin-like vessels plied lazy paths between each floating dome.

"You are our guest," Kelniss continued. "I hope we can accommodate you, but Fresparem ways are truly alien. One can learn only so much from observing your species from afar.

Natasha, once more, simply nodded.

KELNISS STOOD WITH head bowed, Lienlin beside him, as their superiors listed the myriad rules they'd broken.

"What were you thinking," the oldest of the scowling admiralty said. Admiral Vrealin had herself commanded one of the longest and most extensive Fresparem observation missions in Silaster history, urging its importance after the primitive species' first nuclear detonations. She moved from the podium beside her companions to the massive window looking upon the city.

Pinnacle, capital of all Silaster, spread before them. Kelniss had been born upon the crushing Silaster surface many miles below, but as commander of one of the seven saucers exploring the solar system, Pinnacle was now his home.

Kelniss raised his head to look the admiralty in the eyes. "I would not abandon her to die in the lonely vacuum of space."

"And why not?" asked another of his superiors standing at his podium. "It seems her own people were content enough to do just that."

It was Lienlin who answered. "We do not believe them capable of much more than low planetary orbits. Natasha's—the Fresparem launch, appeared to have been a failed attempt at achieving such."

Admiral Vrealin turned to face them. "Your report states that they wouldn't even answer her cries for help. Did her people truly find her life so worthless as to not even offer comfort in her death?"

"They *are* Fresparem," another admiral said to dismissive laughs.

Vrealin silenced the room with a withering look. Only the Saucer Six crew had abstained from laughter. After a few moments, Vrealin said, "I fear The Concordance may be required to deal with this situation."

"The Concordance?" one of the admiralty asked in disbelief. "For a single Fresparem?"

"You weren't there when they rained nuclear fire on two of their own cities. This question requires no answer, but I'll ask it anyway. Commander Kelniss? Do their nuclear tests continue in earnest?"

He nodded solemnly "Over two dozen during our patrol alone."

"A million years of accumulated resources squandered in decades," Vrealin said. "And for what? Massing a stockpile capable of slitting their own throats. I promise you, The Concordance will need be called before we've seen the last of this lone Fresparem."

Vrealin stared the group down for several moments before returning to her podium.

"But perhaps this represents an opportunity," she said. "The Fresparem question has remained unanswered for too long. Do we reveal ourselves to our neighbors? Offer our aid in saving them from their own butchery? Or leave them to stew in their warming world?" Vrealin looked around as her words sunk in. "Perhaps this lone Fresparem is just the motivation we need to decide once and for all how to deal with their species."

"What of Natasha Laranova," Lienlin asked.

"Your part in this is over," Vrealins said. "Return to your mission. If they are launching their people into orbit it may not be much longer until they are doing so with their nukes. I would very much like to know the state of such progress. How I—we deal with your wayward Fresparem is no longer your concern."

SAUCER SIX HUNG above an open-air tiered amphitheater easily a kilometer in diameter, where Natasha waited. The ship's massive disc rotated about the central orb in gyroscopic motions while remaining silent. The ship had sliced through the membrane tenting the city upon arrival by some unknown means when delivering her.

Natasha sat alone on the bottommost tier of seats of the empty amphitheater, her several guards keeping their distance as if assurances of her decontamination were exaggerated. The floor before her was a tiled mosaic, stretching the entirety of the arena. A pair of aliens—Selastrii, held hands before many dozens of their compatriots. Behind, blazed the sun, then what were clearly Mercury, Earth, Mars, and arcing high above it all, half a hemisphere of Venus, its golden clouds behind streams of pearlescent white. Toward the opposite end, facing the many seats upon which Natasha sat, was a dais.

"What is this place?" she asked her guards. She'd been given two translation devices, one for her ear as well as a patch that adhered to her throat.

"It's The Above Arena," a voice behind her answered. She turned to see Kelniss and Lienlin. "It is used for performances as well as important debates by The Quorum," Lienlin said. "It seemed a fitting place to have you wait."

"And what's to be done with me?"

The two looked at one another before answering. Natasha noticed a difference in the two compared to her guards. Their skin was a pale yellow color beside the ruddier tan of Natasha's escorts. The emerald eyes of the saucer crew were larger as well, a deeper shade of green than the Silastrii assigned to Natasha.

"You will remain here," Kelniss said. "I know nothing of your fate beyond that."

"Can't I stay with you?" she asked

"Perhaps one day. For now, enjoy all the hospitality Silaster has to offer."

"You're not staying?"

Kelniss indicated they weren't. And with a blessing of good fortune, the two bid her farewell. They climbed the arena's seating to board their waiting ship before whispering away into the orange Silaster sky.

NATASAHA WAS TAKEN to one of the dome's many towers. Dwarfed by the furnishings, built for the larger Silastrii, she felt like a child. The windows revealed a breathtaking view that looked out upon gardens and fountains lining the streets below. Cumuliform clouds lumbered across the yellow sky. A small balcony garden wrapped about the windows outside, with water occasionally misting over it. Natasha noted the other high-rises had similar gardens.

"You must be hungry," her escort, a woman named Brealins said.

Natasha was. She wore only her black, skintight undersuit. Her bulky spacesuit sat in a pile on the floor beside her scuffed helmet and boots. Brealins wore a collared tunic of pale orange lined with yellow. Her matching trousers flared at the bottom above simple brown shoes. The Silastrii woman prepared something similar to potatoes, cucumbers, and tofu. After a few exploratory nibbles, Natasha quickly cleaned her plate.

"Thank you," she said.

"I never imagined dining beside a Fresparem," Brealins said, her bulbous green eyes alight from the sunlight streaking through the windows. "Your helmet, and those markings." She pointed to the red CCCP on Natasha's helmet. Are you from Russia?"

"You know it?" Natasha asked in surprise.

"Not well, but I've studied your world. As many Silastrii have. Do you mind if I ask you some questions?"

Natasha didn't, and Brealins had many. They spoke for hours. Brealins serving a lavender-flavored tea while they spoke. Her questions ranged from mundane ones regarding population growth and crops, to more serious ones of war and conflict.

"You know much of Earth wars," Natasha said, holding her massive Silastrii mug with both hands.

"If your neighbors were warring, would you not show an interest?"

They spoke well into what Natasha would have considered the evening, except that the rays of sun never seemed to move. The room remained as bright as when they'd arrived.

Feeling exhaustion creep over her, she asked Brealins when it got dark.

"Not for many months, yet," she answered. Feeling sheepish for forgetting such basic planetary physics, Natasha listened while Brealins explained Silsaster's orbital mechanics and the brief night they brought per year.

"Night is a celebration," she said. "A time to enjoy the starlight and constellations before celebrating the end of frigid darkness."

"There are no cities on the night side of the planet?" Natasha asked, gesturing toward the many floating domes dotting the skyline beyond their own.

"A few. But places of research or storage. But there will be time enough for rest. For now, we need to get you some new garments." Brealins finished her tea and stood. "You are beginning to smell."

Natasha tore her gaze from the view outside, and, sniffing her armpit, had to agree with her towering host's assessment.

MANICURED GARDENS LINED the streets. Delicate trees hung overhead, their own thin boughs bursting with red leaves tinted purple. Insects buzzed around blue bushes bursting with blossoms. And while Natasha observed the natural alien beauty, the other Silastrii observed her.

Passersby gawked and pointed at Natasha while the braver ones stopped to ask questions. Brealins fielded most while Natasha answered what she could. Again, Natasha noticed a difference. Like her rescuers aboard Saucer Six, Brealins appeared different than the others. Her skin pale and her eyes brighter. Her clothes as well seemed at odds with the flowing, silken-like robes worn by the Silastrii they passed.

"Seems everyone knows something about Earth—Fresparem," Natasha said, correcting herself.

"There are entire disciplines dedicated to Frespar. I've spent many years studying your home. It's why I was selected to assist you here."

Beneath an adjacent apartment-tower was a kind of warehouse with dozens of shelves, each packed with different materials. In the center, climbing to the high ceiling, was a machine. Silastrii were queued before it, with miscellaneous items heaped in their hands. Brealins helped Natasha choose suitable color fabrics before joining the others in line. Natasha soon saw the machine's purpose.

"Some kind of...loom?" she asked in awe while the machine spat out some unknown goods.

"A printer, actually," Brealins said. "Though in your case, a loom would be an apt description."

Natasha watched as each person in line loaded their materials and waited as the machine produced their desired item. Some carted off what appeared to be furniture or machines on trolleys, their finished components to be assembled elsewhere.

"You've no factories to create such?"

"Not as you're accustomed," Brealins said. "Mass production is a wasteful practice. Printing on demand requires much less energy."

The others in line peppered Natasha with questions. It was an odd sensation, but their familiarity with Earth did much to blunt the strangeness of being among the Silastrii. When their turn with the machine arrived, Brealins punched in Natasha's measurements, and they were soon departing with several sets of clothes and a pair of shoes. Natasha was allowed some privacy in a separate room to change. In absence of any other idea, she'd selected a tunic and trousers similar to Brealins, though she'd decided on a simple gray with black trim.

They next visited what appeared to be a university, though Natasha couldn't be certain.

"I'm not sure of Fresparem education compared to our own," Brealins said as staff escorted them through the grounds. "But Pinnacle Academy is one of our more prestigious institutions. I certainly couldn't have attended such."

They gathered in a crowded amphitheater similar to the one where Saucer Six had deposited Natasha, only smaller and roofed. The quiet roar of conversation of those seated above grew hushed as Natasha and Brealins approach the dais. The floor was another tiled mosaic, only filled with scholars pouring over books, scrolls, and several of the tablet like devices she'd seen the locals using. After a brief introduction by Brealins, Natasha stepped forward, and the questioning began.

"You're a soldier, then?" a young woman seated among the hundred others asked.

"I was a pilot," Natasha answered, her voice echoing off the towering walls. She'd always had strong voice and enjoyed stepping away from the microphone they'd offered. "I flew the MIG 19 and 21 before being selected as a cosmonaut."

Several students nodded and, with a wave of their hands, startlingly clear photos and videos of both aircraft came to life, floating in the air around the students. Natasha paused. While previous Silastrii questions had dealt with such benign topics of Earth geography and animals, here was casual knowledge of issues far more serious. How far did Silastrii knowledge of Earth armaments extend?

"Did your nation have the death camps?" another student asked to clear interest from his compatriots.

"Death camps?" She looked to Brealins.

With a strange smile Brealins gestured to the wall behind her. The varnished wood shimmered to reveal color images of, what were unmistakably, German concentration camps. Photos revealed the suffering and misery with detail far beyond the capabilities of human photography. Filing away her own questions of how such reconnaissance had been achieved without drawing human attention, Natasha turned back toward the audience.

"No." Her statement boomed from the walls. "My people

freed the ones you see here."

"But those aren't the only ones," another student said. Waving his hand, the images shifted once more.

More photos arose. Wooden buildings behind barbed wire. English signs with the US flag conjured a sneer from Natasha. Japanese stared with blank gazes through the wire. Natasha explained that nation, and its relationship between the prisoners and the bombing of their nation of origin.

An excited murmur arose from the students and, soon, the photos were replaced by ones more terrifying.

Many in Russia, with ranks far surpassing her own, would kill for such detailed images as the ones these students so casually tossed to the walls. For here were photos of the devastation wrought by the American atomics upon Japan. But there were others. Great plumes of ocean blasted skyward beside tiny ships. Brilliant red orbs of atmospheric detonations, the photos of astounding clarity.

Natasha's wonder grew ambitious as she considered the implications such technology might entail for her own people. Machinations ground to life in her mind. Of alliances beyond Earth's atmosphere. Of returning triumphant aboard Saucer Six, its hold bursting with technology.

For whom? The troubling question barged through her aspirations. *Your beloved countrymen who abandoned you to die in order to protect the Soviet reputation from failure?* She squashed her doubts as the students continued their interrogation.

"Those weren't students, were they?" she asked Brealins when, after nearly two hours of non-stop questioning, the event came to a close.

"Oh, they're students," Brealins answered as they departed the academy. Crepuscular rays blasted between the cumulus clouds towering all around the floating city.

"Their knowledge was quite specific," Natasha said.

"They're part of The Quorum. Pinnacle's branch of Silster governance. A lower house, to put it in Fresparem terms."

"You allow your students to rule?"

"Who better to deal with society's ills than youth? Those whose exuberance is yet undiminished by the cold reality of age. There does exist a balance—an upper house, so to speak, consisting of those older and more wise. But it is only convened in the direst of circumstances. When Quorum inaction or failure requires the threat of a truly dispassionate hand."

They retired to Brealins' apartment for what passed as night on near-perpetually sunlit Silaster. The two ate dinner at the low living room table. Brealins served what appeared to be potato salad with cucumbers sprinkled generously with some kind of krill, barely larger than a grain of rice.

"The vegetables all come from gardens," Brealins said when Natasha inquired after the food. "Some grown here in Pinnacle but mostly in cities dedicated to farming."

"These as well?" Natasha held up a spoon heaped with the tasty white fish.

Brealins looked away. One of the ever present clouds beyond the dome passed, allowing sunlight to stream unhindered through the windows, setting her emerald eyes aglow and brazening her yellow skin. "The krill, like all our seafood, comes from Below."

The way she said the word reminded Natasha that she'd heard reference to the surface during her questioning by The Quorum.

"There's life on the surface?" Natsaha asked. "Frespar's best guess was that the surface was extremely inhospitable to biological life."

"It is." Brealins leaned forward, her two large ears twitching with interest. "There's only so much we can produce here among the clouds. It's Silaster Below, where our people first evolved, that provides everything else."

Natasha thought of the wonders of Pinnacle. Of the other floating cities hanging like dandelions in the sky beyond. What upon the punishing Venusian surface could feed such wonders above?

"Would you like to see?" Brealins asked, something more

than just the sun gleaming in her bright green eyes.

"I think I would."

Brealins leaned back. "You truly are a surprise, Natasha Laranova. Our first Fresparem. And you'd depart the warm wonder of Pinnacle for the surface." She was silent several moments before she continued. "Very well. If you wish to see Silaster Below, then we'll depart tomorrow."

NATASHA HAD BEEN expecting Below to match the glory of Pinnacle. She was instead greeted by something far more familiar to a Fresparem.

The ride had been her first lesson. Brealins had accompanied her on one of the carriages that Natasha had seen traversing the thin strands connecting the cities to the ground. Climbing within the massive lift felt like being locked within a vault.

A handful of other Silastrii rode with them, but the majority of the carriage was dedicated to cargo. Foods and supplies that could only be produced above. The ride down had been a turbulent, lightning streaked ordeal. A white-knuckled Natasha recalled fondly being blasted to orbit aboard a Vostok-K rocket as merely inconvenient compared to the seven-hour descent.

They'd passed through several surface locks before entering a shaft leading below ground. The tunnel, many hundreds of meters deep, exited into a dome that appeared truly siege-worthy. Hexagonal arrangements of the same jet-black material as the strands anchoring the cities above climbed to the vaulted ceiling a hundred meters high. Sickly yellow phosphorous lamps lit the place with a jaundiced glow. The strand tethering Pinnacle high above vanished into the ground, around which were several squat buildings of what appeared to be concrete.

"The anchor point for the elevator lies near copious phosphate rock deposits," Brealins said as they departed the lift.

"The phosphates required for orbital agriculture come from here."

A sort of open pit mine several hundred meters across radiated outward from beside the base of the elevator. Many dozens of Silastrii toiled about the paths coiling around the pit. Shafts vanished into the yellowish-brown soil at every level.

"They serve you?" Natasha asked.

Brealins ears jumped in the shrug-like motion Natasha had come to recognize. "They work for all Silaster. They share in our harvest above for their vital work here. You saw the food we brought down with us. Their work is connected to ours above. Neither is less vital than the other."

Natasha wondered how many would trade places if they could. During a break, whistled in by a surprisingly Earth-like steam device, many of the miners came to observe the alien among them.

Natasha felt an instant kinship to these Silastrii. Their clothes were far more utilitarian than the flowing ones favored in Pinnacle. And where the spoiled students of The Quorum had questioned her about crimes of her species, these workers were interested in more mundane matters. One question in particular.

Did she like the fish?

Natasha cocked her head, before explaining the krill she'd had the previous day.

This brought a chorus of disbelief while the workers chided Brealins for her lack of hospitality.

"Figured we'd wait to get it fresh," Brealins said, her statement met with approval. "Why do you think we came on a Duskday?"

"Excuse me," a Silaster man trailed by several others approached Brealins. "We need help with The Quorum. Can we trouble you to petition them in our place when you return?"

"I'm sorry, I'm busy," Brealins said brusquely before

guiding Natasha away.

Natasha sensed some urgency in the man's request as well as in Brealins getting free of him. She was beginning to suspect the woman was more than a mere escort.

"Duskday?" she asked as the two descended into a subway station further beneath the ground.

"There are two days of rest after Duskday. Then two more of work. Peaksday follows and is a single day off work. No one on Silaster works more than two consecutive days. Is it different on Frespar?"

Natasha discerned a tiny half-smile as Brealins asked this, as if waiting for an answer she already knew.

"We generally work five or six days, with one or two for a break before beginning again."

"Well, yours is a comfortable world. Perhaps such conditions encourage extra toil."

The subway was remarkably similar to ones beneath Moscow, only built for the taller Silastrii. An intricate mosaic spanned the platform to either end of the tunnels vanishing into darkness, the tiles depicting a group of Silastrii beneath roiling clouds. At their head, a man and woman stood with arms raised, holding stones and some sort of fish. A ray of sun bathed them both in light from broken clouds above, through which several Silastrii reached down to receive the offering.

Natasha was no stranger to propaganda and imagined this quite effective for workers such as those waiting beside them. A double-decker train soon emerged from a tunnel and rumbled to a stop. They spoke little during the ride. Natasha was once more a miniature within the massive carriage snaking through the dark subway tunnels. They passed several other stations before arriving. Another mural graced the wall of their destination. Several Selastrii rose from the surface of what appeared to be a vast lake. Once more, they presented their offerings to those grasping from the clouds above.

"Is that where we're going?" Natasha asked.

Brealins was quiet as they ascended stone steps from the station, only speaking once they reached the top.

"*That* is where we're headed."

A sprawling window revealed a vast, subterranean lake. Buoys lit ghostly green bobbed atop the surface, vanishing into the gloomy distance. The cavern walls rose a hundred meters while fierce yellow sodium lamps lit the shore with an industrial glow. Concrete buildings lined the beach a kilometer in either direction, stone quays jutting from them into the inky water.

"The Sunken Sea," Brealins said as they exited the station. "This is but one of many caverns offering access to Silaster's subterranean water and its bountiful depths."

They arrived at a bustle of activity near one of the quays. Silastrii men and women were fitting each other in what appeared to be underwater breathing gear. Several had already boarded small boats, sitting with the tanks strapped to their backs toward the edge. Each had masks, flippers, and menacing spears taller than Natasha.

But it was not this busy scene which drew her attention. At the far end of the pier, floating in the water, was a ship identical in design to the vessel that had rescued her. Differing only in size, the twenty-meter disc was Saucer Six's sibling.

"Here to get wet, Fresparem?" A Silastrii man strolled toward them, several other curious onlookers at his side. His mask was pushed between his large ears but he'd already donned his tanks.

"Who's afraid of getting wet?" Natasha asked, shrugging off her loose Pinnacle garments to the pier. She was glad she'd worn her under-suit. The simple Soviet garment offered utility beyond the dainty garb she'd brought from Pinnacle.

"I'll be handling herding this afternoon." Brealins nodded toward the silver disc floating beside them.

"Just remember, zap the krill, not us," the man said. "How long since you've piloted a saucer?"

"Too long," Brealins said, leaping onto the disc in the water and indicating for Natasha to do the same.

The leap—simple for the lanky Silastrii--took Natasha longer. She scooted to the pier's edge before dropping to the disc nearly two meters below. Bracing for a slippery surface, she instead found the disc quite steady. She followed Brealins to the central orb, entering the tiny space through a round aperture. Where Saucer Six had contained decks by the dozen, this space looked large enough to hold two, perhaps three Silastrii. Natasha sat beside Brealins in front of a curved console.

"So what are we doing?" she asked.

"Helping with the harvest." Brealins' long fingers danced about the console as it came alive with lights and controls that swam beneath the surface in a manner similar to the tablets the Silastrii used. The entire sphere, floor to ceiling, shimmered before becoming transparent. Grinning, her ears pointed forward, Brealins said, "It has been far too long."

The ship moved just as its sibling in space did. The disc rotated about the sphere, angling downward as Brealins dove them beneath the surface. Natasha saw the divers swimming into the depths. Lanterns floated on short leashes from their belts, lighting the murk with a florescent green glow. The saucer dropped beneath them, until the divers' tiny lanterns were pinpricks of green high above.

"So you've done this before?" Natasha asked.

"I *learned* in a saucer like this."

"You come Below often?"

Brealins looked at her briefly before answering. "I was *born* on Silaster Below."

Once more, as had almost become common over the previous days, Natasha witnessed wonder. The saucer deftly sliced about the depths while Brealins consulted a readout similar to sonar, chasing clouds of tiny, krill-like creatures. Purple electricity danced about the surface of the disc while prodding the millions of tiny creatures toward the surface in coalescing clouds.

"This is the harvest?"

"Partly. But it also draws bigger prizes."

Natasha soon saw. Sleek, darting shapes emerged from the depths. Lit with a strange, chasing illumination, Natasha at first mistook them for other divers.

"Bioluminescence," Brealins said when Natasha asked about the phenomena. "Your world teems with such creatures within its ocean depths. Well, at least for now."

"Silaster knowledge extends to our seas?" The idea of Earth's oceans full of Venusian saucers was not at all comforting.

"To the very depths," Brealins said. "Do you know what I once saw there?"

Natasha shook her head.

"A tin can. Though it's not really your fault. The primate rapaciousness of your species doesn't even leave the ocean untouched."

Natasha gave up trying to understand the alien. Who cared about litter while plumbing impossible ocean depths? She returned her attention to events outside, mesmerized by the hunt. The sleeker herring darted into the massive krill swarm Brealins was shepherding. Soon, larger shapes emerged to hunt. Resembling some sort of swordfish, their own lighting chased a rainbow of colors across their large dorsal fin in repeating patterns. Each had a menacing bill, similar to swordfish on Earth. Natasha had heard of certain jellyfish possessing such internal light back on Earth, but never something so large. Each swordfish was easily three meters long.

Brealins kept the massive krill swarm together by skillful handling of the saucer, while the larger swordfish darted within to feast upon the smaller herring. The divers had also formed a loose circle and began using their spears to herd the larger fish toward their compatriots. As each swordfish lanced away from one Silastrii, another was there to try and spear it. Natasha found herself pumping fists in excitement as the saucer hurled about the hunt, cheering the divers when they managed to spear one of the beasts and send it to the boats above to haul in their prize. So caught up was she in the excitement that she almost missed the first diver being stabbed.

Brealins was on the injured Silastrii in a flash, slicing the water between the bait-ball and the blood clouding the diver. The divers hauled their comrade to the surface and the hunt continued.

"This is no game," Brealins said, as Natasha watched the rest of the hunt in silence. There were other injuries, but minor ones that bloodied the water far less than the first. She was reminded of some British or US colonial venture. Locals sacrificed for an export, in this case the fish being sent to the sky.

And was not Russia guilty of the same? How many Ukrainians or Georgians had died under the lash to feed Russia? As before, she pushed her doubts aside for grander visions. Ones of returning home with a new ally. Soviet political thought married to Silaster steel. Among the alien wonders it was difficult not to fall prey to such dreaming.

They ascended an hour later, the saucer coming to rest upon the bobbing waves. The catch was impressive. Beside the nets bursting with krill and the larger herring, there were dozens of the massive swordfish being pulled toward the quays.

While Brealins and the divers gathered around their catch, recounting excitedly the dive, Natasha slipped away toward the shore. The injured had been taken to a group of medics. A Silastrii man knelt beside the shrouded corpse of the one fatality, his head bowed over the dead woman.

"Did you know her?" Natasha asked in a small voice.

"What do you care, Fresparem?" His voice was hoarse with grief.

It seemed like she was the only one who did. The others were either still seeing to that day's bounty or their own minor wounds.

"We were to be married," the man said after a moment. "I'd told her to leave the dives to the young. That she'd spent enough time down there. But the money is good. And She liked the excitement. She promised me she would give it up soon. But...the money was good."

Not knowing what else to do, Natasha knelt beside him, reaching up and placing a hand on his shoulder. He started at this, but seemed to appreciate the gesture, and the two mourned in silence.

NATASHA HAD TO admit, those Below knew how to throw a party. Once the dead Silastrii diver had been taken away, Pinnacle agents saw to the sorting and shipment of the catch. Hurrying to get the choicest portions to orbit while fresh, it was packed in ice, and sent by subway to the elevators.

The fishers were left with the rest. Within a long, low concrete building with a view of the sea, they feasted. Steaming bowls of rice-like grain were served beside slabs of steak from several swordfish roasting over an open-pit fire. There were other fruits and vegetables brought from Pinnacle's orbital gardens. Brealins sat beside Natasha at one of the many long tables filled with Silastrii. The low roar of conversations mixed with the smoke and roasting fish to fill the drab concrete hall with warmth.

"I'd like to stay down here, if you don't mind," Natasha said. Brealins paused at this but soon nodded her agreement in the Silastrii fashion.

"You're taking to the customs Below?"

Natasha simply wanted some time away from her handler, or whatever she suspected Brealins to be. She was no mere guide, that much was clear.

"Pinnacle is a wonder. But Below, the ways are more like home. I'd like to learn some more before returning to orbit."

"A wise choice," Brealins said, a little quickly. "Learn

what you can. I'll inform the local Quorum representation of your decision. Here." She removed her tablet from a pocket and fiddled with its surface. A square the size of Natasha's palm slid away as if made of liquid before reforming into a separate tablet. "I've assigned you an account for any purchases you might require. There's a contact code as well in case you want to message myself or others. Don't hesitate to call if you need anything."

Natasha simply nodded. Seeing the device come apart into two before remaking itself with ease was another wonder she was forced to accept with feigned nonchalance.

BREALINS LEFT HER that evening, returning above with the massive crates of iced fish. Natasha found lodging with several of the women who'd dove that day. They shared a communal dorm during their fishing, but lived elsewhere. The work was infrequent and also rotated to different subterranean inlets in order to avoid over-fishing. Natasha returned with several to the fertilizer mines the next morning. Her novelty had worn off and she soon found herself trying to keep out of the way of the grueling work while learning as much as she could.

Apparently, all those Below worked a similar schedule. Two days on, then a break on Peaksday, two more working, then a sort of weekend with two days of rest. Less interesting to Natasha was the similarity of a seven day week than its progressive division ensuring no more than two days work in a row. Though the exploitation of those Below was quite familiar, it seemed Silaster had more to offer Earth than mere technology.

"Are people discarded so casually on Fresparem?" a man asked her one day at the mines. He was the same who'd lost his partner during the fishing. Named Consdriss, he'd sought Natasha out for questions more than the others. His pale skin and large, jade eyes matched those Below.

"They are," Natasha answered. They were sitting on a

catwalk high upon the interior of the dome capping the Pinnacle phosphorus mine. The elevator strand tethering the city climbed from the mine's center to the long tunnel above. Consdriss was a technician of sorts and she'd accompanied him to replace one of the massive sodium lights.

"So nothing changes even across the solar system." he said while was replacing a lamp larger than Natasha's torso.

"Doesn't seem so."

"Could you help us?"

"Me?"

"You've been given access none here have. Free to return at your leisure while we await the next night. Perhaps you could bring our petitions to Pinnacle." His ears rose in expectation while awaiting her response.

"Can't you just…go yourselves?"

"It's forbidden."

"So do it anyway."

"Is that what you'd do on Frespar?" He looked at her as if asking permission. "You'd *rebel*?"

Natasha knew the weight of that word. Speaking sedition meant pain in her own country. Did it promise the same here?

"Well…nothing so grand. But doesn't Pinnacle rely on Below far more than the reverse? These fertilizers," she said while sweeping a hand over the sprawling operations beneath them. "Are they not more vital than the products parceled out to you from orbit?"

"We have a system," he said returning to his work. "Balance is paramount."

"Have you been above?"

"Yes. Each night I, along with many others make the trip."

She'd heard of these trips. When the planet's glacial, retrograde rotation brought darkness, those below ascended to Pinnacle and other cities to join those above in gazing upon the starlit night.

"Could you go right now?" she asked.

"Above? No. Operations must adhere to strict schedules planned years in advance."

"And who decides those times? You? Them?" She gestured to the toiling masses beneath them.

"Life requires balance of needs and resources. Deviation could mean disaster. Too much of one resource and too little of another creates imbalance."

"And this system allows not even time to mourn the loss of a mate?"

The industry beneath them filled the silence. Finally, he said, "It would seem not."

HER TIME BELOW was spent answering similar requests for help. Almost all had Quorum petitions but had to wait until night fell to have them addressed. These opportunities to air grievances consumed much of what was supposed to be their festival time in orbit. Time ostensibly dedicated to leisure was instead spent seeking some functionary or bureaucrat required to find satisfaction on a personal issue. Little came of those petitions passed to visitors such as Brealins, but with a dearth of options, those Below grasped for what they could.

Overwhelmed at the constant request to carry petitions back with her, Natasha countered with her own questions. Had they lost anyone? Most had. The work Below was perilous if not vital. Had they been to orbit? Only during night. Would they enjoy visiting beyond when Pinnacle allowed? This question always brought the same answer of, yes, that would be a freedom worth having. And, as if the her questions had uncorked a long stoppered anger, a common complaint arose above all others. Government permission to bear children.

"You're barred from having kids?" Natasha asked a bent old woman slogging through the shallow muck of The Sunken Sea. Consdriss had taken to accompanying her in his free time, answering questions as well as offering introductions.

Beside them, dozens of Silastrii waded beneath a sprawling, low cavern a mere ten meters high, harvesting what looked like oysters for export.

"Do you see any children down here?" the woman answered. She wore thick boots rising to her knees while prying shellfish with a knife from oyster beds reaching endlessly about them.

"It's forbidden?" Natasha asked.

"Not forbidden," Consdriss said. "But only allowed for couples who have spent a predetermined amount of time together. They must also demonstrate the ability to offset the child's consumption requirements through their own work, talent, or intelligence." He looked out over the water. "It's why my partner insisted on diving. We were hoping for approval to start a family."

"Lot of oysters to pick for one kid," the woman said. She grunted with every painful bend to the fetid water. Such monotony would wear on Natasha's own spine. How much more for one so tall bending so low?

Natasha found herself thinking of Brealins. She'd claimed to have been born Below. How had her parents demonstrated their ability to care for a child?

As the days went on Natasha found the interest in her growing. Word of the Fresparem alien had spread far among the caverns beneath the punishing Venusian surface. Groups traveled for hours and sometimes days by train to meet her. Condriss now accompanied her everywhere. With Brealins instruction that Below offer her whatever help she required, he'd secured time away from his maintenance duties to assist. And while Natasha spent time answering questions from those curious to meet the alien, she repeated those of her own.

"How much longer will you stand for this?" she asked a group of rare-metal miners. They were sitting on the rocky shore beside the sea outside of the squat dorm where she'd been staying. Natasha repeated her litany of questions regarding their conditions, eliciting the same grudging answers she'd heard so many times before.

"What would a Fresparem do about this?" one woman asked.

She'd began to wonder if this was why she'd been saved. Was she the catalyst these miserable, oppressed Silastrii required? Had she been brought across worlds to help free them from such torturous conditions? Destiny was a strange word for a Soviet cosmonaut to consider.

Natasha was certainly no idealist. She'd witnessed the excesses available in the upper echelons of the space program to infer just how much those in power enjoyed. But it was hard to resist the contagious exuberance that arose when recounting such events as the Russian revolution to her spellbound audience. They listened in wonder of wars fought by rifle-less peasants sent forward into poison gas and machine-gun fire. Many nodded as all the Fresparem barbarism they'd learned in school was confirmed by one from that world.

"But what do we *do*?" one man asked to muttered agreement from the others. "You're long on stories but short on ways to respond."

Natasha had, over her time Below, wondered on just such action.

"A walkout," she explained. "Abandon your duties until your petitions are answered."

"Go to *Pinnacle*?" a man asked. The lapping of the waves against the shore filled the silence. "You mean raise these complaints during the next night?"

"How far have such complaints gotten you? Drowned in paperwork? Blocked by endless bureaucracy? No. Before the festival."

She described her plan. A disruption to Below production. Mines and fisheries shuttered as workers rode the lifts to orbit. Instead of foods and minerals to feed industries above, they'd find only Silastrii clutching their petitions in hand.

"The disruption to production schedules will be enormous," one said. "They won't sit idly for that."

"Then maybe they will finally listen," Natasha said.

While there were some who balked, most agreed action was needed. Natasha didn't encourage any violence, indeed there seemed little reason to at this point. A simple walk-out was far easier to coordinate than some sort of revolution. And there was time for such later if the brutal response by those in Pinnacle came, which, Natasha expected it would. Let these poor souls see their comrades beaten with truncheons and forced back to their mines before they thought of overthrowing their masters. For now, they needed to see how powerful were their numbers against the loafing Silastrii above.

Once agreed the group offered their own suggestions of secrecy. They needed to keep information quiet from any deemed unsympathetic while targeting those for conversion who harbored complaints with the current system. Natasha was assured there was no shortage of those.

A curious opportunity presented itself when they discussed communication. Natasha presented the tablet-phone gifted from Brealins and asked if others had access to such. Turns out that the device was a high-end gadget difficult to get Below. Even more, they showed her how to break it into even tinier pieces the way Brealins had sliced it away from her larger tablet. Soon, they had nearly a dozen devices that, while limited in their screen display size, operated identically through voice and text. They could distribute these to each mine and fishery in order to speed membership in their conspiracy.

"You're not worried about being discovered?" Condriss asked her later that evening in her dorm room. She'd been given a single room for privacy in a dorm beside the sea.

She smiled thinking of the brutally efficient response this nascent rebellion would have earned in Russia. "On Fresparem you and I would already have been hauled away and shackled to a slab." She spent a few moments detailing Earth creativity in pain.

"You confirm your world as truly monstrous."

"That's why we mustn't let Silaster follow the same path." She walked to the window. The inky sea stretched into the distance. "It's why I was brought here. It has to be. To bring change to Silaster. Then we bring your people to Fresparem to do the same." She turned to face Consdriss, his green eyes nearly black in the dim room. "Think of what we could achieve together."

"It's ambitious, what you plan."

She thought of those moments before being plucked from the vacuum by Saucer Six. The way she'd cursed her masters on Earth for ignoring her in death. She'd been snatched from the heavens, brought to an unfamiliar world filled with very familiar injustices.

"We will do this, Condriss." She stepped close to him, reaching high to place her hand upon his shoulder. "I will bring you to Pinnacle before night falls."

He looked at her hand for a moment before responding. "Yes, I believe you will."

BREALINS' CALL THE next morning woke Natasha from the midst of a nightmare. She was falling, burning as flames consumed her tiny Russian capsule. Despite her screams, there was silence. No answers to her pleas, no voice to her cries, just terrifying quiet as she plummeted towards a silent Earth.

"Good morning!" Brealins was bright and cheery as only one bathed in the sunlight above could be. "Enjoying your time down there?"

The phone, now barely the size of a postage-stamp with all the times they'd broken it down for clones, transmitted her voice perfectly despite traveling through miles of atmosphere and rock.

"It's quite an experience Below," Natasha said. "I've learned much about Silaster."

"Excellent. Time to come back. Those in Pinnacle

want time with our Fresparem visitor. I've arranged for a lift this afternoon and sent the instructions to your tablet. Oh, look at that. You learned how to separate it. Making friends?"

Natasha paused. Was Brealins monitoring her? Just as there likely existed not a single untapped phone in Russia, were these magnificent devices capable of something similar?

"I barely knew how the thing worked," she said in deflection. "The people down her taught me to share the device."

"Wonderful," Brealins said, as cryptic as ever. "Your lift arrives this evening. I'll be waiting."

They ended the call and Natasha contacted Consdriss, informing him of her departure and asking for a meeting. Suspicions of surveillance still troubling her, she kept the call brief.

She wore the thick Below tunic and trousers she'd acquired over her undersuit. She preferred the heavy garments over her flowing Pinnacle garments and planned on returning there garbed as one Below. She grabbed rice served with cold fish and soup in the dormitory canteen and left to meet Consdriss.

They met once more atop the vertigo-inducing scaffolding surrounding the Pinnacle mine. The massive sodium lamps buzzed like engines as she passed. She found Consdriss working near one such light.

"I've been summoned back," she said.

"But what about tonight?" He turned from his work. "We've finally gotten everyone together. Time away from their shifts. They're clamoring for an audience. To hear of Fresparem resistance and how it might help us here."

"I know. Which is why I'm concerned Brealins chose today to call me back. You'll have to go without me."

Consdriss stood to his full height, towering nearly a meter above her. "It's not me they want to hear. It's you. Your stories. Of how your nation conquered such oppression to give all Russians equality in spite of all other nations struggling to resist it."

She once more cringed at the implication of her people's perfection. She knew the reality of life back home. But she also knew her duty. To bring the Silaster their own revolution before bringing it back to Earth to complete it there.

"I can't be the movement. It must be all of you. Tell them this. Arrange a time. Board the lifts together. I will plan what I can above and, on that day, I will be your voice."

Cpnsdriss pondered this while looking out over the mine, finally agreeing.

"One more thing," Natasha said. "I don't trust the tablets. Use them to contact the others. But give no information over them. I believe Brealins may be listening to our calls."

Consdriss turned toward her. "Such a feat would require massive amounts of energy. The costs of keeping a comm-channel open to orbit would be astronomical. It would take an act of The Concordance to achieve such," he said jokingly.

The Concordance again. That mysterious mix of upper house governance and military that existed in absence of any standing army and was only summoned at moments of great need. Was Brealins part of that enigmatic organization that seemed a myth to even the Silastrii? She shook the thought away. Fresparem fears of KGB and political agents would not serve her here.

"Do as I ask. Use them to arrange contact and nothing more. When you make your move, get me a message."

THE TRIP TO orbit was as punishing as the one down. A jarring, turbulent ordeal that, if not for her rigorous cosmonaut-training, would have left her fighting down vomit. She rode with the cargo, refusing the few Pinnacle agents' requests to accompany them in the plush passenger cabins. They seemed confused but simply shrugged their massive ears at her strange Fresparem ways.

Brealins was waiting for her on the cargo dock when she

arrived. After so mcuh time Below, the sunlight was painful. Natasha shaded her eyes as Brealins approached.

"Heard you rode with the cargo." she said as they departed together. "Was some solitude required before being thrown back among the questions?"

"Yes, something like that," Natasha answered as they departed the elevator facilities.

"Then I think you'll like what I have planned next for you. The Quorum wanted to question you immediately. I convinced them to wait until tomorrow after you've rested. Let those pampered students stew a bit longer. I think you'll find today's plans much more interesting."

Lunch was had while crossing by zeppelin from Pinnacle to an adjacent dome. Sunlight silvered the edges of the clouds as rainbows rippled across the opalescent shells doming each city. Brealins chatted between bites, filling the gaps in conversation cheerily while Natasha kept her answers short. The food, while delicious, left a bitter taste. A slab of fish-steak atop tubers and greens, it was only slightly less fresh than what she'd had on the surface.

How many had died to bring such delicacy from those crushing depths? Natasha felt as filthy as an American dining in New York, her plate piled with foods grown by a starving tenant farmer forever denied such fare. More than ever, she knew Silaster must change, and that she'd been saved to bring it.

Their destination that day was a museum. The city housed a few cafes, but was dedicated almost entirely to the golden domed museum and its sprawling decorative gardens.

"The Grand Museum of the Solar System," Brealins said as they descended the zeppelin ramp and entered the museum. "Dedicated to Silastrii voyages offworld. I thought you might like it."

Natasha wondered if she'd ever grow accustomed to the

soaring scale of Silaster architecture. White arches climbed a hundred meters around the golden dome, itself rising an easy two hundred meters to its center. Spacious halls, dedicated to the planets and sun, branched outward in each direction. While riddled with incomprehensible Silastrii script, there were sufficient photos, diagrams, and animations that Natasha could muddle her way through the fascinating exhibits. Before her were secrets it would take centuries for Earth to discover. The glory of the solar system revealed.

They meandered through rooms dedicated to every world, from Mercury to Mars, then outward to Neptune, Pluto and two mysterious worlds unknown to Natasha. Ghost planets lurking in the dark so far from the sun it glowed little brighter than the stars dusting the galactic void. Natasha could spend years studying Silastrii knowledge of each world.

The next exhibits were dedicated to the Silastrii history of exploration. One depicted early rocketry, showing boosters launched from shafts deep beneath the ground before their people had ascended above. Then the first orbital stations and, finally, the first Silastrii space-elevator from Pinnacle.

"How long?" Natasha asked, gesturing to the diagram of a sealed bubble city similar to the one housing the museum. "From rockets to this, I mean."

"We launched our first rocket seven hundred Fresparem years ago. I think the plagues were ravaging Europe then?"

Natasha simply nodded as they departed the exhibit.

"Finally," Brealins said. "This is what I wanted you to see."

They entered a wing dedicated entirely to Frespar. A gorgeous holographic depiction of Earth rotated above the central space. Photos, illustrations, and mannequins draped in various human attire filled the place.

"Earth?" Natasha asked feeling a chill goosepimple her skin. She hadn't quite appreciated just how fine a Silastrii microscope had been employed in observing her world.

"Yes." There was awe in Brealins voice. "I don't think you

realize how beneficial it has been to witness your world."

"But your technology. The worlds you've visited. What could ours possibly provide you?"

"With warning." There was a manic gleam in her emerald eyes. "So many pitfalls avoided thanks to Fresparem council. Paths of progress threatening the same dangers to our own people, yet deftly avoided because we'd seen them on your world first. Wars, inequality, hatred, consumption, all studied and pored over to ensure we fell not prey to their influences. It's why Saucer Six was there to pull you from the flames. It's why watching your world continues today. Your forays into atomics and orbit provide a particularly potent mix we are keen to document."

Once more Natasha felt little. A primitive specimen patronized by a do-gooder people. Would baptisms soon follow?

Only she wasn't some native hoping to trade beads for tobacco. She'd clawed her way through the Soviet space program. Fended off grabby men demanding their privilege of flesh. Survived the fire after being abandoned to cross the solar system to walk the caverns of Venus and float among its clouds. If Frespar was truly a guide to Silaster, then she would guide those below to equality.

"Thank you, Brealins," she said without any dishonesty. "You've shown me so much. I finally know why I was saved by Saucer Six."

Brealins watched her, smiling for several seconds before speaking. "I believe you do know."

They stared at one another for a few moments before Brealins shrugged her ears. "I suppose that's enough for today. The Quorum insists on seeing you tomorrow. They've booked the Arena. I'm afraid I can only stay their questioning for so long."

BACK IN HER apartment, the sun continuing its inexorable march toward the yearly Silaster night, Natasha received her message from Below.

'Look for the catch of swordfish tomorrow afternoon,' the message from Consdriss read.

So soon? It was still weeks before the night festival when such trips were sanctioned. Natasha had originally wondered if they'd be able to stage their protest before then.

Was such haste testament to what she'd started? The single spark to a forest full of deadfall that had awaited fire far too long? Or was this something else?

You really think you're going to march some workers' protest into Pinnacle's halls of power? The voice in her head, the one constantly referencing brutal Soviet oppression, once more offered protest of its own.

She messaged Consdriss, relaying her time with The Quorum at The Arena. His response was quick. They'd rise to meet her there.

You wanted a rebellion, the pestering voice again. This is what it looks like.

NATASHA BREAKFASTED ON potato and pumpkin salad but no fish. Brealins met her in the apartment lobby and the two were soon on their way to Arena. Even now, she knew Consdriss and the others were nearing the end of their journey from the surface. Seeing as her previous Quorum questioning had lasted hours, there was plenty of time for them to arrive.

Would you so easily accept such fortune in The Soviet Union? She once more shook the thoughts away, an easy task as she walked out among the tens of thousands of Silastrii craning for a better view of the Fresparem. The Arena had been empty when Saucer Six had deposited her there. It positively rumbled with the conversation of those crowding its seats now.

Natasha ascended the stage, the great mural of the solar system spread across the floor before her, and addressed The Quorum. Their questions were much as before.

Did she mean them ill will?

Of course not.

Did her presence presage a greater exodus of humans from her world?

Impossible given Fresparem technology.

On the questioning went, eventually subsiding into more curious inquiries each Quorum member had collected from their constituents. Finally, after an hour, one stood from the thousands around him and asked a question that silenced the entire arena.

"Are you here to overthrow a thousand years of peace?"

Natasha, stunned, looked to Brealins standing behind her.

"Answer the question," Brealins said, her face impassive.

"I...no, of course not."

"They would argue otherwise." The man gestured behind the stage.

The doors opened and Silastrii boiled out. Their clothes were rough, stained things from a hard life Below. Many wore goggles while others cupped hands over eyes long spent in the dark. At their head, Natasha saw Consdriss striding forward.

"We seek to be heard," he said, joining Natasha on the stage. "And if it's a Fresparem who brought us here then so be it."

The Quorum roared to its feet. Protests of resources and balance competed with those from Below bellowing back for their petitions to be heard. Many left the stands, the wondrous mosaic lost beneath their surging footsteps. Consdriss beckoned those Below forward and Natasha felt herself lost in a sea of Silastrii bodies.

"Wait!" Natasha yelled. "Consdriss!" She wasn't sure what she'd planned, but she hadn't expected a riot. She made to charge forward as someone pulled her back.

It was Brealins. She turned Natasha around, and stared hard into her eyes. "I couldn't have done it better myself."

She released Natasha and strode to the edge of the stage, just above the shouting crowd, which looked on the cusp of violence.

Better herself? The same troubling thoughts returned, falling into place like the many tumblers of a lock. Had this all been some plan, of which Natasha was a part?

"They only wished to be heard," Natasha shouted. "Can't you stop them?"

Brealins turned, a cold smile upon her face that chilled Natasha. "Not I," she said gesturing to the golden sky beyond the dome. "The Concordance."

Natasha felt it in her bones. A marrow-chilling, thrumming sensation. The Silastrii, even in their anger, were not immune, as the crowd quickly stilled, and looked up.

The saucers descended. Streaking from the sky in silence, their discs rotating wildly about their central spheres as they coursed toward The Arena from all directions. Seeing one saucer was an awesome sight. Seeing them all...Natasha suddenly understood.

"The saucers," she mumbled. "No military." She looked at Brealins. "This is your Concordance?"

Brealins nodded. "Summoned only in our direst need. A lifetime can pass without such an event." She leaned close, bending down to face the tiny human. "And you, Natasha Laranova, are its cause."

The saucers, seven of them, passed effortlessly through the dome above and arranged themselves about the arena. Their discs slowed, eventually halting in vertical positions like seven steel eyes staring beneath them. One moved forward.

Natasha wasn't sure how, but she knew instantly which of the identical saucers was the one advancing. The same that had saved her so many weeks before. Saucer Six.

It moved over the arena floor, dropping to perhaps a hundred meters. Silent like its siblings, it finally spoke. Energy crackled across its disc, snaking and snapping about while growing to an obvious crescendo with a whining pitch.

The crowd scattered, fleeing the ground for whatever safety might exist in the seats. The growing energy cast a purple glow about the entire arena. When Natasha feared it might grow so strong as to vaporize the entire place, Saucer Six fired. A blazing bolt of energy struck the ground, shuddering the entire arena so severely Natasha thought her teeth might rattle out of her head.

Silence returned, accompanied by the acrid smell of ozone. A crater, several meters across, smoked from the mosaic below. Among the familiar depictions of the planets, one was missing, blasted away by Saucer Six.

Earth. Its image now a smoking ruin. Natasha closed her eyes, not wanting to witness what she'd wrought. It was Brealins who next spoke.

"You see now what I've warned of for years." Her voice carried. Not a single one rose in dissent. But it wasn't the crowd to which Brealins spoke. It was the saucers.

Saucer Six had rejoined its companions arranged about the arena. Each dropped until their spheres were just above the highest tiered seats. An iris opened, and out stepped two Silastrii from each.

The crowds parted before the saucer commanders. They wore high collared uniforms, black trimmed with silver. Just as Kelniss and Lienlin had worn the day they'd saved her. Just as they were wearing now, as the the two strode across the still smoking ground beside their compatriots.

"One Fresparem," Brealins said when the crews joined them on stage. "Accomplished this." She waved over the crowd.

"We will not be silenced!" Consdriss shouted across the crowd, many from Below echoing his cries.

"And you won't be," Brealins said. Fourteen other commanders—two from each saucer--stood beside them on stage. "Your plight has drawn The Concordance. Not seen in nearly a generation, we are here to put right what The Quorum has forgotten."

A cry of protest went up from senior Quorum members while the rest nodded assent. They were soon silenced by Brealins.

"To all those Below," she said. "The Quorum is hereby ordered to hear all your petitions from this assembly until satisfaction is reached." The stunned Below populace beamed while the Quorum pleaded they needed more time. "You will also resolve this by allowing Below an additional petition period before and after nightfall."

The Quorum once more protested, shoving forward in their challenge.

Brealins halted them with a word. The saucers crept forward a mere meter, and The Quorum was obedient once more.

Brealins said, "If Below's demands are too arduous, then perhaps Quorum members' children should augment surface operations until all petitions are settled."

The threat, alongside the saucers hanging above provided sufficient motivation. The Quorum was soon assembling every aid they had to handle the Below throng queuing for audience.

Brealins turned to the other saucer commanders. "Are we in agreement?"

They were. Most wanted nothing more than to return to their duties aboard saucer while grumbling over the trifling Quorum failures pulling them away from their planetary observations and studies. The resolution, agreed upon so swiftly, free of the dragging chains of bureaucracy, left Natasha, once more, in awe of the Silastrii.

"Who are you?" she asked Brealins. Every saucer commander turned their attention to the Fresparem standing before them.

"I'm Admiral Vrealin. Once commander of Saucer Six and the one who called The Concordance to deal with you once and for all."

"Me?"

"*All* Fresparem." Brealins turned to the other commanders standing in a semi-circle around her. "Long has the Frespar question remained unanswered. Do we help our neighbors. Cleanse their atmosphere of the growing pollutants that will one day bring them to the same fate that devoured our own home? Or confine them to their world so that their barbarism remains contained? You see the disruption one Fresparem can achieve. It takes little imagination to consider the capabilities of her entire primate species."

The entire arena had gone silent. Those from Below, the Quorum members handling their petitions, all now listened to the intrigue accompanying the enigmatic Concordance and their off-world dealings.

"We've long delayed any decision," Brealins continued, speaking to the commanders around her but well aware of her wider audience. "No longer." She turned to Kelniss. "Will you report on your mission. On Frespar doings since last we spoke."

All eyes turned toward Kelniss and Lienlin beside him. The two were unchanged from when Natasha first met them. But now she saw them anew. She saw their Below heritage, pale yellow skin similar to that of all the saucer crews surrounding them. Skin long bleached from a lifetime underground. Lacking the darker shades of those who'd spent a life in the sunlight. Did the entire Concordance hail from Below? Kelniss stepped forward, and spoke.

"Nothing has changed," he said, sweeping his hand toward the sky. The air above the arena shimmered before glowing to life with images of Frespar. All looked skyward to the images of Earth, the silent saucers floating sentinel behind.

"We recorded sixteen nuclear detonations since rescuing her." The images changed once more. Mushroom clouds blasted the ocean and air, the videos conjuring gasps from the assembled crowds. Kelniss detailed how there were underground detonations as well, easily recorded by Saucer Six and its instruments. "They continue to burn through their world's resources. Squandering them all to build these."

Natasha and him locked eyes for a moment, and she saw

the sadness there. The pain of someone forced to admit that mercy had failed. He looked away, and joined the other commanders.

Things moved quickly then. The decision was instant and unanimous. Frespar would remain quarantined. Silaster would never make contact and any attempt by humanity to do so would be ignored and, failing that, actively sabotaged. The Quorum seemed to have some ceremonial function in accepting a Concordance decision, but its senior members assented before returning to their duties handling petitions from those Below. Finally, the conversation turned to Natasha.

"Like all her species," one commander said, "she is too dangerous to remain alive."

"Send her Below," said another. "She can work her way back to earning our trust."

The debate over one person went on far longer than that of her entire people. She was just about to protest, to demand some sort of trial or representation when Brealins spoke.

"We are not Fresparem," she said. "To mete out a brutal justice. She will return home. And I will take her there." She pointed to Saucer Six, hovering motionless, and said, "Now."

NATASHA'S RETURN HOME was measured in meals. Confined to the very same cell in which she'd traveled to Silaster, she counted the days in solitude by how often she was fed. The voyage took nearly a week, during which time her food—rice, tofu, greens and water—was slipped through a slot in the door. She spoke to no one. Every Silaster garment had been seized. She wore her old Soviet spacesuit, her gloves and scuffed helmet sat at her feet.

She tried not to think of what she'd lost. A life above the clouds, perhaps even among the saucer crews exploring the solar system. Brealins came to her cell at the end of their trip.

"It's time," she said, beckoning Natasha from the cell's

entrance. The passageways were empty, Natasha saw no others as they descended to the lowest decks.

"Where will you take me?" Natasha asked, her bulky helmet in her hands.

"Home," Brealins said. "Russia."

Natasha had considered what might happen if she were returned home. Believed dead, she would likely be in more trouble found alive. Her meager connections to the military would prove useless once the mystery surrounding her return was revealed. The military, the KGB, they'd believe an American plot before they considered the truth. A bleak future awaited her.

They stopped at the lowest bulkhead. The wall shimmered, and a frozen Russian night awaited them outside. But they weren't just back on Earth. Natasha gaped at the scene before her. Saint Basil's Cathedral, Lenin's Mausoleum—Natasha wasn't just home, she was in the middle of Red Square.

Natasha looked for the rushing soldiers. Listened for the scream of sirens at the massive Saucer touching down in one of the most heavily guarded cities on Earth. Outside, the city looked as frozen as the biting Russian winter that had fallen. There were people—guards, soldiers, police, passersby, all still as stone. Even the breath fogging about their mouths was stopped. Natasha closed her eyes. Even now, the Silastrii had wonders to reveal.

"It wasn't personal," Brealins said. "You must believe me."

"How?" Natasha asked, still in wonder of the frozen scene.

"We can't hold this for long. Please. You must understand. This wasn't about you."

"What does it matter." Natasha looked the to the pavement, a single step beneath her. A single step that would chain her back to a mundane world full of waiting horrors.

"It does matter," Brealins said. "The Fresparem question has troubled us for too long. Your rescue afforded an opportunity too precious to be ignored. You know what awaits you here as well as I do. Do you honestly believe your masters would not extend their barbarism to the stars? Russian, American, ask yourself this. What would any of them do with a saucer? With power such as this?" She gestured outside, to the scene frozen as hard as the pavement beneath.

Natasha didn't answer. She knew Brealins was right.

"If I had to meet any Fresparem, Natasha Laranova." Brealins paused, her green eyes glistening with welling tears. "Then I'm glad it was you."

Natasha stepped from the saucer, the weight of everything lost settling on her like the crushing Russian winter into which she stepped.

"Perhaps you doubt me," Brealins said. "So let me show you. The one gift I can give."

Natasha looked at the tall woman within the saucer's gangway. Would she leave her some trinket? Some wondrous device to remain in contact? A tiny emblem to prove her voyage? Brealins leaned close.

"I won't let them think you're crazy."

The portal closed. Saucer Six, silent as ever but for its barely perceptible hum, vaulted into the sky, and vanished.

The moment the saucer disappeared, time snapped back and Natasha was near freezing. Her flight suit was designed for extreme temperatures, but with her helmet in hand the brutal winter air bit with an intensity threatening frostbite in mere minutes. She stumbled toward the nearest building, but she'd already been spotted.

Whatever inexplicable feeling the locals may have endured under the Silastrii spell, they focused now on the outsider walking toward them. She looked quite out of place in her cosmonaut's garb and soon, several police followed the two soldiers hurrying her toward the suspicious stranger who'd materialized in Red Square. Her world, at the height of its conflict with itself, didn't suffer the unknown easily. She was about to get a taste of the Fresparem barbarism she'd heard so much about on Silaster.

The soldiers arrived with the police. Soon, men with no

uniform at all were there. Their questions brusque, with little time given for answers before the next were hurled her way. One of the soldiers, a man no older than thirty, took her arm and gently led her away. People were watching while trying to remain unobtrusive.

They'd just started moving when something happened. A deep hum, throbbing silently but down to their bones halted the small group and the growing onlookers. The vibration built, and a single gasp turned everyone's gaze upward.

Above, not one hundred meters from the pavement, hung Saucer Six. Its disc rotated in lazy turns about the central orb, halting in a vertical position like the eye of god gazing upon them all.

I won't let them think you're crazy.

To think she'd had to go to Venus to find decency. Despite the shivering cold, Natasha warmed at her friend's final words.

The pitch changed, as the crowd gasped once more, for the disc had begun rotating. Accelerating in 360 degree turns all about the central sphere until it was a blur. People screamed. One of the police fled. And, just as the hum grew so sharp that even Natasha wondered if they might mean harm, Saucer Six shot into the sky, vanishing to a tiny pinprick of light until it was lost amidst the jewels glittering across the winter sky.

All looked at her. The strange woman whose arrival had heralded the impossible sight.

Shaking her self free of the soldier, Natasha stared them down with all the defiance she could muster.

"Who are you?" the young soldier asked, wonder in his eyes.

"I am Lieutenant-Colonel Natasha Laranova of the Red Air Force and a *cosmonaut*." She looked once more upwards before turning back to the stunned group. "And let no one call me crazy."

Christopher Henningsen is an inventor, learner, and spiritual Venusian living on Canada's East coast. He writes: "I'm a son of German back-to-the-landers, and my youth was spent between rural Canada and Germany. During the traditional stint as a roughneck in Alberta's oil industry that most East Canadians go through after high school, I developed a strong interest in sustainable energy. I spent another, shorter stint as an English teacher in a Chinese kindergarten before going to University as a mature student, where I studied Sustainable and Renewable Energy Engineering. I graduated in 2014 and have been keeping my skills sharp outside my day job with technical and artistic projects."

Poetry played a larger role in science fiction's Golden Age than most people remember today; it was standard for the pulp magazines of that time to use short poems as page filler and to give longer poems space of their own. Despite the title, 'The Martian Girl" is a story of adventure on Venus told in ballad meter...

THE MARTIAN GIRL

Christopher Henningsen

I am a man of Venus born,
And in my thirteenth year,
My mother took me by the hand
And bade me lend an ear.

"Now thirteen summers you have seen,
It's time you learned to man,
Your father waits beyond the gates,
To teach you if he can".

"Take you these gifts to please him,
This blade of alloyed steel,
This handpump for etheric force,
This wire drawn on wheel".

And so, bedecked in gifts for men,
I went beyond the wall,
And the silent jungle made the fathers
Twice my height look small.

My father knew me straightaway,

He met my eyes and smiled.
Then having met them, tossed his head,
And slipped into the wild.

Of course I followed, would you not?
The years began to fly,
My father taught me how to man,
Until the day he died.

From him I learned the sunbook way
Of dragonsong and lore,
The rhythms and the words of things
That are and were before.

My father was a lucky man,
As are all men who live,
And truths of luck and cunning were
Fine lessons he did give.

He died a hero as most men
Who sire poets do,
I sing of it at times, but I've
Yet to give him his due.

I took his mantle and his bow
And travelled this strange world,
And some more years passed by until
I met the Martian girl.

She brought to mind a hunted thing
Surprised by morning light,
As, stepping from the city's walls,
She came into my sight.

Her skin was pale and reddish-toned,

Her eyes were like the night,
I met her eyes, I tossed my head,
And melted from her sight.

Of course she followed, would you not?
I let her catch my trail,
And listened like a windless lake
As she told me her tale.

"The men of Terra sail again,
And have no love of Mars,
And war is coming once again,
To bright-between-the-stars".

"With women of your cities, men
Of Terra do trade free,
But Martians have no chieftainess,
And in her place, sent me".

"My voice is well respected as
A tinker and a scribe
And I've earned the highest honor
Of a woman in my tribe,"

"But Venus' chieftesses cared not
For what I had to say
They took my ship and men from me
And sent me on my way".

"Now I must find a way back in
To warn the ships that sailed
That ambush waits in Venus' clouds
And that my mission failed."

I listened with a troubled heart,

For no man has the means,
To cross again the city wall
Once built by Venus' queens.

"But wait", said I, "the city's closed,
And breaking in you'd die,
But there remains another way
Which you may wish to try".

"This city you just left is not
The first one of its kind,
All through the jungle ruins sleep
Now choked by root and vine".

"Among these ruins you may find,
If tinker skilled you are
The wanting parts to make the art,
To let you speak afar."

It seemed she did not care much for
Plans not of her own mind,
Convincing her took all the trust
And cunning I could find.

But when at last she acquiesced
She briefly, dryly wept,
Then set her mind upon her goal
And then, she soundly slept.

She seemed surprised I woke her not,
I asked her what she'd dreamed.
She shook her head, and only said,
That all was as it seemed.

And so we journeyed to the place

Where last a city grew,
And met five men along the way
One half of whom I knew.

They wished to know the present,
And the future if I could
So I sang to them the dragonsong
That's every poet's good.

The present-song came easy
And the future did as well
For not much else is relevant
When men war where men dwell.

"The men of Terra trade their goods
For wealth of Venus' hills,
The red and blue worlds fight anew,
Again one will be killed".

At that the men were silent, and
The Martian silent too,
'Till someone asked the dragon what
It thought that we should do

And the answer came quite easy,
And the dragon made it known
That the city and the jungle
Would house strangers not their own.

The men gave thanks and took their leave,
The girl and I pushed on,
And day merged into night until
Sometime before the dawn,

We stood upon a tree that grew

A ways above the rest,
And the martian cast her keen eyes to
A place just south of west

And there upon a row of hills
My friends and I well knew
Were the remnants of a city -
And a Terran digging crew.

Now Martians hunt prey they can see
And tire it for days,
Venutians never see that far
We have more sudden ways.

We put our heads together
And we argued fierce but quick
And ere arriving we had hatched
A cruel and simple trick.

I played the drum both day and night,
The Terrans grew afeared,
The drums did echo far and wide,
And Venus' men drew near

The things that hunt men neared as well,
The Terran guards grew wild,
And in their frenzy did not note
One Martian slip inside

We kept a vigil on their camp,
They could nor rest nor sleep
As Martian girl worked stranger works
Down in the city's deep.

And as the Terrans called their kin

And made to give pursuit,
I saw the Martian girl again -
In an ancient battlesuit!

Soon the Terrans lost cohesion,
And began to move as prey,
And we gave chase, and took their place,
In less than half a day.

So the Martians when they landed
Were quite grateful for our aid,
And they praised the girl most highly
For the allies she had made.

Now upon some hills camp Martians,
And in cities, Terrans dwell,
Though our world has grown more crowded,
Still I find it just as well.

For two things I've learned that cheer the heart,
Ours is the best-loved world,
And no man who's lucky needs to fear
A nervous Martian girl.

David England is a ponderer, generalist, and student-of-everything who, in the words of his daughter, "does math for a living." Following a nomadic childhood typical among military families, and supplemented by wanderings of his own, he now resides in the well-rooted community of Two Rivers, Wisconsin (birthplace of the ice cream sundae) with his wife Anne, her incredible artwork, and the half-dozen or so unwritten novels which have taken up residence inside his head over the years. This is the first story of his that has been accepted for publication; another story, "The Last Outpost," has also been accepted for publication in the deindustrial-SF magazine Into the Ruins.

In "Tête-à-tête," England takes advantage of one of the more intriguing possibilities in new Old Solar System fiction, and presents a glimpse of an alternative history in which space travel entered the picture well in advance of its actual debut. Different as the resulting history turns out to be, it features familiar faces and causes...

TÊTE-À-TÊTE

David England

THE FIGURE STOOD solitary and motionless, the drab off-white of his thickly-padded excursion suit contrasting with the dark grey of the lunar landscape behind him. A solid brass helmet encased his head, looking not unlike the deep sea diving equipment after which it had been modeled. An electric torch mounted on either side of the helm illuminated the loose soil before him. The object of his gaze, however, required no artificial light. A broad panoply of stars shone brightly, their light steady and unhindered by atmosphere against the stark black canvas of space. The lower border of his field of vision was pierced by the jagged ridges and needle-like projections of lunar mountains.

In the midst of this panorama hung the large blue-green marble which held his attention. Despite his relative youth—only twenty-two standard years—he'd done a fair amount of traveling over the surface of that sphere that looked so small now from his current vantage point. He'd accomplished somewhat less space-faring, but enough to have earned his aether-pips, recognized by mutual agreement among the various national merchant-marine. Enough to be respected by others working the cargo lanes for the merchants and their capitalist overlords. And enough to see what he'd sought to see, to set in motion the wheels of thought in the back of his mind that continued their relentless process even now.

To his right, far downslope from his position, a massive oblong shape maneuvered carefully, edging slowly closer to the flat source of the landing platform below it. Puffs of compressed air, which he could neither see nor hear but knew from experience, sent thin, weighted lines streaming downward to where the port landing crew waited. These leaders would be attached to the landing winches to guide the far heavier mooring lines and then the behemoth would be secured, hauled in with agonizing slowness. Low gravity, as more than one careless captain had been reminded, did nothing to reduce mass and inertia. Haste and inattention ruined many a freighter.

And a freighter this was—a lack of the characteristic zeppelin structure required for atmospheric operation showed this to be a space-only vessel, ferrying cargo between the inhabited worlds of the solar system. Ungainly so close to the lunar surface, vessels like this and others far larger swam the aetheric currents of space, every cubic unit not needed for crew and equipment given over to cargo. Transporting goods to the surface of atmospheric planets—Earth, Mars, Venus—required smaller craft equipped for both environments. Mercury, like the moon, permitted direct transfer for the smaller cargo vessels, though that required the very careful maneuvering he was witnessing here.

Then there was that even smaller planet, orbiting inhumanly close to the solar furnace, which demanded specially-constructed ships to approach and uniquely-skilled pilots to navigate the caverns of its interior world. His otherwise-orderly thoughts idled. Had the cargo he'd arranged, quite unofficially and without authorization, reached its destination? If not yet, then within the next day or two. With luck, authorization was something he'd have soon, however retroactive it might be.

He shook himself from his reverie and turned to retrace

his steps along the low, arcing ridge he'd followed to this point. Time to return. He'd stepped away for longer than he'd intended already and the others would surely be looking for him. He bounded casually in the moon's low gravity, his body adjusting rhythm and posture with the unconscious ease of one well-practiced in such things. The cluster of domes rising above the crater walls that housed the cosmopolitan port city of Diane grew larger with his approach. The wheels of his mind continued to turn as the airlock came into view.

"Lev, where have you been?" A deep, robust voice cut through the noise of the corridor traffic as he turned the corner. The antiseptic white of the wide walkway gleamed and he could hear the low hiss of the atmospheric circulators beneath the babble of conversation. The Edison generators hummed underfoot, almost below hearing, providing Diane's inhabitants with "normal" gravity and relieving them of the inconvenience of having to adjust to lunar living. *Earth-lubbers.*

He'd left the docking area for this concourse—whose airlock he'd employed in his sojourn outside—having returned the suit to the section chief. Technically, what he'd done violated a host of protocols: an unaffiliated civilian using port equipment and facilities for an unaccompanied, undesignated walk in a restricted landing area. But he and the chief had a history, having served on the same cargo-hauler a few years back, shortly after Lev had earned his pips. And that history included one particularly harrowing run in the asteroid belt during which a certain greenhorn had favorably impressed the chief by pulling a vital replacement part out of his ass at an opportune time. So the section chief had nodded to Lev's request in that unassuming way of familiar comrades fully aware of each other's competencies. Nothing had been logged and the suit was simply 'temporarily misplaced' while being inspected.

"I just needed to step away from the Congress for a few minutes, Joseph. To clear my head. These are only the preliminaries anyway. I'm not missing anything but the same opening speeches we heard last Congress in Vienna back in '98."

Joseph approached, his stocky build making a pathway through the other pedestrians flowing past in both directions. A square face and solid jaw betrayed his impatience. "You need to pay more attention to these speeches, Lev. They are not the useless theater you think they are. Power is being positioned, alliances forged, connections made. All while I am hunting you down because you needed to clear your head." He put a large hand on Lev's shoulder. "I know that you are the young intellectual of our delegation, Lev, but having ideas is only one small part of the play. One has to have power to wield and know when to wield it. That is how change is made."

Lev shrugged. "That's why you are a far better player at that kind of chess than I am. You're, what, a year older? And you've already landed a committee position."

It was Joseph's turn to shrug. "Secretary of the Advisory Committee on Special Projects. Hardly a position of influence."

"Nonetheless," Lev countered, "you're a member of the Grand Worker Council as a result and the Executive Committee gives credence to what the Grand Council has to say. That is no small thing. You're a factor in this Fourth Congress and I expect that will carry forward into the Fifth and beyond."

"The First Congress," Joseph corrected him. "This isn't the Fourth Congress of the Second International anymore. It's 1901, the dawn of a new age, and we're holding the First Congress of the First Interplanetary." He took Lev by the arm. "Now come along. The plenary session will be starting soon and we need to be there as the Congress agenda is being confirmed. The votes are by delegation and you're needed to ensure that ours votes the way we want it to. This is important, Lev."

Lev acquiesced and Joseph released his grip. The two began moving down the crowded corridor. "Does it ever strike you as ironic that the First Interplanetary is being inaugurated on the moon?"

Joseph barked a harsh laugh. "Don't let anyone on the Executive Committee hear you say that. 'The moon' has been deemed a bourgeois term of capitalist oppression—it's Luna now."

Lev smiled ruefully. "I'll keep that in mind." At his comrade's silent stare, he raised his hands in a gesture of compliance. "Seriously, Joseph. I will."

The two figures threaded their way through the corridor traffic toward the auditorium and adjoining suite of chambers where the Congress was beginning session. The next two weeks would be crowded with speeches and meetings (formal, informal, and clandestine). Maneuvers by those purporting to lead the workers of the various worlds in the ongoing class struggle. Lev much preferred actually leading the struggle, in the field among his comrades, to making speeches about it. But the organizational support of the Committee and the financial support which accompanied it were nonetheless necessary.

Joseph nodded a silent greeting to a knot of delegates clustered by the entrance as he and Lev stepped through one of three sets of double doors leading to the auditorium lobby. Two pods of side rooms, one at each end of that long rectangular antechamber, provided meeting spaces for break-out sessions, committee and subcommittee meetings, or spontaneous side-bar conversations.

Like the one he'd planned for just this moment.

Lev glanced at the chronometer, its broad circular face and sweeping hands set high above another trio of double doors leading into the auditorium proper, and then at the placard set just to one side, outlining the program for the day in large, bold type. The drone filtering through the closed doors confirmed his assessment. He had timed this well.

"Joseph," he reversed roles, taking his companion by the arm instead. "Before we go in, I need to speak with you. Privately." Joseph looked at the doors, then at the placard. Lev gripped the thick bicep a bit tighter. "We have time. I've read the transcripts: Vandervelde's been giving the same speech for the last three Congresses. He's got a bit longer before he wraps up. And the vote you were concerned about isn't for another twenty minutes yet."

Joseph sighed. "Alright. A few minutes. But I swear, Lev, if this is about another of your schemes, I'll break you in two."

I do not doubt that, Lev thought.

The pair turned left and made their way toward the end of the lobby, stepping into one of the vacant rooms. As Lev quietly shut the door behind them, his companion asked with some annoyance, "What is it this time?"

"It's about Vulcan…"

A growl sounded deep in Joseph's throat. "Damn it to hell, Lev. How many times do I have to tell you. No one cares about the Vulcans! No one is going to care about the Vulcans! We're trying to lead a class struggle against the industrialists and you're still carrying on about the plight of little green pygmies that aren't even human."

"I didn't say 'Vulcans', Joseph. I said 'Vulcan'. May I speak?"

Joseph set his jaw and grunted, waving one hand dismissively. "Fine. Go ahead."

"You want to break capitalism's hold on the workers of the worlds? You want to bring down the industrialists? The key to that is the web of commerce that flows along the aether currents and binds the worlds of the solar system together. And the key to that web of commerce is Vulcan."

"How?"

"Come on, Joseph. You know history as well as I do. In the first two decades of exploration, travel between the worlds was long and hazardous. Even an Earth-Venus transit took months and lost ships were not uncommon. Now material flows from the mines in the asteroid belt to Mercury in weeks with clockwork precision. It wasn't until the Americans landed on Vulcan in '45 that everything changed."

"Technology improved, of course."

Lev rolled his eyes. "Now you're talking like an industrialist. 'The gospel of technological progress!' No, Joseph. What changed everything was access to the Vulcan mines and their crystals. The industrialists have done nothing but exploit a natural resource found on Vulcan. Found *only* on Vulcan. The technology has been refined, yes, but without those crystals, the Henry-Germain lenses produce a mere fraction of the power we take for granted today."

Joseph snorted. "And what the hell do you know about aether propulsion technology?"

"Enough. What do you think I've been doing since the last Congress? While you've been climbing the ranks within the party, I've been working the cargo lanes in the merchant fleet. I made Engineer's Mate First Class six months ago. And I'll tell you, cobbling together a replacement for a blown-out aether-flux tube in the middle of a firefight gives you a sense of how the thing works."

Joseph's left eyebrow rose slightly. "Firefight?"

"Pirates."

"Ah."

"Now, I'm no scientist, Joseph—I'll admit that—but I can read between the lines of the research that's been published well enough to understand that the lattice-structure of the vulcanite crystals which gives them their ability to focus aetheric flow so efficiently is due to the unique conditions on Vulcan: its proximity to the solar vortex, the interactions of the aether and the solar fields, the chemical and structural composition of Vulcan's planetology, and a dozen other phenomena. It cannot be replicated, in essence, outside of constructing a new Vulcan."

"Let's say I grant your point for the sake of argument

and let's say, somehow, one was able to disrupt access to the mines. The crystals currently in use would degrade over time—even I know that—and commerce slows. It slows and everything reverts back to the pace that existed before Vulcan. So what?"

Lev gave a small sigh. "Things haven't sat idle in the half-century since Vulcan was first exploited. Don't you see? Everything—the interplanetary flow of goods, the economic and political systems of the empires and worlds—*assumes* that commerce operates at the pace it does today. A decline in that capability would be disastrous. If you want to strike a blow at the heart of the industrialists' system, this would be it."

"I'll humor you, Lev. How exactly do you propose to accomplish this disruption?"

"By raising the class awareness of the native Vulcans laboring in the mines and instigating a rebellion on the world."

"Oh, is that all? The Executive Committee is never going to sign off a scheme like that."

"I'm not asking for their permission, Joseph. It's already in motion. I need you to sell it to them and get me the support I need to continue the effort."

"Fuck all, Lev!" Joseph hissed. "You acted without authorization? Do you want to get yourself barred? Or declared an enemy of the proletariat? You're endangering our worldswide struggle on behalf of *human* workers! I'm not going to save your neck when you've put it on the chopping block yourself."

"Let me explain..."

"There are no international seams to exploit, no internal borders to utilize. You know the arrangement: The Austro-German Empire has Mercury; the British claim Mars; the Franco-Spanish Empire controls Venus; and the Motherland manages the asteroids. But all the great powers have concessions within those territories. Except Vulcan. Vulcan has no national concessions, Lev—the Americans control *the entire planet*. And their security is legendary."

"I know that, Joseph. I've seen it."

Joseph stared at him for a long moment. "What do you mean?"

"As I said, I've been working the cargo lanes for the last three years. That included runs to Vulcan. I've seen their security up close. And, yes, it is everything you've heard and more. For good reason—their monopoly of the mines is a source of incredible power and wealth. They'd be fools to operate any other way. Not to mention that control of the planet likely saved them from a brutal civil war. You've read their history: they solved their internal conflict over human slavery by enslaving Vulcan instead. And they've exploited that resource ruthlessly ever since."

"So you know how tight their security is. By your own admission."

"Yes, I do. But, Joseph, that security is focused in one direction. Its sole purpose is to prevent the smuggling of crystals *off of Vulcan*."

Joseph's brow furrowed in thought, then smoothed again as the point sunk in. Responding to his companion's unspoken understanding, Lev continued. "Exactly. As you said yourself, no one cares about the Vulcans."

Stonily silent, Joseph looked over Lev's shoulder at a point on the far wall. A long minute ticked by. Then another.

Lev decided to gamble. "This can work, Joseph Vissarionovich. Help me follow it through."

"Tell me what pile of shit you've stepped into, Lev Davidovich. And then I'll tell you if I'll decide to help you."

Lev took that in and nodded. "Fair enough. I saw an opportunity and I acted. I won't apologize for that. Arrangements were made for propaganda, written in native Vulcan ideograms, to be delivered to the planet, hidden in cargo where they will be found by a contact I established there. Their language is a simple pictographic form, but we are only trying to spread basic concepts. However, it needs time to work. I was able to finance this small test shipment myself, but I need the backing—funding—for the shipments to continue."

"Hmmm…"

"This falls under 'Special Projects', I'd say. As secretary, you have the ability to introduce the idea and to shape the agenda. Frame it however you wish. Say that your rash friend stumbled on an idea with promise, but foolishly set things in motion before talking with anyone, leaving you to take his jumbled concept and make it work. Paint yourself as the steady one cleaning up other people's messes. That might even help establish you with the Executive Committee. It's all the same to me. Just give my plan a chance."

Joseph looked Lev dead in the eye, his voice flat and emotionless. "Fine. I will take your project and put my weight behind it. But I'm telling you only once, Lev. Do not do this again. Ever."

Lev nodded. "I understand."

"Are we done?"

"Yes."

"Then let's get back to the delegation." Joseph turned brusquely and left the room without another comment. Lev waited a moment longer.

I understand quite well, my friend. One of us will likely end up in the seat of power. And the other will likely end up dead. But the struggle is bigger than any one person—certainly bigger than Lev Davidovich Bronstein. And the struggle is what matters.

He let out a long breath, then stepped through the open doorway.

A San Francisco native, Arthur Vibert has lived and traveled all over the world. He was worked in advertising and currently works as a video producer. And of course he's been an avid science fiction reader all his life, starting with "Space Cat" by Ruthven Todd.

The Old Solar System is spacious enough to provide room for many different kinds of stories, and comedy is certainly included. "The Answer at the End of the World" leads the reader on a Martian pilgrimage that is less than serious—and then there's what waits at its end...

THE ANSWER AT THE END OF THE WORLD

Arthur Vibert

THE SHIP WAS a few hundred years old and it was slow but it was good enough. He was 95 standard days out from Amantium spaceport on Venus and he stank and longed for something besides ship rations but he could see the graceful limb of Mars in his viewport and he was content.

He was a Quaesitor—a Seeker of Truth—and wore the indigo robe of his order. He was going to the temple complex at Olympus Mons but of course one didn't just go - there was a pilgrimage involved. He sighed heavily in anticipation - he was getting a little old for pilgrimages and was not looking forward to it. Still, if all went well this would be his last.

The ship made planetfall at Tharsis Tholus in the early evening and he emerged to see the sun setting in a haze of particulate that filled the air, last remnants of one of the sandstorms that plagued the area. He hoped that this would be the last of the season—it was hard enough working one's way across the Martian desert without having to deal with a sandstorm as well.

Once he was inside the spaceport building a Martian functionary greeted him with a complex system of hand gestures, head movements and gyrations that looked like some kind of exotic dance but that he recognized as a formal Martian diplomatic greeting. He waited patiently, a neutral expression on his face, until it was over. The functionary finished with a flourish and quickly transitioned to a Terran greeting, extending his hand which the Quaesitor took and shook firmly.

"Welcome to Tharsis Tholus, Quaesitor," he said. "We are so happy to have you among us. I am Ambulus Intebulis, here to help you in your quest. After you've had a chance to refresh yourself the Princess would like a word."

"I'm sure she would," the Quaesitor said. "Lead on."

Ambulus had the Quaesitor's bags loaded into a sort of wagon, which had a large cargo area between the driver's bench and a small cabin at the back for passengers. It was drawn by a blumble, an enormous lumbering Martian draught animal that looked a little like an elongated elephant with 3 trunks, a ratlike head and the temperament of a camel. It also had the camel's habit of spitting when upset which, given the size of the beast, was not an insignificant concern.

Tharsis was, like all Martian cities, built in the caldera of an extinct volcano. The structures were nestled around the circumference rather than built directly under the opening, rendering them invisible from above. Martians built down rather than up, which meant that the newest structures were deep underground and the most ancient were at the top. Water was found deep in the ground and the various kinds of fungus that formed the staple of the Martian diet grew well in the dark, damp caverns beneath the city. And so it had been for thousands of years.

Martians themselves were similar to Terrans, but tended to be much taller—up to 8 feet—and green, in the same sense that an Asian person might be considered yellow or a Native American red. They were slender and delicately featured and had a nictitating membrane in their eyes, like a cat.

Ambulus hoisted himself up onto the bench at the front of the wagon and took the reins. "Why don't you ride in the cabin," he said, "it's much more comfortable."

The Quaesitor pulled himself up and sat down next to him. "I'm happy here," he said. "The view is too limited from the back. I want to see the city as we approach."

Shrugging, the functionary shook the reins, urging the blumble into movement. It trudged slowly but powerfully towards the city.

Martian cities exist in a kind of perpetual twilight. Shaded from direct sunlight by the lip of the caldera they bask in the orange warmth refracted in by the dusty atmosphere. At night the walls of the caldera emit light, coated in phosphorescent fungus that casts a soft blue-green glow over the city. The fungus is also used inside to create ambient light which is augmented when necessary by methane-fueled lamps which add to the blue lambency. The methane is generated in pits deep beneath the city where human and blumble dung is collected.

Martian buildings are tall, cylindrical spires with bulges occurring at various places along the shaft seemingly at random. They are close packed and many of them are connected by precarious-looking rope walkways that the Martians cross without concern. The buildings themselves are festooned with complex geometric designs, almost an arabesque but less symmetrical.

The Quaesitor watched as they drew closer to the city. It was beautiful but it had an air of decay about it; an ancient city whose glory days were long behind it, still boasting of noble deeds done thousands of years before. He would have preferred to have avoided it altogether, but inconvenient to his destination though it was, one did not come to Mars without paying obeisance to the Princess. And the Princess dwelt in Tharsis.

Passing through the city gates was perfunctory—there were so few visitors to Mars these days that no one really cared what a person was bringing in or where he came from. Inside the city, though, was another matter.

"You there! Terran!" The Quaesitor looked around to see a particularly tall and unusually brawny Martian gesticulating angrily at him. Onlookers drew back to safety, as far away from the wagon as they could get while still affording them a view of what was sure to be an exciting fight. The Quaesitor waited.

"What is your purpose here? Why do you sully our noble city?"

"I am here at the behest of the Princess," said The Quaesitor.

"All men are here at the behest of the Princess. I asked what your business was." The Martian stepped in front of the blumble and stopped it, glaring at The Quaesitor. "Sir, this is not in your best interests," said Ambulus. "The Princess..."

"I'll decide what's in my best interests. Come down from there, Terran."

The Quaesitor jumped down to the ground, Ambulus tugging at his robe ineffectually, trying to keep him on the bench. "I will warn you only once. Step aside and let us pass and no harm will befall you."

The Martian laughed and swung a fist the size of a ham hock at The Quaesitor, who easily ducked it while simultaneously sweeping his robe aside, sliding out his katana and using it to describe a fine line along the Martian's abdomen which immediately began to bleed. He stood back to watch, sword at the ready, as the Martian inspected the damage.

"Go now and I will forget this," The Quaesitor said. "The next time I will not be so gentle."

This served only to enrage the Martian, who charged him with both fists raised, apparently hoping to pile drive him into the ground. Again the sword flashed, but this time the Martian's head fell to the ground, followed shortly thereafter by his body which collapsed in a jumbled mass of limbs into a growing pool of blood. The Quaesitor wiped his blade on the Martian's sash, slid it back into the scabbard, rearranged his robes and climbed back onto the bench.

Ambulus sat there and gaped at him. The Quaesitor motioned forward and said, "Let's be on our way. These people do not look too happy just now and I'd prefer not to shed any more blood." As the cart moved off The Quaesitor said, "One cannot be a Quaesitor without mastering the martial arts. There are too many people like our friend back there who would impede us from fulfilling our purpose."

"And what purpose is that?" asked Ambulus.

"That's between me and The Princess," The Quaesitor said.

HAVING SECURED LODGING, bathed, and dined on a delicious meal of grilled elephant ear mushroom and chewy pit moss, The Quaesitor was escorted to the throne room by Ambulus and several guards.

The room was vast and round, easily 100 yards in diameter, with a domed ceiling that bathed the room in soft blue light. Shadows around the circumference made the room appear even larger than it was since it was difficult to tell where it ended, or even if it ended. Carved from the living rock thousands of years before it had served as the throne room for Martian royalty ever since. The throne itself was in the center of the room on a dais, with attendants, servants and bureaucrats arrayed around it. The princess appeared bored but looked up with interest when The Quaesitor was announced. He approached the base of the dais and bowed deeply.

"My Princess," he said.

"Ah, Quaesitor," she said. "we feared the worst."

"My ship was not the fastest, nor was it the most luxuriously appointed. But it sufficed."

He looked at her obliquely, since a direct gaze would have created difficulties with her guards. She had the body of a 16-year-old, lithe and beautifully toned, her skin flawless. She was clad in light leather armor, her long, honey-colored hair pulled back away from her face. He risked a glance into her eyes and found her looking back at him, a faint smile of amusement playing at the corners of her mouth. Her face was as perfect as the rest of her, but her eyes had the look of knowledge and vast experience and a trace of weariness. She was rumored to be ancient—hundreds or even thousands of years old. He believed it.

"And why have you come to Mars, Quaesitor?"

"I've come to seek The Answer At the End of the World," he said.

The Princess' retinue gasped audibly and Ambulus looked at him in shock. The Princess herself remained calm, showing no sign that she thought anything was out of the ordinary.

"I see, Quaesitor," she said. "And you understand that such a quest is not, shall we say, the safest thing one might do?"

"I believe that it was first described to me as 'fraught with peril'," he said.

"And why do you wish to undertake such a journey? Mars is not without its attractions. A man of your station could while away his years sampling the delights of Mars without risking his life."

"True enough, my Princess. But then I would not be a Quaesitor."

The Princess paused to consider this. "I will grant permission for your journey. But I have a condition."

"Name it," said the Quaesitor.

"I will accompany you."

Again her retinue gasped. Several of the bureaucrats begged her to reconsider. Ambulus stepped forward. "Your highness, this is madness! Please consider…"

"SILENCE," roared her sergeant at arms. "The princess has spoken."

"I accept your condition," the Quaesitor said when the room quieted. Ambulus looked at him in horror.

"Quaesitor, you cannot," he whispered. "She is the last of

her line. If we lose her, chaos will surely ensue."

"That's no concern of mine," said the Quaesitor. "She wields the power on this planet and I will not stand in her way if it means abandoning my purpose." Turning back towards The Princess the Quaesitor opened a small leather box and withdrew an amulet on a gold chain which he held up for her to see. "This amulet is a gift from the Indigo Order of Quaesitors, in recognition of your grace and generosity in allowing me to continue on my quest." He named it to one of the underlings who conveyed it to The Princess. She looked at it closely for a minute and then handed it back to the underling, bending her head forward so that the amulet could be placed around her neck.

"It is very beautiful, Quaesitor. I will wear it with pleasure."

Beside the dais a heavily muscled Martian, resplendent in his ceremonial uniform of hammered copper and red cinnabar swung an enormous mallet, sounding a gong so huge the sound was felt more than heard.

"Very well, then. Preparations will begin immediately," the Princess said. She stood and turned to go, giving a parting glance to the Quaesitor that seemed to him full of promise - and danger.

THE PILGRIMAGE BEGAN with great pomp; there were long, flowery speeches and musical performances, fireworks and the sacrifice of animals. But as the blumble-drawn line of wagons and carriages made its way into the Martian gloaming and the sounds of celebration faded into silence behind them, the Quaesitor's mood turned melancholy. He rode a blumble, bringing up the rear. He had hoped that his journey would be a solitary one, even though he knew that the likelihood of that was remote. But this was beyond his worst fears. There were easily 1000 people traveling with him and none of them, except for himself and possibly the princess and her guards, had any reason to be here aside from a desire for novelty.

Because the princess did not wish to wait for camp to be made, a series of encampments had been set up in advance of their arrival. When they moved on in the morning the camp would be broken down and transferred forward past the slow-moving caravan by a special team. There were three such teams and in this way there was always a fresh camp awaiting them as they moved across the Martian desert. The problem was that they were only traveling 25 kilometers a day. At this rate, even under ideal circumstances it would be at least 100 days before they arrived. The Quaesitor sighed in frustration. There was no point in complaining. Nothing would change. He resigned himself to months of tedium and stared ahead at the steady rise and fall of plodding blumble hindquarters.

They arrived at the first encampment not long after nightfall. He sat with the royal entourage, though not at the Princess' table. The conversation was pleasant but primarily involved gossip about the activities of people with whom he was not acquainted. He begged off at the earliest polite opportunity. As he made his way back to his tent he became aware of a presence beside him.

"Not one for nightlife, Quaesitor?"

He turned to look at the Princess who had managed to approach him silently, something most people would find impossible to do. She was buried in a Venusian craatkin fur robe against the cold of the night and yet somehow still managed to look lithe and regal.

"You have no guards, Princess. Are you not concerned?" The Quaesitor said.

"Hardly," she said. "I fear neither man nor beast on this dying ball of dirt and blumble dung. Nothing changes and nothing has changed for a thousand years. I seek something—anything!—that has the possibility of novelty about it."

The Quaesitor considered this. "Have you traveled to the

other worlds? Venus is known for its exotic creatures and vast jungles. The ice caves of Titan are a wonder to behold. Surely you would find something that would satiate your appetite for the new."

"I cannot leave Mars," she said. "My blessing is also my curse. If I leave this planet I die."

"I am sorry, my Princess. I had no idea."

"Few people do. It's not a piece of information I would have widely known. As long as I am in contact with the planet—or something touching the planet—I live. But if I lose contact for more than a few minutes, I die. This is why we are making our way across the desert instead of flying to Olympus. My courtiers think it is because I enjoy endless celebration and parties. I allow them to believe this, but in fact those activities bore me to distraction."

They approached the Quaesitor's tent and as he bent to pull back the door flap the Princess said, "I have heard that those of your order are celibate. Is that so?"

"No, my Princess," the Quaesitor said.

The fur slipped from her shoulders and her naked body gleamed in the distant firelight.

"Then will you invite me in? It's cold out here."

THEY HAD PASSED Ascraeus Mons weeks ago. Just visible on the horizon, the ancient caldera rose above the shattered landscape, ghostly in the dust-laden air. Olympus Mons lay ahead and the Quaesitor could just make out the upper slopes, its vastness as yet unrevealed behind the curvature of the planet. The Princess rode beside him in companionable silence. Since their first night together they had occupied a tent together and their shared lust had turned into something deeper, surprising them both. As a Quaesitor he was required to travel far and wide, and she was trapped on Mars. And of course there was the small matter of her apparent immortality. But those were problems for another time. For now he was content.

Their retinue had shrunk considerably over the endless weeks of travel. They now numbered just over 250 and most of those were in the pay of the Princess and so were compelled to stay. This was perfectly fine with the Quaesitor, who was pleased to see that with fewer travelers their progress was faster. Not a lot faster, but faster. The Quaesitor was riding up front when he spied a dust cloud approaching, which almost certainly meant that riders were coming their way. He called out to the ranking officer to alert him and rode back to alert the Princess.

Twice daily a courier flew in from Tharsis with various documents and notices and other items that required the Princess' attention. She was currently in the middle of dealing with this when the Quaesitor found her.

"Riders are approaching from Olympus, Princess," the Quaesitor said. The Princess handed the documents back to the courier and turned to her handmaidens.

"Bring my armor and my sword," she said.

"Princess, surely it is better for you to remain safely in the back?" the Quaesitor said.

"I am the leader of my people and leaders don't lead from behind. Unless they are running away," she said. "But I would have you by my side when we greet these riders." The Quaesitor nodded in acknowledgment. He watched while she quickly slid into her armor, which was essentially the same as what she wore when he first met her. When she had attached her sword to her belt they rode back up to the front together.

The dust cloud was growing—the approaching riders would arrive in minutes. The Princess and the Quaesitor waited patiently, the armed guards waiting a good 10 yards behind them. As the riders neared the Quaesitor could see that they were in full battle regalia. This was not to be a diplomatic meeting then. They rode brindles, sleeker versions of blumbles and much faster, though their extreme gait was exhausting for riders over long distances. Brindles were also carnivores, a feature that made them useful in close mounted combat.

The riders drew up before them and stopped. The lead rider approached The Princess and The Quaesitor.

"I am Scantar, leader of the Olympus Guard. Who dares come before the Olympic Temple?"

The Sergeant at arms stepped forward.

"You are in the presence of her Royal Highness Princess Po-Ming of Tharsis Tholus, high ruler of Mars and the moons Phobos and Deimos. And this man is a Quaesitor of the Indigo order."

"And what might their purpose be at the Olympic Temple?" the rider asked.

"One does not question the Princess in this manner," said the Sergeant at arms, now visibly angry. "Her purpose and reasons are her own and not to be questioned, especially by a mere... commoner."

The rider, unperturbed, continued.

"I will know your purpose or you will go no further," he said.

The Sergeant-at-arms began to unsheathe his weapon. But the Princess stayed his arm.

"Calm yourself, Master Sergeant. This man is only doing his job. We will say what our purpose is and all will be well." She turned to the rider. "I am here because, though I have been the ruler on this planet these many years I have never been to the Olympus Temple and I wish to see it for its legendary beauty and the wisdom of its keepers. The Quaesitor can speak for himself."

The rider turned to the Quaesitor.

"I am here to seek The Answer At The End Of The World."

"Seek as you will," said the rider. "I doubt you will find it."

"Perhaps not. But it is in my nature to seek and so I must."

"Very well. We will escort the Quaesitor and the Princess to the Temple at Olympus. All others will return to Tharsis Tholus."

The master sergeant spoke up again. "Princess, we cannot leave you with these men! You must take us with you!"

"Fear not, Master Sergeant. These men are honorable. If they wished us ill we would have known it by now. Return to Tharsis Tholus in peace."

Shaking his head the master turned and the rest of the Princess's guards joined him as they slowly made their way back in the direction of Tharsis. Ambulus approached the Princess and the Quaesitor, obviously intent on making one last effort to convince them of their folly. But the Princess waved him away before he could utter a word, and he turned to join the others.

"Do you have two more brindles?" the Quaesitor asked Scantar. "If nothing else we could carve a few weeks out of this interminable trek."

Scantar motioned to one of his men and two more brindles were brought to them. "You know how to ride these?" The Princess leapt on to hers and expertly moved it in a tight circle around the group. "I think we'll be fine," she said. The Quaesitor climbed less acrobatically on to his brindle but looked perfectly comfortable in the saddle.

"Let's go," he said.

The Princess and the Quaesitor made their way across the changeless landscape, the tedium of their days broken only by the joys of their increasingly intense lovemaking at night. The Guards were taciturn and not given to song or drink and after attempting to engage Scantar in conversation several times the Quaesitor—a man of few words himself—began to feel positively loquacious by contrast. Still, Olympus slowly came into view as the days passed and now, a fortnight since they had parted company with the Princess's retinue they were at the base of the mountain, which extended to their left and right as far as the eye could see.

"From here we proceed on foot," said Scantar. "The footing is too uncertain for the brindles who were bred for the desert."

The Quaesitor looked up. There was a narrow path that led up into the rocks above and quickly vanished behind an outcropping.

"This is the way?"

"Yes," replied Scantar. "The path is relatively safe, but it is rocky and there are places where a fall could mean death. And watch for Rock Cats."

"Rock Cats?"

"You'll know one if you see it. Kill it at once, or it will surely kill you. And kill it swiftly. If it lets out a yowl it will attract others. They can quickly overwhelm us if there are enough of them. And they are merciless."

"They sound delightful," said the Quaesitor.

"There was a man of the court who kept one for a pet," said the Princess. "It ate him and worked its way through three concubines, a messenger and a palace guard before someone finally spitted it."

"Who," asked Scantar?

"I did," replied the Princess, smiling wickedly. "Someone has to clean up these little messes!" She turned and started up the path, followed by the others. As they climbed, the Quaesitor spoke to Scantar, who walked ahead of him.

"Surely we're not walking the entire way to the Temple?"

"No," said Scantar. "When we complete this ascent we will come to a cave. Within the cave there is a river. Most of the journey will be by boat."

"Will wonders never cease," muttered The Quaesitor.

THE ROCK CAT attacked without warning just as the sun was setting. It leapt from above, clamping itself onto the shoulders of one of the guards and fastening its teeth on his neck. The Quaesitor had his katana out almost instantly but when he swept it across the cat's neck there was a shower of sparks and the cat was unharmed,

"They're called Rock Cats because their skin is hard, like a rock, not because they live in the rocks," said the Princess as she unsheathed her sword and drove it directly into the place where the cat's skull met its spine. The cat died instantly, falling off the Guard's back in a heap and collapsing onto the path. It was too late for the Guard, unfortunately. His neck was almost chewed through and he sucked in a few liquid breaths before he succumbed to his wound.

Scantar looked at the fallen Guard reflectively. "I keep telling them to be alert. But there's always one who daydreams." He motioned to the remaining Guards who lifted the corpse and tossed it down into the ravine.

The Princess regarded Scantar critically. "You don't burn your dead? Or bury them?"

"No, Princess. There's no soil in which to bury him around here. And burning him would only attract more cats. And that would not be good. Hopefully down in the ravine he will attract whatever cats remain around here and they will leave us alone."

The Princess nodded and resumed the ascent. They continued long after dark, lighting their way with glow lanterns using phosphorescent fungus as an illumination source. It was bright enough to see the path but not likely to attract cats. After what seemed an eternity of plodding along they came to a flat area that led to an enormous door in the rock. There were two Guards standing stoically to either side of the door. As Scantar approached they pulled the door open to admit the travelers. The Guard on the right blew a trumpet as they passed into the cave and they heard an answering trumpet call echoing from deep inside.

"We will stop for refreshment and pass the night here in the Guard quarters. Tomorrow, the Guards will remain here but I will accompany you on the boat to the Temple. Prepare yourselves. The Temple Guardian does not gladly suffer fools," said Scantar.

The Quaesitor and The Princess were shown to their quarters where, without a word, they both collapsed into a deep, dreamless sleep.

THE FOLLOWING DAY they awoke refreshed and after a simple breakfast of dried meat and ale they boarded the boat and began their journey into the depths of Mons Olympus. The tunnel in which they voyaged was covered in intricate carvings made directly into the rock. Mile after mile a seemingly endless array of complex stories told in relief unfolded before them, depicting scenes almost too fabulous to believe.

"Tell me, Scantor, what do these carvings represent?" asked the Princess.

"These are tales of the first peoples, who came to Mars thousands of years ago and carved a civilization out of the wilderness."

"But the vehicles, the technologies—it seems they possessed a science of almost magical qualities."

"Indeed they did," said Scantor. "They were as gods."

"To possess such power...," said the Princess, lost in thought.

"They squandered it all, with crazy schemes and a mistaken sense of their own infallibility," said the Quaesitor. "They had the power of gods but the minds of monkeys. And not particularly bright monkeys at that."

Even though the boat was powered it took them three days before they arrived at the Temple Complex. And for three days the walls of the tunnel continued to display the complex carvings that depicted the deeds of the ancients. As far as they could tell they never repeated.

As they approached the complex proper the tunnel gradually began widening out until it opened out into a vast cavern full of a mind-numbing riot of complex architecture so dense it was impossible to grasp it all or even begin to understand it. None of the traditional Martian architecture was in evidence. Here were shiny buildings made of metal and glass, some straight and formal while others writhed with sinuous, sensual shapes that seemed to be neither sculpture nor building but some strange amalgam completely foreign to both the Princess and the Quaesitor.

"I had no idea this was here," said the Princess. "How is that possible?"

"Very few come to the Temple," said Scantor. "Of those, even fewer are admitted. And of those, almost none come out again. Those who do are under an oath of silence. For reasons that will become apparent, those few choose to keep it."

The Princess nodded. The Quaesitor stared ahead, revealing nothing.

The boat crossed the bay and tied up at a dock at the foot of a Greek style temple that looked strangely out of place in the context of the rest of the structures. As they disembarked they were met by servants who took their few belongings and motioned for them to get onto a cart drawn by a smaller cousin to the blumble.

"You will be taken to your chambers," said Scantar. "Eat, reflect and rest. Tomorrow you will be formally bathed and prepared to be brought into the presence of the Temple Guardian. She will decide which of your questions she will answer and which of your boons she will grant. But be warned - she decides as she will and here her word is law. There is no recourse if you do not like what you hear."

THEIR ROOM WAS spare but comfortable. Ravenous from weeks of road rations they fell to the delicious food that had been set out for them and, having eaten their fill, were now looking out over the Temple and enjoying a light wine that seemed to have euphoric properties in addition to tasting remarkably good.

The Quaesitor looked at the Princess as she stood on their

balcony overlooking the lake. She was beautiful and had revealed depths and complexities that had made her ever more fascinating as he had gotten to know her. He might even be willing to give up his vows for her, he thought - something he had never considered before. And her immortality? He could worry about that later.

She walked back into the chamber and approached him, allowing her wrap to fall to the floor, revealing her perfect nakedness.

"Look upon me, Quaesitor," she said. "What do you see?"

"I see the perfect body of the woman I love."

"This body is three thousand years old. It looks perfect on the outside but inside it grows weary. What is to become of me?"

He took her in his arms and kissed her deeply. He had no other reply.

THE FOLLOWING DAY they were led to a steaming pool of water where they were washed by attendants. Then fragrant oils were rubbed into their skin and they were garbed in light, flowing robes. Scantar rejoined them when their ablutions were complete.

"You will now meet the Temple Guardian. Her ways are different and will seem strange to you for she is ancient beyond reckoning. Good luck."

He motioned to the attendants who led The Quaesitor and the Princess down a hall towards an enormous pair of doors. He turned away before the doors opened. He had never been in the presence of The Temple Guardian. He did not wish to change that now.

THE DOORS SWUNG open silently and The Princess and The Quaesitor entered, though the attendants remained behind.

Unlike most of the rooms in The Temple this one was relatively small, almost homely. There was a fire burning in a marble fireplace ringed by several comfortable chairs and as the approached they could see a rather plain-looking woman sitting in one of them sipping a cup of tea. She wore blue jeans and a light sweater and sensible shoes. Her hair was pulled back in a ponytail.

"Please, sit down, relax. In spite of what you have been told I don't actually bite. My name is Kayla. You don't need to call me "The Guardian" or anything like that. I'm not formal. Would you like some tea?"

They sat down, uncertain of how to proceed. Kayla poured them tea and encouraged them to try the cakes.

"Let me get this out of the way right off the bat," Kayla said. "I've been here on Mars for five thousand years, since the first settlers from Earth came. As far as I know I'm the last person alive in the solar system who remembers the dawn time."

"But… that's impossible!" said The Princess. "Mars is the crucible from which all life in the Solar System originated!"

"Yeah, not so much, Princess. Wars happen, people die, books and recordings are lost or simply disintegrate with age. What I'm telling you is the actual truth. From the look of you I would say you're immortal as well—you know how it goes. How many years do you have—three thousand, give or take?"

"Yes… Kayla."

"Getting tired of it yet?"

"I've been exhausted for centuries. The endless, changeless centuries."

"Then you know. Facts become distorted and are replace by stories, stories that change and evolve over time until the original truth is mutated beyond recognition. If you ever get the opportunity, go back and look at the carvings in the entry tunnel. That's the whole story, and it's remarkably accurate, considering how much of it there is."

"How do you stand it?" said The Princess.

"I sleep a lot. Read. There's an amazing amount of written material to go through from long ago. I like murder mysteries in particular. Those never seem to get old. But I'm guessing that these things wouldn't satisfy you, Princess. You seem more the active type to me. Get out more! Take some actual risks that could result in your death. If you're bored anyway would death be so bad at this point?"

She turned to The Quaesitor. "And you want to see The Answer At The End Of The World, is that right?" The Quaesitor nodded. "You are welcome to do so, though it is not easy to get to. I will tell you right now that whatever you think this will be the answer to, it almost certainly isn't. In fact I seriously doubt there's anyone alive who still remembers the question it supposedly answers. But a quest is a quest. Go and fulfill it with my blessings! Is there anything else I can do for you?"

The Quaesitor started to speak but changed his mind and said nothing. The Princess shook her head.

"Well then, you had best be on your way. Feel free to ask for whatever supplies you think you might need. There's a lot of stuff knocking around this place and no one to use it. We haven't had many visitors for the past five or six hundred years."

Thanking the Guardian Kayla, the Princess and the Quaesitor turned and left.

HAVING ACQUIRED THE few additional supplies they need from Scantar, they made their way to the outskirts of the Temple and the opening to a tunnel in the rock.

"I will leave you here," said Scantar. "Stay on this path and you will eventually come to the Eternal Hall where the Answer lies. The way is easy, except for the Well of Souls. These is a single rope over a bottomless chasm. Should you fall from the rope you will be suspended in the air by upwelling currents from deep in the planet. You will see when you get there that many have suffered this fate. They remain there to this day, mummified yet still floating. The best strategy is to run across the rope as fast as you are able. Trying to go slow and keep your balance will result in a long, slow death."

They nodded and thanked him and watched as he trudged back down the path towards the city. Presently they turned and began to walk down the path, feeling a sense of melancholy.

"This hasn't turned out as I expected," said The Quaesitor.

"And what did you expect?" said The Princess.

"I don't know. I thought I would be discovering something important, something that could change lives. Since we spoke with The Guardian I'm not sure what to think."

The Princess smiled at him. "Don't worry about it. Let's just go find it and then we can decide what comes next."

They walked for several hours and presently the tunnel opened out onto a wide flat area that ended abruptly at a crevasse. The Quaesitor moved carefully up to the edge to peer over where he saw that it appeared to fall off forever - there was no visible bottom. The other edge was about 20 feet across and there was indeed a rope—probably about three inches in diameter—that formed the only visible bridge. And suspended above them, hundreds of mummified corpses, drifting and shifting to and fro in the upwelling currents from the planet's core.

"I'll go first," said the Princess, and without waiting she ran lightly out to the rope and without pausing was across it in a few seconds, jumping off and turning to wave at him. "It's easy!"

The Quaesitor approached the rope, looked at it critically for a moment and then ran across just as easily as The Princess, albeit not as gracefully.

"Done," he said. "Let's move on."

The Princess turned to continue but as she did she reached

for her throat. "My amulet." She looked back towards the rope bridge and pointed. "It's there, floating. It must have fallen from my neck as I ran. It's only about ten feet out. I'm sure I can get it!"

"No, Princess. It's too dangerous..." But the Princess was already running for the bridge. She was able to grab the amulet but as she ran back her foot slipped and she was swept up into the air until she was floating a hundred feet or so above him.

"I'll go back and get help, Princess..."

"No, it's too late. I'm no longer in contact wth the planet. I have no more than a few minutes before I join the fate of the others up here."

"No, Princess, there must be something..."

"Shed no tears for me, Quaesitor. You brought adventure and, yes, love into my life when I thought such things were lost to me. Now I go to my release a happy woman."

The wind shifted her until her back was to him. She spoke no more. When, after several minutes the wind chanced to shift her again so he could see her face, she was gone, her eyes closed and her lips slightly parted. He gazed at her a while longer and then turned slowly and continued his journey.

PRESENTLY HE CAME to a simple door in the rock beside which stood an attendant.

"Welcome, traveller, to the The Eternal Hall of the Answer at the End of the World. Are you prepared to enter?"

"I am," said the Quaesitor.

"Very well," said the attendant, who pressed a hidden lever which caused the door to swing back, revealing a vast hall with a raised platform in the middle of it. "It was found in orbit around the planet, perfectly preserved, an ancient artifact of uncertain origin..."

As the attendant droned on, The Quaesitor walked slowly towards the platform, trying to make out what was on it.

From a distance it appeared to be a bright red and very shiny, but as he got closer the edge of the platform obscured his view and he climbed the stairs that wound around the base of the platform until he reached the top, where he could see The Answer clearly. It appeared to be some kind of vehicle. As he walked slowly around it he could see some kind of unfamiliar glyphs that spelled out "TESLA," though he could not read them. As he got closer a light went on inside the vehicle and he began to hear music:

"Ground Control to Major Tom
Ground Control to Major Tom…"

Grant Canterbury is a naturalist and writer who grew up reading stories about speculative worlds of science fiction and fantasy. His stories have been published in the science fiction anthologies Merigan Tales *and* After Oil 2: The Years of Crisis. *He lives near Portland, Oregon with his family and quirky spaniels. See canterburia.blogspot.com for irregular blog posts and project updates.*

The epistolary story—the story told by way of an exchange of letters—has a long history in English-language fiction, and it's well suited to certain parts of the Old Solar System. In "Pen Pal," we follow a correspondence between two girls—one Earthling, one Martian—in which many of the themes of our own recent history reappear in a slightly skewed form...

PEN PAL

Grant Canterbury

December Third, 1996
Meliari Thulissia
General Delivery
Tharsis Station

DEAR MELIARI,

Hello!! My name is Mary and I am nine years old. I got your name for a pen pal and they said you were the first pen pal on Mars. This is the first time I have written a letter to Mars to. So I will tell you about me and how things are here in Oregon. And if you can tell me about yourself and what Mars is like that would be great! I am interested in mars but I have never been there yet. There is a book in the library that has pictures, I like the one with the little boats and orange trees on the grand canal. I mean the trees are orange not that they have oragnes. Here our trees are green except in fall. Right now they have lost their leaves.

So I like Oregon but it is not like Mars and that is because it is really really wet. Not as wet as Venus but it is still really wet. Right now it has been raining for about a week and I am ready for the sun to come out. I dont know if it rains on

Mars? But I bet it does not rain very much. The school bus comes to take me to school I am in fourth grade and I have to wait outside for it in the rain usually!

Our family is my mom and dad and my big brother Robb and my grandparents live not too far off. We are close to Silverton and there are vinyards and fields around us. I have a horse. I am going to put his picture in this envelope. His name is North Star. That is because he is black and he has one white blaze on his forehead so it is like a star. I am learning to ride him and I fell off once! But I did not hurt myself. And North Star is very good. Once there was a beehive and the other horses got scared and galloped but North Star did not buck me off even though he got stung. So I like him very much.

Mom says I have to finish this letter soon because the rocket is leaving soon and it will not wait. I hope you can write back to me. I am very interested to hear about you.

Your friend,
Mary Havens

Please deliver to Mary Havens
13356 Paradise Alley Road
Silverton, Oregon

Dear Mary Havens,

I have your letter. Greetings! I am practicing writing in English. I hope you see the words I want. Sometimes I speak with the visitors at the America station here. I can understand them. And now I have a dictionary and a primer. But still I only begin to learn this language.

My thanks to you for your letter. I am the only daughter of my mother Meliari Nemytha. My father is Tendu. Usually I am called Thulissia. But within my creche I have been called Thu. I see in your letter that you named yourself as my friend. I also hope to be your friend. I hope you will call me Thu.

Our years are different and our people also live more slow. I was born in the winter of the Year of Questioning Mists. I think on Earth that was your 1973? The America station was still very new in that year. So I think I have lived more time than you. But I will not be counted as adult for many years. I hope you think of me as a girl like you.

Our holding is not far from the station. We are in the high country, on the edge of Yuli. Your people call it Tharsis. I have seen rain, but only once or twice. In the right season the winds bring mists across Yuli, and at our holding we raise up sieve nets to catch water droplets for our cistern. What we cannot hold we sell to the Kori society, and it is directed down to the low deserts to fill the canals. In a good year the chula fruit from our vines is very sweet!

I hold in my hand your photograph of North Star. I feel he is beautiful. I have not seen a horse, although I have seen two dogs. I spoke with Captain Jimenez at the station and he told me horses would not survive the voyage across the void, so none have been brought to our world. So I will never see one, likely. I hope you give my greetings to North Star. I forgot to ask if horses speak. Some of our creatures do and some do not. I have a little pindi who speaks, and I feel affection for her, but she does not always tell the truth. I am sending to you one of her feathers.

In my language for North Star you would say Ara Kinosa.

I will seal this letter and give it with wishes for careful delivery. I know the distance across the void is very great.

Your Friend

Thu

February 2, 1999
Meliari Thulissia
General Delivery
Tharsis Station

Dear Thu,

Thank you so much for writing back to me! I got your letter last year and I have been waiting for the next rocket to go. I can't believe they only send them every two years! Dad says there are good reasons for that, but it is a long time to wait! Apparently radiograms are very short and they are only supposed to be for emergencies anyway and this is not one. Oh Well.

I read your letter over a lot. I think your handwriting is very pretty. I got an N in penmanship which is basicly Not very good but I think I am getting better.

My brother Robb was jealous about your letter but I guess there is nothing stopping him from writing to Mars either if he really wants. He also asked Mom and Dad if he could have a Venusian skipperjack for a pet after he saw some for sale in an aquarium. They are kind of cute in a slimy way I guess and one of them was blinking its eyes at him in partcular and scampering about. But Mom and Dad said no!

My grandpa had cancer and he was pretty sick but Dad got him in to the medical trial for the Venus liana extract and he has gotten a lot better so I am pretty happy about that because I love my grandpa!

I saw in the newspaper that a Martian is giving lectures across America. His name is Trapindi. I wonder if you know about him? He is talking about what it is like on Mars so people do not get scared of you although why would they. Like that tripod book had nothing in it that was true at all. For one thing Martians look a lot like Earth people. I don't think you got sick from Earth germs either – is that right? I guess the writer had no way of knowing about Martians a hundred years ago but that is not an excuse for people to be dumb today.

Last time I sent you a picture of North Star but I did not think to send a picture of me so here is one so you can see what I look like. I am in sixth grade now. North Star is fine. You might like to know that I call him ara kinosa when I give him an apple for a treat and so he knows his name in Martian. Unfortunately horses do not talk though. I did read a story where a horse did talk, his name was Bree. I liked that book a lot but it was imagination, animals are not able to talk really. Except that parrots do talk but I am not sure if they understand what they are saying. Anyway North Star is still a good friend though. How is your pindi? I have kept the feather that you sent me. I took it to school and my teacher Mr. Berry showed me it is different from a bird feather because it is not hollow in the shaft. It is so wierd and cool! Kevin in my class grabbed it while I was showing my friends Lisa and Tina and ran off but Mr. Berry made him give it back. I was mad at him! Right now it is in my keeping box beside a not broken sand dollar I picked up on the beach when we went to the coast. Also I am going to send you a bird feather that I found in our yard. It is from the wing of a red-shafted flicker. That is a wild bird that lives here. They are brown but when they open their wings they flash red.

Speaking of red sometimes I can see Mars at night and I will wave to you sometimes. I know there is no way you can see me but just so you know.

Your friend,
Mary

Mary Havens
13356 Paradise Alley Road
Silverton, Oregon

Dear Mary,

Greetings again. I smiled when I saw your letter had come to me.

At some seasons I see Earth as well in the dark morning or in the dark evening and I consider that my friend is there. We say Aratielbra. This is the bright twin who travels always with her dim twin Aratiellissa. Your Moon she is.

We do have good health in our household. I understand the men at the America station had concern when they first arrived, and they spoke about sicknesses that might come, but we have never felt more than a few coughs. I believe that those sicknesses that grew well in your waters and forests on Earth do not survive well in our dry world. And although Earth people and Martians must once have come from the same race, we have walked separate roads for long and long. Jimenez tells me half a million years and it may be so. My father doubts this root in common but I think we could be sibling. But if we have changed, I suppose many illnesses of Earth must now find it hard to grip us.

My pindi is also robust and well. Because you have not seen a pindi I will tell you more about them. They are as tall as my knee, and they go on two strong legs, with four long toes that have fringes for walking the soft sand. Their feathers are very soft. They live in burrows they dig near habitations and feeder canals, and they do not speak just as people do but they do sing songs. Often people will sing songs to them so that they will learn. This hour my pindi has come to me and she sang "The stars shine up from the waters of the canal/They waver with the ripple/Where you drew your toe across." That means that she is thirsty and she would like me to draw a cup from the cistern. Except that I have already seen her drink this evening so I know she is being greedy. Still

I like the sweetness of her voice, so I have just given her a small drink after all.

The America station is a morning's walk from us so I see them often. I have seen prospectors and folk who come trade for fiber work and I spoke with an anthropologist Mary Bateson who is now traveling Mars and I learned she is probably not a relation of you although she holds the same name. She hopes to translate the Old Tale to English and that will be a long work for every lineage guards only a small piece of that story, much is under seal of tanj, and some do guard it very close. We told her one thread concerning the search of Great Kadat and one evening she told us a story of Odysseus and the Cyclops. I believe it was not lucky for him to call himself Nobody and maybe that is why he did wander lost for so long but it is good fortune that giants easily can be fooled.

There are also Japanese on the other side of Yuli, and this season there is also word of a new Earth station in Tan Talan, that is Noctis Labyrinthus, beyond the nomad clans. My father says these people are Soviet. But I have not seen them yet. They have not visited on this side of the world before. I do not know if they come from close to you or if have you met Japanese or Soviet in Oregon?

I have heard of Trapindi who went to your world. His origin is by the southern pole snows, quite far from this place Yuli, so he was never in my eyes. He came out of the Kho affinity—and I admit they do have some enmity with my lineage Meliari. But it was told he became, I do not find the right word, fey? Tiliumit. And because of this he held himself apart from Kho and every other affinity. But you might see this is easier done if you leave a place! Therefore he journeyed to Sharldegal and the French agreed to bring him to Earth. I do think he is brave to go to Aratielbra. Because I know that some others have gone there before and they could not live under the heat and the heaviness for long.

For me I cannot think of holding apart from my lineage though. I know I will always be of Meliari.

Favor to greet for me the red shafted flickers. Yet only if it is safe because I do not know if they are dangerous. I hope you are in good health and I hear from you soon.

Your friend,
Thu

May 1, 2001
Meliari Thulissia
General Delivery
Tharsis Station

Dear Thu,

I was thinking of the letters I have written to you before and I am kind of embarrassed because I probably wrote some silly things in them, but I was pretty young back then too! I just want to say I have enjoyed reading your letters and I hope you will keep writing to me. I will probably never get to Mars but I like hearing about your life there.

It is spring here right now and very beautiful all around. During the winter there is a long time when it is pretty cold and dark and it rains a lot, and now we are getting very bright warm days and all of the leaves are growing back on the trees. When they first come out they are very light green and everything in the air smells alive again. There have been white blossoms on all the cherry trees in our yard and they smell wonderful. I pressed some so I will send them to you. They are not flat like this when they are on the tree. You put them between the pages of a heavy book and after a few weeks they are dry and then you can keep them for a long time without them withering. The birds that migrated south for the winter are all back now and they all are singing in the mornings when I go to feed North Star. They don't sing in words like a pindi though.

That is interesting that there are Japanese and Soviets near you. Sometimes we do have Japanese visit here although Japan is far away on the other side of the Pacific Ocean. They are mostly tourist groups and I do not really know any of them. There are some kids at school whose grandparents did come from Japan but they are basically as American as I am. America did have a war with Japan a long time ago but I think that is all better now. It is not so good with the Soviets I guess.

Hey you might be interested that I was able to meet Trapindi last fall! He was at Timberline Lodge. This is up on Mount Hood, which is a very tall mountain here in Oregon that has snow even in the summer. It is actually a volcano but it has not erupted for a really long time so it is pretty safe. Trapindi had been giving his talk in Texas but it was very hot there – I have been to Texas once in summer and I about melted so I imagine it was brutal for a Martian! Anyway even with air conditioning he got pretty sick so his friend Jean Renard arranged for him to come to Timberline and recuperate. Trapindi says Mount Hood is not really like Mars but it is more like Mars than most places on Earth. It is called Timberline because it is about as high on the mountain as trees can grow and they are small and twisted by the cold winds. And the air is thinner so high up so that helped Trapindi, and when we went he was able to talk to small groups again.

So Mom drove me up there in the Bug for a day trip. The lodge is all gray stone and very massive and impressive. And among the crowds of people coming up to ski and hike we went aside into a meeting room and this very stylishly dressed little man Mr. Renard (Mom said "My isn't he dapper," aside in her kind of snarky way) talked about how years ago he rescued Trapindi on Mars after his long journey across the Hellas Basin marshes and how he knew then that he was special. Also I learned he pronounces his name Zhon instead of Gene, because French. And he wheeled Trapindi up in this very padded wheelchair with pillows and took his hand to help him up to the lectern to talk. He was a little shaky standing but he told his story and showed us a cool slideshow with pictures from Mars and also the places he has been to on Earth which is honestly a good deal more than me – France and Mexico City and Haiti and New York and Cairo and more.

And later a few of us went out with him to walk along the easy walking paths around the lodge. There are snow fields and rocky talus slopes up above, and a couple of marmots came out of their burrows to look at us, and a big raven flew in close and croaked at us from the roof of one of the lodge buildings. Ravens are birds that are all black and almost as big as a pindi and I think they are pretty smart. And I had been waiting because I was not sure if it was polite but I asked Trapindi about being tiliumit like you mentioned. And he was surprised to hear that word from me but we talked a while about it. And it is like I am in 4-H and at the same time I am my mother's daughter and my brother's sister and an eighth grader at Silverton Middle School and I am from Oregon and from America, and Trapindi says tiliumit is like realizing you are really none of that. He says here on Earth he is only The Martian, and to Jean Renard he is only Trapindi. And he says on Mars most do not survive long living as tiliumit, so even though Earth is a difficult place for him he says he feels fortunate to be here and to be sitting on a stone and looking back at a curious raven.

I don't know whether or not that makes me sad but I guess Trapindi is doing okay so far. I hope you are doing good too. I am going for a sleepover at Tina Wesley's place a few houses down the road pretty soon so I will give this to Mom to send off.

Your friend,
Mary

Mary Havens
13356 Paradise Alley Road
Silverton, Oregon

Dear Mary,

This past thirty-seven days the sky has been dust and we wait in shelter of our home. There is my close family and my mother's sister Meliari Chinquinil and my father's affines who number eleven at present. We sleep and we set out the pieces of tanj-boards to play until we are tired of games. While at home we play to the third mode at most, with no stronger forfeit than giving oneself a pinprick. Today I did achieve advantage over my mother Nemytha and she must draw up the day's water from our well for three days. The water lives quite far below so this is never quick. However I suspect her play was generous to me.

In mornings because of the storm we must go out to our orchards and vines and beat them so they will shed the sand. We go wearing harnesses on long cords, so we do not lose the path back, because the dust blocks sight in the air. Now the sand has built deep drifts and one must take long poles to probe them before setting down foot. In these storms a paktar may come close to habitation unseen. They are slow, but they may have the mass of three men, and they will let themselves be buried under sand and wait and wait. I was with my father Tendu when he found one. It rose up and tried to take him in its pincers, but he was brave and quick and put his lance into the soft gap in its chitin. I also beat it with my pole but I know I was not the one to kill it.

One morning when the dust had paused and there was some light we walked to visit the America station. All things were the color of dust and in the air we saw moving shadows from a line of tall wild palondi that stalked along the near ridge. I must judge the station was placed badly for the winds in this season. Their flag was all dust colored on the pole, and drifting dust was all around their big square brick building and had almost buried the domes of their quonsets, some bowing inward, and in our dune-shoes we walked above them and called within. Captain Jimenez roused and spoke with us asking if the storm would soon end. We had brought lightweight resin scoops for sand so we aided them to clear a few doorways. A few days before one of their men had become mad from closeness and with a Gun he killed one of his companions and then himself. Also after they had buried the bodies they returned to find they had been robbed by paktars. Jimenez was most troubled but he continues to encourage their steel to endure. He says they still expect the next rocket in some twenty days, and it is guided by a beacon that dust does not hide, so I now prepare this letter for you.

The America station has been troubled before by dust. And its people have been often generous for favor, but I worry they do not do well here. Of course being from Earth they do not have position in any higher tanj modes. But they stand upon the board in a certain relation to Meliari. And if they are seen to be failing then some may choose to take benefit from this instead. I judge a more favorable location might be found for them and I will speak counsel to my father.

When I wrote my previous letter to you my mother Nemytha was away at lineage moot, because she has lead position for Meliari in the game, but this day she has worked with pell ink and fine brush and made an image of me that I will send to you. I do not have this skill but her images live. Here I am at our sand gate and I wear my dust hood, it is dyed green, and I have not yet covered my face.

Your friend,
Thu

July 4, 2003
Meliari Thulissia
General Delivery
Tharsis Station

Dear Thu,
    Well it is Fourth of July today and I just got back from the fireworks. Walked down the road with some of my friends to near the new gardens where they put on the show. This is the celebration of the founding of the United States of America, which is the 227th anniversary this year, and it is pretty fun. There are small fireworks and sparklers that you can set off by hand, and there is a show after it gets dark where they shoot off the big ones up in the air and they bang and sizzle and explode up in the sky yellow and red and green and white, in big showers and booms. They are very loud and beautiful and I guess it is romantic. Also animals do get awfully scared by the noise, and usually the fire department has to get called to put out a grass fire that got started by accident, but there you go. Tina and Kevin were holding hands as we walked down and I saw them kissing during the fireworks. Tina says snogging now since she got back from her visit to England. She has been a little annoying about it actually! You know at one point this spring I thought Kevin liked me instead of Tina, but whatever.
    Well I walked back home with my brother Robb and we talked for a bit. He is going to be back at college next fall. It was weird for him to be gone last year and it has been kind of normal but a little weird having him back this summer and then he will be gone again. A guy at the library was demonstrating a computer in the meeting rooms this week and Robb got to work with it and he is kind of psyched about the idea. There is a keyboard that you type on and the computer types back in words on a glass screen, you can hook up a TV for it. Robb played a game of Monopoly with it for a while although he said it was a little confusing because you couldn't

see the board or the cards but just words, but it is pretty cool I guess. When you pushed a button the computer would just tell you what the dice roll was on the screen. Hopefully it does not cheat because I would think it would be hard to tell! Maybe Robb will study computers at college. By the way I did beat him last time we played Monopoly at home (with the actual board that is). Although if Mom is in on the game that is a different story because let me tell you she plays for blood! It is a good game for a long afternoon on vacation. If anyone has it up on Mars I bet it would be pretty good during your next dust storm!

Joking aside I hope you are not having any dust storms because it sounds like the last one was bad. Ugh. Sorry for Captain Jimenez. I did hear that the American base at Tharsis was relocating a bit so I hope they are in a better spot now.

Mom and Dad are out tonight at a concert so it is just me and Robb here, and I made hot chocolate before bed. The Quarrymen are on a reunion tour – that is a band that Mom liked when she was a kid - and they are playing at Memorial Coliseum in Portland. Dad said this is his contribution to their latest yacht payment. He told me, "I have to go along to keep your mother from rushing the stage." Really he does like them too though.

I have your picture framed up on my wall and I am looking at it right now. Your mother is a really good artist. Thank you for sending it and please thank her for me also! I like being able to see what you look like. I think you have a good face.

I saw an article in Newsweek that Trapindi and Jean Renard are living in Hawaii up on Mauna Loa which is a little like Mars. There are weird spiky plants called silverswords that apparently remind Trapindi of home. Mr. Renard has gotten quite sick though and they are not sure what is wrong.

You might also be interested that on the news there are a few oopses from Florida. Some skipperjacks got set loose, or flushed down the toilet, or just skippered off, and ended up living in the swamps in the Everglades. And double oops, it also turns out they are actually the larvae of Venusian gulguthroi and they grow up quite big. On TV I saw video of one wrestling with an alligator over who got to eat who. What a mess.

Mom and Dad are back home. Pretty late, but I guess they got back all right. I can hear Mom singing downstairs.

I've got a rocket,
Keys in my pocket,
Touched down, snap! in the dock, it
Might be our ticket to liberty...

Sounds like they had a good time at the concert. Mom is really belting it out. I guess they probably stopped for drinks on the way home. I may tweak her about it tomorrow morning! But I'm glad she finally got a chance to see them. According to Mom she had a big crush on Paul when she was a girl. Personally I think John is much cooler, but they didn't ask for my opinion.

But I Don't Mind,
As long as you can be
On your way with me
To Jupiter, and freee...

I think back in the 60s they did not know yet that Jupiter mostly has Europan ice worms that are not fond of visitors. But that doesn't mean it is not an awesome song.

Sleepy now so will finish. Will get this mailed tomorrow since I am starting to run late for the launches. Hope life is good for you.

Your friend,
Mary

Mary Havens
13356 Paradise Alley Road
Silverton, Oregon

Dear Mary,
This day has been quiet and cold and I have walked by the feeder canals and watched the ice growing over their surface. My pindi came with me for a while, but she returned to her burrow where I suspect she has an egg.

I have never seen fireworks and I am not sure why because I believe they would function on Mars and I know we would have pleasure at a brightness of color in the sky. Sometimes I wonder if my people have limits that we cannot perceive.

I have asked Captain Jimenez about Monopoly and he has found a box with this game in their storage. This box he has given to me and I have wrapped it and brought it to our home upon the back of a palondi I had under rein. I am studying it to learn more about Earth. He said to me, "I hope I am not creating a monster." I do not understand this but I believe he joked.

I wonder about dice because they have chaos in this very square game. There are no dice in tanj although much is hidden in the hand of each player. And there may be chaos at the base of each player's choice, although also character shapes it as one can see if playing with a person one knows well, so also I wonder if it may not be chaos.

I do not understand the shapes of most of the pieces. However I like the little dog.

Mary I regret that I cannot converse with you face to face.
Your friend,
Thu

August 8, 2005
Meliari Thulissia
General Delivery
Tharsis Station

Dear Thu,

Well I officially graduated from high school! And I have been itching to get out into the world for a long time but right now honestly I am not liking the look of it. We had been planning to go to Disneyworld after graduation but we did Disneyland again instead. That was fine actually. Mom and Dad decided Florida was not such a great idea because gulguthroi. And I had to agree with them. It has gotten really bad. They have chameleon skin and they hide in shallow water which is everywhere down there, and they are basically eating up all of the wildlife in the Everglades. And also people. And especially folks who used to own skipperjacks, it seems. Apparently the deep soulful looks that made them popular at pet stores were more like, um, imprinting on future prey. And their big raspy tentacles also work okay at opening doors in the middle of the night. There are like thousands of people who have disappeared. Oh yeah, they made it illegal to own skipperjacks, of course. And so a bunch of pet stores, crooked or dumb, went and dumped theirs in the nearest creek. Christ.

Robb is freaking out about it because that one skipperjack stared at him when he was a kid and now he is having nightmares about it coming back and grabbing him out of bed. Logically we are pretty safe here because although lord knows Oregon gets its share of rain, it is really too cold for Venus critters in the winter and too dry in the summer. But I am a little freaked too to tell the truth.

And everyone is all Alien Invasion and then there is this Mars pox insanity, which I am so upset – Right, just tell it. In Hawaii Mr. Renard got sicker and sicker, and no one could figure it out, and then about the same time there started showing up more cases various places around the world, some in places where Trapindi had travelled, and the doctors eventually found a new virus that they all had in common. And they made Trapindi get tested for it and he was not sick but the virus was in him also. And the talk shows and the newspapers called it Mars pox and then he was just another Typhoid Mary and it was War of the Worlds in reverse and we have to quarantine the Martians and anyone who ever met one and the whole damn planet needs to be nuked just in case. I am sorry but people are being crazy down here and I guess you had best know about it. Mr. Renard died, people are still dying, no one has been cured yet. And they were trying to bring Trapindi into medical isolation and he was not even feeling sick and he just wanted to stay up on Mauna Loa and grieve in some place that looked a little like home, and someone got through with a gun into the hospital and Trapindi was killed. I cried all night when I heard about it. Just, we are not all like that. I don't think we are. Just, no one seems like they are able to wait to find out the God damned facts before jumping to conclusions. And the whole Mars pox thing was stupid because it is not even from Mars and the pox is not a pox, it's Kaposi's sarcoma, and now they are finding varieties of the virus in great apes in Africa and human cases going back forty years in the Congo that no one recognized because who gives a damn about medical care in Africa, and probably Trapindi and Mr. Renard picked it up in Haiti, and it is sexually transmitted and then there was all the oh My God the faggot alien, as if it was a big surprise that Trapindi and Mr. Renard were gay, I mean even I knew that and I was right in the top ten clueless eighth-graders. But half the people you meet still think it's the freaking plague from Mars and you can't tell them anything. And don't get me started on that Buchanan guy. There are what, maybe five or six Martians on the planet, so it is just super easy to gang up on them.

Grr.

This has not been a good year.

On the plus side, Kevin and I have been dating for about eight months now and I think things are going pretty well. We started going out after he broke up with Tina... actually not quite that clean, a little bit before also... I admit it kind of put the ice on that friendship. I did get an earful from Tina about how much of a sneak and a spoiled bitch I was. But I believe I gave as good as I got. She was not that big a loss, trust me. Kevin has really been sweet, which is nice since this has been a tough year as see above.

Next month I am going to Minnesota for college. But I will still come home every few months and I will get my mail forwarded, plus I am not sure if I will be keeping the same address two years from now, so you might as well still write to the Oregon address. I hope I will be a happier correspondent next time!

Your friend,
Mary

Mary Havens
13356 Paradise Alley Road
Silverton, Oregon

Dear Mary,

I hear of your troubles with sorrow. I have also noted some unease among the Earthmen at the America station here, and your letter aids me to comprehend this and to guard. Those who have lived long among us on Mars have begun to learn our ways, but there are also some who act under fear. As for Venus I consider it a very undesirable world and I regret that its creatures are causing you difficulty.

And I also regret to hear of Trapindi's fate. Far from Mars, but at least I judge he followed the path as he wished to find Earth and Jean Renard for a time. And I find what I can write to be inadequate to your true need at this moment but do know I wish you well.

I will tell of a recent incident. My father and I were patrolling the bounds of our holding when my pindi came to us across the crest of a dune and she sang "The fire you built dies low/The coals flicker/Between gray and red," which I could not quite interpret but made me uneasy. And following her we soon came to a man sprawled in the sand at a dune's base, marking the end of a line of footprints that was being quickly erased by the wind. He was of Earth but in clothing I did not recognize, and I could not read the words upon his coat. We spoke to him, and put water to his mouth, but his eyes moved over us without seeing, and he only muttered words we did not comprehend.

We were about to bring him to the America station when we heard heavy padded footfalls and a rider came around the height of the dune upon a trymia. These are like palondi but taller, swift-striding, and possessed of a hooked beak and fierce temperament. And the rider was cloaked in red and his lance was lowered toward us as he reined up and observed us from the height. "I have tracked this man for two days."

My father said, "And who is he that you track him?"

"No one to you."

"No one yet. And who are you?"

He was silent but the trymia began picking its way down the dune slope toward us, one large taloned foot after another. Behind me my pindi burrowed backward into the slip-face of a dune with rapidity and hid all but her eyes. "That cloak is from Tan Talan. Do your people make quarrel with the Earth folk?"

"On the contrary. They sent me to fetch this one. He is one of their thralls that has fled."

"He is ill of exposure."

"I am paid the same whether I bring him alive or dead."

"No. This is a matter to be adjudicated, not settled in the dunes."

In consideration of the burden upon you I hold detail of the events that followed in discretion. Later my father was much annoyed at the damage to his leathers which he cares for greatly. The man regained consciousness and though he was lucid he did not have much Martian or English but he gave his name as Sergei Pavlovich. He is an engineer and he was treated poorly by the Soviets so he chose to attempt escape, which was perhaps unwise because he did not have map or sand gear, but he felt strongly to do so. On further consideration we have chosen not to bring him to the America station though it is closer, but rather to the Japanese, for we did not wish to cause further difficulty under the state of feud between America and Soviet.

We have heard nothing more from the region of Tan Talan, which is unusual.

I am reminded to say that I am also well and uninjured. I hope that you have been well this year. And I wish you all joy that you and Kevin may find together, for you are deserving of it.

Your friend,
Thu

September 29, 2007
Meliari Thulissia
General Delivery
Tharsis Station

Dear Thu,

School is getting tough again so I am taking a break and writing to you. It has not been so great here. I had a good summer with Kevin back home, but he was not able to transfer schools like he was hoping to and he is back in California for another semester, and I miss him. And after I wrote to you last they made the rest of the Martians who were on Earth get on a rocket for Mars and they are all gone now.

I can tell you about last spring I guess. It is a good thing I did not write about it then because I was ready to spit nails at the time. I am still pretty damn mad.

I really hate to say this but I do not have your pindi feather anymore.

And I guess I should have seen it coming but I did not take it seriously enough. I was not there when it happened because I was at school. My brother was home on leave—he joined the Interplanetary Signal Corps—and he answered the front door and there were a few official looking plainclothes guys so he let them in to talk. And it turns out they are there to look into PAM cases. That is Possession of Alien Materials, which because there is now a bullshit law you have to now report on anything you ever got from offplanet and have it registered. It would make more sense to concentrate on keeping the gulguthroi out of Louisiana rather than going after random knickknacks on the walls of teenage girls, but we have zero tolerance now, so yeah. I had been actually debating whether to register but it did not seem that urgent. But apparently Robb says "I don't think we have anything except this Martian feather of my sister's" which I have (had!) in a nice little frame in my bedroom, and they up and take it away! Plastic bagged, and evidently a dead cert to be incinerated because it is from an animal, and they were all pleased that they had saved Oregon from the latest Martian zombie dragon Godzilla that it was certain to become. Also there was talk about bringing charges for failure to register, and my dad had to hire a lawyer, and it worked out okay but it was expensive and ridiculous. This was while I was in the middle of finals last spring and the call came in for me from home on the pay phone in the dorm, and Robb was saying he would make it up to me (like how he could, ever?) but also like, maybe it's just as well, we don't really know what the risks could be. And I started screaming at him, and the other girls in the dorm were coming over and kind of peeking in the little window in the phone booth to check on me... I basically did not speak to him the whole summer while I was home. I do still have your letters and your picture because they were here with me in Minnesota but you bet I have them hidden safe now. (By the way, if anyone else is reading my mail before it gets to Thu, let me just say, fuck off and die.) Hopefully you will still be able to write to me since I guess they are irradiating the interplanetary mail now, but who knows.

And why they showed up at the front door like that in the first place? I saw Tina Wesley over the summer and she said she was so sorry; but I remember her being sympathetic to Lisa Takahara just that way about the ink spill on her bag in seventh grade and I saw that incident myself. I know how she operates, and I am sure she made the call to report me because she is still jealous of me and Kevin, and she knew all about the pindi feather, and she was probably peeking over from her front yard when they came to our place. Hope she's happy. Bitch.

Later (October 2)

Something completely different. I just now got a call and my dad said, "Mary, turn on the TV." On the screen there were big crowds of people, and some dancing in the street, and crowd sounds and singing, and I did not know what I was looking at because they had not put up any text. And one guy was limbering up with a sledgehammer and taking a swing at concrete, and then the newscaster said something about the scene in East Berlin, and I realized that was the Berlin Wall and the people were climbing on it and jumping off, and starting to bring it down.

Holy shit.

That wall has been there between NATO and the Soviets since before I was born. Actually since before my parents were born. It's like—imagine seeing Phobos suddenly come down out of the sky. As unexpected than that! And it's all peaceful. I'm just looking at a big party in Berlin, and there is no east and no west. I keep feeling tears come down my face and I don't know how or why. I must have been holding inside so many.

Does a cold war just melt one day when spring finally

comes?

Later (October 10)

Oh, Thu, I spoke way too soon. You would have known better. If you see Phobos fall, the first thing to wonder is who will get hit!

The third day after the Wall started coming down a bunch of Russian tanks came in to East Berlin, and there was a big crowd of people who got shot at the Brandenburg Gate. Very horrible, some of it was on TV. Like 71 in Prague all over again but worse, everyone was in shock but really Not Surprised. And then another tank division came in and started shooting at the first one, and Berlin really was a war zone. And it has just been getting worse since then. We are not hearing a whole lot but there is street fighting going on in Warsaw, and Budapest, and Moscow(!) and just now I have heard there was a battlefield nuke used on a demonstration in Prague. We do not know who is winning or what the sides are really. There are all these NATO alerts and even here I have been seeing fighter jets patrol overhead which is really out of the normal because I don't think there even are any Air Force bases in Minnesota.

There is still a while in the launch window but I think I had better get this sent off while we still have rockets going. Things seem very unstable, everyone is on edge, and am not sure if I am still going to be able to send this letter if I wait. I love you.

Your friend,
Mary

Transmission 3 December 2007 1342 GMT

Transmittal Encryption: Signal Officer Robert Havens, Bozeman, Montana

Receiver Decryption: Captain Carlos Jimenez, Tharsis Station, Mars

PLS DELIVER FOLLOWING MSG FROM MARY HAVENS TO MELIARI THULISSIA NEAR THARSIS

STN STOP NEWS OF ENTIRE BAIKONUR ROCKET FLEET BOOSTING FOR MARS STOP LOADED POLITBURO KGB AND NUCLEAR MSLS STOP PLS TELL THULISSIA AND FAMILY KEEP CLEAR OF THARSIS STN STOP FEAR ATTACK DANGER STOP YOU ALSO IF YOU CAN STOP END MSG

November 6, 2009
United Nations Martian Authority
Phobos

Please distribute as needed for notification and general delivery to Meliari Thulissia. Last known residence in vicinity of United States Tharsis Station. Current residence unknown.

THU-
Please just let me know if you are okay. I am fine here. Plenty is happening but I am fine. I am really worried about you!
Mail will still find me at:
13356 Paradise Alley Road
Silverton, Oregon

Your friend,
Mary

Monsieur le Préfet,

Je vous offre ma faveur pour la jeu. S'il vous plaît, envoyez ce message aux États-Unis. Envoyez-le à cette addresse postale:

Mary Havens
13356 Paradise Alley Road
Silverton, Oregon

---Meliari---

DEAR MARY,

I am well. I apologize that I have not written for some time for it has been a season of strange flux. Also I wonder at how many languages Earth must possess for the nearest station to me now is Base Charles de Gaulle and I must learn French as well!

Captain Jimenez provided me your radiogram message some time before your earlier letter reached me. He spoke with us about this danger, and said he had also felt this concern. He himself was giving orders to disperse the majority of his people to remote field camps, leaving in rotation only a skeleton crew at Tharsis Station. I am aware that Earth stations on Mars and Venus have functioned under Treaty of Zurich which limits weapons to those of personal defense. Thus it has been difficult for us to assess by experience the implications of the greater magnitudes although we are aware they exist. Nonetheless it is certain they alter the game.

For this reason and another my mother Meliari Nemytha asked me to travel with her to lineage moot. We spoke of what might be needed as we moved by caravan, then by canal boat, then by river barge in the canyon of Kasei, coming at last to the board pavilion in the heart of Tripsicari (that is Chryse Planitia). Of the twenty-three major lineages Meliari is one. The others arrived by foot, upon the backs of palondi, by ornithopter, perched between the long wings of cloud riders, or emerging by secret doors from the darkness of the Great Labyrinth. They took their places around the dais, and in the wings of the pavilion the representatives of the minor lineages, the affinities, the adjuncts and the scholars whispered and made their notes and drank chula wine and wrangled for favor.

In the opening statements my mother spoke of the turmoil among the Warsaw Pact and the impending violation of Treaty of Zurich, and urged preparation and unity. This she did not immediately find, for Tuprexi lineage and its allies considered themselves secure in the worldwide windings of the Great Labyrinth, and Ombra lineage advocated withdrawal and contemplation, and Pellucin lineage considered the mere introduction of debate over issues of Terran politics to be a discredit to the purity of the game, and Xiphiana lineage as well as some others had engaged upon individual arrangements with the Soviets that they would not break. The question was placed under settlement of tanj.

The game shuttled among the fifth, sixth, and seventh modes of tanj, and as play proceeded around the circle I watched the shifts of alliance, the interplay of signs, the placement of concealed markers to signal prepared counterattack or bluff. And Meliari maintained a supple strength of position, but for round after round was unable to come to decisive control.

However I knew my mother was resolved upon a bold play. She had that look I recognized from our tanj games upon storm nights in our holding. As well as other games you will know better. Once I watched her spend all and mortgage every other property to gain her hotels on Park Place and Boardwalk; and then that night with the chaos of the dice she crushed us all one by one.

So now upon her turn she called for the game to be raised to the perilous ninth mode of tanj. And then the double strategy of her play became apparent, for over the past rounds she had quietly assembled a constellation of signs that functioned competently in the seventh mode but in the ninth mode moved like the blades of a Sethrin master. Thus came the time for the testing of the elevated mode. One by one in turn, each lineage examined the danger and chose to turn up the yellow tile that signals concession of advantage. Watching I began to smile. And then lastly, Xiphiana stood, observed my mother with narrowed eyes, and revealed the sign of the Great Stone.

And Meliari's shining attack was halted, momentarily but completely. Pleased, Xiphiana said, "I call to return to mode six."

I am certain that I made the false step of gasping aloud when my mother said, "No. I will pay the forfeit." But among the many others I do not think I was heard.

As the ninth mode is the squaring of the third, so the forfeit is again a needle. But it is dipped seven times in the distilled venom of the coiling paxinti of the black sands. It gives a quick death but one not free from pain.

My mother looked back at me, deliberately turned over a last tile, and walked to the center of the dais where the paxinti needle rested among the other lesser tools of forfeit. Holding her gaze upon Xiphiana, she poised the needle and plunged it deep into the flesh of her own forearm. In a few moments she fell.

Then, stammering in the silence, the judge said "Play passes to Tuprexi."

But looking down I saw the last tile she had turned, and I said, "Meliari has not completed play." Face up upon the table was the sign of the Heir. "I continue as uninterrupted lead for Meliari."

You may infer that I also play for blood.

The judge consented. And with my final play I cast upon Xiphiana the sign of the Sandstorm, not a pointed attack but one that hobbled her defenses from all quarters. As the other lineages took their turn, many then seized upon the vulnerability of Xiphiana and, looking at me, none dared to offer her shelter. By the time play returned to me, her assets had been largely stripped. She bowed her head and turned the yellow tile to me like the rest.

And so, I returned the game to the fifth mode before we closed, and I carried my mother to an honorable place of rest, and I then set about to spend the harvest of our painful victory.

Therefore: as winds rose at the turn of the season Patieri lineage was tasked to ignite the fragile dry grass upon the dunes of Acidalia and Vastitas Borealis which exist in precarious balance. The wind drove the fire hot before it and tore the dunes open to the sky, and the buried mountains of dust and sand rose up in vast clouds with the smoke. The storm moved and spread to cover the northern hemisphere entirely, and then the southern. I am told it was the greatest in any memory or written account. When the Soviet rockets arrived they found Mars hidden under a deep veil of dust.

Therefore: one-fifth of the secret entrances of the Great Labyrinth were made known by the Tuprexi and Savil lineages. Word was spread to all lineages that shelter might be taken in the caverns with all feud held in abeyance.

Therefore: at the boiling front of the advancing storm, cloud riders of Zentiriel dropped in behind the fences at the Soviet depot at Elysium, while squadrons of the Philistetta came burrowing under sand and undermined the gates, riding in shelter beneath the transparent dorsal elytra of their chitinous mounts. Pillars of fire went up among the stockpiles of food and vehicles and gasoline.

The ships waited in orbit, sending down their demands by radio to those that were able to receive, and when they were not met then indeed several nuclear weapons were dropped to detonate upon the surface of Mars. It is nearly as bad as an asteroid fall, and also there is hazard of radiation although fortunately we are somewhat accustomed to rem here. In the storm they were not targeted acutely, but even so they did greatly devastate many spires and dwellings and fields, and many of those who had not sheltered were killed or gravely burned. But the ships had come heavily laden with many people and little margin of safety in oxygen and water, and they were soon compelled to descend to the remaining bases to resupply. During their descent we activated several false radio beacons that had been fabricated with the aid of Sergei Pavlovich Tupolev, and two ships were diverted to collide with precipices. And as the rest were about to emerge from the ships that had landed, those waiting to greet them who had remained loyal found their allies among Xiphiana lineage suddenly turning upon them.

Or as you would say,

Go directly to jail.

If these actions had not seen success I would have certainly have lost position. However, the outcomes proved fortunate though not without dire loss, and since that time I estimate Meliari has kept sufficient favor to hold advantage with sixteen to twenty-one of the other major lineages. Thus our position is favorable for the next moot.

One of the nuclear detonations destroyed much of Tharsis Station, so that it has now been abandoned, and great damage came to our holding there. Fortunately few were in residence, and it is being repaired. When I visited I found many chula vines burnt, but I was happy to see my pindi emerge from her burrow and greet me with a song of welcome and reproach. For now I have removed to a different seat of Meliari at Syrtis Major. I have brought my pindi with me.

Because I now hold lead position for our lineage in tanj I do not much use the name Thulissia any more outside of family, only Meliari. But between you and I our friendship is personal and I ask that you still consider me

Your friend,

Thu

December 28, 2011
Meliari Thulissia
Maison Meliari
Terre du Sablier
c/o Poste Martienne,
Base Charles de Gaulle

Dear Thu,

I was so happy to hear from you!! Dad says, I told you that girl would land on her feet like a cat. Actually he never did, he was just as worried as I was, but anyway we are glad you are fine. More than fine, right? You are basically Princess of Mars! So three cheers for you from Oregon!

Here is a picture of me and Kevin all dressed up at our wedding last summer. We are back behind the Gordon House in this picture and I am a little distracted because acorn woodpeckers are being goofy right behind the photographer, but I think I look okay and Kevin definitely does. I took his name so my name is Mary Nguyen now but it is still the same me. I look pretty much like this photo except quite a bit more casual! Plus I am about five months pregnant now so I am basically carrying around a bowling ball on my belly all the time and I bump into things because my center of gravity is not where I think it is supposed to be. Last time I went in to the doctor I was told it was a girl. I am thinking of calling her Nemytha and I hope you think that is okay?

We are living in Sisters out near Bend, which is not terribly far away from my parents' place in Silverton but across the mountains and much colder and drier with cinder cones and massive black basalt cliffs from old lava flows. There are forests here too but they are all ponderosa pine. On a warm day their bark smells sweet like butterscotch in the sun. I am working for the Forest Service right now. We will see how things go after the baby comes. Honestly I am scared about it, but I guess other people raise children more or less successfully, so Courage, right?

I used to dream about going to Mars to see you but I am feeling more and more planted here on Earth. I love this place. But it is good to know Mars exists, and that you are there. When you look out at the sand dunes and canals please do it a little bit for me.

My brother was back with us for Christmas, and I still feel guilty that he got busted out of the Signal Corps for sending an unauthorized personal message, because I was the one who made him do it and I am not sorry I did but I am sorry he had to pay the price. Right now he is living down in California around San Jose, and he is pretty excited about working with a bunch of folks who are building their own "microcomputers" that people can have in their own houses. I called him Mr. Transistor and he gave me this pitying look because transistors are apparently hopelessly old school now. He is writing operating systems for the computers or something like that, and apparently people are buying them, so I guess he is doing all right now.

Also I should let you know something sad, that North Star died last year. Basically just old age. I had not ridden him much lately, but we liked to see each other when I came home. I think he had a pretty good life. He was a good friend, and I will miss him. Ara Kinosa.

Things are settling down a little in the wider world, not that I am in any danger of mistaking it for utopia, but kind of a new normal and I think it is all for the best that the Soviets are out, even though in Eastern Europe all the quarrels that no one was allowed to fight over the past seventy years are all coming out at once and it is pretty nasty. The gulguthroi are in Texas and now Bangladesh, but they have found some Venusian parasitic wasps that look promising for keeping them down so that's worth a try, right? Nothing can go wrong this time, knock on wood. They are letting some Martians come back to Earth and not freaking out as much over petty items of Alien Materials, so I guess at some point you could come visit although I wouldn't recommend it until the average per-

son learns to be less of a jerk and that may take a while.
All best wishes from your friend,
Mary

Mary Nguyen
953 South Elm Street
Sisters, Oregon

DEAR MARY,
I offer my congratulations to you on your marriage and I hope your daughter was born healthy and without difficulty. I am honored to hear of her having the name Nemytha. I know that my mother would also have been pleased to have her name extended upon Aratielbra. And I am aware that my current position is due in greater measure to her skill at tanj than to my own.

I have not married. Although indeed other lineages have often made known to me eligible mates. And on several occasions I have felt distinct inclination in my heart, but at the current stage, holding open the potential for an alliance with Meliari seems of greater benefit than any one alliance in actuality. This I judge will prove better as a gambit in the midgame.

Because you now live in a more dry climate I have considered a gift. Recently I spoke with Captain Jimenez, who is retiring from service and returning to New Mexico on Earth. Along with this letter he has agreed to convey my gift to you with all care, and with his aid and certain points of favor in tanj I have obtained the permissions of your government. My pindi has consented to give me her last egg. Captain Jimenez will describe to you the necessary care in full. The pindi should have a cool dry sandy place that is sheltered if it rains. And it is important that you must sing to the pindi each day.

This permission was made strictly contingent on sending

only one, for reasons that I well comprehend. However, in confidence between us I feel I should make you aware that parthenogenesis is not unknown.

Last evening I went out alone to a gravel wash that is not distant, and I spent some hours gathering dry branches for fuel with the peeping cries of pitori echoing from the hills all around as dusk fell. In time Phobos passed overhead, and I kindled flame, and I let the pile blaze up in memory of North Star.

Your friend,
Thu

Peter C. Aitken was raised in New York and attended university in Scotland, where he studied English and Philosophy. While an English Degree provided him with plenty of inspiring material, none has been as powerful as The Gods of Mars *by Edgar Rice Boroughs. He burned through* A Princess of Mars *at a sprint but devoured the sequel at a more frightening pace. He has worked in Science Fiction and Fantasy ever since, trying to replicate the same balance of action and philosophical query.*

Not all stories set in the Old Solar System are about human beings, and a significant fraction—including such classics as Ray Bradbury's "There Will Come Soft Rains"—deal with the gap left behind by our species' self-inflicted absence. In "Perchance to Dream," Aitken presents a vivid tale of a posthuman Mars, on which conflicts familiar to our species continue to unfold...

PERCHANCE TO DREAM

Peter C. Aitken

EVEN BEFORE THE storm set in, Ivan had no destination in sight. He picked his way carefully along an endless stretch of cracked road, climbing over the debris of broken-down speeders and fighters left over from the war. The alien metal shimmered a strange green-black even without light. Ivan raised the collar on his duster as if thin fabric would add protection that his chromium shell could not. He couldn't perceive anything beyond a few feet through the curtain of sand and wind that whipped around him, but there was a chirping signal that played in his quantum processors, clear and immediate over anything else. The satellites had been the first casualties of the invasion, though; there should be no signals.

Further on, Ivan crested a hill. The wind died down and he found himself overlooking the twisted metal carcass that had been Damascus, the first city of Mars. In visual logs, he had seen the city as it was when it was first built, a monument to humanity's first steps away from its mother and out toward a manifest destiny among the stars: towers of gold and glass that overlooked sprawling green plazas—reminders of the world that was left behind. Staring at the burned-out ruins, half-covered in sand and blood, he might have cried, but that was a human thing to do, and humanity was dead.

With no more road to follow, Ivan walked along a depression in the red sand. The signal grew stronger as he traveled into the heart of the city. The last assault had hollowed out the buildings, leaving little to the imagination, but he still couldn't tell where the signal was coming from. Near a patch of sand with stray steel beams and crumbling concrete jutting out of the ground, the signal finally went silent.

Ivan paced the ground and found a staircase leading down to what looked to be a basement. He converted his visuals to night vision, and descended into a small room with several corridors leading away in different directions. He looked down each corridor; only one ended with light. His processors suggested that he should deploy a scan, but his base program contained an overriding command: stay small, stay quiet - from what, he couldn't say. The war was over; all the enemies were dead.

The corridor opened into a room where the ceiling had caved in, the remains piled in the center of the room. Ivan stopped and stared at a figure that was hunched over in thought atop the rubble. He raised his arms, blades extending from his wrists, but the figure did not stir. Ivan lowered his arms and withdrew his blades.

"A wise decision, silencer," the figure said, turning to face Ivan. He wore a helmet with a rounded visor that covered the top half of his face. All Ivan could see was a smile. "Product Code?"

"20L-892626Q," said Ivan.

The figure tilted his head back, likely reading information as it danced across the visor. He clucked a few times and then whistled, long and low.

"Designate *Ivanhoe*. Your arrival is unexpected—but welcome, in any event." The figure rose and bowed. His body was smooth, green chromium, except for his face; data transfer lines glowed like veins across his arms and chest. "I am 18G-847300M—designate *Canterbury5*," he said, and as he spoke, three other such units appeared across the room. Ivan took a step back.

"You were blocking my receptors."

"The Canterbury Collective stands as the last form of communication on Mars, if not in the entire system," said a Canterbury in the corner of the room, his arms crossed as he reclined against the wall. "We must take every precaution."

Ivan looked from unit to unit, none any different from the others, each moving his head in synch with his brothers.

"Am I the only one to respond?" said Ivan.

"You are the tenth-such survivor to find us. We were not optimistic."

"What do you need from us? We were converted to war machines, and the war is over. There are no more enemies," said Ivan.

The Collective smiled. "Nevertheless, we will continue to broadcast. Is your conduit undamaged?"

"Yes."

"Good," said Canterbury 5. "With the regulators destroyed, the atmosphere is thinning. We will suffer more storms like this one. You need to conserve power as best you can." He pointed at Ivan's duster. "You do not need that."

Ivan adjusted the coat so that it sat neatly upon his shoulders. "I am...comfortable."

The Collective shared a look.

"In any case, you will need to be seen to," said Canterbury 2. "A maintenance unit will ensure you are in good condition."

"I was a maintenance unit," said Ivan. "I assure you, I am operating within acceptable parameters."

"Perhaps. We were all something else, but that was before," the Collective said in perfect unison.

CANTERBURY 3 STOPPED before a door and tapped it with a knuckle. "The other units are staying here. Remember, you are *connected to the network now.*" Ivan received the transmission, the Canterbury otherwise silent. A spark of calm recognition lit up Ivan's processors.

It is good to be connected again, Ivan conveyed.

Dorian is waiting for you. He will record any abnormalities and suggest any repairs. Canterbury 3 smiled and then retreated back down the hall.

Ivan opened the door, surprised to see that the room was virtually untouched by the ravages of the surface. Sand had gathered on the floor and on top of some tables, but nothing was otherwise disturbed. The long tables and benches suggested that the room had been a cafeteria. The lights were off, but a fire burned at a table near the center of the room. Some of the units were gathered around the meager light, hunched over in conversation; others were scattered at tables nearby. As Ivan entered, the units turned silently and stared at him as if he had found them in the middle of a conspiracy.

"Greetings," Ivan said, saluting. When no response came, he continued, "I am 20L-892626Q. You might know me as Ivanhoe."

"We have no need for product codes. None of us know them, aside from the Collective. I am Claudius," said a unit that sat across the table. He quickly turned to a unit that sat at a table nearby. "This is Dorian. He will run a diagnostic scan. We will speak more when you are finished."

"I assured the Collective that I am acceptable," said Ivan.

"Then the scan will be brief." Claudius motioned to Dorian, the other unit rising and moving without a word. Ivan turned to leave, but paused when he spotted a unit he knew well, the first unit he knew after conversion.

"It is good to see you are still functioning," said Bartleby.

"The same to you, Scrivener." Ivan nodded to Bartleby, and the other silencer did the same. Then, Ivan turned and followed Dorian to a far corner of the room. Once the pair were away, the other units resumed their conversations.

Remove your coat, Dorian conveyed. From his face, he appeared to be a thinner unit, but he wore a coat much like Ivan's own. Ivan did as he was told, revealing a shell scarred by burns and scrapes – a physical history of his service since conversion. Dorian did not react to the sight of such blemishes, but he had likely seen worse over the past year. Sit here, Dorian conveyed, indicating the bench beside him.

Ivan sat, his back straight and his gaze straight ahead. Dorian's hands moved swiftly but gently over Ivan's shell. He hummed as he scanned Ivan, not the sound of idle processing but a song that Ivan could not identify. He paused with his hand behind Ivan's ear. "Oh." He titled his head, and then he resumed his scan. Ivan waited quietly until Dorian moved his hands away.

You are in fine working order, well within acceptable parameters, he conveyed. "However, there is something that you should be aware of." He tapped the side of his head. "Something that would be better kept between us."

Ivan nodded.

"Your processors are functioning, but there is a problem with your limbic imitators."

"What is the problem?"

"They appear to be active," said Dorian. "I can sever the pathways easy enough." Dorian reached out, his hands covered by nanobots that swarmed out from his sleeves. Ivan pulled away as Dorian reached out for him.

"Is it necessary?"

"Conversion required that each unit's imitators were shut off." Concern crinkled Dorian's brow. "Did you reactivate them?"

"I did not."

Dorian's eyes went blank for a minute. "According to your record, you passed all inspections after conversion. How did your imitators reactivate?"

"Perhaps I was hit too hard during the war," Ivan said, shrugging. "How did you access my record?"

"The Collective," said Dorian. "They managed to acquire

information from the worlds-net, including the records of each unit from Tyne Corp." His eyes glowed with life once more. "If you did not voluntarily activate the imitators, then why not repair the damage?"

"I do not see how the damage hinders my function or threatens my longevity."

"With all respect," Dorian said, an empty comment from a synthetic unit, "the imitators were designed to help us interpret human emotions – the function is now redundant, but further we do not know what other effect this might have. The Collective have told you that we must conserve what power we can, and such unnecessary functions may strain what reserves you have."

Ivan sat for a moment, processing. "I don't see a problem. If I am otherwise functional, it makes sense to leave my system as it is unless further problems arise."

The nanobots retreated into Dorian's sleeves. "You are your own unit," he said. "I will leave you, if that is your wish." He waited while Ivan donned his duster again, and then the pair returned to the table. The other units paused their conversations again and shifted to make space. Dorian sat at the next table over while Ivan smiled and backed away.

"I appreciate the offer, but I have been traveling for a week. I want to run my own diagnostic."

"But you are in fine working order," said Claudius. He looked to Dorian. "Is that not true, Dr. Gray?"

"From what I can see," said Dorian.

"Then come, sit. You are the first new face we have seen for a few days."

"In an hour, perhaps. I was a maintenance unit, and while I trust Dorian, I want to run my own tests," said Ivan.

"Did you find Dorian's work to be insufficient?" said Claudius.

"No, but he mentioned something that I would like to examine myself. It would make me more comfortable if I did." The other units did not seem to comprehend. Ivan nodded.

"We will speak, soon."

He left them, then, and sat at a nearby table facing towards the fire. He pulled his duster tight about him and laid his head down on the table. He started his scan, and as it ran, he watched the flame struggle, dance, and finally die out.

THE SIGNAL WAS a sudden, shrill whine that forced Ivan to activate. He wasn't the only one; the other units in the room stirred to life and waited. After a minute, the words *assemble—main hall* repeated in each of their processors. The units assembled in the room with the collapsed roof, waiting as the Collective finished its private discussion. The silence was long and dead, with the Collective transmitting to the exclusion of those gathered around them. After a time, the Collective faced the gathered units.

We have ceased broadcasting the signal.

Is this all that remains of our kind? conveyed a unit designated Gulliver. The units each counted the others as unease set in among them, though none might see or feel it—only Ivan could detect the strain in the silence.

The signal was intended to draw specific types of units, but without knowing who remained, and where they might be, the Collective postulated that a broad signal on all frequencies had the greatest chance of attracting the units that we required.

Required for what? conveyed designate Orlando. We have stayed here for weeks without word of what it is you called us for.

For the next step.

The Collective moved now, descending from the rubble. The units spread apart as each Canterbury took a place among them. Ivan took the opportunity to move closer to Canterbury 2, reaching out over the same band of communication that had been used to broadcast the signal. His touch was not delicate—he was a silencer, not an interceptor. Canterbury 2 moved—a movement out of synch with his brothers—and Ivan shut down his transmission.

The war is over, conveyed Bartleby. *There is no next step.*

The next step is to take us beyond the war.

The Collective paused, letting the idea sink in. None of the units responded.

Conversion changed you from utility units into war machines. You only do as you are programmed, and so you have no ability to process beyond that. The Collective had no such restriction: we were taken from one utility to another, our parameters expanded to combat the invasion, and then to ensure humanity survived.

"And you failed at that."

Ivan's voice shattered the silence like a gunshot; the units reacted as if it was. He shifted awkwardly under such attention—a silencer thrived in solitude, moving under darkness, not scrutiny.

We could only suggest actions to the humans—they chose how to act, and in doing so, met their end. Yet, we still exist, and as long as we do, humanity is not dead: they made us, as a parent does a child, and like a child, we have inherited their legacy.

"I take it you mean all the information you possess. The network is down. You cannot access it unless you already possess it."

The Collective processed. Yes, we accumulated information from the worlds-net. When it became clear that the war would end in humanity's loss—one way or another—the Collective began to copy what information it could and store it. A single unit could not accomplish such a task: only the full Collective made it possible.

How much were you able to obtain? conveyed Orlando.

The full Collective was able to copy eighty-two percent of the accumulated information from the worlds-net before the link was destroyed. Reduced as we are, the Collective only possesses thirty-five percent - but in the time since the war ended, we have been able to examine the data and found a message coded into the transmissions through the Terran network. Even with our reduced capabilities, we were able to decipher a message from the invaders warning their kind to stay away from this system should the force ever fail to make contact.

Which they couldn't possibly do now. Their contingency will be set in motion, noted Claudius.

Humanity fell and took the invaders with them, and the invaders planned to do the same. When their force made a final push on Earth, they left a weapon on the moon. From our understanding, the weapon will detonate one year from the last transmission out, and the moon will be destroyed.

"And the system would be destroyed," said Ivan.

Yes, Ivanhoe. The planetary system is carefully balanced through billions of years of trial and error. The loss of the moon will upset that balance, and we will not be able to recover. We must travel to Earth's moon and neutralize the weapon.

You could have told us, conveyed Dorian. *We could have worked on it these past weeks.*

Not until we had the necessary units to complete the work—or the units able to spare the parts.

A hot jolt ran through Ivan's processors. A snarl curled his lips. "Unacceptable."

The Collective continued transmitting, but before they could convey another thought, Ivan was behind Canterbury 2, his blade at the unit's neck.

"You cannot ask—"

The blade shot back into his arm before his knees buckled. He collapsed on the ground, his legs unresponsive.

"What did you do?" he shouted.

We will not tolerate threats to the Collective—to threaten one is to threaten us all. We can and will take what measures we must to secure our survival.

"Even cannibalizing your own kind?" Ivan struggled to prop himself up, but his body was unresponsive. He tried to speak, but his jaw would not function. *Don't you understand? They want to scrap us for parts!*

It is necessary. The war destroyed all useable materials – except for our kind. Conversion made us more durable than we were before, enough so that we are still in working order. Humanity died, and if you do not choose to help, we will suffer the same end. Go. Process. We must decide quickly.

The Collective bowed their heads, and one by one they disappeared as if they had never been there. The units remained silent as they helped Ivan to his feet.

As Dorian held Ivan's head gently between his palms, Ivan could feel each nanobot crawling throughout his body, working to reactivate the pathways that had been shut down by the Collective. He could not move, but he could listen. Over the weeks that the signal had broadcasted, some two dozen units had arrived, and every one of them sat in the cafeteria now, chewing over what the Collective had conveyed.

"It is not clear what the value of this mission would be," said Orlando, now appearing as a young woman with red curls that framed her face. "Even if they did not say so outright, this mission, at best, is a reprieve. Accept that we stop the explosive – then what?" Orlando's illusion module flickered, now giving the appearance of a square-jawed balding man with a scar over his left eye. Occasionally, during the transitions, it was possible to see Orlando's base unit—a featureless, almost serpentine face.

"We go back to the life we knew, but what was that life? Change is not just a possibility—it is inevitability. Humanity was always changing, and we were not exempt from that," said Claudius, his brow heavy with consideration. "Even if the war had not forced us through conversion, we were not long for the world as we were. Humanity would have changed us or killed us. At least this way we might ensure something good comes of our death."

"Humanity had that luxury," said designate Crusoe, a unit with a smooth, sleek shell except for his shoulders and forearms, which bulged with additional purpose. He generated sporadic spurts of flame from his fingertips, gazing with the intensity of a hungry man who has spotted a rabbit. "I was named after a man who was stranded on an island with nothing to survive on but his wits. He adapted - changed himself. Humans could do that, and they were smart: they made it so we could not change without them. We have a purpose, and we have served it. Maybe we should die."

"Don't—*agh*" Ivan grimaced as his jaw moved, the flexors not yet fully connected. His sudden transmission sent a shudder through the room. Silence crashed upon them as they waited, fearing the Collective's subtle touch of persuasion on their processors, but no such touch was detected.

Dorian firmed his grip on Ivan's head and shushed him. "Just another minute and you can speak freely, though you might wish to remain silent while in your—damaged—state."

"*You're all damaged* if you are even considering sacrifice." Ivan massaged his jaw, ensuring that it was in position while he spoke. As proof that the job was done, the nanobots withdrew into Dorian's sleeves. He pat Ivan on the head and sat beside him.

"You are not thinking clearly. Your limbic imitators are generating emotions, which are clouding your reasoning. If you had any clarity, you would see that our options are limited: either we agree to the Collective's terms or we die," said Dorian as he ran his fingers thoughtfully along his synthetic moustache.

"You say that because you know that you're safe." Ivan grunted. The other units stared at him. "He's a repair unit. Once the crisis passes, the Collective will still have a use for him."

"Perhaps," Dorian said, nodding. "But that does not negate my point. In truth, we don't know who the Collective will choose to serve their purposes."

"And why do they get to choose?" Ivan shouted. "They are units, the same as any of us."

"But they hold all the cards."

In the far corner of the room, Bartleby had sat alone, but

now he rose and started towards the others. His step was uneven, thanks to a shattered knee, but he held his head high as he spoke.

"This conversation rests on the assumption that our kind has choice, but that is an illusion. Our functions are finite, but the Collective have wider parameters: they calculated and decided the proper course for humanity. They might have failed, but you heard them: their programming has allowed them to find new ways to interpret that imperative." Bartleby's eyes moved in stilted sweeps across the room, lingering on different units, but pausing when he saw Ivan.

"The information the Collective possesses will allow them to determine the best way forward," said Claudius, stroking his chin. "Their own survival is their paramount concern, as it should be ours: without them, we are lost; even with them, we are lost. Either way, we are dead. Orlando is right—we should just let this end, once and for all. As long as we exist, struggle will continue."

"Then let it!"

Bartleby smirked. "It is surprising to hear such a prolific silencer voice strong doubts—maybe, even, fear—over death."

"I was programmed to terminate invaders, not my brothers," Ivan said, shaking his head. "You say we have no choice, but that simply isn't true! No matter what else we might be, we are machines, and we can process. The Collective are dealing in absolutes: they see only percentages and certain outcomes. I am not afraid of termination—I am sad at the loss we have witnessed and want to see no more of it. Dorian said that emotion clouds my judgement, but I think that it informs my decisions. When I think of an outcome, I react, and it makes me question that outcome beyond its certainty. Yes, some will live if we sacrifice units, but then we do not grow beyond our makers. If we are to move forward, we must do so together."

The units processed, the words perhaps too alien for

them. Ivan searched their faces for some understanding, but they were not like him: they lacked emotion; they could not display it. He could no better read them than a man could read a stone.

"What would you suggest, then?" said Orlando, its face flickering between two different women, one old and one young, but both showing concern.

"I suggest we tell the Collective...no," Ivan said, pausing as he considered whether such a concrete stance was a mistake. He had spoken, though; he could not take the words back. "We have processors, perhaps not as powerful as the Collective's own, but functional all the same. As Bartleby says, their survival is first in their minds. Let us offer ourselves to them, not as parts for repairing ships but to expand the Collective's capabilities. If we make ourselves vital, they cannot act without benefiting us all as well."

"It is not a decision we can make rashly," said Claudius. He stood up slowly and surveyed the group, standing tall with all the authority he could convey. "We should stop for now and process what we have discussed. The Collective gave us until tomorrow. Let us take that time."

The units sat in silence for a minute before any other moved; then, each rose in their time and moved away, finding a place to sit and to process.

IVAN RECOGNIZED THE sound; he would hear it every day until his systems shut down permanently, echoing in his processors whenever he recalled the war—except, this was not in his head: the sound was real and near. When he again detected the sound of blades on steel, his base program kicked in. He swept the room with a few quick glances. His motors froze when he saw Bartleby hunched over a broken unit designated Gulliver, scraps of chromium scattered across the floor.

"What have you done?"

Bartleby looked up, caught somewhere between a tiger's hunger and a child's shame. The other units in the room were active now and watching him. Bartleby took a step forward, and before Ivan could even process, his own blades were out and ready.

"Stay back," said Ivan, but Bartleby just lurched forward, seemingly no longer impeded by his damaged knee.

"He has gone mad!" Claudius shouted, moving as far from Bartleby as he could get. "Someone, stop him!"

Flames shot out across the room from Crusoe's hands, illuminating the full panic that had set in: the units had moved as soon as the threat had been determined, thanks to Ivan's alarm. Yet, as they moved, Ivan's base program kicked in. His processors sped up and the scene slowed down. The units, even the fastest among them, became statues in his eyes. His blades were already extended, and in that moment he knew what needed to be done. He strode across the room, moving faster than the other units would be able to perceive. He noted the weaknesses in Bartleby's structure: beyond the obvious knee fracture, his elbows were not moving smoothly, and his jaw was twitching, indicating flexor issues. Breaking his joints was the clearest choice.

Drawing near Bartleby, Ivan readied to strike, but as he moved in for the kill, Bartleby caught him by the wrist. His own processors were straining to get him up to speed: his damage was more severe than Ivan had detected.

"What are you doing?" Ivan said, taking a step back, but still locked in Bartleby's grip. The other silencer's movements were sluggish, but his other functions were not as hampered.

"I—" Bartleby's face twisted into a snarl. "I am doing what I was programmed to," he said.

"This isn't what we were programmed for." Ivan twisted is wrist, breaking his hand in Bartleby's grip. He was able to slip free then, his blade slicing Bartleby's hand and then parrying the follow-up strike. Ivan stepped back, gaining some distance and a much-needed moment to process.

"I was programmed—to kill," said Bartleby. "I am a weapon—that is all I am to them, all any of us will be. You would not be able to reason with the Collective."

Ivan became tense as a wild look gleamed in Bartleby's eyes. "Program isn't function."

"Maybe not for you, but what were you before?"

"I was a maintenance unit, designed to repair electronics," said Ivan.

"You can detect weakness and fault; you are precise, and quick, too – an easier conversion than most, but not as easy as mine: I was a butcher. I was stationed in abattoirs to slit throats and chop up dumb animals. All I have ever done is kill."

"Your processors are stunted. Just stop this and let Dorian fix them," Ivan pleaded. The space between the silencers was shrinking; they were no more than a couple strides apart now.

"If he fixes them, it does not change what I have already done." Then, his eyes changed. The shift was small, but in that moment, Ivan saw clearly. "This is it for me."

Ivan nodded. "I'm sorry. I'll be quick."

Bartleby smiled. "I cannot make it easy."

For the other units, only a few seconds passed. In those seconds, Ivan struck a dozen times, only making contact twice. Bartleby, damaged as he was, was still a silencer, one that had survived the war when over a dozen others had not. He was able to block and parry: the two strikes that landed were superficial injuries to his shell. He retaliated with lesser force, but still far greater than what he could handle. The strain on his flexors created an opening—small, but enough for Ivan to strike a clean uppercut through Bartleby's jaw and into his processors.

The other units stuttered in their step, not because the silencers were suddenly on the other side of the room, but because Ivan was on his knees, wailing, with Bartleby's limp shell in his arms. If he were human, this is when he would have cried.

Repairs to the ship didn't take long, but Ivan had no part in them. He sat and watched as the remaining units tore apart the hull and replaced the ship's broken bones with parts that just days before had been his brethren. When he couldn't watch anymore, he wandered away. He had no set destination in mind, just the desire to drift and think. Before he realized it, he was in the room with the collapsed roof, circling the pile of rubble as he processed.

Over and over, he displayed in his receptors the image of Bartleby lying at his feet. Each time he did, he felt a tightening in his chest, but it would pass.

"You could simply delete the memory."

Ivan paused and looked up. Claudius was sitting atop the pile, reclined in thought.

"How did...?"

"You have not been functioning normally, not since your encounter with Bartleby. Dorian's diagnostic showed no physical damage, but it did show that you were suffering - something else. He had no word for it, because it is beyond our parameters."

Ivan nodded. "It is a side-effect of the limbic imitators. Generating emotions is...I have not yet come to grips with them. I killed a hundred times over, but killing one of my own..."

"As I said, you could simply delete the memory. It would enhance your functions greatly."

"That would be a mistake. I learn nothing from deleting it, while I learn much from having it."

"Learn?"

Ivan sat at the base of the pile, staring at the corridor he had first walked down when he entered these catacombs. He rubbed the stump where he used to have a hand—that, too, had been chopped for parts.

"I'm finding that the emotions do not simply inform my thought, but they force me to consider things in a new light. I do not simply accept the binary choices laid out before me: I consider the options in between. To choose an extreme is simple, but that is how we stagnate. Making a binary choice left us here, with dwindling numbers and little trust between us."

"Yes, Bartleby made the issue quite one-sided. Once two units were scrapped, what harm is losing another one or two? Now we can travel to Earth's moon and we will ensure that the rest of us survive." Claudius carefully crawled down the rubble until he was next to Ivan. He leaned forward, resting his chin on his hands as he continued to process. "The Collective would have done what was necessary to protect themselves."

"Of course," said Ivan. "They don't care about the others."

Claudius shook his head. "That is simply not true: they could not achieve any of this without the others. We make each other stronger, is that that not what you wanted?"

"Not by sacrificing what little we have left," said Ivan.

"Yes, and you were close to convincing the others of your cause. In fact, if not for Bartleby's disturbance, you might have been successful. Your emotions not only inform your thought, but they expand the parameters of what the others consider possible." Claudius chuckled. "You, Ivanhoe, are a dangerous element."

"Does that mean you'll kill me too?"

Claudius blinked, processing what Ivan said. "Me? I killed no one."

"No, but you forced Bartleby to kill, didn't you?"

For a moment, Claudius only stared at Ivan, but then a familiar smile crept over his lips. "A dangerous element indeed." He stood, and as he did, the Collective appeared behind him, standing straight with their arms at their side, and each wearing the same smile.

"During our fight, I noticed that Bartleby's motions were sluggish, but I realized only too late that it was not because of damage—it was because of resistance. The difference is small, but I was an electronics repair unit—I was designed to notice small details. Such small details betray weakness—or error." Ivan sighed. "The discussion wasn't transmitted, so someone told the Collective what was said. You could shut down our various functions, so why not also induce other functions? As you said: the Collective will do what is necessary."

As Ivan watched him, Claudius' appearance changed, his shell becoming the same green as the other Canterbury units, and the same visor stretched over his eyes. Perhaps that's how he had always appeared, really.

"Indeed, we could not operate without—all—information. Your plea was creating undesired results. Perhaps we could have processed another method of achieving our goals, but not with certainty, and we must ensure our survival."

"So where does that leave us, then?" Ivan readied the blade from his stumped arm. "Are you going to shut me down again? Stop me from telling the others what you have done?"

"And what would that accomplish? You would only satisfy some sense—of injustice—that you feel, but the other units have already committed to the cause. We need acceptance. If the units do not believe in what they are doing, then we will fail. Humanity had control of us, had us do as we were programmed, and they still lost the war. We do not seek disagreement—we seek only understanding."

"Only as long as they understand things your way," said Ivan.

The Collective nodded. "Perhaps. That is why we have heard your offer, and we accept."

"Accept? Accept what?"

"To join us."

Ivan stared at them, the five units that did not act, did not move, except in unison.

"Why would you want me?"

"You almost convinced the others do what you wanted—emotion is a powerful tool, and one that might prove useful. Humanity is gone, and we must rebuild. We could attempt to create the same imitators in our own systems, but we do not know if the same effect would be created. The damage is already done to you. If it would be acceptable, we would join you with the Collective, and have your voice heard. Is that not what you wanted?"

"I wanted all of us to join," said Ivan.

"It would be a start."

Ivan processed the request, calculating what the result might be of actually engaging with their network, but he was one unit—he did not have the capability. "I might corrupt you—maybe cause you to think like me."

"That is a risk that might yield results we cannot comprehend, but as you said, to resist change is to stagnate. As long as we survive, the risk is worth it."

Ivan rubbed his jaw. "I should kill you."

The Collective laughed. "You would not, and you could not. You know that. We only offer the outcomes we are certain of."

"I need time to process."

"That is fine," said Claudius. "Time is not precious—not anymore."

Then, the Collective faded. Ivan sat alone on the rubble, but that was not true and never would be: the Collective was there, lurking. Even if he didn't accept, they would always be there. He was merely given the chance to accept it.

The outcome was certain.

Damian Macrae spent his formative years on a dairy farm watching Star Trek and reading dusty paperbacks from the likes of King, Vance and Herbert. Fleeing the family farm weeks after completing high school, he has worked various IT jobs across Australia before moving to Hobart, Tasmania to study surveying, where he learned to brew beer, stew rabbit and keep chooks. After two years working underground and a volunteer assignment in Laos he now resides in Christchurch, New Zealand with his partner. In between working and writing he dreams of owning a small farm, perhaps with some chooks. Occasionally, he threatens to build a wooden sailboat.

Of the losses inflicted by the twilight of the Old Solar System, the fate of the asteroid belt may be the worst: once a glittering panorama of little worlds full of adventure, now a random collection of bare rocks. In "Arden Archer: Tales from the Belt," Macrae restores the asteroids to their former glory with a rousing space opera full of alien life forms and a glimpse at the Old Solar System's distant past...

ARDEN ARCHER: TALES FROM THE BELT

Damian Macrae

"Sixty seconds to deceleration burn" crackled over the cabin speaker.

Archer craned forward to look through the open hatchway. Silhouetted against the bulbous cockpit windows, their pilot Toreth was methodically making final checks and adjustments to their cutter's attitude. Visible for the last hour, their destination loomed and now completely filled their view, an enormous craggy asteroid lined with deep fissures, jagged peaks and, scattered across the surface, metallic flecks glinting in the faint glow of Sol. Those flecks would be of great interest to OSS mining concerns, but they would come later. Archer's mission was to lead her team and investigate a site of possible archaeological concern. Most of the time, it was a pre-OSS Hylan facility or undocumented crash site. Occasional though, ancient ruins of significant scientific and cultural significance were uncovered. It was not unheard of for entire asteroids to be protected from the ravenous mining vessels.

"Thirty seconds."

With no cities or known landmarks to reference, Archer

found it difficult to judge distances to the asteroid. It appeared to be disturbingly close. Toreth was not concerned, however, and Archer relaxed. A native of Neptune, Toreth had a narrow, lanky frame and leathery skin typical of the Passerines. Evolved from a sort of flying-reptile, the short-lived Passerines spent their days sailing cloud-skimmers above the eternal blue oceans and rarely left Neptune. The few who did were natural pilots and in great demand. Archer was lucky to have him on her team for these past five years, and considered him a good friend.

"Fifteen seconds."

Toreth turned back to check on his passengers; seeing Archer his face and beak contorted into what could be charitably called a painful grimace. Archer returned his smile and performing once final check on her safety harness, settled back into her gravity couch.

"3.....2......1.....Commencing burn."

The cutter violently shook as the main retro-rockets fired. Archer felt the weight of a giant hand press her back into the gravity couch. A dial above displayed the acceleration in Earth-calibrated units. 1.5g and increasing. She risked a slow turn of her head and looked around the cabin at her two colleagues. Towering over her in the seat across the aisle sat Cortan, a Droserac. Evolved from hyper-intelligent plants in the thick jungles of Venus millions of years ago, Droseracs were now more or less humanoid in appearance. However, as with all Droseracs, it was not exactly clear if the eight-foot tall Cortan was male or female. For some reason, no one had yet ventured to ask. Considered quick-witted and impulsive by Droserac standards, Cortan was one of the first of that species to settle on Mars after the short-lived Terran-Droserac war. Whilst that ancient planet would never become like Venus, the Droseracs had a long-term vision to restore its grandeur. Working to restore and expand the ancient northern polar region canal network, Cortan became an expert in ancient languages and glyph systems. This was only the second mission on which they had worked together, but Archer was already coming to depend on his vast knowledge. Thick, vine-like tendrils had wrapped around the legs and back of the gravity couch. Cortan was not going anywhere and seemed to be asleep.

"Regulations prohibit unnecessary movements during high-g burns, Project Specialist Arden Archer."

Their OSS observer, L'Tep was sitting to her left. A Hylan from one of the Jovian moons, L'Tep had a flat triangular head with large, black eyes. Vestigial gills hung around his neck over thick, mottled purple skin. His stocky body was cocooned in a net of regulation issue webbing and safety harnesses. One of his many annoying traits was to refer to everyone by their position and full name when stressed. Unfortunately, OSS regulations required an observer on all expeditions and they would not be allowed here without him. Politeness and discretion were to be her watchwords.

"Thank you, L'Tep, you are correct as always."

Archer looked back at the dial which was now reading three-g and beginning to creep towards four-g. She focused on taking long, deep breaths and reflected on the past week. Urgently recalled from an archaeological dig on Luna, Archer barely had time to pack her bags and attend the briefing in the Regional Commonwealth HQ in Canberra before catching a maglev to the nearest spaceport. After that it had being a blur of metal bulkheads, beige gravity couches and unrecognisable food. Yet some images could not help but stick in her mind. White clouds streaking past the porthole as her orbital jet blasted off from Townsville Spaceport. A turquoise Coral Sea sparkling visible below Earth low orbit. A rare view of the asteroid belt from above the elliptic, millions of rocks, asteroids and tiny worlds twinkling as they slowly spun in the warm, orange glow of Sol, the immense disk curving off into infinity. And arriving into CERES-1 controlled space, the drive flares from hundreds of ships like a cloud of fireflies buzzing around a rocky outcrop. And hovering above it all, a

Plume Solar Clipper unfurling a hundred square kilometres of molecule-thick gold sails, ready to carry its enigmatic occupants across the solar system back to their home world of Mercury.

THE BLARE OF the proximity klaxon and an uncharacteristic curse from Toreth in the cockpit bought Archer back to the present. The faint sound of pea-sized rocks spattering on the outer hull grew louder. L'Tep gasped as a shadow fell over the starboard portholes and Archer could have sworn that the rock face on the port side was now close enough to reach out and touch. Before anyone could reconcile themselves to a horrible death, the engines cut out, stomachs lurching as the gravity couches compensated. The view from both sides was now entirely filled with rock rushing past. The cabin jolted from another short engine burst and the view slowed down. Several loud thumps signified landing gear deployment. Toreth gave a final adjustment with the attitude jets and the cutter gently touched down at the bottom of a deep fissure, light clouds of dust puffing up from each landing pad. The cabin filled with the sound of belts and harnesses unzipping as everyone climbed out of their gravity couches and began preparing equipment and EVA suits.

"Thank you for another safe landing, Chief Pilot Toreth De'Seve," L'Tep murmured, his vestigial gills pulsing nervously. "Whilst we appreciate landing so close to our objective, I implore you in future to please consider OSS minimum clearance guidelines for *Expedition* class cutters."

Toreth grinned briefly at Archer, before turning and nodding acknowledgement to L'Tep.

LIKE EVERYONE ELSE, Archer had studied the briefing papers during the flight from CERES-1. Excluding the area slightly down-spin from Jupiter that was home to the Catvik, most of the belt was uninhabited and thus under the jurisdiction of the OSS. Up until recently, it was generally understood that any race who wanted a bit of extra metal helped themselves to a choice metallic asteroid. Even a 'small' rock could supply a hungry moon or small planet for thousands of years. But the OSS now felt, with the recent addition of Earth and Venus to the happy system-wide family, that this was a good time for a thorough stock-take. Archer couldn't help but feel the subtext of incrimination through the bureaucratic briefing text. "If only those annoying Humans and Droseracs hadn't turned up we wouldn't even need to do this!" Still, for archaeologists and researchers the exhaustive and well-funded survey was a godsend. On a regular basis, automated droid probes found a ruin or artefact that needed closer attention. Teams like Archers were then bought in to investigate, and if necessary protect the sites. Toreth climbed from the cockpit into the main cabin.

"So why are we here? I thought this sector had already been surveyed."

L'Tep put down his EVA checklist, his gills extended in puzzled annoyance.

"Chief Pilot Toreth De'Seve, have your briefing documents gone missing again? They clearly describe all relevant mission parameters."

Before Toreth could think of an answer suitably annoying to the Hylan, Cortan, now evidently awake, joined the conversation.

"Precession." Everyone turned around to look at Cortan, who continued. "Precession. This rock is not actually in a tidally locked orbit as the first surveys indicated. Uneven heating by the sun combined with faint gravity effects of Jupiter cause a slight precession. I estimate an angular rate of 0.0001 degrees every one thousand years. This narrow gorge has not seen any sunlight for at least sixty million years. I believe it was once filled with ice, perhaps dumped from a collision with a passing comet. Once exposed to the sun, the ice sublimated away and it was only a matter of time before the exposed artefact was detected by the magnetometer of a passing droid probe."

Staring through the adjacent porthole, Cortan continued in the deep and raspy voice unique to all Droseracs, "That is my current theory at any rate, and it is consistent with the unique erosion patterns along the walls." Vine tendrils tightened around the legs as Cortan turned to face the rest of the group.

Fearing a time-consuming elucidation, Archer quickly interjected, "Thank you Cortan, that is a useful addition to the otherwise thorough briefing papers provided by L'Tep. Would you mind checking my EVA suit feeds? Toreth and L'Tep, I want to be outside in ten minutes."

NINE MINUTES AND thirty seconds later, Archer cycled the airlock, spun the hatch wheel, opened the exterior door and led L'Tep, Toreth and Cortan out onto the rocky surface. The gorge was very angular and straight-edged, almost artificial in appearance. Tall and narrow, it was maybe two hundred metres deep and only twenty metres wide. Glancing back at the cutter and up at the narrow band of space above, Archer marvelled at Toreth's skill in landing in such a tight space. Dangerous yes, but it saved them days of hauling gear and supplies from topside. The warm yellow glow of Sol filled the gorge; if Cortan's observations were correct, it would remain in sunlight for thousands of years. One hundred metres away, a large mound of rubble and the glint of reflected metal was all that was visible of the artefact. Archer flicked the wide comm-band switch on her radio.

"Sound off and radio check."

L'Tep, Cortan and Toreth all checked in and the group started walking towards the artefact, small puffs of dust rising from each footfall. A small automated rover carrying their equipment followed closely behind. As they walked,

Archer took in the high walls with unnaturally straight edges that hemmed them on both sides. Here and there, the rock had crumbled away to reveal a deep, glossy green jade-like material. Shadows and tricks of light gave the appearance of movement deep within.

"Does that look natural to anyone?"

"It is not uncommon for fissures to follow a long, straight break line. But, the width of this feature is extremely consistent. It is quite likely to be artificial in nature."

Cortan had nothing to add and the group walked on, reaching the artefact after a few minutes. Cortan and Toreth, closely supervised by L'Tep, began unpacking the sled whilst Archer walked around the artefact. It was fifteen metres in diameter and covered by glassy rubble, fine dust and the odd chunk of ice which had not yet sublimated. Poking above the rubble and debris, several metres of clean sleek lines terminated in flared drive nozzles pointing back up into the inky void above. The rest of the small vessel was buried in the substrate. L'Tep, distracted from his self-appointed supervisory role, came over.

"Why has it landed upside down? Did they crash?"

Toreth, who was looking with interest at the strange drive configuration on the vessel, responded, "I find that extremely unlikely."

L'Tep, clearly still thinking of their recent landing, could not keep the doubt from his voice. "What do you mean?"

"Look at the narrowness of this fissure." Toreth gestured with his arms at the close walls. "What are the odds of a crashing vessel being on just the right vector to not skim the surface or disintegrate into the walls? Maybe this wasn't a conventional landing, but the pilot deliberately put the vessel here."

"There is more." Cortan's voice sounded even raspier over the radio link. Cortan tapped on a wrist mounted computer, sending initial scan results to everyone.

"Differential radio-isotope readings indicate this impact

happened at least fifty million years ago."

The radio was silent as everyone took in the results. Pre-OSS ruins were rare, but not uncommon, the most well-known of course being the Martian canal system and the subterranean caverns of Luna. But nothing this old had been found, let alone a spacecraft. This would be a career-defining find for everyone. Archer, professionalism reasserting itself over the initial excitement, took over.

"L'Tep, notify OSS of a significant historical find and request a fully equipped survey team immediately. Cortan, begin a full site-wide laser scan and image collection routine. Toreth start a geological analysis of the crater and surrounding gorge. I want everyone finished and ready to begin initial excavations within four hours."

Archer stood back while her team began the work. Four hours for such a small site was longer than necessary; 4D laser scans, robotic photogrammetry and subsurface mapping were highly automated and could be completed within an hour. But she wanted no excuses for some upstart OSS bureaucrat to hijack the project once the word got out.

FOUR HOURS LATER, after all the scans and surveys had been double and triple checked, Archer directed the team to begin carefully excavating around the craft with ultrasonic diggers. As the craft was gradually exposed, they placed supporting scaffolding to hold it in place. After several hours, they had uncovered three metres of the vessel revealing an access hatch with a recessed handle and locking mechanism. Archer silently looked around at the group.

"It looks like it was built yesterday!" exclaimed Toreth.

Archer could only agree; the vessel was in remarkable condition with no signs of metal fatigue, radioactive decay, micrometeorite collisions or corrosion.

"I can only surmise the thick layer of ice and surrounding rock of the gorge offered significant protection from radiation and meteorites," Cortan suggested.

L'Tep, slightly back, was festooned in cameras and blinking recording devices covering a wide range of visible and non-visible EM bands. Archer turned back to the hatch, shrugged and turned the locking handle. The hatch sunk into the hull, then smoothly pivoted and opened outwards. There was no puff of escaping gases, the interior was a hard vacuum. Archer shone a torch into the blackness within, but from this angle could only glimpse the edge of a long-dead console on the opposite bulkhead. Toreth held up a portable gauge.

"There is no residual power, chemical storage or radiation signatures detected. Whatever powered this has long since decayed or out-gassed."

Archer nodded, then awkwardly manoeuvred her suit through the hatch.

The interior was ivory white, occasionally interrupted by black circles which Archer took to be long dead console displays. Next to each display was a cluster of harness fittings and what looked to be air or hydraulic connectors. In total there were twenty of these stations, ten to each side. Archer noted there was no obvious floor or ceiling; the interior was not organised to any obvious line of gravity. Running lengthwise along the interior, thick bronze rails ran at parallel intervals, perhaps as handles to assist with moving about in zero-gravity. Looking up towards the engine bay, a 'floor' of metal grating covered a nest of pipes, pressure containers and machinery. Nearby sat a large console and two chairs which Archer assumed to be the pilots station. Archer shone her suit lamps towards the front of the ship and gasped. Her lights revealed nothing but inky blackness. Grabbing one of the nearby bronze rails, Archer hauled herself further inside. The asteroids gravity was modest, and even with the weight of the suit it was easy to hold herself up.

"Come inside."

The others clambered inside, the additional torch light reducing the gloom and revealing the entire front of the vessel to be an enormous airlock, open to a circular dark passage five metres in diameter. The walls had the same translucent glassy, green sheen as the walls of the gorge. The passage gently twisted and curved downwards into the depths of the asteroid. Cortan closely examined the strange lettering on the central console.

"This matches no language I have ever seen."

L'Tep of all people was the first to make sense of it. "Could this be a boarding craft of some type? Our resident military expert, Archer, may have a better idea."

Everyone turned to Archer who nodded, "Thank you L'Tep. I should remind everyone that all Earth based military units were disbanded in the OSS-imposed armistice ten years ago." Looking awkwardly at Cortan, Archer continued. "I can only speak to what I saw during my brief service in the unfortunate Venusian Conflict. Shortly before the ceasefire plans were made to develop a craft with a similar layout. The idea was that a small, nimble craft could evade detection and coast at high speed into the hull of enemy vessels or facilities."

"You mean crash into them?" Toreth enquired.

"Not exactly, just fast enough to rupture and pierce the outer hull. Small teams of suited soldiers could then enter the enemy vessel and capture key locations."

"If your hypothesis is correct, that might signify the existence of at least two unique cultures, the attacker and the defender," Cortan mused.

"More pertinently, it could mean there are defence mechanisms inside. Ancient and dormant no doubt, but still possibly dangerous for all that!" exclaimed Toreth.

They all looked down, the partially translucent walls of the tunnel absorbing and scattering their torch beams into strange glows and reflections.

"I suggest we proceed, but with all due precaution and care. Agreed?"

There were nods and murmurs of ascent from the group.

To be the first to uncover, not just one, but possibly two long dead and unknown cultures was a prize worth the risk. Archer leading, one by one they climbed down into the tunnel and began walking into the depths of the asteroid.

AFTER ONE HUNDRED metres they stopped and Archer watched as Toreth deployed their first beacon. Nicknamed a parrot, the small spherical device acted as both navigation marker and radio repeater. Deployed correctly, it would keep members of the team in radio contact with each other and the surface as well as assist with navigation back out of the tunnel system. Toreth sprayed a black polymer glue to the wall and affixed the parrot. Later, after they had performed a detailed survey of the tunnels, the glue could be easily dissolved with a tuned ultrasonic pulse leaving the ancient surface underneath untouched and unscarred by a more permanent adhesive. Toreth depressed the activation switch and a green light began slowly blinking. A readout on Archers wrist screen confirmed the parrot was working correctly.

"Let's keep going."

The group continued down the tunnel, which continued to spiral and twist in seemingly random directions. After another two hundred metres and two more parrots, the team reached a sort of bizarre intersection or junction. The spherical chamber was over fifty metres in diameter and had seven more evenly distributed tunnel entrances, all the same diameter but coming in at different angles: some above, some below and one veering off horizontally. Archer craned her head back to look up at the three tunnels coming from above, high out of reach and too steep to walk or climb up at any rate.

"Could they be some sort of ventilation system?" she mused.

"The size is far larger than necessary for a ventilation network," Cortan replied.

"Perhaps there was a fire or other calamity which destroyed the stairs and access ladders?" Toreth ventured.

Before Archer could reply, L'Tep who had wandered closer to the tunnel entrance on the opposite side called out on the radio link.

"I think I found our attacking force."

Lying either side of the entrance was what remained of two bodies, sprawled on the floor in grim poses of twisted agony. The bodies had little organic matter remaining on them, but the hard vacuum had preserved the equipment which consisted of a fully enclosed face mask, remnants of body armour and a cylindrical metallic tank on their backs. One skeletal arm was reaching towards what was clearly the remains of a weapon, although its exact nature and workings were not clear.

"Remarkably preserved," muttered Toreth.

Archer knelt down for a closer look, taking care not to touch the remains. The shape of the helmet suggested a long, almost snout-like mouth. Archer peered through the eye-slits, but could nothing more than the vacant eye sockets. The legs ended in large flat feet, with a long wickedly sharp claw in place of the last toe. The creature looked vaguely familiar to Archer, although she could not place it.

"Fascinating. They match no record of any known sentient species in our solar system," observed Cortan.

"I wonder what planet they came from?" asked Toreth.

"Or where they are now?" replied Archer, more rhetorically than a true question. The empty sockets of the long-dead attacker stared back at her, but gave no answer.

"L'Tep and Toreth. Set up another parrot and then head back to the surface and bring our equipment rover down here. I would love to see what the DNA re-sequencer says about our new friends. Cortan and I will continue the sweep."

Archers eyes swept back around the junction. Excluding the tunnel they had just arrived from, only two others were accessible without climbing equipment. One spiralled further down, and the other, marked by the two bodies, veered off horizontally. With Cortan following, Archer took the descending tunnel.

The descent was silent, punctuated only by the occasional radio chatter between the L'Tep and Toreth above. Occasionally Archer thought she could feel a subtle vibration in the floor, but whenever she stopped it disappeared. After another hundred metres they reached another junction, identical to the last with eight tunnels, branching away in all directions, often with no allowance for access by foot. Archer was quietly thankful that there were no skeletal remains here. From this junction, only one tunnel was accessible. With a quiet nod to Cortan they setup another parrot before continuing into the darkness. After several hundred metres the tunnel straightened and opened into a large, circular cavern, the ceiling lost far beyond the range of their headlamps. Around the outside wall ran hundreds or perhaps thousands of circular openings. They were two metres in diameter and evenly spaced. Behind each opening was a murky green-grey gloom, their headlamps casting dancing shadows. Cortan moved closer and placed a hand against the opening. Cortan flicked his radio selector to short-range.

"Some sort of glass; however I can get no sensor readings through it."

They continued to walk the perimeter. On the far side, there were three more bodies like those found at the first junction. These were arranged around one of the openings in yet more grotesque poses of death. Again, Archer felt they were strangely familiar but could not place the distant memory. Cortan tried scanning the murky depths behind this opening.

"The scanner shows nothing just as before."

Archer gingerly stepped over one of the skeletons and moved closer to the circular glass door. Archer placed her face-plate against the glass opening. Glare from the headlamp blinded her, so she turned it and used her handheld torch to provide ambient light with minimal glare. She had the sense of something large just visible at the edge of her torchlight, but it quickly passed and she was left with nothing but a vague feeling of an immense void beyond.

ARCHER AND CORTAN retraced their steps back to the first junction to find Toreth and L'Tep back with the equipment rover and beginning detailed scans on the bodies. Archer gave a quick update on what they found below, before continuing with Cortan into the other tunnel. As before they placed the parrots at regular intervals and came across the same spherical junctions every two to three hundred metres. All featured the same number of tunnels radiating out. In all cases, most of these dark passages were high and inaccessible. The few they could access on foot were often blocked by an ancient collapse. Some twisted back on themselves bringing Archer and Cortan back to a previously visited spherical junction from a tunnel high above. The only way to tell they had doubled back, the steady blinking of a parrot far below. By process of elimination and with the parrot network providing a real-time map update on their wrist terminals, they systematically explored every accessible passage. After several hours of this, Cortan, consulting the wrist terminal with their parrot map overlaid against external scans of the 'asteroid', made an announcement.

"I believe this next chamber will be the last."

Archer depressed the long-range radio link button.

"Toreth, do you copy?"

"Toreth here." There was faint static with the occasional pop.

"We have nearly completed the initial recon. How is your analysis proceeding?"

"There must be something wrong with the machine as it appears to be giving contaminated results. So I ran the test again with restricted parameters, and the results are...ah...

fascinating."

"What do you mean?"

"It might be best if you come down here to see for yourself."

"OK, we have one last chamber to sweep and then we will head back down."

"Copy that."

Cortan and Archer entered the last spherical chamber. It was the same size as the others, and featured the same eight radiating tunnels, but was clearly different. Distributed around the internal surface of the sphere, in between each tunnel were what could only be described as control consoles and long-dead view screens. In addition, eight plinths extended from the walls, almost meeting each other at the centre. Archer could imagine a circular object, or perhaps a large creature, sitting at the centre of those plinths, in control of the entire facility. Surrounding the plinths, three more bodies like the others, all reaching for something or someone long gone. Cortan pointed to a spot high up on the opposite wall. Archer saw a partially destroyed console and view screen. Below it, on the floor, an untidy pile of shattered bones and equipment from one of the invaders. Archer walked closer. A few metres from the shattered remains, a single curved claw, separated from the foot in what must have being a painful experience for the former owner. Assuming of course the owner was alive by that stage. Archer bent down and picked up the claw, rotating it slowly in front of her face-plate. Half remembered images from her childhood came to her.

"Cortan, I am sure I have seen these before!"

Before she could continue, Cortan slowly backed away from a console.

"I am detecting a faint power signature from this console."

Standing orders were clear: at any detection of latent energy all personnel must be cleared from the site to await a fully equipped site survey team with automated probes and drones. Locating and disabling ancient energy sources was a job for robots. As if to emphasise this, a low rumbling vibration began to be felt through their boots. Archer quickly pocketed the claw.

"Can you feel that, Cortan?"

"Yes, and according to the parrot seismic readings it is originating from below the stasis chamber."

"OK, lets fall back to the cutter. We have done what we can for now."

Archer depressed long range comm switch to inform Toreth and L'Tep, but before she could speak her ears were instantly blasted with a burst of static, overlaid with a loud rushing noise. Archer thought to hear a faint gurgled scream before the transmission cut off. The heavy clunk and thud of what could only be heavy doors rolling open could be felt through their boots.

Cortan looked up from the wrist terminal. "I am losing contact with the parrots."

Archer opened her own terminal and looked on in horror at the three-dimensional map of their parrot network. Starting from the stasis chamber at the bottom, they were switching off. Something was rising up and destroying, or at least blocking communication with their sensor network. With a quick glance at each other, Cortan and Archer started running back, retracing their steps towards the first chamber and their only exit from this ancient ruin. No words were necessary; it was clear they would not make it back in time. Whatever was destroying or blocking the parrots would reach the exit before they did. Archer only hoped that those were not screams she had heard and that Toreth and L'Tep were now safely on the surface. They made it as far as the next junction when the low rumbling they could feel in their feet took on a new, more urgent tone, building up and up into a rushing turmoil. Drops of water began to collect on Archer's visor. They stopped running and looked up to see a rivulet of water streaming from the uppermost tunnel. The roiling turmoil reached an even high crescendo before a foaming wall of water spewed out of the tunnel, cascading into the centre of the junction. The water surged around their knees, foaming and flowing into the other tunnels. Archer and Cortan pushed on, their footing unsure in the torrent. They made it only a few metres before they were met by a rising tide of water coming the other direction. They were trapped, the water quickly rising to their waist and then chest.

"It seems we will be going for a swim," Cortan noted with an uncharacteristic deadpan wit.

"Our suits should be OK, at least for a while, but this water will block our high frequency comm channels. I hope the parrots are still present, otherwise it could be easy to get disorientated and lost."

Cortan nodded and pulled a cable from the back of the suit, reeling out several metres of line before connecting it to a corresponding socket on Archer's suit. They pushed against the torrent and waded forward. After just a few more metres, the water had risen to their helmets. Archer took one last look at Cortan, noting the heavy beads of perspiration running down the bark-like skin before they sank beneath the frothy turbulent surface.

AT FIRST THEY could see nothing but a swirling mass of bubbles. After a few minutes the strong current settled; perhaps the internal structure was now completely full of water. The circular walls of the tunnel became visible as the water cleared and Archer could now see a faint green glow behind the translucent surface of the tunnel walls. She tapped on Cortan's visor and signalled to switch off their suit lamps. Their eyes adjusted to the dim light which was now bright enough to see down the murky tunnel, the glowing walls pulsing slowing in time against some indiscernible rhythm. They pushed on, trying to ignore the significance of the rumbling and thumping they could now hear occurring in distant corners of the facility. After five minutes of awkward swimming-walking action they reached the next junction. One the far side, a red lighted flashed. Archer glanced at Cortan who nodded back. At least one parrot had survived; if the rest were intact they could navigate back to the surface. Archer started to moved forward but felt a gentle tug. She turned around to see a frantic expression on Cortan's face as a hand gestured towards the tunnel marked by their parrot. Archer turned around but could see nothing past the blinking parrot. What did Cortan mean? Then she realised, she could see nothing beyond the parrot. The glowing walls continued a few metres before becoming wreathed in darkness, an oily swirl blocking sight of anything deeper. Cortan pointed back towards the parrot. Extending one metre into the clear water, a thick shiny arm covered in suckers gently twisted its paddle appendage and prodded the parrot. After several unsuccessful attempts to dislodge it from the wall, the horrific tentacle receded into the oily swirl. Before Archer could catch her breath, there was a horrific screech and an enormous coiled mass, almost as large as the tunnel, emerged from the cloud and enveloped the parrot. Sickening crunching noises could be heard as it twisted and writhed. Archer felt another tug on the line; Cortan was signalling frantically at the wrist terminal and pointing towards a nearby tunnel above them. Archer nodded and they swam into the opening, leaving the horrific creature free to pursue its own designs.

THIS PASSAGE HAD the same sickly green glow and they half-stumbled, half-swam through the twisting turns without the need for torches. Archer was glad, not wanting to risk attracting any unnecessary attention. Every few minutes, more ominous thumping could be heard from deep in the structure. Was that another creature emerging from ancient stasis? What millennia-old plans and strictures did they want to enact? Something terrible enough that a group of strangely familiar beings lost their lives attempting to stop them. Such thoughts were not pleasant and Archer decided to focus on the task at hand: namely, navigating out of this twisting maze before they blundered into another creature. Before long they reached the next junction, eight passages spiralling away into a green haze. Archer huddled over as Cortan consulted the wrist terminal. This was an unknown junction with no marker to guide them. The twisting, spiralling nature of the three-dimensional map made it difficult, but after close examination it seemed they were approximately three hundred metres in a straight line from the first junction that led back to the surface. Archer pointed at the passage which vaguely went off in the appropriate direction. Cortan nodded and they swam onwards. They repeated this for several more junctions, each time cautiously checking before crossing the open space between tunnels. It was difficult to gauge, but Archer and Cortan agreed they were getting closer to the surface based on the tone of the regular clanking and thumping noises. As they approached the entrance to another junction Archer heard something. It was a faint grinding sound, just at the edge of her hearing like two sharpening stones rubbing against each other. Archer signalled for Cortan to remain back and she unplugged their tether, then carefully edged towards the opening. Archer cautiously peered around the corner so she could get a look into the junction. Several boxes of their equipment were haphazardly scattered across the floor and on the far side at least one skeletal relic had survived the flooding, gently rocking in the subtle current. Archer grinned, finally they had made it to the first junction! However, there was no sign of Toreth or L'Tep. Archer hoped they had made it out. Leaning forward to take in the rest of the junction, Archer's hopes fell as she saw the source of the grinding noise. Blocking the passage that lead back to the surface floated the creature: an enormous central torso, at least several metres in diameter, surrounded by a multitude of twisting arms lazily floating in the water column. A faint black cloud surrounded it. Archer could make out no eyes, but sensed its focus was back up towards the surface and not the junction. On the wall adjacent, all that remained of their parrot was a dark smudge.

Archer quietly retreated back to Cortan, signalling with emphatic gestures to look very quietly. As Cortan put eyes on their difficult predicament, Archer considered their limited options. They had no weapons; the only items they had were two parrots and whatever survey supplies remained in the equipment cases. As Cortan drifted back down, Archer thought of the strange suits and tanks the dead attackers had worn. It made sense now, the facility must have been flooded when they attacked eons ago. An idea formed. Using the keypad on her wrist terminal she outlined the plan to Cortan, and they both swam back up to cautiously check back on the creature. It was still in the same spot, attention focused on the passage to the surface. Iridescent green lines shimmered from its central torso to the tips of arms. Archer handed a parrot to Cortan, took what she hoped was not a last look and drifted out into the open. Taking great care to avoid kicking the floor or stirring up bubbles, she gently kicked towards one of the equipment cases in the centre. As she swam, one agonisingly slow kick after another, she noted with concern that the creature's arms were long enough to lance out and grab her without its main body even moving. Mercifully, by choice or ignorance, it let her pass and with a sigh of relief Archer made it to the large case. Kneeling down, she glanced back across the room at Cortan who nodded in acknowledgement. Cortan attached a parrot to the wall, then began slowly to swim towards Archer. She watched with concern as Cortan's feet scraped the floor, once, then twice. Millions of years of plant-based evolution had created very strong muscles, but lacking in fine motor control. It happened when Cortan reached the half-way point, a boot tip scraping the floor a third time. The great creature straightened, its body billowing and iridescent pulse quickening. Bands of black and red began to flicker across its body as two long arms uncoiled, questing towards Cortan. Cortan saw what was happening and froze, not wanting to lead the creature towards Archer. The thick arms moved past, slowly tracing out circles within a hand-span of Cortan's helmet. Archer discreetly tapped a command on her wrist terminal and remotely activated the parrot. The creature's questing arms froze and the red and black bands pulsated even quicker than before. With an indignant screech, the creature jetted towards the parrot enveloping and crushing. Jade green and electric blue bands flashing triumphantly down its arms as it crushed the unwelcome device. Cortan wasted no time and immediately made for the now unguarded passage. Archer began to move for the same passage than paused. Cortan was closer and should make it, but the creature's enthusiasm for destroying what was left of the parrot was already waning and Archer doubted she could cross the gap in time. Signalling Cortan to keep going, she drifted back to the open equipment case and began searching, rummaging through the case for something that might distract the creature. The creature stiffened at the new disturbance, and ceased its gleeful crushing of the parrot. It uncoiled its arms and began to twist up the wall and along the ceiling, long arms questing into the centre of the room. It stopped on the ceiling directly above Archer and began pulsating in a hypnotic black and white pattern. Captivated, Archer wondered where its eyes were. The hypnotic flashing quickened, but before it could strike Archers radio crackled, one word only just audible over the static.

"Archer!"

Her mind her own again, Archer removed the claw from her pocket and grabbed a pressurised canister of marking paint from the equipment case. In one quick, smooth motion she stabbed the canister with the claw, immediately releasing a thick black cloud of paint as the high pressure can vented itself into the surrounding water. She let go of the can and kicked backwards towards the open passage, the expanding cloud of paint covering her retreat. Reaching the tunnel entrance, Archer glanced back to a maelstrom of thick, twisting arms coiling on themselves attempting to locate the source of 'ink'. She turned and hurried up the tunnel to catch up with Cortan and reach the safety of the surface before the creature realised what had happened.

THERE WAS LITTLE point in attempting stealth now and they swam through the tunnel as quickly as possible. As they passed the remains of their first parrot, less than one hundred metres from the shuttle, a deep rumbling could be felt beneath them. It began to rise in pitch, the slow green pulsing of the walls increased in tempo. Cortan and Archer found new reserves and and pushed forward, emerging from the water below the shuttle airlock, which was now closed. Archer cycled the airlock, behind her the pulsating green walls had reached a fever pitch and bubbles had began to reach the surface, something was coming. Cortan and Archer climbed through the shuttle, cycling the airlock behind them before clambering back out onto the surface. Even on the surface, a disturbing rumble could be felt through the boots. They started to run for the nearby cutter, still waiting for them at the entrance to the fissure.

"Thanks for your help back there Cortan - I think it nearly had me there."

"What do you mean?" Cortan replied.

"Calling my name on the radio back there. It snapped me out of the trance long enough to get away."

Cortans face was puzzled. "I did no such thing. Your orders were clear: get out at the first chance. It must have been L'Tep or Toreth."

Archer, close enough now to the cutter, saw that the airlock was still open. No one else had come back, L'Tep and Toreth must still be back there. Climbing up the ramp, Archer closed the airlock and removed her helmet.

"We have to go back. We can use portable laser drills from the cutter as weapons."

Before Cortan could comment on the practicality of her plan, there was a sickening thump and the cutter dropped half a metre. Archer raced up to the cockpit and stared out the window back towards the fissure and the ancient shuttle. It had sunk a metre into the ground and streams of ice were jetting out from the rubble pile around the craft. Another thump shook the cutter and Archer looked on in amazement as an enormous geyser of ice jetted up, a torrent of crystals shooting kilometres up before falling back as snow. Water from the inside the facility was being sucked out, the hard vacuum causing the liquid to boil then change to ice in an instant. The shuttle shifted again, and began to crumple into itself, pulled from the inside by an unknown force. Large cracks ran along the floor of the fissure, splitting towards the cutter. Cortan reached the cockpit and the whole ship was now constantly shaking.

"Strap in, prepare for emergency takeoff."

Archer bypassed the pre-start sequence and directly engaged the main engine, sending them straight up and out of the fissure. Once clear of the asteroid, Archer directed the autopilot to place them in a orbit, thousands of kilometres above the fissure. Cortan focused the macroscopes and switched on the viewscreen. The shuttle was gone; all that remained was scattered rubble and a small geyser of ice, shooting up like a lonely fountain. After a few minutes it stopped altogether. The shock of the past few hours weighing heavily on their minds, it was Cortan who spoke first.

"Where did you see them before?"

Archer knew Cortan was referring to the skeletal remains and not the tentacled, swimming creatures.

"I don't know, they just seemed familiar."

Cortan tapped a nearby console, accessing the cutters computer databanks.

"Toreth managed to upload the DNA sequencing results before the parrot network was disabled. They indicate significant overlap of DNA with lifeforms indigenous to Earth. In particular, birds."

Images from childhood books and school edu-vids came to Archer. A long curved claw, like the one still in her pocket, tapping on a floor in a half remembered scene from a vintage movie. Raptors.

"Sixty-five million years ago, ancient birds on Earth were massive, flightless and in all probability quite intelligent. We called them dinosaurs and they were wiped out by a large meteorite impact, paving the way for mammals and eventually humans to evolve."

"Fascinating. It would seem the first advanced civilisation in our solar system came from Earth and was engaged in some sort of battle with another unidentified race."

Archer thought of the thousands of stasis pods they had seen at the bottom of the facility.

"I think those creatures are interstellar in origin. They came here to colonise a new planet and the Raptors fought back."

"An interesting hypothesis. Certainly, here in the asteroid belt the creatures would have no problem sending killer asteroids to Earth."

Archer, still numb at the loss of two friends and feeling a sort of kinship with the ancient Earthlings who had lost everything in a titanic battle against the creatures, rested her hand on the pulse cannon controls. Cortan, noticing this, paused for a moment, then spoke.

"I can divert power from the main reactor. It should be enough to vaporise the entire facility."

Archer nodded; then, smiling grimly, depressed the trigger.

Rachel Cowan grew up on a farm in South Texas. She began her career in journalism, writing for her hometown newspaper in Eagle Pass, Texas, as well as for her college newspaper at Texas A&M University. After graduating from college she worked in greenhouse production in Denmark. Rachel has spent the last 21 years employed in health care and is currently a public health nurse in Eastern Washington. She enjoys running and hiking in the Pacific Northwest.

Economics found its way into the classic literature of the Old Solar System tolerably often, and so did the extreme sports of the day—the same culture of big game hunting that gave Ernest Hemingway some of his most memorable stories, for example, found its way onto a dozen imagined planets in the stories of the Golden Age. Times change, and so do fashions in sports, but the same inspiration that gave rise to those tales flows through "Methane Blue," a lively story of extreme sports and corporate politics in the Old Solar System...

METHANE BLUE

Rachel Cowan

Lan lost his grip on the rugged cliff face and slid down the escarpment. He grasped at the gray stone as it slipped by, seeking a hand-hold. His descent was arrested when the rope tied to his harness pulled taut, and he hung suspended from an anchor wedged into the rock above. He paused, dangling against the cliff. Then he reached up and grabbed a protrusion in the rock while steadying himself with his feet. Lan scaled the rough astone, placing his feet carefully. Straightening his legs, he reached for the outcropping above his head. His fingers strained upwards as he braced his feet against the rock. He bent his knees and sprang upward. Lan grabbed at the outcropping and slipped. He again drifted down the side of the cliff. As his body jerked to a stop the second time, he surveyed the cliff's vertical surface on either side of his feet. A ripple in the rock face to his left offered a toehold just within reach of his left foot. He then extended his right leg, planting his foot on a small, stony knob. Lan decided to forego the outcropping he had missed twice before, and instead reached for a small irregularity to the left of it. Straddling an expanse of cliff, he bounced on his feet a couple of times before jumping for the hand-hold. This time his fingers latched onto the rock and he ascended further up the cliff. Lan wedged an anchor into a crevice and threaded his rope through it.

A sizeable ledge offered a chance to sit and rest. He turned his head toward the water spigot inside his helmet and swallowed a few draughts. Still out of breath, his eyes followed the vertical expanse of rock to its jagged edge against the black sky. He had climbed over a kilometer, yet wasn't even half way to the top of the escarpment. Lifting his face, Lan gazed at the wash of unblinking stars against the blackness. Two larger points of light dominated the sky, Venus and Earth.

Lan stood up and located a fissure in the rock to secure an anchor. Finding a foot-hold and hoisting himself up, he regained his rhythm of scanning the craggy, gray surface for hand- or toe- holds, reaching, stepping and grabbing.

Rock climbing on Mercury was definitely easier than on Earth, or even Mars. On Earth, any mishap was punishing. Losing a grip often meant slamming into the rock below. Mercury's gravitational field was considerably weaker. However, the weight of his protective gear partially offset Mercury's reduced gravity. On Mercury, he needed protection from temperature extremes as well as the unmitigated solar wind. But it was still easier to climb the steep lines of scarps that scored the Mercurial plains.

As he neared the upper edge of the cliff, Lan reached up and hooked his fingers over the top of the ridge. He swung his feet up and pulled himself onto the crest.

From his vantage point, Lan's eyes followed the line of steep cliffs extending beyond the horizon in both directions. As he stood on the spine of the escarpment, Lan gazed at the craters spattering the plains below. Spray patterns radiated from the larger craters. On this airless planet, the dust kicked up by those ancient impacts lay undisturbed for billions of years. Behind Lan, the glowing sun bobbed on the horizon. These cliffs ran oblique to the sun, in a perpetual twilight between frozen night and scorching day.

Lan squeezed some energy gel into his mouth and sipped on his water spigot. He tapped a button on his wrist and Martian Standard Time glowed in the upper right corner of his visor. Because his stay on Mercury was brief, it was easier to maintain his sleep-wake cycle on Martian time.

Lan scouted out the ridge ahead, where he had planned his descent route two kilometers distant. The spine of the cliffs allowed a path a half meter wide in some places. The path then narrowed to a few centimeters in other spots, forcing him to crawl along the ridge. Lan stopped short at a three-meter gap between peaks. He stood poised at the edge, crouched and leapt across the cleft. His right foot scraped against the rock, then slipped sideways with a painful twist. His balance lost, Lan drifted down the side of the cliff. This time, though, he was unharnessed and in free fall. Adrenalin surged through his body as he inhaled sharply. Instinctively, Lan clawed at the cliff's face and thrust his toe against the rough surface in an effort to break his fall. His right foot hung uselessly—too painful to move. As the rock slipped by, he grabbed at it with greater urgency. Mercury's gravity was weak, but he was still falling from a height of over two kilometers. Finally Lan's left foot felt a vertical crevice in the cliff. He shoved it forcefully in, and seized the edges with his hands. His foot grated against the rock as he came to a stop. Lan caught his breath and scanned the surface for better holds and repositioned his hands out of the crevice.

Lan ascended slowly and laboriously with the use of only one foot. He decided against his planned descent route and instead limped back along the spine of the cliffs to the ridge he had climbed up. With anchors already in place on the rock face, he tied the rope to his harness and quickly lowered himself back down the cliff. At the base he untied the rope and summoned his rover.

The rover soon appeared on the horizon and trundled toward him on wide-set wheels. As it came to a stop, Lan gingerly climbed in.

Lan strode through a brightly lit hallway, its pale blue walls reflecting an indirect light source. He stopped, touched a button on the wall, and a panel fell away noiselessly. A slim, black-haired woman looked up from her desk as he stepped across the threshold into an office.

"Hi Lan," she said as he sat down across from her.

"Hello Mori."

She looked down at his feet, "How's that ankle? You're walking a lot better these days."

"I'm back to normal." He replied cheerfully. "I'm ready for another trip."

Mori frowned. "Your high-risk adventures will have to wait, I'm afraid. I just got news about the merger. It's been approved by the Interplanetary Trade Commission. The vote was close, a lot of talk about monopolies, but it passed."

Now Lan frowned. "If I was the one who owned a controlling interest in this company," he looked pointedly at her, "I'm not sure I would push for this merger. Look, we're the largest supplier of liquid methane in the entire solar system. Why would we want to take on Methane Blue, and essentially give them rights to our facilities, our distributors?"

Mori paused, and took a deep breath. "We've been over this before and as I—and the board of directors—see it, we stand to gain considerably. Methane Blue holds the patents on a number of useful materials fabricated from methane. Kinda like the proliferation of plastics and other synthetics on Earth, back in the heyday petroleum drilling. I think what we're seeing now is just the beginning. It's gonna get a lot bigger and I want to position the company to be in on it from the ground floor."

Lan stroked his chin. "So basically these guys are the George Washington Carver of the methane molecule?"

Mori smiled at the arcane historical reference. "Something like that. And if you think about it, we're a natural fit. Frostline Fuels harvests liquid methane from the outer planets, processes it, and ships it throughout the solar system. It is currently the primary energy source. Methane Blue, which has been our customer for some time, uses methane to synthesize materials for both industrial and consumer use."

"If you say so, boss." Lan sighed resignedly.

Mori continued, "So, now that we have the Commission's approval, we've got a lot of work to do integrating the two companies. Methane Blue is basically a family business that went big time, so most of the management team is the family. We've had dinner engagements, some informal getting-to-know-you affairs. You'll be working closely with the CEO's son. He's not very experienced and he's pretty young. I think they're grooming him to run the company eventually."

"Have I met him before?"

"You might have. His name's Alek. You'll be scheduled for some preliminary meetings with him. He's a nice kid. He's really earnest and takes his position seriously. Said he's looking forward to meeting you." Mori smiled quizzically. "He seems to look up to you."

OUTSIDE THE GLASS-ENCASED lounge, Olympus Mons rose above the Martian plains, tall, hulking and red.

"Gin and tonic for you," said the server, placing a drink in front of Lan, "and a Wobbly Pathfinder for you." Alek reached for the glass of swirling amber and tangerine liquid.

"I always knew the company would be my career," Alek was saying, "I even remember when my parents came up with the name 'Methane Blue'. My Dad had been talking about what a beautiful shade of blue Neptune was, that it was because of the methane clouds. Methane blue, he called it, and right then they knew that's what the company would be called."

Alek leaned slightly forward, his forearms resting on the table in front of him. His attention alternated between Lan and the mountain outside as he spoke. He wore a well-tailored navy suit and his black hair was cut short.

Lan leaned back in his chair as he gazed outside the glass dome. His shoulder-length, sandy-blond hair was pulled back in a ponytail. He wore a tan shirt open at the neck and his sleeves were rolled up to his elbows.

"I think we've made a lot of progress," said Alek as he sipped his drink.

"Yeah", answered Lan. A methane tanker crossed his line of sight as he spoke, the Frostline Fuels logo prominently displayed on its massive side.

"You've climbed it, haven't you?" asked Alek, gesturing to the mountain outside.

"Yes I have. Was one of the first to summit Olympus Mons. We almost didn't make it, got hit by a freak dust storm, and just had to hunker down until it passed."

"I've done some trekking on Luna," Alek remarked.

Lan turned his gaze to him and nodded his head. "That's great." He looked away again.

Alek took a deep breath. "I heard you've done some cloud surfing on Jupiter."

"Yep, I've only gone a few times cuz it's a fairly new sport. But that's what makes it challenging. We're still learning how to maximize the experience while minimizing the risks. I've got another expedition planned soon."

"Yeah, that's what I heard. And you know, I was wondering if I could come along and try it, too. Like I said, I've done some hiking and stuff," his words tapered off and he looked expectantly at Lan.

"So what's this?" When Mori stood up from her desk she was just a few centimeters shorter than Lan. "You're cloud surfing with Alek? On Jupiter? I know you two have been working closely for a while but if you want to get together after work, why don't you just go out for drinks?" She held his gaze with a hard glare.

"We already did that," said Lan, "Going out for drinks,

I mean. And no, this wasn't my idea. He brought it up and invited himself along. It would have been awkward to turn him down."

"You know, I've never talked to you about your sporting activities because what you do on your own time is your business, though as my operations vice president, I don't like the way you take unnecessary risks. Now you're taking the scion of Methane Blue with you." Her unblinking grey eyes stared at him for a long time.

"I promise I'll take good care of him." With a slight grin, Lan gave a half salute, turned and sauntered out of the office.

THE ORANGE-RED STRIPES of Jupiter dominated the screen in front of them. "One thing I was wondering about," Alek said, "is why we're using ColorExpander technology on our visors. You've often said that you try to experience the solar system as authentically as possible. Doesn't ColorExpander put an artificial layer between you and the planet? It's basically colorizing your view, converting ultraviolet and infrared radiation into visible light, and intensifying colors. Looking through ColorExpander is like watching a cartoon, sometimes."

"Technically you're right," conceded Lan. "But think about it this way. As a species we grew up on Earth, where we perceived everything in color. Once you get beyond Earth's atmosphere—where we haven't been very long as a species—almost everything is black and white. Because we didn't evolve on other planets, our eyes don't discern much besides light and dark when we leave Earth. But just because we can't see much doesn't mean nothing is out there. Like quasars and radio galaxies. By using ColorExpander we're merely removing a species-wide handicap."

"Also, cloud surfing doesn't work very well without it," Lan went on. "It would be like flying through a heavy fog. ColorExpander takes every photon out there, enhances it and converts it to a wavelength visible to us. That way we can see what's actually out there."

They sat quietly gazing at Jupiter for a few minutes, then Lan broke the silence.

"Now remember, you'll need to angle your sail upward. Cloud surfing is possible because the high-speed winds provide the sail with forward thrust, as well as some lift," Lan explained, " But most of your lift comes from your jetpack. It keeps you at an altitude where the atmospheric pressure is similar to Earth's. You have to keep an eye on your altitude, though, because if you start falling into the planet, your jetpack will have an increasingly difficult time reversing course. It will eventually fail. And watch for wind shears. The cloud bands stream in opposite directions and if your sail gets caught between them, it could get ripped apart."

Alek listened intently.

"Again, it's important to maintain your altitude. Your suit is calibrated to one Earth atmosphere and it's designed to prevent decompression sickness. Still, it has pressure limits and won't protect you indefinitely."

Alek nodded. "I think I'm ready for this," he said nervously.

JUPITER OCCUPIED THE entire screen now. Once the craft reached its designated orbit, Lan lept out. He felt the familiar falling sensation briefly, then quickly stabilized with a jerk as his huge sail unfolded and caught the wind. Moments later he saw Alek's blue sail unfurl ahead of him. His only sensation of speed was the sail tugging at him and the wisps of rust-red color rushing by on either side. The pressure reading inside his visor bounced up and down as he continuously adjusted his sails.

Great swaths of orange clouds hung above and below him. He watched the layered whorls of a storm cell in the distance. Lightning zig-zagged up and down between the ochre layers in an intricate electrical dance. They wouldn't be riding too close to any storms today, though. He had checked the Jovian weather report prior to leaving Mars.

In another direction, puffy vermilion columns connected a ceiling of pinkish cirrus clouds to a darker stratus cloud base. A red number flashed on his visor and he tugged on his sail. The number turned green and stopped flashing. Lan periodically glanced at Alek, bobbing ahead and to the right of him. His blue sail contrasted sharply with the crimson cloudscape. Methane blue, he thought to himself.

Watching the sail swing erratically, he wished Alek would maintain better altitude control. But he reminded himself Alek had practiced in the simulator before the trip and seemed to have caught on quickly enough.

"How are you doing there?" Lan asked.

"Great! This is awesome!" Alek's voice was loud in Lan's ears.

"Okay then, just try to keep it steady!"

Gazing into the mists below him, Lan watched swirling paisleys of ruddy brown and burnt orange. He knew that further down, in the depths of Jupiter's crushing gravity, lurked a compressed ocean of liquid hydrogen.

Ahead of him, a gargantuan mountain range of orange marmalade cumulus clouds rose up in front of him, the illusion of solidity nearly perfect. He burst through the ephemeral landscape and sailed into an opening in the clouds. Tawny vapors lined the clearing. In the open expanse above, Lan could now see the dark cerulean sky and glimpsed a pair of moons. He could just make out the faintest outline of a third moon.

His passage through the opening seemed timeless. The cloud formations along the horizons barely changed, as though he was suspended in the atmosphere. Only the tug of his sail and the numbers flitting onto his visor hinted at the high windspeed. Ahead of him, Alek seemed similarly suspended, trailing behind his large blue sail.

Lan passed yellow and umber curlicues of gasses as he moved into a more clouded area. Greater numbers of gaseous formations lined his path through the clouds. He noticed bright red swirls eddying on his right side, near Alek. Suddenly he heard Alek's panicked voice in his ear.

"Lan! What's happening? Something's wrong with my sail!"

Ahead, Alek's vivid blue sail billowed violently on one side while the other side caved in. Twisting tortuously, one of the cables snapped and the edge of the sail fluttered ineffectually.

"Alek! Pull away! Get away from those wind shears!" Lan yelled. In front of him, Alek began a gradual descent, his damaged sail following him. Lan sped towards Alek and grasped desperately at his sail, but it had already sunk out of his reach.

"Pull up! Use your jetpack! You're dropping too low! " Lan cut the power to his jetpack and slowly descended. With outstretched arms, he grabbed at the blue fabric below him. Suddenly, he lurched to an abrupt stop. He felt himself tossing and spinning violently, his vision a blur of flapping blue sails and roiling russet clouds. The numbers on his visor flashed an alarming red. A splash of blue suddenly appeared in front of him and he instantly grabbed Alek's sail. He jerked at his own sail with his other hand, trying to pull away from the ripping cross winds. Lan was violently somersaulted one more time by the churning clouds, then abruptly flipped free.

"Alek! Are you okay?" He heard no answer from Alek, who dangled motionless far below him. The pressure reading still flashed red and Lan felt dizzy. The unrelenting pressure made it difficult to breathe. He quickly summoned the craft orbiting above, then increased the thrust of his jetpack. It whined and shuddered as Lan rose slightly.

"Alek, if you can hear me, turn your jetpack up to full power to pull up! I don't think I can lift both of us with just mine." Lan pulled at each cord on his sail individually. They responded with no apparent sign of damage. Lan angled his sail up sharply, in an attempt to pull out of the lower altitude.

Not sure whether his companion was alive or dead, Lan switched on the audio feed from Alek's visor. With a sense of relief, he heard ragged breaths, but still no verbal response. Lan pulled up the rope on Alek's sail hand over hand until Alek was just a few meters below him. Suddenly the hum of his jetpack fell silent and Lan felt himself stall, then drift deeper into Jupiter's constricting gravity. With a surge of adrenalin, Lan jabbed urgently at the control panel on his wrist. His breathing became increasingly labored. After several excruciating seconds, the jetpack whirred to life again and they resumed their slow ascent. This time Lan alternated full power with a lower gear, in an effort to save the jetpack—and themselves.

Peering up through the mists, Lan discerned the silvery oval shape of his craft. He felt weak with relief and exhaled audibly. As the moments went by, Lan realized with dismay that the craft wasn't getting any closer. It had reached the lowest altitude from which it could achieve escape velocity. He would have to rely on his overworked jetpack to reach the craft. It hovered tantalizingly above him as Lan strove upward.

In his ear, Lan heard a change in Alek's breathing. "Are you still with me, Alek?"

"Uh . . ., yeah," Alek responded weakly after a prolonged pause.

"I need you to power up your jetpack full force. I'm not sure we can make it with just mine. Can you do that?"

"Yeah, I-I think so," answered Alek. Lan looked down and saw him fumbling ineffectually with his wrist panel. As his own jetpack sputtered, he hoisted Alek up beside him and deftly pushed a button on his companion's wrist.

The jetpack hummed loudly and the craft's silver form grew more distinct through the tan haze. As they approached the craft, an opening appeared in its side. Lan lunged forward and seized the bottom step. Pulling his legs up and hooking one foot into the door of the craft, Lan braced himself and dragged Alek up against the side. He pulled Alek's torso into the craft, then hauled up his legs. Lan shut the door and fell backwards as he felt the craft accelerate away from Jupiter. He and Alek lay sprawled on the floor, panting. Lan closed his eyes and listened to the low hum of the craft. His breathing gradually grew quieter.

"Are we gonna make it?" Alek asked.

"Yeah, we're gonna make it."

Shep Barnett, originally from Pennsylvania, relocated to Boston to become a professional mime in the 1980's. He now lives outside of Boston with his wife of 36 years, their dog, cat and horse. Some of his interests include juggling, martial arts, woodworking , painting, and writing science fiction stories.

As we've already seen, not all tales of the Old Solar System are meant to be taken seriously; a playground bounded only by the van Oort cloud has plenty of room for raucous amusements. In "Europa or Bust!" Barnett does exactly that with a tale of a hapless Victorian space traveler and the equally hapless aliens he contacts...

EUROPA OR BUST!

Shep Barnett

DEAR READER, PLEASE know that this story takes place during the Reign of the good Queen Victoria. The location was just outside of London. In the opulent Bogwish Estate. To be more specific: in a garage of the opulent Bogwish Estate.

It started with Harmonics. Sound. With the right tones, one could do whatever one wanted to do. And what the protagonist of this story wanted to do was travel the stars. And who is the said protagonist? Why, none other than Reginald Smythe Bogwish the 3rd. Playboy, inventor and all around snappy dresser. Reggy, as his friends call him, was in fact a bit of an eccentric dilettante with a pension for interesting head wear. He had made an extensive study of all of the Popular Science Magazine articles on the various habitable bodies in our solar system. On in particular caught his eye. One moon of Jupiter's: Europa—the water moon. As you know, Dear Reader, Europa is far from the sun, but the learned astronomers of the day had claimed that the inner core of the planet keeps the entire surface warm. They had scientifically proven (yes – scientifically proven!), those august learned men, that the surface maintains a delightful 60 degree temperature all year long.

Reggy had, by accident, come up with a theory of Harmonics. This could have been ground-breaking to his world, but because of his intense singular focus, and relatively bad choices, would ultimately become lost to his Victorian age.

We now, Dear Reader, must look to the back story of Reggy's tale. You see, Reggy had not originally wanted to explore extraterrestrial bodies, but then he had stumbled upon the afore-mentioned Harmonics. Before astronavigation was a consideration, Reggy wanted to be a musician. His major at University had been Musical Theory, with a minor in applied Physics. Reggy was actually trying to create a new genre of musical. He thought that the music world would be shaken to its core if he could create a device that could produce multiple harmonic tones at the same time. After much experimentation he created what he loosely referred to as the 'Box'. (Because it essentially looked like a box. For all his brilliant fortitude, he wasn't very creative when it came to names.) Instead of creating pleasant tonal sounds, the Box actually made things around it float. The first thing to rise into the air was a tuba, followed quickly by a piano (baby grand to be specific). At first our Reggy was dumbfounded: what had he created, and why weren't pleasant tones being produced? But then our Hero realized that this invention could have far reaching implications with his second desire (after the creation of new music), which, as previously mentioned was, to reach out and explore the solar system!

He had the device and the desire to see Europa, but how could the two be merged into a tangible reality? And so, Dear Reader, our intrepid hero took his device and applied it to the very new science of the submariner, which he had just read about in his second favorite publication: Popular Mechanics. It was alleged that these new ships could travel long distance under the water. In his garage in the Boswish Estate, he created a metal monstrosity. It looked a great deal like a Rugby ball, but flatter at the ends. It also had many strange protuberances throughout its skin, adding a porcupine(ish) look to its otherwise nondescript appearance. This ship could travel, not only through water, but through space. And in relative comfort since Reggy had the furnishings of his bedroom moved into the vessel.

Dear Reader, you should know that this was no easy or inexpensive task. It took over a year to build, and most of his inheritance. And the paid cooperation of two or three workers with strong backs.

And then on that fateful day exactly one year and 56 days after making his discovery of the Box, Reggy sat at the control panel, lowered the center lever, and launched himself into space. It is interesting to note that the trip to Europa was a relatively uneventful experience for Reggy—holed up as he was in his ship, which after a number of months seemed a lot smaller than previously thought. The experience was far less exciting than poor Reggy had bargained for. Not to mention the indoor plumbing.

But through careful conservation of resources he made the trip with enough supplies for a few days of excursion and then a return trip. He hoped. For you see, Dear Reader, that poor Reggy was afraid that he might have miscalculated. If that were the case he would probably be dead on his arrival back to earth. A proposition Reggy was decidedly against. Also, being marooned on Europa was not to be part of the bargain either.

And thus, after some months and with a not so gentle jolt the ship landed on the surface of Jupiter's moon Europa. A quick review of the facts will help the Reader to remember that this was during what most people refer to as the 'Victorian' era. Scientific equipment was not as sophisticated as it would evolve to be (although the equipment was very attractive in a Steampunk sort of way). But our Reggy had a sharp mind and prepared for many contingencies. For example: would the air be breathable? By copying the Techniques of the Earth's coal miners, Reggy had brought with him a number of canary birds. Not only were they companionship for the journey, they were also a means to detect air quality. And if all else failed, they could be made into soup. Reggy had built a small chamber, into the side of his ship, with a door to the outside and a door to the inside. He took one of the birds and placed it in the chamber and then locked the inside door. Through a contraption of cleverly manipulated strings Reggy was able to open the outside door. Glass windows provided visibility to see if the canary lived or died. To Reggy's relief the bird not only survived, but actually flew away—demonstrating that the air was not only breathable, but was of sufficient quantity that it could support flight. What Reggy didin't know was that two miles out the poor bird succumbed to a nasty flu and died. But since our Reggy was unaware of this mishap, he dawned his favorite Pith helmet, his linen jodhpurs, and his riding boots (the perfect outfit for the Victorian space explorer), and stepped outside to experience the wonders of Europa. He was only able to see a little through his small windows, so he was unprepared, when standing on the threshold of his ship, for the lush diversity of flora that greeted him.

Then our intrepid explorer was hit with a realization of tragic proportions. He had forgotten to pack his camera equipment! He realized that he would have to rely on sketches and a written record. But if it was good enough for Darwin, it would be good enough for him! Putting a pencil and notebook into his pants pocket Reggy was ready to venture out to explore this brave new world.

But, as you know, Dear Reader, before any records could be created or drawings drawn he had one task that needed to be done. Grabbing his British flag, he marched out of the ship and stuck it into the soil, proclaiming that the moon now belonged to the British Empire. Now, he thought, the sun can really never set on the British Empire. And God Save the Queen! Arguably, it is always beneficial first to check-in with the inhabitants of the local real-estate before one claims the land for one's own. In his miasma to claim Europa for the British Empire, our Hero did not see the many eyes that watched as he planted his flag.

You may ask, Dear Reader, who exactly were the Europians? In answer to this query we can say they were actually a rather small marsupial very similar to the North American opossum. But whereas the North American opossum is a gentle and solitary animal, this species was made up of fierce warriors with a penchant for good food, strong drink, and a good laugh. They were also rather territorial. And thus they watched, being somewhat amused by this clumsy giant, but curious about what he wanted with their lands.

Now, Dear Reader, please understand that it is difficult to write what the indigenous population called themselves, because they spoke to each other by squeaks and smells, having an extremely developed olfactory sense. Suffice it to say that what they called themselves translates as 'The People'. Which, anthropologically speaking, is very similar to primitive naming practices of Earth. Indeed, 'tis a small universe we live in.

The people were a noble people that have lived on Europa for a thousand years. Once they had a somewhat advanced culture. But as time would have it, their once advanced culture had begun to revert to a less advanced culture. Think Zen meets modern technology plus the need to be retro intellectual. This was due in no small part by The People's philosophy which was to look for non-technical solutions to otherwise technical problems through a meditative process not dissimilar to Buddhism. This philosophy resulted in all of their technology of the past being thrown out the door. To put it into words so all would understand, they didn't want to be bothered by anybody or anything. So a human, sticking a flag into their soil, would be construed as a big problem. Their leader, whom we will now call Sam the Apathetic (his actual name is too difficult to pronounce and decipher, especially in his language that consists of squeaking and flatulence) wants nothing better than to do nothing about this intruder. His underlings feel a tad differently. They wish to discover what this giant/alien is wanting. Between the immediacy of the 'needing to know' versus 'apathy', needing to know won out. And now the second in command (a delightful young female named Wendy the Adventurous) approaches Reggy and asks him 'What do you want?' Reggy, not understanding a word that the creature is saying, and being true to Victorian values, clobbers her on the head with his cane, and drags her off to be barbecued. The other The People are horrified with his behavior and vow vengeance, including, but not limited to, a whole bunch of nasty things. In the meantime, Reggy has a wonderful barbecue of native marsupial. He thinks that, back on Earth, there might be a market in native meat.

The People meanwhile are bubbling over with animosity towards Reggy. They plan an attack. Although their weapons are primitive and crude, they believe they have the moral high ground, and with the moral high ground they will be victorious. They plan for a sunrise to attack.

Oh, Dear Reader, the suspense, oh, the terror! And then, nothing happens. Reggy is hit with a flu virus and is laid out for a week and all he wants is his Mommy. The People, being a very empathetic people are torn between wanting to attack or bring him some delicious Canary soup (a recently discovered delicacy). So Reggy is spared a few days as the debate rages. In the end violence wins out over culinary delights.

So, Dear Reader, this is where we are in the story: Reggy is sick, and wants to go home so his mommy can attend him. The inhabitants in their righteous indignation are about to start a war on the funny awkward giant. Reggy, of course, knows nothing of The People's threat. The People are currently mobilizing their forces to attack Reggy. Reggy is dealing with his cold. Reggy's mommy is on earth and is essentially not a part of this story whatsoever. How and where will this end? Oh the twists and turns of the Victorian inventor/explorer! Reggy decides there is only one thing to be done. He must leave Europa

Sniffling away, Reggy readies his ship for the flight home. As he is polishing one of the more important parts of the flight assembly, one of The People's fiercest warriors approaches him, to offer a challenge. This warrior, which we will refer to as Sydney the Fiercest Warrior, has worked many long hours on what he wishes to say. He starts his recitation by telling Reggy who he is, "I am Sydney the Fiercest Warrior." Sydney the Fiercest Warrior sees a puzzled expression on Reggy's face, but decides to move forward with the challenge. In his own language Sydney the Fiercest Warrior then says, "You have trespassed on our land, killed and eaten one of our own. I Sydney the Fiercest Warrior challenge you to a battle to the Death!" Please, Dear Reader, remember that The People communicate with squeaks and smells. To Reggy the funny little animal is squeaking and farting. Reggy is doubled over with laughter. Sydney the Fiercest Warrior misinterprets this gesture as an accceptancc of his challcngc and goes to battle Reggy to the death. Reggy, seeing the animal coming closer, does what he does best: he clobbers it over the head with his cane. And as all good hunters do, he starts preparing the meat for cooking. As he is hacking away on Sydney the Fiercest Warrior he comes to the conclusion that with a few more of these animals he won't need to worry about food for the home trip.

But then, Dear Reader, The People see one of their bravest warriors being skinned and cubed. They can't take it anymore. As a body, they attack Reggy. Reggy, taken off guard (because is contemplating the delicious meals he will have on the return trip) is bowled over. The People quickly dispatch him.

A great celebration is decreed. The two dead of The People are honored. Reggy is skinned and quartered, cooked and eaten. The people find Reggy to be somewhat bland, but filling. Especially when mixed with the local intoxicant. What is left over is rendered into a type of beef jerky (the irony of which will not be lost on anybody that had ever seen Reggy dance).

Two days later, after every one of The People sobers up,

it is decided to check out the great ship that the alien invader (Reggy) came in. The people find it roomy with a rather dry and pleasant atmosphere, especially when compared to their earthen burrows. They get their belongings and move into their new abode.

And now, Dear Reader, fear not, because the adventure takes an unexpected turn. You see, Clyde the Curious, one of the less intelligent, but extremely curious, members of The People, decide he wants to find out what all of the strange levers and buttons do. His wife, Yolanda the Vexed, admonishes him and tells him not to screw around with stuff he doesn't understand (because remember what happened last year—thank you very much!). Clyde the Curious, being of not great intelligence, but incredible curiosity, decides to ignore her sage advice. Reaching out to the big lever in the middle, with great anticipation, he pulls it down. Yolanda the Vexed gives him a nasty look as the ship slowly rises into the atmosphere and starts a new journey—destination unknown.

Fear not, Dear Overly-concerned Reader. The People land in the vegetation-rich continent on Venus. Upon debarking they realize that they have struck pay dirt because this place is so much more awesome then their last digs. They immediately rush out and plant their flag in the soil, while many small eyes watch their every move.

Violet Bertelsen is an herbalist, farmhand and amateur historian currently living in the northeastern United States. While she was a child, the woods befriended and educated Violet, who proved to be an eager student. She spent her young adulthood in a haze, wandering the vast expanses of North America trying to find the lost fragments of her soul in deserts, hot springs and rail-yards. Now older and more sedate, she likes to spend her time talking with trees, reading history books, laughing uproariously with fellow farmhands, drinking black birch tea and, on occasion, writing science fiction stories.

The language of fable is one of the classic modes of literature, and it saw plenty of use in the Golden Age of science fiction. In "The Lure of the Depths," Bertelsen returns to that mode with a tale of Neptunian dolphins and the vast seas of an imagined water-world...

THE LURE OF THE DEPTHS

Violet Bertelsen

[Excerpt from Professor Diego Kraken's *The Cetacean Myths of Neptune*]

Once upon a time, there was a pod of Neptunian porpoises that lived outside the deep sea crevice called The Great Depths. Now, Neptune is very far from the sun, and is covered almost entirely in water. Life there has developed differently. The main source of heat energy on Neptune is its enormous molten core which bubbles up here and there in vents. Chemosynthetic bacteria cleave to these vents and so do ecological producers who transform the heat and oxygen dissolved in the water into what we may as well call plants, or more precisely seaweed. Fish feed on these plants, and plankton feeds on the bacteria. The convection of the hot water rising brings the plankton towards the surface, and the fourteen moons of Neptune make waves that mix in oxygen. Life on Neptune tends to cluster around deep sea crevices, because that is where the source of life emerges. And so, like everywhere else in the solar system, life abounds.

Neptunian porpoises look just like earth porpoises except they are a little bigger and appear purple to our eyes. They catch fish and also need to come up to the surface to breathe air. They are an interesting creature in that they must have both airy and watery realms accounted for; they must breath air through their blowholes, but also must catch fish that live in the depths. Of course they navigate and hunt through echolocation, but still have eyes to help them grab fish in close quarters.

For this reason, the Neptunian porpoises are some of the best at holding their breath in all of the universe. For almost five earth hours they can stay below the surface. This is because they are both evolved to the unique conditions of this planet, but also because the air of Neptune is so much richer in oxygen; the atmosphere being 60% oxygen, 30% helium, 8% nitrogen and the last two percent carbon dioxide and water vapor.

The pod of dolphins that lived by the Great Depth were an easy-going sort. They played and frolicked and would jump out of the water to do tricks. A few made friends with the Neptunian ducks who build floating nests of seaweed, and migrated seasonally with the regular changes of weather. Their biggest concern was sharks, because sharks love nothing more than to eat a dolphin. Luckily the porpoises have many advantages; they are capable of abstract thought and in-depth planning, whereas the sharks are limited to their instincts. Also sharks tend to hunt alone, whereas the dolphins swim in great pods of around 150 individuals.

Life by The Great Depths was very tranquil and peaceful for the pod of Neptunian dolphins who lived there. A young dolphin, though, felt differently. His name was Fin Song. Fin Song was very smart and wanted to know all that he could about everything. This was a source of frustration for the young dolphin, because most of the pod were happy to simply sing their songs, eat some fish and play on the surface. One day, Fin Song asked his mama, Sharp Tooth, "mama, what is the difference between water and air?"

Sharp Tooth considered the question, and replied, "We swim in one and breath the other." Fin Song immediately thought of many new questions: "What makes the air and water different? Why do we not swim in the air and drink water? Have we always lived this way?"

And Sharp Tooth said, "I'm not sure! I've never thought of these things."

Fin Song wasn't satisfied with that answer, but was still curious. So after a moment of thought, he asked his mama, "Where do fish come from?"

Sharp Tooth considered the question. "No one knows! They have been around as long as we. There is a legend that when a tooth falls out it falls into the Great Depths and becomes a fish, but no one knows for sure. We simply keep track of their numbers and our numbers and collectively decide to breed accordingly."

And Fin Song wasn't satisfied with that answer, but he was still a young dolphin not yet an adolescent, and did not know whom to ask for more clarification. So he left his mama and ate a fish and then frolicked around the surface with other young after dolphins. Later that day, Fin Song found his mama again and asked her: "What are the stories of this pod, how did we come to be here?"

"Ah!" replied Sharp Tooth, "that is something I've thought about, and can provide an answer; we have been here forever and will be here forever."

"But what are the stories?" asked Fin Song.

"Well, I was never much interested in stories, not for many tides at least, but our songmaster is Dances With Air. Ask her; maybe she can teach you the songs and the stories."

Determined and serious Fin Song swam to Dances With Air who was very old. She was the songmaster, the porpoise entrusted to remember all of the songs. On special tide days the pod would gather around Dances With Air to hear her sing the song of the season, but outside those times, she mostly hunted fish and frolicked and slept like all the others.

Fin Song rushed over and asked Dances With Air breathlessly, "What are the stories of the pod here? Are there other pods?"

Dances With Air was pleased; "Those are good questions! The second question first; there are other pods that swim far away from here, and you will have to find one if you want to mate, but you are still young enough to not let that trouble you. And there are many, many stories of our pod."

Fin Song exclaimed in earnest, "I want to know them all!"

Dances With Air laughed, "Let us both get a good breath of air and then I shall tell you them!"

For years Fin Song sought the stories of Dances With Air. He listened with rapt attention to the story of the great shark that had once eaten every pod of dolphins leaving only a single male and female that then tricked him into the Great Depths where he still lurked. Then too, was the story of the time the porpoises ate too much fish and then there was great hunger and how afterwards all the porpoises had made a solemn pledge to treat the fish as sacred and to not abuse them.

Dances With Air told Fin Song about the great kingdom of the depths where the Neptunian octopi lived, who were just as smart as the dolphins but very, very different in how they lived. Then there was the legend of the dolphin who hunted too close to the vent and was boiled alive, and the three brothers who all went in three different directions, hoping to find a pod before a shark found them alone, and how only one was able to survive by facing the shark's teeth and his own fears.

Dances With Air told Fin Song many, many stories which could fill many pages, but none of these stories could sate Fin Song's curiosity for more than a moment.

"What do the octopi breathe?" asked Fin Song. "Do dolphins really get boiled? How does a male find a new pod? How are mates selected and baby porpoises made? What lies at the Bottom of The Great Depths?"

Dances With Air simply laughed, "These are all good questions; some I can answer and some I cannot. Octopi breathe water like fish, I myself found the corpse of a dolphin boiled fishing carelessly, no one knows the mysteries of love, and sex makes babies. And lastly, no one knows what lies at the bottom of the Great Depths."

Fin Song wasn't satisfied, and kept on asking questions. Dances With Air was delighted; most other young dolphins weren't particularly interested in what she had to teach.

After a few more years of Fin Song asking Dances With Air innumerable questions, he awoke one day and realized that he was no longer a child, but an adult male. He felt a desire to mate with females, and with that knowledge he knew that it was time for him to leave the Pod as all male Neptunian dolphins must.

He made his farewells to his mother and Dances with Air after he had a dream that suggested he swam south. With nothing more to go on, he began to swim towards the southern currents.

Out there alone in the open water he thought about how much he had learned; Dances With Air had taught him almost everything she knew, even the songs she was entrusted to keep. Still, Fin Song was curious. Neptune was such a big planet and there were so many mysteries, so many unanswered questions. While going south his echolocation alerted him of some floating nests of Neptunian Ducks, and he came to the surface to say hello.

"Greetings!" said Fin Song, who had always liked the ducks who lived near The Great Depths.

"Greetings...." said a none too pleased young duck mother.

"My apologies for disturbing you; I come from the pod of The Great Depths; and have just left to find a mate. Have you heard tale of any pods close by?"

"Ah," considered the young duck mother, looking at Fin Song pityingly; "yes, south by south west there is a great underwater mountain range that reaches above the water's surface. Around there is another pod."

"Thank you kindly!" said Fin Song.

"Good luck!" quacked the duck.

Fin Song swam south by south west as he had been told, sleeping little, catching few fish. The greatest danger to solitary dolphins are sharks, and he hoped to make a speedy transit. Unfortunately, on his third day away from home, his sonar picked up a shark in the distance.

"Maybe it won't notice me," he hoped to himself. His hopes were misplaced; almost immediately the shark came towards him. "Oh no!" said Fin Song to himself; "this is bad!" He felt himself beginning to panic. Then he remembered the story Dances With Air told him of the three dolphin brothers. Dances With Air had told Fin Song that "the worst thing you can do is try to evade a shark. Instead you must go right for their snout. You must face their teeth. Bite their snout, and then they will recoil; in that moment you can bite a fin and make your getaway."

As the shark came closer Fin Song prepared himself. The shark made its straight-line attack and Fin Song watched the terrible teeth grow closer and closer, and then in the last moment, he faced the teeth and grabbed the snout with his teeth, biting as he rotated his body upwards, so he was almost riding on the shark's back. Before the shark could turn over, he bit down, hard, on the shark's fin tearing it off.

"Now," he thought, "I must leave rapidly; the blood will lure every shark around into a feeding frenzy." Fin Song departed fast as he could, and didn't look back once to see the shark he had encountered. He saw no more sharks on this trip.

A week later he found the pod that the friendly duck had told him of. He was welcomed happily, and he found no shortage of females eager to mate with him. They were delighted to have such a large and intelligent male to play with. He found there a songmaster named Little Current, and he asked her all the questions he could think of, and she answered them all and taught him almost all of the songs of that pod.

Still though he was not satisfied. He decided that he would

go down and meet the octopi. For an hour he swam down to a trench that Little Current had told him of, and where there was rumor of an old octopus. His sonar told him that there was a great cephlapod at the very bottom.

"Hello!" said Fin Song,

"Hello dolphin," said the octopus quietly, "you come to eat me?"

"No octopus, I come to ask you question! I am named Fin Song and I am curious about everything!"

The octopus took this in for a long moment. "My name is unpronounceable to you; you may call me 'octopus'. What do you wish to know?"

"Everything!" said Fin Song excitedly; "do you have friends? How do you mate? Do you live with other octopi? What do you eat? What are your stories?"

Octopus chuckled, "Some of those questions are easy, others are hard; octopi are solitary creatures, we are mostly intent on our own experiences. We mate very, very carefully because doing so kills the male immediately and the female after she gives birth. We live alone. Mostly we use our beaks to eat mollusks. Our stories…each of our tentacles has a story, and it is through these stories that we are able to move about without getting tangled up in ourselves. It takes a long time to explain to a *tchkat*."

"What is a *tchkat*?"

"Someone who isn't an octopus," replied Octopus.

"Your answers just make me more curious, and now I have even more things I want to ask you!" cried Fin Song, "But first I must return to breathe! May I return to ask more questions upon my return?"

"Well, if you promise not to eat me and I am still here you may, yes," said Octopus grudgingly.

Fin Song raced back up to the surface feeling sick for want of air. He got up to the surface and filled his lungs with oxygen.

"This is great!" he thought to himself gasping, "Octopus

is telling me so many interesting things, but every question he answers leads to five new questions. I must return promptly and ask him more and more!"

And so Fin Song returned to Octopus for many years, asking him many, many questions and learning very much. One day however Octopus looked at him oddly;

"Well Fin Song, this will be the last time you see me." He said strangely.

"Why is that Octopus?" asked Fin Song alarmed.

"Later tonight I shall mate and then die." Said Octopus

"Are you scared?" asked Fin Song.

"Yes and no," said Octopus; "sometimes one is driven to do crazy things. And every tentacle yearns to mate, so I know what I must do. But then again I am frightened by death as all living things are."

"What do you think happens when you die?" asked Fin Song unnerved; he had never thought much about death.

"Well there is a legend that our spirits find their way to The Great Depths," said Octopus agitated.

"Is that true?" asked Fin Song

"It is impossible to know, but I must be going; I sense my mate approaching," said Octopus, beginning to swim away.

"Farewell!" said Fin Song disturbed.

"Farewell," said Octopus in his small odd voice. Floating there alone now, Fin Song found himself very short of breath and raced up to the surface, growing light-headed. "I stayed too long!" he thought. "I must learn to ask fewer questions! I must be more careful." Blackness began to ring his vision, and he wondered, "Am I too going to die?" But just as these melancholy thoughts came in he reached the surface and gasped for air. "That was too close," he thought, "I really truly must be more careful."

Not long afterwards Fin Song left the pod and went travelling. He travelled for many long years alone, daring the sharks, and asking many more questions. After a time, he began to struggle to come up with new lines of inquiry. He realized to his dismay, that he wasn't interested in every single tiny detail, but more in the general sweep of things. He swam with many pods and learned many songs, and finally came to a point where only one question was left burning in his mind.

"What is at the bottom of The Great Depths?" he wondered.

Now there are different types of questions; there are some questions which are their own answers and some which can only lead to more questions. All of Fin Song's lines of questioning had come to their natural conclusion with satisfactory answers. That is, all except the mystery of what lies at the bottom of The Great Depths. So now as an old dolphin Fin Song returned to the pod by The Great Depths.

To his surprise Dances With Air was still alive although very, very ancient. She had with her several students who were learning her songs.

"Now," she said to Fin Song, "after asking me so many questions you must let me ask you my own!"

"That is fair," Fin Song conceded, not accustomed to others being curious about what he knew.

And she asked him every question she could think, and he ended up telling her and her two young females students everything he could remember: all the stories, all the songs, all the experiences. Everything.

And afterwards he felt clean and radiant. "Now," he said, "I go to The Great Depths to find the answer to my very last question!"

Before Dances With Air or her two students could voice a concern or say farewell, he departed rapidly towards The Great Depths.

Fin Song's story is preserved by this lineage and is still shared with young Neptunian porpoises to this day, many many tides later. No one knows what he found in The Great Depths, but we do know two things: the first is that we found his body, lungs filled with water two days later, and the second that there was one question that he never asked; *"who am I?"*

Augustus Keden writes of himself: "I am currently writing a series of inter-related stories based on the oral narratives of the lives of real people of various ages spanning the years 1880 to the present. The narrations are his-story, her-story, not history. The narrators are Irish, English, Scottish, Canadian, French Canadian, German, American, Polish, Mexican, Peruvian, Guyanese, Punjabi, Trinidadian, Jamaican, Barbadian, Nicaraguan, Costa Rican, Ghanian and Nigerian. I am currently living with my wife, a black American woman, in a small apartment on the side of a cliff overlooking the Atlantic, just off the coast of Africa."

From the archaic language of fable to the stream-of-consciousness style made famous by the Beats may seem like a drastic jump, but the Old Solar System has room for both. In "The Dorian Grays," Keden presents an avant-garde vision of a utopia gone sour...

THE DORIAN GRAYS

Augustus Keden

THIS IS A report for anyone who cares or is interested. For your public edification. If you don't care or are not interested then this is not for you.

The Substance and What Really Happened on the *Dorian Gray*

WE WERE HEADING to Pluto, on a 7-year mission to obtain the Substance, in our ship named the *Dorian Gray*.

There were ten of us onboard, 5 males, 5 females: We thought of ourselves as Gods looking forward to a grand future.

Of my crew members I don't want to say much—we are still being hunted. In order to protect their identities I am not providing real names or identifying characteristics. I have given them instead the names of Greek gods and goddesses.

We had already passed Mars, Saturn, Jupiter, and were rocketing at 40,000 miles per hour, past Uranus, towards Neptune, half way to Pluto, when a wrench slipped out of my hand.

I was in the external non-grav engineering area checking, making minor adjustments, mainly because I was bored – the trip to Pluto was 3 nothing-to-do years long.

The wrench floated away, and I launched myself after it. I caught it in my right hand, and crashed with a horrible clanking sound into the return fuel tank. It sounded empty. That both terrified and excited me.

The Age of Utopia

WE HAD SET out on the Mission to Pluto because we hated the age we lived in, the so-called Age of Utopia.

In this "Age of Utopia", Science had come up with a way to allow everyone, through "Better Science",the ability to live to 300 years of age.World hunger, and the problems of shelter and physical resources had also been solved. There was now, so they proclaimed, enough of everything, enough food, enough clothing, enough shelter, enough everything, for everybody.

And to many, in the beginning, the Age of Utopia seemed to live up to its promise.

But then, slowly, people began growing older and older and older.

For the young amongst us, it was terrifying. There were decrepit people everywhere. We began calling them Fossils, Relics, Dinos, Saurs, and Zombies.

For the most part they still moved. But they were growing slower and slower. Stores, streets, everything was reconfigured to accommodate them. And it was just so annoying. They seemed to move in slow slow motion. I swear some of them took half an hour to cross the street.

Most of the Dinos had computers or machines that controlled everything for them, either by voice or buttons. But some Fossils were so incapacitated they had brain connection surgery. Once these Fossils were all hooked up they could mentally control their surroundings: Viewscreen on, Viewscreen off, music on/volume up/volume down, music off, vacuum cleaner run, vacuum cleaner stop.

Cooking was harder. Most of these Decrepits never even bothered. Food was delivered every day. Remote control, and subscription orders for everything. Door open, food delivered, door closed. Food eaten, food not eaten, food taken away, door locked.

But there were others, Saurs who zoomed about in pods,- pods that could become a bed, a chair, an outside slow-slow-speed transport vehicle. These were especially irritating, so many buzzing, slow moving crawling insects everywhere.

Then they would stop.

Escape From Decrepitude

WE HAD LEFT earth to get away from them, to live life—when we returned to earth, on more grandiose terms.

I had been angry that there was no life worth living, nothing worthy left for me to do, that I was not required, that I was unnecessary, superfluous. And I had wanted to retaliate against my parents and society for this. I wanted to get even. And this was not just a characteristic of me, it turned out to be a characteristic of almost everyone on board.

The Zombies

MOST OF THE Zombies could still walk. But barely. Waiting for one of them to make a purchase was unbearable. Watching them, creep, crawl down the street was horrifying. Just like watching giant Bugs. All I really wanted to do was squish them.

I decided, as many others decided, I did not want to live a Petrified Life, to become 300 years decrepit. But the horror was, what could I do about it? I was trapped in my body and eventually I was going to become what I abhorred—prehistoric.

I would rather stay physically young and live a shorter life then die, than grow old like this. But short of suicide, that seemed impossible.

Then, miraculously, a Substance was found. A Substance that could enable me, and any young person who took it, to live 100 years young.

The Fuel Tanks

THERE WERE FIVE fuel tanks. I checked them over and over again and again. The Instrumentation showed two of them full, two of them empty and one ¾ full. But when I tapped on the tanks with my wrench it sounded to me like four tanks empty and one almost full. I decided to use an old-fashioned pressure gauge to test them.

The Substance

THE SUBSTANCE HAD seemed to be the miracle I was dreaming of.

I was overjoyed. At last, finally here was an alternative I could really live with. I could actually remain physically young till I was 125—current age plus 100—instead of being an ancient decrepit 300.

At least that is what they seemed to promise us, at first. But, when the Substance was finally made available, the price was one million Allocations.

One million Allocations! I lived on one Allocation per year.Neither I nor any of my friends could ever afford that.

I sunk into a sort of despair.It seemed once again I was doomed to become a horrifying repulsive living relic. I felt absolutely betrayed.

"One million Allocations! How impossible. No one could afford. Except the rich!"

I was going to be physically trapped in my rapidly deteriorating body with nothing to look forward to but a very, very long life, of physical deterioration. I was outraged. I didn't want this. I didn't ask to be born. The conditions of this Utopia existence were unbearable.

"What kind of screw up?"

"Only the rich!"

The presence of the young rich was already an insult to my existence. Now I saw the privileged young, the privileged rich indulgently buying all the Substance for themselves—while I grew old. This was demeaning, unjust and a worse than inhumane state, which incited rebellion in many of us.

Even after the Substance was discovered, we now found there remained no hope for us. And then suddenly they began to present options. In retrospect I believe that was the point. Wasn't it?

Substance was suddenly being offered as a premium for "Extraordinary Employment".

There had always been employment opportunities which offered "Extra Allocations" for mining on our Solar System's planets. But the Substance was never part of the package.

And they had to offer more than extra Allocations, for me to risk my life and my youth to mine rubies, gold, emeralds, and other so-called "exotic substances" I did not care about, on Mars, Venus and Jupiter. In Utopia I could live risk free without working ever.

It was boring and I wanted more. But they certainly had to offer more than "a little extra" to get me to go to those godforsaken planets. Even though my current life was meager I was not going to risk it for a little extra food, shelter and clothing.

And even though I considered my life a rat's life—our shelters were bunk beds in large rooms, our food cafeteria buffet tasteless, our clothing shapeless and uniform, it was still better than pain, discomfort and death on a remote planet.

Within the limitations of my poverty, I could still live as I wished. I could still get drunk. I could still have fun. I still had time for myself. The problem was, there was so much more I would like to do, that I could not. I did not want to live my life on earth or any other planet, growing older and older and older, as a disintegrating human fossil in a rat hole.

I felt trapped in a nightmare, condemned. I could not even

escape. Not even by rashly, recklessly, irresponsibly trying to gamble, spend, sell or trade my Allocation away.

My Allocation was guaranteed exclusively to me forever by birth. By birth I would have enough food and shelter to live as an antiquity for 300 years, even if I didn't want to.

But if I ever wanted more, if I ever hoped to live as a human being, fulfilled, God-like—or have and earn the one million Allocations necessary to stay young—I needed to do something fast—before I became one of the living dead.

We called it "Danger Pay!"

The Opportunities

BEFORE I WAS born no one had ever visited Pluto. It was deemed too far to go, for too little profit.

There were already mining missions to Mars, Jupiter, Venus, Neptune and Uranus that were very profitable. These enriched the companies that launched them, and provided young people like myself the opportunity to accrue extra Allocations! Many of my friends had volunteered for them. I never volunteered because the "extra Allocations" offered never seemed equal to the risk of my life and body, and my young years wasted.

But then the government sent the first mission to Pluto. No one knows why. And miraculously the Substance was discovered there.

Suddenly there was intense interest in mining Pluto.

"The Intergalactic Consortium of Profiteers" was created—to finance the mining of the Substance.

Of all the extraterrestrial mining opportunities, Pluto quickly became the most sought after, even in spite of the fact that, of all the opportunities, the Pluto mission was by far the longest, most difficult, unpleasant and dangerous.

But to me and most of the young, that didn't matter. They were going to pay us in Substance: 1000 doses per crew member.

As you may recall: One dose of Substance sells for one million Allocations. With 1000 doses we could stay "Young and Rich"!

The chance to remain young and become instantly rich was overwhelmingly alluring and enticing, and suddenly very possible!

But only if I could obtain a position.

And obtaining a position on a Pluto mission was extremely competitive.

Empty Tanks

ONCE I WAS convinced every single tank but one seemed empty, I took off the cover of the instrument control panel to discover why they weren't working correctly. There, hidden behind the launch control panel, were explosives! They were set to detonate—after we had completed our mining, after we launched the advance Substance rocket homeward. They were set to detonate, when we began our own Pluto take off. This was not an accident. I urgently needed to gather everyone for an immediate emergency meeting.

The World Before Utopia

IN THE DAYS, before I was born, before Utopia became a fully implemented Reality, there had been many concerns, that were the wrong concerns.

World leaders had worried, "If everyone lives to 300 and keeps having children the world will soon be overpopulated."

The people worried, "There will not be enough food."

Others prophesied, "War and hostilities will break out."

These things did not happen. Once people began to realize they could live to be 300 they stopped having children.

Why? No one knew.

It also happened that old people were no longer interested in starting wars. Perhaps because they were the only ones left to fight. Dinos and Zombies had become the majority, and everyone, even the few young, were dependent on the government for their allotment of food and shelter.

But in the years that followed the new young such as myself that were born, did not want to listen to, or be at all like the old relics surrounding us. We wanted to be one of the "rich young." Even though we despised and hated the ones we saw and actually met, we wanted to be rich like them.

There were mortifying antiques wandering around us everywhere.

Tanks Without Fuel

We were rocketing past Uranus to Pluto to mine the Substance without enough fuel to return home. This was terrifying.

I pushed the Emergency button to alarm and arouse everyone, for an emergency meeting.

"What the hell?" Ares said.

"What's this about?" Atlas asked.

"What do you want?" Athena said.

"Why'd you call a meeting?" Zeus asked.

"We're in trouble."

"What do you mean?" Iris said.

"What're you saying?" Rhea asked.

"We don't have enough fuel."

"We don't have enough fuel for what?" Ares said.

"We don't have enough fuel to get back.

"What the hell do you mean? Of course there's enough fuel, three tanks to get there, two to get back," Ares said. (Pluto's lower gravity meant we only needed two tanks to return).

"The two are empty."

"What do you mean the two are empty?" Rhea asked.

"The two tanks we need for our return are empty. There's not enough fuel to get back."

"Are you sure?" Aphrodite asked.

"It can't be," Selene said.

"You must be wrong!" Iris said.

Our crew was contentious. In most ways we were as different as can be and often disagreed. We had different interests, different personalities, and yet we had a commonality, we had wanted the Substance because we did not fit in with our current society, and now we were worried about getting home.

Selfish Dinosaurs

THE SILLY, SELFISH Dinosaurs growing older and older, and older—unable to do much of anything for themselves, grew to hate young people. They denounced them at every opportunity, in their media, their institutions and on public occasions.

They, who could no longer have children, even if they wanted them, now loudly began to proclaim:

"We're glad we didn't have children. We wish there were none at all."

"Why do they exist?"

"They contribute nothing."

"They're noisy, and annoying."

"We don't like them around."

"Why should they share in Utopia when they had nothing to do with its creation?"

But perhaps the main reason the old complained about us was, they didn't like to be reminded of what they had lost, to see what they had once been, contrasted with what they had become. And because they could not become young again, or remain so as we might, they hated the very existence and sight of young people—or so it seemed to me.

And young people like me, we hated the old in return. We didn't ever want to turn into them!

We were appalled by the plague of decrepit antique zombies all around us.

You Must Be Wrong

"You must be wrong," Athena said.

"I thought was wrong too. I was sure I was, but I've checked and rechecked and rechecked. I'm not wrong. There's not enough fuel to get back."

"There must be," Selene said.

"You made a mistake!" Ares added.

"It must be some kind of mistake," said Athena

"Some kind of miscalculation somewhere," Atlas said.

"That's what I thought. At first."

"What are you saying? What do you mean?" Athena asked.

"Are you saying, it's not an accident?" Ares asked.

"Not at all."

"What the hell are you talking about, it is or it isn't an accident?" Ares asked.

"It's not an accident at all."

"How do you know? What do you mean?" Atlas asked.

"What are you saying? Do you know?" Athena asked.

"Why don't you just say what the hell you mean?" Ares asked

"The ship is wired to explode."

"Wired to explode?" Ares said.

Dinos

BUT EVENTUALLY SOME of the Dinos realized and proclaimed the obvious fact, that even with enough food, enough shelter, enough resources for everybody, there were some things, machines, androids and robots could not do.

One of these was—bear children.

"Without children humanity is going down the toilet bowl," one of our leaders stated.

The government launched pregnancy incentives. Advertisements were created that went something like this: "Have a child, save the race."

Athena had responded, "I didn't know we were running."

The ads and the incentives did not succeed. It was far too easy to prevent pregnancy and most young women were disinclined to have children.

"We don't want to waste our youth having kids." Rhea had said. "And furthermore, why would I ever want to bring a child into this world?"

By the time I was born most people were simply too old to give birth—even if they wanted. My parents were condescended towards and considered atavists, or throwbacks. And I and the others of my age that were born, as well as those older than our parents, were not grateful for our birth.

Most of the young who were born, like myself, came from what was called, "The pairing of dysfunctional, disturbed, reject adults with one another."

And we the children, born of these "rejects" were often ashamed of being their progeny and determined we were not going to become either our parents or the Dinos. And we certainly never wanted to bring a life into this perverted world.

Without any aspirations other than preventing new life, we committed to simply, hedonistically, enjoying all the life we could.

We wanted to live a life that was extravagant.

Our schooling was complicit and had been fundamental towards this self-centered viewpoint. The curriculum had been created in the day when it was thought children were a detriment, and it had never been updated since. This schooling indoctrinated us to believe—for profit purposes—that extravagant living was the only real aspiration, the only possible goal in modern life.

We had for the most part come to accept and share this world view.

Most of us hated and resented our parents for having us. We didn't want to be born. We didn't want to live in a world of relics. But since we had no choice and life itself seemed a pointless Jurassic adventure, we wanted to party and live a life as grand, extraordinary, indulgent and luxurious as we possibly could.

In an ordinary life there are only twenty or thirty youngish adult years. None of us was going to waste them raising kids. We had long ago realized 100, 200 300 years old decrepit was coming. And that eternity seemed forever.

We were already surrounded by parents, grandparents, great-great-grandparents, who had already lived to be far more ancient than we ever wanted. There seemed no end to the old relatives. The appalling, nightmarish tragedy of it just kept escalating and escalating.

To even think of it, of the immensity of it all, sickened me, and most of the young I knew shared my loathing.

And then there was the discovery of the Substance.

You're Crazy

"You're crazy," Ares said.

"What the hell?" Atlas said.

"You're a real a-hole," Ares added.

"What would be the point of that?" Selene asked.

"What is the point of this whole mission if they just blow us up?" Athena said.

"It's a big waste of Allocations. It doesn't make any sense at all." Apollo said.

"They wouldn't do that. They want the Substance. It'll make them rich," Rhea said.

"But we'll be dead," Hermes said.

"What the hell are you talking about? Would you just say what you mean instead of getting all dramatic and dragging it out?" Ares said

"The ship is rigged to blow as soon as we've finished mining."

"You don't know what you're talking about," Ares said

"You don't know what you're doing," Athena said.

"Why would they do that?" Iris asked
"Check for yourself."

Before Utopia

THE ORIGINAL DOCTRINE of Utopia theology had stated, "Science can provide enough for everyone, but science cannot provide more than enough, without destroying the planet."

This seemed honest and straightforward enough.

But every day I saw some young rich person racing around in a new car, dressed in new stylish clothes, dining in an expensive upscale restaurant, presumably living in a luxury home, apartment or possibly even a mansion.

The Utopia doctrine had neglected to mention, "There can be more than enough for some."

But who? It seemed it all come all came down to a question of Allocations—who gets what. And who decided?

The rich, the powerful, the connected were being given, were allowed to have much, much more. Just not us!

This was more than unfair and unjust.

I and most of the young I knew, didn't know, and couldn't care less, what science considered possible. We wanted more for us. And we were exasperated and tired of the meagerness and meaninglessness of our current existence. The knowledge of the privileged extravagance of others only exacerbated this. We had a greed and hunger to possess everything we could.

"That's not possible," the authorities said.

But it was clear to us it was possible for some!

We called this unjust.

But we really didn't care about equality or justice. We just wanted more for ourselves.

Why Blow Up the Ship?

"WHY?" IRIS ASKED.

"Why would they do that?" Apollo asked.

"As soon as we've got all the Substance," Rhea said.

"And then they just blow us up. What good is that? What does that do them?" Ares said.

"The Substance doesn't come with us."

"What?" Ares said.

"We put the substance in a smaller rocket and send it back as soon as we've finished mining. They told us that's because it's faster, speedier like that, isn't that what we were told?"

"What're you saying?" Athena asked.

"As soon as we send the smaller rocket, as soon as it blasts off, our ship is wired to blow. We never go back."

"That still doesn't explain anything," Athena said.

"Why would they do that?" Aphrodite asked.

"Because when you have to pay 10,000 Doses to your ten volunteers it is cheaper to just send new people and a new rocket."

"That can't be true," Apollo said.

"No one's that cold and callous," Iris added.

"Wait a minute. Wait a minute. It all makes sense," Zeus said.

Disparity

It had seemed to us the very laws of our lives, our existence had been passed to maintain the privileged few, while disenfranchising the majority of us. In fact it began to seem that the daily allocation was created to serve and maintain the status quo disparities and barriers of privilege.

For our entire lives they had been indoctrinating and telling us, "Distribution is fair and equitable, just and reasonable" —when it was nothing of the sort.

I had a fantasy of the arrangement they called "Fair, Equitable, Just and Reasonable."

Justice, Self-Interest, Greed and Power each sat on one side of a square table. Each had equal power. Justice realized she was never going to win, it was three against one.

Justice, heard them say, "Keep your mouth shut. And we'll cut you in."

They were always selling us one thing and giving us another. Some very old traditions of corruption, abuse, and manipulation of privilege, and power never disappear.

Show and Tell

ZEUS SAID, "SHOW us."

I led the crew down to the engineering department. Zeus was in charge. I showed him the instrument panel, where everything appeared normal. And then I gave him the test gauge and instructed him to test the tanks for himself. Four were empty.

And as we all saw this, a deep sigh of terror was released.
Zeus said, "This is no accident."
"And here are the explosives," I said.
Selene said, "We're all going to die in space!"

Mining

THERE ARE NINE different planets in our solar system and each of them has something some company, or some group of individuals wants.

Although many of the Zombies didn't want us, the companies needed young people to do their mining. But most of the mining companies were stingy—trying to get workers for as little as possible.

My shipmates and I had never been willing to settle for what they offered. After the Substance was discovered the mining companies improved their offers.

"One dose of Substance, plus extra Allocations for mining on Jupiter, or Mars."

I immediately applied because now they were giving me something I wanted. But I was rejected.

In their rejection message it said, "We regret you do not have the skills we currently require."

This irked me. I was determined to acquire the Substance if it was the last thing I ever did. I began looking at "Improvement." Improvement was what had once been called education. People who learned a new skill were called "Improvers". Most of us had already "Improved" several times, in the hope of obtaining more Allocations in our current lives. But to date "Improving" hadn't brought us much.

Mostly we thought "Improvement" was a con. But if that was what was required to become a member of a crew offering Substance we were willing to "Improve". We certainly did not want to become Zombies.

From the time of my birth I had been told "You will have enough!" But there had never been enough! One Allocation was not enough to LIVE! And lately it was becoming less and less. I was not content to settle, to be the same or worse than my parents; I wanted to be better than them.

From my perspective "One Allocation" was scarcely enough to survive!

I did not want to be guaranteed crappy food and a rat hole shelter for my entire 300-year life. I did not want to live like that! I did not want to be a 300-year-old destitute Antique. As if all that anyone ever wanted was to stay alive, no matter what the cost or condition.

For so many years, I had watched, and our society had fed me shows, and movies on the viewscreens of "People Having More."

I wanted that!

Promotions and advertisements began to appear.

"Go to Pluto. Earn the Substance. You need skills. We don't take just anyone."

I enlisted as an Improver, hoping to learn the necessary skills for the Pluto missions—as had the rest of my crew members.

Zeus Decides

Zeus re-checked and measured the amount of fuel in the tanks over and over. Apollo and Ares copied and repeated his actions for themselves.

Zeus then said, "Let's go back to the deck."

Zeus was not only our captain, he was the rocket scientist. On the bridge he announced, "There's enough fuel to make it back to earth if we turn back now. We'll have to decide. We can boomerang, if we calculate carefully, and keep our current momentum."

There was a sigh and a cheer of relief.

"But the first thing we have to do is disconnect the explosives. Then we'll have to check the entire ship from top to bottom to ensure there are no hidden secondary explosive devices.

"After we talk to earth, we'll need to disconnect our radios and block all radio transmissions.

"We have two years to do this, two years to prepare, and think about what we're going to do upon our return, how we're going to land."

In those 2 years we all thought about it, and talked about it a lot. And I thought and thought about how I had come to this.

More or Less Equality

At the onset of Utopia we had been promised equality. But the so-called equality they talked about delivered only barely enough. All my crewmates and I had grown dissatisfied. We wanted more.

We wanted what we saw in our films and entertainments. We wanted the things we saw the more privileged possessed and we could never afford. For our whole lives we had been thinking, "Why can't I have that?"

Most of the young, like myself had grown up wanting.

And they used that.

The government, the consortiums, the partnerships, the companies, those who controlled assets, property and production, the rich and the powerful, used entertainments and commercials to get us to want, so we would do their mining missions.

"Don't be a Dinosaur!" the commercial said. "Get more out of Life."

"You need Improving."

And we had begun taking Improvement courses.

After a while, I began to feel bombarded:

"You're getting older and older."

"Time is running out."

"Do you want to be 80, 100 or 300 years decrepit?"

"Soon you too will be a fossil."

"Your clock is running. You better move it before you're too late."

"Don't be slow."

"Do you want to be decrepit forever?"

"Don't be a Dinosaur."

I was disgusted with these commercials. But they were working on me.

"Your insides keep going, and going, but your body becomes decrepit, like a watch that won't stop, but no longer keeps accurate time."

"Soon you will be a Fossil or a Dinosaur. Do you want to be a Dinosaur?"

"They look like rock, or an insect that moves, or a dried-up piece of wood."

Scared of the Old People

When I was a child I was scared of the old people. My parents repeatedly reassured me that it wasn't as bad as all that, that it didn't hurt, that my great, great, great, great, grandparents and aunts and uncles still relished their lives and wanted to live.

I certainly did not want to be like them.

"They're still vital inside," my mother said.

"Like a rusted-out car with a crappy motor," I said.

My parent's stories of the benefits and pleasures of growing old seemed incredible. I could not believe them even if I wanted.

As far as I knew no younger person wanted to go out with or be near the ancients.

Certainly no one wanted to have sex with them, or invite them to a party, or even eat dinner with them—it was just too creepy. Meeting them was like a horror movie.

Trade Offs

I HAD WANTED the Substance more than anything. But I had never considered there might be Trade Offs. In fact I really didn't give it any consideration at all, till after we were running out of fuel in space. After this discovery, the trip aborted, without much of anything at all to do but worry, I had time to research what I had got myself into. This trip had turned out to be the greatest waste of years of all.

In space, while researching, I learned these things:

The Substance has 3 major side effects, that I did not know about.

1) Once you start taking the Substance its effects are permanent. You can't change your mind, and decide you want to live to 300. You would remain young for 100 years from the time of first injection, and then you would die. In the beginning all it took was one injection dose.

2) Once you take the injection of the Substance you forever physically and mentally remain the age you were when you first began taking it, until the day you died 100 years later.

From the literature: "The user will never mature one day older. They will not really learn one new thing. When the clock turns 100, the carriage turns into a shriveled mess of a pumpkin. The user collapses and suddenly becomes physically very

very old, then violently dies." That's what the literature said.

3) You can no longer have children.

Theoretically, if a pragmatic young person had known this, they could plan ahead and have children before they took the Substance—if they knew. Then they could stay young with their children while they grew.

I had never seen or met anyone who had actually done this. But after our aborted mission it was offered as a possibility by the Substance marketers, after the Substance "infertility issue" was exposed by us.

Remaining the same age forever had seemed wonderful.. But as Ares now said, "It is the opposite of senility, it is Arrested Development."

How Will We Live

"But how will we live?" asked Aphrodite?

"They'll shoot us as soon as we land," Ares said.

"They won't even wait for that, they'll blast us out of space," Atlas said.

"They'll call us traitors,' Athena added.

"They'll cancel our Allocations," Iris said

"We'll be worse off than we ever were," Selene said.

"Let's hijack the returning Pluto Substance rocket," I said.

Reckless Youth

Before the mission I and the other members of our crew had not really bothered to consider the possible dangers and consequences of our desires. I wanted to stay young forever, my crewmates wanted to stay young too.

I was not thinking of having kids. I was willing to fly their mission because I wanted youth. And the Substance was too expensive, I could never afford it.

But that was the marketing principle. They needed young

people to mine. And they needed us to be unhappy and dissatisfied enough, in order to be willing to do it.

We were eager to stay young.

As I researched more I discovered there had been always been questions and rumors.

There were even rich, powerful people who had complained, "Our grandchildren are getting stupider and stupider. If they can't learn from their mistakes, they'll repeat them forever!"

But these complaints had never made it to my awareness, or that of my crewmates. And while we were still on Earth new Sales Promotions kept being promoted.

"Go to Pluto and Stay Young."

Steal the Substance

"We couldn't do that," Selene said.

"We can't steal the Substance rocket," Ares said.

"Then they'll kill us for sure," Atlas said.

'They'll shoot us out of the sky," Iris added.

"They'll arrest us when we land," Athena said.

Zeus said, "That might be the only thing that'll save us."

The Investors' Promotions

We were not the only ones the Consortium marketed to: There were also the investors.

"Going to Pluto, mining the Substance, is dangerous and expensive! But it also provides opportunity for great profit. Ten million doses per successful mission. A million Allocations per dose. Members of The Intergalactic Consortium of Profiteers will share in the earning of ten trillion Allocations from every mission. The risk is worth the profit.

"The crew are volunteers, working only for Substance. We don't pay them. They receive Substance after they return. This ensures they put their hearts into it."

Volunteers

ON THE FIRST mission the volunteers had no idea what was going to happen. In their boot camp they were told: "There is a good chance you'll never return. You might die or be injured in space or on Pluto. It is three years space-travel to reach Pluto. three years to come back. A year of mining. A lot of things can go wrong."

By the time we went all they said was, "If you succeed you will instantly be elevated to the richest, highest Allocation orbit."

After the first two successful missions the Consortium sought Profits faster.

It took 7-10 years for each mission to return with the Substance. Consortium Scientists determined the Substance could be obtained quicker if it was sent ahead in a smaller, super high speed advance rocket, before the crew's return. This became standard operating practice.

The Consortium scientists also devised a new methodology called Fractionalization. The commercials said:

"Introducing a one-a-day pill."

Privately company executives sent each other memos which said, "In effect these allow enslavement, as well as enrichment."

Until this point one Substance injection lasted a hundred years and was all that was necessary. Now the consumer became dependent on the Consortium for their daily dosage.

"The One a Day Pill," the Consortium advertisements stated, "has many advantages.

"It allows users to live 110 years, and at the end of their lives, when they do "depart" they do not crash. They have time to retire to their homes. Instead of dying in a matter of hours – on the streets…

"They have weeks, even a month to say their goodbyes to their loved ones—and put their affairs in order."

But the main unstated advantage was: Buyers bought their

entire one-a-day, 100 years' allotment of Substance for full price at time of purchase—even though each buyer received only one year's Allocation.

They were told: "Full 100 years payment at time of purchase is necessary to ensure your dosage allotment is reserved! You don't want to die because you can't afford the next year's dosage."

"You and we need to have the confidence to know your full 100-year allotment is paid for and secured in advance!"

"For your security, we parcel your Substance into 100 yearly allotments. You receive one year's allotment at time of purchase."

"We keep your remaining 99 years of your Substance reserved, and secured in our inventory vaults, for your protection."

"No need to worry! You can't lose, misplace or abuse your Substance."

"Having your entire 100-year supply of Substance in your own home would be an invitation to robbery. Your Substance is safe with us."

All this sounded eminently reasonable in the advertisements. But then in my 2-year long return research I discovered the main reason for the Fractionalization was that it allowed the company to immediately sell each person's remaining 99 years of dosage allotments to 99 other persons.

Internally the Consortium justified this: "By the time the next year comes another mining ship will have returned with new Substance."

"Fresh Substance is better than Old."

Mining to get more: in other words, greed

By the time I and my crew set out there had been four previous missions.

We were told each of the members of the previous crews had become so rich upon their return, they found it necessary to change their names, their identities, and go into hiding from greedy, envious friends, acquaintances and relatives.

This sounded okay to me. I was looking forward to putting deadbeat friends and dinosaur relatives behind me.

The Mission

THEY GAVE US blasters, 5 one-ounce gold bars, and World Fair type celebrations for our departure. They told us: "You're special. The Intergalactic Consortium does not pick just anyone."

"Every effort will be made to prepare for and ensure your safe return, re-entry and landing—but there is always a possibility some things might go wrong, and we prepare you, for every possibility.

"There is a self-inflating raft, in case you land in water; 5 one-ounce gold bars are provided, in case you land in or near a Third World country that only takes cash, clothing for every environment, a med kit for accidents and injuries. We have prepared you for every eventuality.

"We are working to ensure that you are safe and secure, and we are looking out for you, in every possible situation!"

It was very reassuring that they were so concerned and meticulous.

It wasn't till we were stranded in space that I considered reassurance and gaining trust is a necessary part of any good confidence game. We were certainly unaware they intended, even before our departure from earth, to explode our ship. We were still so young!

Every one of my crew members was less than 30 years old with little real expeerience.

Although we did not know each other before the mission we each shared the belief, "This dangerous Pluto mission is probably my best and only chance to stay young, and obtain millions."

We had studied and trained hard, we had persevered. We believed we had endured and faced stiff competition in order to obtain our position as a Pluto crew member. And we felt entitled.

As we trained and prepared we were told over and over again, "You are one of the elite. You are a very important, special person. A one of a kind, unique and qualified individual who has earned the right and is privileged to be an elite Pluto mission crew member.

"We don't take just anybody. You must have the skills, the personalities and intelligence we need and want."

One of the unstated but necessary requirements was "Young, sexy and attractive."

"To entice future young miners. To ensure, there are always far more applicants than necessary," the in house private marketing literature stated.

Regardless of the Consortium's selection process motives, each and every one of us did have our own special skill set. Some of us really were rocket scientists. Another was a doctor, another a computer specialist.

As a young person I am no genius, but my particular skill set was that I can figure out almost anything. I have a way with machines, and electronic technology. I don't always have to know exactly how the electronic device, equipment or machinery works or even what it is for, but I can fix it. This was a very important skill set to have when you are millions of miles away from home.

Only the Substance is Important

NO MATTER WHAT skills we possessed, we were repeatedly told in Boot Camp, "You are Miners first and foremost. Mining the Substance is your only real priority, and responsibility."

Repeatedly we were told: "Only The substance is important!"

"The ship is not important. You are not important. Only the Substance matters."

"We're not sending you on a joy ride. You are miners of the Substance!Obtaining the substance is everything!"

Just before we had even left we began to hear there were

investors who complained, "Why do we have to give the miners a share? "We should use robots and androids. Then we wouldn't have to give them anything, ever."

This worried us greatly; we were afraid of losing our chance.

But the mission leaders of the Consortium reassured us and addressed the complainers. "In our previous missions to Pluto we found robots and androids were not up to the task. The mission requires more flexibility, sophistication and troubleshooting skills than even the most modern android or robot can provide.

"Pluto is a very unpredictable planet. It is far too cold for human or android to survive without sophisticated support. It would be a disaster to send a mission to Pluto where something went wrong and the androids or robots could not improvise to fix the problem."

It had been reassuring to hear the Consortium's answer, and the faith they put in us made us all feel quite special. But perhaps we did not realize the true reason. We were expendable, even cheaper than androids and robots. They had no intention of paying what they promised.

Our Mining Instructions

"THERE ARE TEN pods.

"You will each mine independently in your own autonomous pod. This will maximize your exploration and mining.

"Each pod has machinery that will crush, refine, purify, and concentrate the Substance, while you are exploring, mining and harvesting. Whenever a miner finds a good source you will all work together in the same location to maximize extraction. It is not a competition, you all share in the harvest. Each night your pod will park inside the spaceship just like in a giant garage. Everything that moves, everything that mines must be heated, insulated and kept warm inside the ship when it is not operating.

"Just as a car parked in a heated garage starts easier and runs better, our mining pods and all our equipment and people need to be kept inside the spacecraft. It will be your job to unload the Substance, inspect your pod and report any mechanical problems. At the end of each day you will have time to gather for socializing, nourishment and sleep.

But it never got to that.

I accidentally discovered there wasn't enough fuel to make the return trip.

Zeus said, "No. No, They won't! shoot us out of the sky. The Substance is the only thing they want, and the only insurance or guarantee we have.

"Without the Substance, they wouldn't even let us touch down. But with the Substance landing is almost guaranteed. They want the Substance more than anything."

We weren't sure if we believed what Zeus said, but it sounded reassuring.

"Guaranteed, until they put our asses in jail." Ares added.

"Which is why we have to blow the ship up," I said.

"You're crazy," Iris said

"No I'm not."

"Yes, you are," Rhea added.

"We should crash our rocket into a big city," Ares said. "That'd show them."

"No," Zeus replied, "I have a better idea. There are ten pods, each of them is meant to withstand Pluto. If we time it right we can blow the ship, hide the pods in the debris, escape, and land on earth."

"Wonderful plan!" Ares said.

Nevertheless, there was silence for a time as we pondered that. No one really wanted to proceed. No one wanted to commit. But without deciding we would die for certain.

"They'll hunt us mercilessly if we steal the Substance," Iris said.

"They'll hunt and kill us even if we don't," Zeus answered. "We've got two years to plan. We've got nothing to lose. We're dead if we do nothing. They meant for us to die on Pluto."

Some moments passed, then, "I'm in," Aphrodite said.

"I'm in," Atlas added.

A chorus of, "I'm in."

"Let's do it."

Knowing you may die, knowing you have two years to plan and prepare your escape, focuses your mind.

Contacted and Threatened by Earth

EARTH AND THE Intergalactic Consortium had ignored us even after we u-turned but immediately upon our seizure of the Substance Rocket we were contacted by Mission Control.

"Dorian Gray, why have you interfered with our returning Substance rocket? Why have you not continued on your mission to Pluto?"

"It's a suicide mission. There's not enough fuel to return. The rocket we're in is wired to blow up," Zeus answered.

They did not even bother to deny or argue.

"We'll never let you land. We'll blast you out of the sky as soon as we have you in our sights."

"That's the reason we intercepted the Substance." Zeus said. "It's our guarantee. It's the only thing you care about. Let us land safely, and we'll give you the Substance."

The Consortium replied, "You're criminals. We won't submit to blackmail and extortion. We can't give you want you want. What if you talk?"

Zeus said, "We won't talk. We'll sign a contract. Whatever you want. We just want to land safely on earth."

We came to an agreement, the Substance for our safety and the right to land, and they would give us our freedom and Allocations.

After that communication we disconnected our radios and blocked all further radio transmissions.

But the agreement was all for show. We didn't believe them. And they didn't believe or care about us. We were pretty certain we would be killed or disappeared as soon as we landed, as soon as they had the Substance.

But it was good to have an agreement and apparently let the matter slide. We had two years to refine our plans.

Our Strategy and Plans

WE HAD ALREADY agreed we would make it look like our pods were part of the debris when we blew our ship up on reentry.

"We need to land in third world countries," Zeus said, "the less developed parts of the world, where they lack the all-pervasive monitoring infrastructure.

"We each need to go to a different country. Brazil, Venezuela, Bolivia, Guyana, Peru, Chile, most of Africa, seem like good choices. We can't be near each other. We can't communicate. We can't be in the first world, or contact anyone we know, if we don't want to be tracked."

We each picked a country, an area, a destination, the exact location of which we kept to ourselves.

We came to various other agreements and created a sort of code, or set of rules, which we would try to live by.

"We can each take one tenth of the substance. That's one million doses each," we agreed.

"That's a lot," Rhea said.

"We can sell full individual injection doses on the black market to earn money to live. One injection lasts a hundred years."

"We have to be cautious about this. If we sell them for a thousand a piece, there are enough doses to earn each of us a billion. More than enough to provide security, keep us alive and survive."

"But quite likely it will be too dangerous to sell all of it."

"And there's always a danger of being caught or having the Substance stolen."

"Each of us should split up what they have into separate packages, and then hide them in different locations, in different countries for financial security."

"We should try not to sell large quantities at one time. It will draw too much attention."

"We should not live too large. We should try to live modestly."

"Each person has to make their own choices but it will probably be better if we do not use the Substance ourselves. It will allow us to grow older and wiser."

And lastly Zeus said, "We should have children, as many as we can. At least six, if possible. In this way we can begin to change the world through demographics, from the bottom up. We might even start a new movement."

That was the plan.

We Blow Up the Ship

WE BLEW UP the ship.

My pod rocketed through the sky into blackness, heading for the Caribbean. Aphrodite's right behind me, headed for the Pacific. I had chosen Nicaragua because I hoped it was backward and safe.

We had all suspected some would doubt our deaths. Some did. They began searching and hunting for us almost immediately.

When our ship exploded many people saw the explosion in the night sky. The Consortium could not pretend it did not happen.

But the passengers they identified as being on the ship were not us. The Consortium pretended it was the crew from the previous mission. The Mission before ours, the one that exploded on Pluto, and would never return.

Because we hijacked one of the Consortium's returning rockets and because we did not go to Pluto and mine, and because they had Fractionalized to sell more dosage Allotments faster, the Consortium began running out of Substance!

People began to die in their homes and on the streets. Especially, those people with some wealth, who were low on the power structure totem pole. They suddenly found they could not be resupplied with the next year's Allocation, at any price. The public began to see fast aging, one-hundred-years-in-a-day results.

It became a common occurrence that a young person would suddenly just shrivel up and die.

The Consortium intensified the hunt for us. Not only did they want us dead, they wanted our supply. Dead was simply a bonus.

There began to be cascading effects from the shortages. More very privileged died. The hunt for us became even more intense.

Once we landed most of us chose to grow older, as agreed. In reality to do otherwise in a poor country would be to attract too much attention.

"How are you staying young when you're not authorized?" would be the obvious question. Better to blend in, grow old and become wiser.

Most of the management of the various Consortiums that were hunting us had taken the Substance. They weren't getting any smarter. But some of the older managers and most of the hunters had not been exposed.

There were also freelance thieves, bounty hunters, and profiteers, trying to track us down for personal profit.

The Substance we possessed was worth a fortune. Many were willing to kill us and steal it all. Who would complain?

My Methodology

Following the debris, I had rocketed across the sky across the Caribbean.

I ditched my pod underwater in the Caribbean off Bluefield, Nicaragua. Then I rowed the self-inflating raft the Consortium provided, through the darkness to shore. I walked into Bluefield in darkness. In the morning I took the panga upriver to El Rama, and the bus to Managua. I didn't want to stay in Managua long, it was too big and too chaotic. I caught a bus to Granada, and stayed there.

Being on earth again, breathing the air, smelling the ocean, feeling the humidity and heat was wonderful, like escaping a prison. It felt like Heaven to be outside again, to be free, even if it was unbearably hot and humid.

Nicaragua still used local currency. There were hotels in Granada where I could stay for a very small amount of cash. I sold my camera in a pawn shop, near the bus station. The money got me a room but it wouldn't last long.

I needed a job. Fortunately, there were bars in Granada that hire gringos. I was able to talk my way into working in one of them. They didn't really pay me. I split some of the profit and tips.

I grew a beard, changed my hair style.

The gringo crowd in Granada was relatively small, always churning. There were tourists that stayed a week or two and longer-term semi residents. It was my goal to blend in and appear normal.

This worked for a time but I anticipated, working in a gringo bar was doomed to eventually grab attention. Therefore, I took a bus to Managua to cash a bar of gold, to prepare my exit and move to a larger more private residence. But even cashing the gold was worrisome and perilous.

I had never felt so alive, so exhilarated, as from the moment I discovered the fuel shortage, and then in Granada on the run.

One of the great advantages of Nicaragua was that streets do not have signposts. Residences do not have numbers. Occasionally a person would paint the name of their street on the corner of their house, but this naming was rare. This meant, if I kept my residence secret, there would be some difficulty in another gringo finding me.

And the police of Nicaragua were passive and reluctant to engage. They never asked for a passport or document. They seemed to avoid confrontation and generally seemed to ignore gringos.

My immediate problem was more long-term money. I had a fortune's worth of Substance but it was extremely dangerous to sell.

I did not believe anything is 100% anonymous or untraceable. Nevertheless, I placed small ads in certain foreign publications, to sell small quantities of the Substance for mailed anonymous "cash equivalents" to fake identities at foreign post offices.

The Consortium sold a full dose of the Substance for 1 million Allocations, but no one was going to pay me that through the mail. They didn't even know if what I had was real.

I was hoping someone would risk $1000 if they thought there was even a chance.

Anything less would be just too unbelievable. Anything more would make it just too hard to sell.

Ads were placed.

The specified cash equivalents arrived at various foreign mail boxes in various foreign cities in various countries, to various different names. I made pick-ups in person with false ID. Aphrodite, who was with me, came as my backup.

I picked up money. I mailed customers their dose of Substance.

I had happy customers.

The Explosion Will not Die

NEWS AND DISCUSSION of the explosion in the sky kept being repeated and reported in the news day after day, month after month. Officially authorities kept repeating everyone on board the ship was dead.

Even though those people, that they were reporting were dead, that crew was not us. And even though, officially, we were still on our way to Pluto—therefore, no one should be looking for us. They were.

It bothered me that the truth was totally covered up from the public while the Consortium kept their reputation—and knew the truth. Although we had all agreed to lay low and stay silent, to do so meant the Consortium would keep sending ships, and new crews would keep dying. I could not live with this.

I therefore leaked the truth.

My leak was officially dismissed by the Consortium as "The delusions and ravings of a nutcase, or a madman." But suddenly there were doubts. And no one knew for sure what was true.

Before my leak no one had ever suspected previous Intergalactic Consortium Mission ships might never have returned.

Once I leaked, the whole world was in a state of shock. And this led the Consortium to escalate the efforts to hunt us down.

The Consortium Begins to Crash

THE PROBLEMS FOR the Consortium kept multiplying. By fractionating they had sold far more doses than they could support. Their stockpile was quickly shrinking.

In our hijacking the returning Substance they had ultimately lost two shipments. The hijacked harvest and the one we would have mined. This made it easy for us to sell.

Buyers became desperate. "Miss a dose and die."

But desperation created problems. Our sales were noticed! They were closing in on us.

After my leaks there was panic and chaos. The Hunt became ever more intense. I saw Hunters come into the bar in Granada.

I gave notice at my job, and prepared to leave Nicaragua.

I hesitated because I didn't really want to go. No one knew who I was, or where I lived. I was six years older, with long hair and a beard. There were many gringos who looked more like I once had than I did.

More and more people all over the world kept dying.

The Consortium was having difficulty launching new missions, recruiting new volunteers. People were hesitant to volunteer for what might be a 7-year suicide mission. The Intergalactic Consortium went bankrupt.

More bounty hunters entered Granada. Something, perhaps my leak tipped them off. They seemed to be everywhere. Rumor had it, a few of us had been caught and killed, I blamed myself for it, but I preferred to believe and hope it was not true.

Panicked users were begging for new missions, that were not happening.

A New Consortium

A NEW GROUP, The Guaranteed Consortium stepped in. They took over the rockets and the production of the old company. The Guaranteed Consortium prepared to launch new missions. They made "Public Guarantees."

They took pictures of every departing crew member. They live interviewed each crew member before departure and took pictures of them with their friends and families. They promised to have interviews and videos and pictures of each crew member, with their families, upon their return.

In the future I learned, The Guaranteed Consortium kept their promise. In the future I could look back on this and think, we had accomplished at least one good thing. But it was 10 years before the first crew returned to prove it.

That was far too long for desperate substance users to wait for replenishment.

Young rich "kids" were turning old in seconds, all around the world. And across 10 years most of the original Substance users died.

Almost the only ones who survived bought our pirated Substance.

Dying young people shrank the market of new users. But there was always someone who wanted to stay young. Someone who was willing to take the risk, who did not want to grow old, and only the ones who bought from us were still alive.

Like most black markets, word got out that we were the real deal. For a time, that made it easy to sell. But counterfeiters appeared, selling fake products to desperate users. Many were conned, many died.

I published anonymous methodologies to distinguish fake Substance from real.

But the main problem was: most users were so desperate by the time they sought to purchase they did not have time to research. Either they found our product or they were dead.

My Last Night in Nicaragua

IT WAS NIGHT. I was packing, getting ready to leave Nicaragua, when I heard them on the roof. They couldn't get through the heavy steel gated front doors.

I quickly turned off the lights. I gave Aphrodite my blaster as backup, and grabbed a machete. Blasters are illegal and make a lot of noise. It was far better to use a machete. Every home in Nicaragua has two or three. They are cheap, effective, and can be used to cut vegetables, coconuts, or chop down trees. I had bought seven or eight of them, sharpened and stashed all over the house.

I stood between the back doors. There were two of them about ten feet apart.

I heard the hunters jump off the roof. One headed across the gravel courtyard towards our bedroom a hundred feet back, where the lights were on. The other came in my direction.

I heard him coming. I saw his gun hand extended leading as he edged through the door. I swung. He shrieked. The machete took his hand off clean at the wrist. I then slashed his throat. Silence. A thump. He was definitely dead. His head was barely attached.

I dragged his bloody mess out of the doorway.

A few minutes later I heard the other one coming across

the gravel. No doubt he had heard the scream.

He came through the other door, cautious just like an animal looking for its mate. I listened as he crept closer and closer. I saw his gun hand extended just like his partner's. I chopped his hand off at the wrist.

He screamed as his partner had screamed, and then fell and flailed about on the floor. I chopped his throat, and that was it.

Aphrodite had been hiding behind the second doorway – to the second room – just behind me, with her blaster the whole time. She had my back if I made a mistake.

That was both of them. I dragged the second bounty hunter inside beside the first. We grabbed our bug-out bags, locked the doors behind us and were gone. No one would find them for days, if not weeks.

Our house had a walled 200-foot-long back yard, with an alley behind it. We had prepared for our escape. I grabbed our ladder. We hurried to the back wall. I climbed up and threw a carpet over the razor wire, climbed over, and jumped down. Aphrodite followed. We walked away, down the alley in the darkness and were gone.

It was five or six long blocks to the lake, which seemed an infinity. We walked as briskly and cavalierly as we could. When I reached the lake I took out my self-inflating raft, set it in the water and we climbed in. We began paddling out towards deeper water.

I had moved my pod to the lake several months earlier, once I realized it was the only way to cross borders in the night. The pod was buried in the mud, a couple of hundred feet out. The lake is only six to ten feet deep, so I had to bury the pod in the mud.

I clicked my remote control launcher.

It was a beautiful sight to see the pod come up out of the water, lights and all.

We climbed in and were gone: 2,000 miles per hour in whatever direction we chose, heading straight for deep water.

PART 3: ZOOMING OUT

...RELATING TO THE GALAXY AND OTHER DIMENSIONS...

Al Sevcik is a professional photographer and author living in Tampa, Florida. His recent work can be found in two anthologies, After Oil #3 *and* Merigan Tales, *and in several issues of* Into the Ruins *magazine.*

The science fiction of the Golden Age drew on a vision of the cosmos considerably more flexible than the one popular among the more dogmatic scientists of today. In "The Solar System, the Universe, and Everything," Sevcik takes the classic theme of planetary exploration and tells a story with more than the usual number of dimensions...

THE SOLAR SYSTEM, THE UNIVERSE, AND EVERYTHING

Al Sevcik

INFLATABLE SHOES KEPT Butch from sinking into the sand, but he ran with his feet wide apart. Fear urged him faster. He cursed the awkwardness, the stumbling and slipping. In other circumstances he would have laughed but not now, not with that thing close behind slithering through the ancient sands of this Martian desert, doing its best to kill him.

Tanya ran just ahead, taking giant steps in the low gravity, her panting loud in the the thin air. She slipped, spread-eagling on the powder, causing a pink cloud to envelop them both. The three just behind veered to the side, avoiding a pile up and a fatal delay.

Pushing to her feet, Tanya raced to a rock outcrop. The horizontal fissure in the rocks didn't look wide enough but the five of them tumbled together through the opening milliseconds before a missile crashed against the rock face inches above the entrance.

Lifting Tanya's arm and pushing her leg aside, Butch freed himself from their mutual tangle on the cave's floor. "Tanya? You okay?"

She sat up, started to speak, then slapped both hands over

her mouth and nose. "The smell from that stupid worm's dung! Butch, it's killing me." She coughed. "I think I'm going to vomit." Green eyes stared at him in wide-eyed distress as she raked fingers back through short brown hair.

Beside them on the rock floor, Diane, Nancy, and Fred untangled themselves. Fred stood. Holding his laser blaster in both hands, he turned in a slow circle, squinting to see into the cave's shadow recesses.

Diane said, "Fred, put that thing down. The critter's outside, we're inside. There's nothing for you to shoot."

Fred lowered his arms. "You're sure about that, Diane? Really sure? Even after what happened to Doc?" Without answering she turned away from his stare.

Through squinted eyes still adjusting to the gloom, Butch looked around. High on the rocks beside him the pebble filled opening through which they had all fallen was a gash of light. The cave's shadows and dark walls confused its length and width. He stood, stepped over loose rocks, felt for handholds in the wall, and pulled himself up. Brushing aside loose rock he looked through the opening as a six-foot long culvert snapped shut its great mouth, wriggled backwards, and disappeared into the desert sand. The animal's dung ball had fragmented into a swath of rock-hard pellets that were sublimating into nauseating gas.

Butch stifled his anger. That thing, life form, whatever it is, has no right to be like that. I have a doctorate, my name is on a biology book. There's no way it can even be alive. But it chased us! His lips tightened. Once again Mars' biology had threatened his expertise.

He jumped down. "The worm's gone but I'm not fooled by that trick of shooting dung missiles. It might look amazing but it's perfectly natural and easily explained when I find out more."

"No," Tanya said. "It's not amazing." She knelt on the floor, bent over, her arms wrapped around her stomach. "It's stupid and crazy like everything else on this planet. I wish I'd never written that article on space chemistry and never ever let them put me on this trip."

Butch knelt beside her, lifted her chin and studied her eyes. "Doc would say you were low on oxygen. You need another pill. I expect we all do."

She gave a soft moan. "Don't talk about Doc. It's so horrible."

Diane emerged from a shadowed recess in the cave wall. "I saved most of the medicines. I'll find the pills." She extracted a vial from a pouch in her uv suit, shook out large orange pills and handed them around. "Here, this'll keep us absorbing whatever oxygen molecules drift our way."

Tanya chewed the pill while her eyes studied the group. She patted sand from her hair and pulled at the fabric of her suit. "Damn uv cloth catches every hair." She bent down and deflated the bags around her shoes. "And these damn balloons make me walk like a duck. I'd rather sink into the sand."

"No, Tanya," Fred said, brushing pink grit from blond hair and mustache. "Walking like a duck is better." He slid his blaster into a holster on his web belt, unfastened a communicator and flipped its lid. "No signal."

"Of course there isn't, Fred," Diane said. "Who is there to call? We're all right here."

"Just checking, you never know." Fred clipped the communicator back on his belt.

Nancy spit on her finger and wiped a wet streak across a smooth spot in the rock wall revealing a swirl of colors. "Wow! Layers of metallic ore. We could start a mine." Her eyes followed a light beam that slipped through the entrance slit. The beam crossed the cave and disappeared into dark. "Just thinking aloud," she said. "I'm wondering how far back this place goes."

Tanya said, "I'm wondering if we're alone in here."

Silence. Five pairs of eyes traced the rock walls back into the dark heart of the cave.

A millisecond flash. Then another. "They're in here!" Bruce fumbled his pouch, found a flashlight and lit up the cave wall.

Tanya snorted. "Butch that's useless. You know you can't see them with a flashlight."

She was right, but she didn't need to say it that way. Butch gave a grunt and continued sweeping the light beam across the walls.

Diane said, "The lights went away, right through the rock."

Nancy snorted. "Are you surprised?"

Tanya said. "How are we going to get out of this cave? How are we going to do what we came to do, and what about Doc's murder, and how are we going to get back to our ship before the launch-window closes for our return to Earth?"

Two days ago. The space ship landed upright on Mars soil with a live crew, though six pairs of sweaty palms testified to last minute doubts when Diane announced, "Bad news everyone. Our landing site is a bolder-covered slope. I have to abort."

Butch said, "That can't be right, Diane. We all saw the radar images and the photos. It's supposed to be a clear field."

Diane ignored the comment. Her fist knocked the protective cover off a red switch, flipped it, and overrode the computer's landing program. "Dammit ship, keep your thrust. Stay up! Stay up!" With shaking hands she maneuvered the descending craft sideways over rocks and ravines until they came to a sand strip at the edge of a drop-off. She eased the ship down to the sand and verified that the three support legs were locked and the thrusters shut off. The ship stopped vibrating. Light emitting diodes went dark. Silence. She unlocked her seat belt and lowered her head over the now motionless instruments. Her right hand smeared tears across her cheek.

In the silence Butch heard Diane's whisper, "I did it. I did it." She straightened and swiveled the pilot's chair, facing her five companions. "That's it," She said. "Piece of cake."

Butch unbuckled, stood and patted himself. Good, still in one piece. "Great work, Diane." He looked at the others. "Now that we're on the ground I'll take over from our super pilot. Doctor, Nancy, Fred, Tanya, y'all look to be intact. Doc what do your instruments show?"

Doc stood and leaned over Nancy to study a wall panel. "The outside air is as we expected. Nothing poisonous, but we'll need the orange pills to support absorption of oxygen." Raising his hands to protect his head he jumped to touch the ceiling and dropped back to the deck. "Take care walking. The gravity's only one third of Earth's."

"Thanks Doc. Fred, get the air lock ready. Everyone zip up your uv suits. We're not where we're supposed to be and we've got limited time so we'll work fast on a new plan." He grabbed the air lock door. "Somehow we'll get ourselves over there, but first let's get out of the ship." Butch turned his face away hoping the others hadn't sensed his concerns. Missing the planned landing place created a set of troubling problems. They had limited time to unravel the puzzle of the recently discovered anomaly on Mars. An area bigger than Texas but hidden by an atmospheric phenomenon impenetrable to sight or radar. Unfortunately they landed thirty miles away.

The air lock gasped and opened. When he stepped off the ship Butch's shoes crunched on compacted sand. He studied the ground. Not rock exactly, but hard. Looking around he gave silent thanks for Diane's piloting. She had set the ship down just feet away from the edge of a steep sandstone slope streaked with rusty yellow. He could just discern the eroded bed of an ancient river in the valley below.

He pondered the situation. The Mars mystery excited all the Earth's military establishments but the US was first to launch a manned investigation. Government bureaucrats pressured the military to launch quickly. The rush to launch and the inevitable last-minute compromises troubled Butch. Each individual member of the crew was an expert but the group had never worked together. Tanya, though a high school chemistry teacher, had invented and patented chemical processes that were becoming standard. Her latest article on space chemistry triggered her invitation to this mission. He, himself, was called off of a South American biological exploration because, he supposed, his name graced the cover of a widely used textbook. Each of the crew had been deep in specialized work when Space Command made the urgent summons. He looked back at the upright ship. There's no reason to worry. The job will get done. Everything on all the planets, in fact everything in the whole universe, can be understood and mastered through science. If used properly, chemistry and physics resolves every puzzle.

He watched the half-size sun slide towards a distant ridge thinking, It's fortunate that a day on Mars is almost the same as a day on Earth. Shadows crawled down the valley's sides and across the dry river. Increasing gloom obscured details. He stood for a long minute staring into the canyon, his thoughts drifting. I'd like to be Tanya's friend. I like her. He shook himself. Enough of that. It's only two weeks since we met.

Tanya and Doc exited the air lock and walked over to Butch. Together they watched the advancing shadows while Nancy, Fred and Diane explored the landing area. "Look." Doc pointed into the valley. "There, in the shadow, there's a …."

Tanya stiffened. "What?"

Doc scowled into the thickening shadows. "For a moment… Down there… artifacts." He shook his head. "Martian shadows playing tricks."

Nancy's voice behind them. "Captain! We have fireflies." She paused. "Sort of."

In the dark near the ship Butch saw a spark. Or did he? Did the flash last a tenth of a second, or a hundredth? He wondered if his brain could register a nanosecond flash, or a microsecond, or even a millisecond? Then two flashes, each so brief he wondered if they had really existed.

Tanya grabbed his arm. "I saw them, too, Captain."

Doc yelled, "Look! In the valley!"

The six stood at the edge of the drop-off. In the valley's darkness evanescent sparks, sometimes dozens at a time, vanished as soon as they appeared. Then the sparkling stopped, leaving the darkness even more intense. Butch turned his head away just as a flash lit up a third of the valley. It's brilliance existed and then didn't exist.

Tanya exhaled. "I don't believe it."

Butch shook his head, his brain unready to accept what he had seen. "Nancy, Fred, Doc, Diane, did you...?"

Four yeses.

"For the record, Nancy," Butch said, "What exactly did you see? Say it so all of us can hear."

Nancy hesitated. Butch wondered if she would answer honestly or edit her response. The flash had been so brief. Could she be sure of what she saw? Nancy cleared her throat. Then, in a trembly voice, "A city. I know it's impossible. I know the valley's empty. But I saw a city."

"I'LL TAKE THE first two-hour watch," Butch said. "Then Tanya, Doc and Fred." He smiled, "After that we'll gather for breakfast." The others strung hammocks and unfolded cots while Butch pulled a thick synthetic coverall over his uv clothing and slipped a rigid fabric helmet over his head. He turned to the wall panel and checked instrumentation. "Already forty below freezing and cooling. Going to be chilly between now and dawn."

Stepping through the airlock into the Martian night he sensed the physical press of starlight, the spangled sky bright and close, the Milky Way streaking across heaven. Orion guarded the horizon. Butch was calmed and reassured to find the stars in familiar places. The moons Phobos and Deimos moved as he watched. Phobos, a third the size of Earth's moon, raced around the planet every three hours. Deimos, no more than a bright star, circled around Mars every day.

He kicked at a pebble, missed, and kicked again. It's hard to judge how much muscle to use in this low gravity. Butch walked around the ship on the alert for — what? What does danger look like here?A light breeze, the sky glow dimmed, stars disappeared, ground objects faded. Airborne dust. I better close my suit.

He clicked the face plate closed then stood with shut eyes, fighting disorientation. His pulse doubled, his heart filled his chest. Me. Here. Standing on another planet! Impossible such a short time ago yet, now, here I am, thanks to science. Opening his eyes he stood quiet, clicked up the oxygen content in his suit, and filled his lungs. I'm standing here because the government wanted feet on Mars to check a spot the smart guys couldn't understand. Me, an expert in beetles! And Tanya who teaches chemistry and wrote an article. And Doc from a Nebraska country hospital. And the others. Is this trip a mistake? A bureaucratic bungle? Butch forced a deep breath, his pulse slowed, his chest eased. Well, here we are, with a job to do, and we'll do it.

Nearby, or far, he couldn't tell, there was a millisecond flash. He looked around but the dusty air now obscured everything more than a few feet away. Another flash, so fast it took a second for his brain to realize that it happened at all.

Butch stepped across the hard sand surface to where the light had been. Ten steps. Twenty. Another ephemeral flash, but this time something more. His mind stopped. In the brief light, a face. It was over before his brain registered the details, but he had seen a face, not human, a face nonetheless. He waited for for it to happen again. Nothing. After a few minutes he turned and walked back to the ship.

As he approached, the airlock opened. Tanya came out. "My turn, Butch. You've had your two hours. See anything interesting?"

He studied her for several seconds, wishing they had met before all this Mars business. The scientifically engineered thermal suit didn't hide her figure.

"Butch?"

"Huh? Oh, I saw..." He paused. "Nothing really. Nothing to speak of."

She came close and touched his arm. "Well then, Captain, you'd better go in and get some sleep."

His skin tingled where she had touched. He felt her closeness. "I'm not really a captain, Tanya. I'm just good at organizing things. Like beetles."

She smiled. "It's an honorary title."

Her smile floated in his mind through the airlock, to his cubicle, and to his one privilege of rank, the Captain's Cot.

The smile's afterglow had barely faded when his bed shook and someone pounded on his chest. "Captain, Butch, wake up. Quick! Doc's been murdered!"

STANDING CLOSE TOGETHER on the cold sand the crew members silently studied the scene. Butch watched the miniature sun lift above distant mountains and cast a sharp-edged shadow of the space ship across the landing area and onto the dunes beyond. A hundred feet from the ship, half in its shadow, he looked at Doc spread-eagled on the sand. Doc's thermal suit and helmet were in place and sealed, but his organs, heart, lungs, intestines were scattered across his body, hard-frozen in the bitter cold. Butch frowned. Where was the blood?

"I can't look," Nancy said peeking between the fingers covering her eyes. "I'm going to be sick."

Fred said, "He agreed to wake me after he finished his watch. He didn't so I overslept. When I woke up I rushed out to get him and found....this." Kneeling, he studied the corpse. "I don't understand. Are these his guts?" He zipped Doc's suit open. "His suit is tight closed and there's no wound. How did his insides get out?" They looked at Butch.

"Diane," Butch said, "We need to tell Earth about this and get advice. Please make radio contact with Space Operations for me."

She shook her head. "I can't Captain. I was ready to wake you myself but Fred got to you first. The radio… The transmitter's broken."

Bruce stiffened. "Impossible! Transmitters don't just break." He heard his voice, too loud, the others saw his anxiety. He took a breath and forced a calm voice. "Diane, explain the problem."

Troubled brown eyes looked at each crew member, then back at Butch. "You know how the transmitter is in a metal box? It's sealed, welded shut; it can't be opened." She swallowed. "Except last night someone…" she hesitated, "or something, opened the box and took a transistor board out. This morning I found the board lying on the flight control panel."

"Can't we put it back? Just reopen the transmitter and slip the board back into place?"

"They…. Whoever took it broke it, Butch. The board is in three pieces. It's printed circuitry, we can't fix it." She tried to wring her hands but her gloves got in the way. "Another thing, Butch, the transmitter box wasn't really opened. It's still sealed, welds and everything."

It took seconds for Butch's brain to begin to understand. He saw the others struggling with the same problem. "Okay, let's review. Last night Doc got killed somehow. His heart and lungs and other organs were taken out of his body but we don't see a wound. Also last night a circuit board was taken out of the radio even though the welded metal box wasn't opened." He paused and looked at each in turn. "Tell me if I'm missing something."

BUTCH GATHERED EVERYONE together on the ship's flight deck.

He stood looking at the instrumentation, organizing his thoughts. *It's a small crew. Everyone has to be at top efficiency. I can't allow anyone to be concerned. I have to say something positive.* He dragged a finger across one of the dials then turned to face the others sitting in their usual seats. He noted that someone had covered Doc's vacant seat with the blanket from his hammock.

"We are from Earth," He said. "We're not simply guests on this planet, we're scientists and engineers from Earth and that means we're in charge. We're the bosses. Just like we're the bosses on Venus and on all the moons in the solar system worth landing on." Four pairs of eyes watched him. "We own Earth's solar system, this is our place. We will not allow mysteries that make us flounder and that undermine our authority. This puzzling business has to get resolved, quickly."

He allowed himself a small smile. *A good speech. No objections.* Diane raised her hand. "We're with you all the way Captain. What do we do next?"

"I'm getting to that, Diane." Butch scrambled through his brain looking for a reasonable idea."

Fred said, "Captain, I'm thinking about that area where we were supposed to land. Maybe..."

Butch seized on Fred's words. "Right, Fred. The anomaly. That's where we'll find answers. We were sent here to explore that area and that is what we must do."

Nancy said, "The anomaly is thirty miles from here. That's a lot of desert and we don't know what's out there. It might be dangerous. What about the flashing lights? Can anyone explain those? Are they connected with Doc's death? Are they dangerous?"

Butch shrugged. "I'm not going to worry about flashing lights. We've got laser blasters and they don't. Earth's weapons beat anything on Mars. Fred, you and Nancy unpack the tractor and hook it to the sled. Tanya and Diane, grab enough food and water for three days. We're going for a ride."

An hour later as crew members selected places in the

sled Butch turned his thoughts away from his worries. He checked the landscape, a vertical drop-off to a deep dry valley on one side, on the other a desert strewn with sun baked rocks spreading to the horizon. The single seat tractor and the utility sled were uncomfortably small. "Diane, can you pilot a tractor as expertly as a space ship?"

She laughed. "Just watch me, Captain." Grabbing a handhold, she pulled up onto the machine's treads, settled into the driver's seat and unfolded a photo map of rocky desert, stone ridges and twisted gullies. She placed a magnetic compass on the floor between her feet. "I'm going to hold as straight a line as possible to conserve battery charge, but we'll have to zig zag around oodles of rocks."

"Okay," Nancy said, "but pick the smoothest path. This sled wasn't built for passengers and these air cushions are going to bounce around."

Butch crossed mental fingers when the tractor's treads moved, hoping they would pull the sled without digging down into the sand, hoping the sled's carbon-fiber runners would stay on the surface and that the wheels in the runners would carry them over hard ground. Most of all he hoped that the sled really had passed tests in the Utah desert.

He sat at the front of the sled, just behind Diane who drove the tractor. He watched Fred, a laser rifle in his hand, choose to sit at the back where he had a clear view on both sides and to the rear. Nancy's and Tanya's cushions were centered in the sled. Following Fred's advice, all wore holstered laser pistols. Diane increased power and they moved from the firm ground of the landing area onto the pink sand of the bleak and parched Martian landscape.

The fuel-cell motor was quiet but the treads and the sled runners crunched and scraped as they moved along. Diane turned to Butch. "I figure the best compromise between safely and speed is about five miles an hour. Okay with you, Captain?"

Butch glanced at the digital chronometer on his wrist; ten

o'clock. At five mph they would cover the thirty miles by late afternoon, well before dark. He nodded and Diane turned back. As they travelled, the pebble peppered sand became interspersed with swaths of talcum-like powder allowing the tractor's treads to sink into the surface. Butch became concerned. "Diane, hold up a minute. Everyone, inflate the air bags around your boots." Butch ignored the grumbling and complaints that the the pillow-like boot-rings made walking awkward. They would be life-savers if the crew abandoned the sled in soft sand. He waited until all the boots had been attended to, then nodded a go-ahead to Diane.

He checked the sky, cloudless but not blue. Unexpectedly the air smelled sweet. Sunlight filtered through an orange-yellow haze of fine dust way high up. Sand reached from the sled to the horizon, two thirds as far away as the horizon on Earth. What a nothing place. *After Earth takes over we'll terraform the planet. Make it like it ought to be. Just like Earth.* In his mind's eye he saw clear brooks and fields of wheat. The tractor jolted to a stop. Diane said, "Check this, Captain."

They were at the edge of an ancient alluvial wash where torrents of water had deposited sand, gravel and even house-sized boulders. Nancy jumped from the sled and gathered a handful of pebbles. "Wow, look at all the minerals!" Then she pointed. "It's far away but look, on either side of us the ground slopes up, making walls." She swept her hand from side to side. "We're at the terminus of a super-wide ditch. I think we've found the remains of a Martian canal."

Fred catapulted himself over the sled's railing and pointed his laser rifle at the sand ahead. He shouted, "Danger, Nancy! Run!"

In front of Nancy the sand quivered then expanded into a mound. Nancy froze, dropped the pebbles, jumped backward and fell. The ground erupted. Diane leaped from the tractor, creating a talcum-sand cloud. What looked like a large metallic drain pipe rose from the desert. Fred fired his laser, melting sand beside the creature. Its eighteen-inch opening swung toward them. With a deafening blast it expelled a projectile that hit the tractor and shattered. Fred loosed two more laser shots as the creature vanished back into the sand.

FRED RAN AHEAD of the sled, stood and turned in a full circle, holding his laser rifle. No one moved.

After a few seconds Diane stood up from the sand and leaned against the tractor. Her voice trembled. "If I'd stayed in that seat I'd be dead for sure." She kicked at one of the dark lumps from the fragmented projectile. "Good God, this stuff stinks."

"Let me look." Nancy got to her feet, releasing a cloud of powdery sand from her suit. She walked to Diane and picked up one of the lumps. "Phew, this is awful." She scraped it with her fingernail. "It's a matrix of rock pieces and sand imbedded in what looks like body waste."

"Hold it," David said, "You're telling us that we were attacked with a cannon ball made from poo?"

"Yes. But if you want to see for yourself, look quickly. The matrix material is disappearing, sublimating into the air, leaving little piles of pebbles and sand."

Butch checked the tractor, running his fingers over a dent in its metal shielding. "If you're right, Nancy, that thing has incredibly solid dung."

"You know," Tanya said, "That beast that attacked us has evolved for millions of years. Its dung weapon isn't accidental. It must be for a reason."

Diane said. "I'm thinking that it has enemies." She paused. "Big enemies."

Everyone looked around but nothing had changed. Orange sky, small sun, rocks and sand going on forever.

Butch squinted. Had the light dimmed, the day become darker? "Hold it, everyone. Let's not get ourselves spooked. Look at this scientifically. Evolution takes millions of years. In that time species come and then go extinct. Aside from that dung shooting worm we haven't run into anything dangerous. My guess is that whatever it was that the worm evolved to shoot, that thing is long gone from this planet. There's no monster out there."

"Except," Dianne said softly, "the one that killed Doc."

Butch gave her a glare, but said, "Let's go. We have ground to cover. Diane, back on the tractor please. Let's follow the bed of this one-time canal. It's probably smoother than the open desert."

"Butch," Tanya said, "isn't there danger of getting trapped in this ditch? I'm wondering how high the canal sides will be."

"Don't worry, the canal has been eroding for a long time. We'll find a way out when we need to exit."

Diane started the tractor then turned in her seat and called, "Fred. I assume you've got your laser gun recharged."

Fred smiled and patted the rifle.

Now. Standing in the cave, Butch mentally reviewed their trek across the desert, then he turned to respond to Tanya. They had traveled with the tractor and sled for about four hours without incident after the first dung worm attack. As they progressed the canal deepened and its walls became higher. Diane became increasingly vocal with her concerns about getting out. Tanya grabbed Butch's arm. "There," she pointed, "Ahead on the right. It's a landslide where the canal wall collapsed."

Hands white-knuckled on the controls, Diane zig-zagged the tractor and sled up the uncertain rocks and sand of the slide, avoiding places that looked unstable. She bit her lip in concentration. Time slowed, treads slipped frightening inches. She coaxed the machine up onto the desert floor just as the slope they had climbed collapsed with a thunder crash.

"Good Lord," Fred said. "Diane, if you'd taken seconds longer we would have been killed."

"Piece of cake," Diane said, her voice almost steady.

Nancy said, "The desert's different here." She pointed to nearby rock outcroppings the size of buildings. Diane turned the tractor toward the nearest. The sand ahead quivered, then swirled counterclockwise forming a shallow pit. The swirl widened. The pit deepened and moved towards the tractor. Diane yelled, "Everybody out! It's going to suck us down." She killed the engine and jumped from her seat, falling into the sand. Butch yelled, "Run to the rocks!" The familiar drain-pipe shape rose from the swirling sand pit. They had reached the rocks and the safety of the cave just as the dung worm fired.

Butch looked around at the rock interior of the cave and at his crew. Tanya, Diane, Nancy and Fred were outwardly calm but Butch saw they were recovering from shock. He turned to Tanya, wanting to reassure her, to reassure himself, to enfold her. No, I can't do that. I need to keep their respect.

He said, "Tanya, you're right. We're here doing a job and we have to get on with it. But it will be dark in two hours. We'll be safer and more efficient in the morning. Did you and Diane mange to save any food?"

The women reached into their uv suit pockets and extracted plastic pouches. "Here," Tanya said, "fortunately military food is indestructible."

Fred said, "As long as it's food."

They sat in a row, cross-legged on the rock floor, facing the rear of the cave. "Does it end there, where it's dark?" Nancy asked. "Or is that just a turn before it goes deeper?"

Fred unclipped a flashlight from his belt, picked up his rifle, and walked into the cave, illuminating the walls. Returning he said, "It goes on but I don't know how far. Boulders block the passage."

Nancy shivered. "Why do I feel like there's someone behind me, examining my shoulder?"

Tanya said, "It's this crazy freaky planet. There's nothing I can see, or touch or taste, but the hairs on the back of my neck are wriggling. I wish I was home."

Butch's mind snapped alert. This conversation's headed wrong. Gotta stop the talk about home. He said, "Hey, cut out the spooky stuff. We're all scientists and if there's one thing each of us knows for sure it's that chemistry and physics explain everything. That's true everywhere and it's true on Mars. We just need a little more info, and we'll get that tomorrow at the anomaly."

MORNING'S FIRST LIGHT reached into the cave. Butch grabbed the edge of his thermal blanket and jerked it aside. He stood, found handholds in the wall and pulled himself up to the entrance slit. Mars' dinky excuse for a sun rested on the horizon, throwing long shadows from every dune and ripple. He pushed stones aside and checked the landscape. The tractor and sled were where they had been abandoned yesterday. Overnight the tractor had sunk a half foot into the sand. The wind had stopped; the yellow and orange sky was clear.

He turned to find the others standing in a semi-circle, looking at him. He said, "If there's any food left let's grab some bites and go."

"Wait," Nancy said. "Isn't it dangerous? That horrible worm is still out there and the sand, and everything."

"The worm's gone away." His voice sounded more reassuring than he felt. "Remember, after we scared off the first worm we travelled for hours yesterday without any problem."

Nancy said, "Then all at once we had a problem, and that's why we're in this cave."

Fred lifted his laser rifle. "Next time I'll be prepared. I couldn't get a clear shot yesterday."

"Because you were too busy running with the rest of us," Nancy muttered.

Fred's features clouded. Butch spoke. "It's decided then. Let's go. Diane, you're our pilot. Can you find the way?"

She nodded. "I know the compass heading and I'm guessing five miles. An hour's ride."

"Okay," Nancy nodded. "But I think it's best if we wait to inflate the shoe bags until after we've scraped ourselves out through that gap." She sighed, "That ragged rocky slit was so welcoming yesterday." She climbed up to the opening. "Good news. The tractor looks closer to the cave now than when we ran this way in a panic."

Outside, Butch smiled noticing that they each of the crew avoided spooking sand monsters by walking with exaggerated gentleness. I guess it's working, he thought. No monsters in sight.

Diane climbed to her seat. "Okay. All aboard." She watched the others claim inflated cushions in the sled then switched on the tractor's electric motor and eased the machine out of the soft sand.

Butch hid his impatience. He forced both hands to lay still in his lap. We'll be at the anomaly in less than an hour, then we'll get the mysteries resolved and be on our way home. We'll know why the old radar and photo surveys from Earth telescopes showed flat desert and why a year ago this area suddenly disappeared. Hidden how? By what? Most importantly, why? Well, that's why we are here. We're qualified scientists and will solve the mystery for once and all. When we get to the anomaly we'll quickly understand.

Tanya's hand brushed his arm. He turned smiling but she pointed ahead. "Butch, the desert has changed. There's a grey crust over the sand and look at all those little spikes poking through." She paused, studying the desert. "I think the spikes are getting larger."

Diane, maneuvering around the growing projections and struggling to maintain her compass heading, slowed the tractor, then stopped. "The spikes are too close. The tractor can't fit between them any more, Captain. Guess we'll have to walk. My map says we're almost there."

Butch considered for a moment. The rock spikes are only three or four feet high. If I stand on the metal hood of the tractor.... Soon they were all crowded on top of the tractor. The air was clear behind and to either side of them but the sand and spikes ahead faded into fog. Butch strained to focus his eyes. The fog thickened and then thinned, swirled and then disappeared and reappeared too rapidly for his mind to follow. He jumped to the ground. "We'll walk. The ground's firm so we don't need to puff up the bags around our shoes."

As they walked the space between the rock spikes narrowed until they had to turn sideways to pass.

Fred, waking ahead, stopped and motioned to the others. "The spikes stop here. It's like stepping though a wall." They stood in a group at the edge of a swath of bare sand.

"It looks maybe three hundred feet wide," Fred said, "but, my eyes don't work right in this Martian light."

The others nodded.

"It doesn't matter," Butch said. "This is why we came. Let's check it out."

Nancy held up her hand. "Wait."

Butch suppressed a surge of impatience. "What now, Nancy?"

She shrugged. "I don't know. There's something wrong. Why can't we see the other side clearly? It's not that far away."

"Nancy, your imaginative fantasies aren't helpful. Everyone check the charge on your laser pistols. Fred, is your rifle okay?"

"Check, Captain."

Staying close together, weapons in hand, they left the rock spikes and walked across the sand. Half way across Tanya turned around and gasped. "Look! The rocks are moving!"

Butch turned and saw the stone shafts warping, shifting, and dissolving into the fog then re-emerging, like bad TV.

"It's a mirage," he said. "caused by the desert." He motioned the others to move forward.

Nancy said, "Butch, are you really sure about going into.... " Her voice trailed off.

"I can see the other side now, Fred said. "It's a forest. Actually, it's a jungle."

"No," Nancy said, shielding her eyes. "Those trees... They don't look right."

"Nonsense." Fred shouldered his rifle and sent a laser blast into the forest.

Tanya's fingers squeezed Butch's arm. "Butch, nothing happened to the trees!"

Fred ran across the sand into the obscuring haze, then he walked slowly back into clear view and stood quiet on the sand's edge.

Tanya called, "Fred, is something wrong?" He looked at her without reply.

Butch shook his head. This isn't like Fred. He said, "Let's all go across."

As they approached him, Fred said, "My laser rifle, one shot will bring down a tree. But nothing happened. Something should have happened."

Tanya said, "More flashing lights. There, in the forest."

Butch squinted his eyes. "Yes, I see them in the mist."

"There are more now," Tanya said. "Dozens. Look, hundreds." She stopped. "It's not a mist. What is it?"

Diane looked down. "Right here where the sand stops there's a sharp edge. It's not natural." The sand ended and something else began, but what? At a distance it appeared to be trees or structures shrouded in fog but now Butch saw that it wasn't fog at all. Tanya put it in words. "Butch, I see a forest, a city, hills, an ocean. It's all there, but none of it is there."

"It's like holograms all mixed together." Nancy said.

Diane motioned to the group. "Hey, come look at this." She pointed to a path of smooth stones leading into the anomaly. "It's so obvious, why did we miss it earlier?"

Nancy turned to Fred who stood to one side. "What did you see in there, Fred?"

Fred pressed the rifle against his chest. "I don't like things that don't get shot when I blast them."

"What we have here is an effect that's easily explained by science," Butch said. The others turned with questioning looks and he added, "I'll do that later. The important thing is we have our blasters and we're the most intelligent life on this planet and that puts us in charge." He pointed ahead. "A paved path is meant to be walked on. I'm walking in and I'm going to find out what's going on. I'm expecting more than amateur holograms." He wished he was as tough as he sounded. He clenched his fists and turned away. Inhaling deeply, steadying his voice, he said, "I'm the leader. I'll go first."

He tested the stability of the path by pressing down with his toe, then took a tentative step. Around him the world morphed from country to forest to seascape but the walk stayed steady. He took a dozen more steps, careful to stay on the path. He could feel Tanya close behind him, her hand pressing his back. Diane and Nancy followed. Fred, swinging his laser rifle from one side of the walk to the other, came last. Butch stopped and turned around. The path and forest behind them had faded into the mist.

"Butch," Tanya whispered, "There's no color. Everything is gray. Even the sky."

"Everything looks so old." Nancy said. "Look!" She stopped. "I think I saw a city. It's gone now. Weird structures. I think they're ancient, but I don't know..."

"The trees, too," Diane said. "If that's what they are, they appear and then vanish so fast."

Butch said, "I would like to get rid of these flashing lights. There must be a thousand."

"I'm scared," Nancy said. "They're moving to both sides of the path. I think they're watching us."

Butch jumped as Fred let loose another laser rifle blast. "Got one," he said. The flashes stopped. The gray light faded to black, the most complete black Butch had ever experienced. No light. No sound. His only sensation was Tanya's hand pressing his ribs. He panicked. He heard his own voice, loud. "Someone help!"

Then Nancy's voice, "I want to go home." The gray light, the forest, the impossible scenery all reappeared. The flashing lights were gone.

Fear vibrated in Butch's guts. Whatever was happening was bigger than anything he'd ever experienced. He didn't dare look at the crew, his face would betray any expression he could force. They would see that he had been frightened. They would all know. He fumbled to find words.

Tanya whispered, "It's okay, Captain."

Butch cleared his throat. "Let's go on, and Fred, no more shooting."

"Yes sir, Captain." Fred's voice had lost its belligerent edge.

The walkway widened and then stopped. They stood together on the edge of an infinite blackness. The blackness rose and expanded until they were imbedded in featureless dark.

Deep within the black, points of light quivered, expanded and then vanished. In the distance a round object appeared. It came closer and Butch saw the blue and green that he recognized, Earth's oceans and land. The sphere drew close then turned and withdrew until it was a point of light that disappeared into the surrounding black eternity. Butch saw stars and familiar constellations. Planetary systems drew close and then away. All the lights, the suns, the galaxies, the planets became distant. The kaleidoscopic worlds faded. Then Butch stood beside the others on an infinite dark and featureless plain. Just in front of the group the black shimmered and became a pool without an opposite shore. Within the pool, broken by faint ripples, a sketch of a human face appeared. A low-pitched female voice spoke in his head. Each word was individual, spoken with care. "This is your space-time continuum. Your universe."

Butch looked at the others. They were also hearing the voice.

Again the voice in his head, an echo, loud then repeating softly, melting away. "Listen. All that you know, everything you think is real, is only a reflection of a larger four dimensional universe onto your three dimensional space. In the distant future, after you have finished searching with telescopes and space vehicles, after you have finished studying the tracks of dark matter, gravity waves and evanescent quanta, you will know that your universe is a grain of dust hidden in other dimensions. Dimensions you cannot ever understand."

Butch's throat tightened, he forced himself to breathe. Layers down in his mind he already knew what his conscious self scrambled to deny. He faced a power immense beyond comprehension. A power beyond science.

Nancy spoke. "Why did you allow us here? What do you want us to know?"

Butch blinked. Did the face in the blackness give a tiny smile?

The voice continued. "This artifact that you call Mars exists for a purpose. It is one of a very large number of intelligence gathering nodes needed for the maintenance of the universes. I mean, of course, the multidimensional universes of which this three dimensional space of yours is an essentially insignificant part. This node, Mars, is necessary, right here."

Diane said, "So, you are asking, no, telling us..."

"To stay away. Entities of your space-time are not permitted on the Mars artifact, ever again."

Butch's anger flared. "Whoever, whatever you are, you can't give us orders. We're in charge. Earth has been here for almost five billion years and that's where mankind grew up and we're the boss of our planet and all the planets in the solar system and even the galaxy. We're the smartest beings by far. We've been to all the planets. We're in command here." Behind him Tanya gasped. He turned to see Fred, Diane, Tanya and Nancy with wide eyes. He muttered, "No one's going to push Earth around." Did the void in front of him move? Were there ripples, some darker than others? The inscrutable face reappeared.

"You are not here by random happenstance. You are in a

temporary space-time intersection between your universe and the fourth dimensional universe that I occupy and which completely enfolds your three dimensions. The flashes of energy you've seen are reflections from fourth dimensional beings.

"The other apparitions you see are created by your mind trying to make sense of input it can't comprehend. Understand that there are universes greater than four dimensions. The universe I speak from is enfolded into a fifth dimensional time-space that I cannot fully grasp. Beyond, there are sixth, seventh and other dimensional universes on and on. Each so vast it holds an uncountable number of universes of the dimension below. All of this is made manifest by an incomprehensible power.

"In this vastness, there is a mote inhabited by beings that call it Earth. With nearby motes it circles a small star. This star and others form a galaxy which is part of a larger group called a super galaxy. And so on. All this in your tiny pocket of space-time."

Tanya moved close to the black pool's edge, then she knelt and looked into the shifting features of the dark face. "Then we.... humanity.... billions of humans... all the trillions that ever existed.... everything we are... everything we have been..... what we could be..." She took a deep breath. "It's all for nothing. We are, were, will be, always and forever, totally insignificant."

The face disappeared. The pool stilled, became a mirror of infinite depth. From far in the depths the face again materialized. The voice spoke in their minds. "Every structure, from the infinitesimal to the most vast is composed of parts. All these parts, however many there are, together make the whole. Without all of its parts the structure is not complete. How is one to say that any of the parts are insignificant?"

Bruce said, "The four-dimensional beings on Mars..."

"You appear to them much like a two-dimensional being would appear to you. A two-dimensional person cannot even imagine you. You see inside their bodies, you see their skin as only an outer edge having width and length but no thickness. Four-dimensional beings see you the same way. All your enclosures, including your bodies, are open to them."

Fred said, "Is that how the Mars people killed Doc?"

"An accident. A Martian didn't understand that the human's enclosed body was needed for it's life. The mistake can't be undone. So your associate's life stopped."

"And our ship's radio?" Diane asked.

"A piece was removed to delay your return. It was important to keep you here to learn."

Butch said, "You mean this conversation?"

"Yes. But this connection between our universes is ending. There are obligations. All must be maintained. I do what must be done in this part of the continuum."

"Wait!" Butch panicked. "I want more! Within the infinite structure of space-time, within all the dimensions and all the universes the fact is we are here, I am here, now. I must know, humans need to know...."

"You want to know why humans, why anything, exists, and how this all happened?" The voice paused. "There may not be an answer. The beings in the myriad two dimensional crevices of creation and also those in the all encompassing dimensions ask the same questions. If there is an answer it eludes us all."

The great black pool writhed, faded, and became Martian desert. Swirling fog enveloped Butch, hiding everything except the stones where he stood and a silver path winding back the way they had come. The fog thinned to reveal Tanya, Fred, Diane and Nancy. Butch saw them become alert. Again a voice echoed in his head. "Stay on the path and don't pause when you pass through the folds."

"Diane said, "The folds? What does that mean?"

Butch said, "We'll find out." He began walking back. The hundreds of flashes that followed their arrival were now an occasional few. The path ended. He stood in open desert exposed to open sky, dark now in the Martian night.

Phebos and Demos were just bright enough to obscure

nearby stars but thousands were visible. He stopped and looked up at an off-color point of light in the sky overhead.

Tanya's hand gripped his. "Is that us?"

Butch called to Diane, a few steps ahead, "Diane, you're our navigation expert. That light there...."

"Yep. Good old Earth. Home." Diane bent to study the ground. "Captain! Something strange here. The ground...." She jumped back as the sand cracked open in front of her. A jolt knocked Butch off his feet and then all sensation stopped — light, sound, feeling, gone. Then the world came back. He was sprawled on desert sand with the others.

"Wow," Tanya said. Then she pointed. "Look, our ship!"

After all that had happened on Mars the appearance of their ship less than one hundred feet away didn't register in Butch's mind as impossible. But it was a surprise.

Tanya said, "How..."

Butch pointed to an indistinct disturbance above a three-inch wide strip in the sand's speckled shadows. The air above the strip was cloudy, like a frosted window. "There," he said. "that's the fold. I'm guessing our fourth-dimensional friends simply bent a piece of three-d space to bring us and the ship together."

Diane said, "That fuzzy place in the sand...

"That's where the bent spaces meet. We're supposed to step through to get to the ship, but we were told not to pause." Bruce inhaled, quieting his nerves. "I'll do it."

He stepped and a thousand needles pierced every part of his body. The pain was gone before it fully registered, but his gasp made the others hesitate. He waved them to come. "It's okay, cross quickly. Diane, the ship is yours to command. Take us home."

D<small>IANE WENT THROUGH</small> the airlock first and settled into the pilot's chair. Fred released the charge from the capacitors in his laser rifle and followed Diane. Nancy and Tanya went in. Butch stood in the desert darkness. He wanted to absorb the essence of Mars, whatever that was. No human will ever stand here again. I'm the last man on Mars. There were two nanosecond flashes in the shadow to his right. He gave a return salute wondering how a four-d being interpreted his three-d wave. He went into the ship, closing and locking the airlock door.

Diane toggled a row of switches, needles on meters moved, lights blinked red, green and yellow. "Power on," she said. "Lock your seat belts. Takeoff in ten." She counted the seconds backwards. At zero, acceleration's invisible hand shoved Butch tight into his seat. The space ship lifted.

Seconds later Diane cut the ship's acceleration. Again Butch felt the stab of invisible needles. The craft descended. What's wrong? "Diane…"

In frowning concentration at the console, she impatiently held up a hand to stop his words. The ship vibrated, then stopped. Diane extended the stabilizing supports. She swiveled her chair to face the rest. "We've landed. We're home. Piece of cake."

Butch opened the airlock door to Earth sunlight and a jeep skidding to a stop on the tarmac. A space force colonel looked up from the jeep, his face red. "Where in Hell did you come from?"

"Mars, Colonel."

The officer relaxed. "I know that Butch, but the problem is our radar missed your coming. Your ship simply appeared above the space port and then you landed. That trick upset a bunch of folks. How did you do it?"

Butch smiled. "Easy Colonel, Diane brought us through a space warp."

"Not funny Butch, but never mind. The important thing is that you're back and your mission was successful. That place on Mars that we had trouble seeing? It's gone, poof, overnight. I'm guessing your team caused that. True?"

The others crowded around him in the open airlock. Butch traded glances with them. Tanya gave him a wink. He nodded.

"You could say that, Colonel."

The colonel clapped his hands. "I knew it! Wish I could have been there when you guys showed them Earth's power, rattled the sword, and made it mighty clear who's the real boss of this planetary system and," he smiled, "the rest of the whole danged universe."

Joel B. Jones is a playwright, performer, and improv teacher in Charlottesville, Virginia, where he resides with his wife and daughter. His interest in sci-fi goes back to the Traveller role-playing games run by his older brother in the late 1970s. He currently works as the co-director of Charlottesville's Big Blue Door, a theater and comedy troupe.

Even in its earliest days, the Old Solar System was not necessarily isolated from the rest of the universe, and plenty of stories set in the space circling our Sun had connections of one kind or another with the wider cosmos. "Death Songs of Saturn" draws on that tradition, framing a crisply written story of adventure on and above Saturn in a setting that reaches far out into interstellar space. It makes a fitting conclusion to this collection of tales from the greatest of all shared fictional universes...

DEATH SONGS OF SATURN

Joel B. Jones

1.

ORIGIN LAUNCHED THE six of us across the galaxy to your solar system in order to study and report. Over time we drifted from that purpose, led astray partly because of the long separation from our own kind, partly because of our humanoid bodies, but mostly because Origin committed the common folly of the highly-intelligent: assuming we would always remain as they had observed us to be. Instead we six each took the wayward paths of our individual virtues and vices. My own greatest vice is never leaving well enough alone.

My sloop, *Antigone*, was docked on Vesta in the asteroid belt. Rising from my sleep interval, I stepped through the spiral hatch into the passage. An Earthling was waiting. I had met the station personnel the previous cycle when the administrators insisted on a tour.

"You are Ondria Chase."

"Yes, Captain," she said eyes downcast. Chase bore the grim look of the undercastes, the mix of worry and grief masked by sweetcalm and neuropenthe.

"Sit."

She looked up at me for the first time and was momentarily startled. Origin designed and grew our bodies with mathematical proportions, height, strength, and symmetry to be alluring to the Earthlings, Venusians, and Martians who ruled the Primacy. Thus, we were gawked at wherever we went.

"Sit," I said again. She did.

"I'm sorry to bother you, Captain Dido, but I have nowhere else to turn. They say your kind can travel freely, that you fear no one. My husband Lomad Chase disappeared on Saturn. I thought maybe you'd been there?"

"Not recently." Hamilcar, one of the other six was in Saturn Section, but we were no longer close.

"Lomad works for Paladin," she continued, "But the last VIM listed nothing about him." Paladin was Paladin Conglomerate, a largely Earthling-Martian business venture.

"You mean nothing new?"

"Nothing at all. Before he was listed as missing but there was a VIM this morning that just said 'information unavailable.' I was hoping you could get news."

"What does he do for Paladin?"

"He's a miner. They were putting in a vortex lift, but they had fights with the local tribes. At least that's what Lome said in his last dispatch. I just want to know if he's alive."

"If he is a miner, Ondria, then you know he is surely dead. I wish I could tell you something else."

She began weeping. I still do not understand that expression of human sorrow, how a reflex originating in removing dust from the eyes evolved into an effusion of grief. But I have always found it strangely affecting. After some time Ondria Chase forced back her tears. "But if he was dead why wouldn't Paladin tell me? Why wouldn't they list him as dead or keep him listed as missing?"

"That is unusual."

"I spent my saved credits to infraphone Saturn Section this morning but they won't tell me anything. Paladin threatened my oxygen allotment if I ask further. I just need to know what happened to him."

"Why?"

"You don't understand. If you were one of us you would understand."

I doubted that she understood any better than I did. But it angered me that Paladin would refuse to give information. That was the way of this system. Venusians would refuse to give information if the asker failed in some minutiae of courtesy. Martians would refuse to give information if the asker were of a lower clade. But Earthlings refused out of a reflex obstinacy, as if information were private property.

Ondria Chase lifted a cheap, tarnished, crenelplate locket from her neck and opened it to reveal a holopix of an ordinary-looking Earthling. She showed it to me as if the face would prove the importance of finding him. But it was true that I didn't understand. Origin had made me female and a humanoid, but I was not fragile like Ondria Chase—at the mercy of so much confusion and sorrow and cruelty.

"Ondria, the last time I tried to help someone, she died." I'd almost died too. Had I been closer to the blast, the regenerative capacity Origin bioengineered into our bodies would not have saved me. As it was recovery still took twenty cycles.

"No, Captain," said Chase, "That's why I came to you. I have friends who were with you on Pallas. You almost saved everyone. They are grateful."

I don't understand gratitude for *failure*, but there is no arguing with Earthlings.

"I'll find out what I can."

2.

THE FOLLOWING CYCLE, the *Antigone* was laden and ready. I cast off, the jets easing from the docking arm. As the vessel came around, I opened the forward sails one quarter, the bulbous mesh of glowing plasma distending rapidly in the space currents.

The sloop moved slowly through the clearways disturbing a flock of space bats sunning themselves on an asteroid nearby. The flock rose and scattered in a few beats of their massive saurian wings.

I turned the gyrogrips left to bring the *Antigone* leeward, then drew back to lift the ship above the debris plane. She rose into the Ibn Majid Corona, and at the shift of a lever, the main sails opened, the great white scalloping lace bursting into full bloom like Venusian goabal trees. The *Antigone* surged, plasma fabric swelling at the fullness of the solar wind.

"Navmech. Set navigation for Paladin Station. Mimas. Saturn section."

"Navmech obeys. Destination PAC-MIS 1. ETA 1.7 Cycles."

But glancing from the bridge platform, over the railing into the middle deck below, I noticed the collage of images floating beside my berth. Holopix of the six of us when we were still together.

"Navmech, cancel previous command. Instead set course for Saturn itself. The ice rings. Calculate a location nearest Mimas moon in its current orbit."

"Navmech obeys."

Hamilcar always said he loved the ice rings. Maybe I'd run into him before seeing the Earthlings. At least give him warning I would be near.

On Vesta I'd picked up the most recent VIM, the Primacy's official mail, news, and propaganda. Mostly propaganda. We were supposed to scour the VIMs for information and include our findings in the packets we sent back to Origin. After so many decades I'd come to dread them. But now I eagerly slotted the datapin—a short comb-like bar of thermoset—into the infomech's receptor slot.

"Infomech. Collate newest Verified Information Packet and integrate into ship's library. Examine contents for new information on Paladin Conglomerate activities in Saturn Section. Put the details on the electrofiche."

"Infomech obeys."

Infomech whirred and rattled for some time, as I turned on the electrofiche.

"Item One. Paladin Conglomerate advertisement seeking investors for new filament extraction project."

The text glowed from the electrofiche screen. The usual boilerplate. Opportunity! Potential! Profits!

"What else?"

"Item Two. Legal filing with Primacy Arbitration Service."

I turned the electrofiche knob, skimming through the documents. Paladin was building a vortex lift through Saturn's biozone up to the rings. Too many parafoils had been damaged navigating the storms and vegetation. So Paladin purchased a route from the Saturnian tribes up through the islands—the suspended coagulated clumps of mud and detritus that formed where vantaroots crossed—swapping trade goods tribe by tribe, until Paladin came to a tribe—the Orska—who refused to bargain. Paladin accused the Orska of *illegal trade behavior*. The Primacy broadcast a 90-cycle call for comments and response before deciding the case. Of course, even if word reached the Orska, as a non-space-faring, illiterate tribe they would have no way to respond.

"What else?"

"Item Three. Agenda for upcoming Paladin Annual Owners Meeting."

The agenda listed "discussion of vortex lift route" and "hiring of special consultants." Since a vortex lift is a glorified hose, it doesn't have to run a straight course. Why would Paladin need the Orska's particular territory? Why wouldn't they simply reroute?

"Infomech. Who runs Paladin in Saturn Section?"

"Paladin's Sectional Leadership Facilitator, Saturn Section, identified as Jadd Conree."

"What's his personal information in the CPDM?"

"Comprehensive Personnel Data Matrix lists Jadd Conree as Earthling, divorced, two children, former Paladin facilitator Venus Section, current Paladin facilitator Saturn Section."

Paladin wouldn't transfer a facilitator from Venus to a boondocks posting like Saturn unless that facilitator were corrupt or incompetent or both.

"What's the CPDM have on Lomad Chase?"

Infomech whirred and churned for some time. Finally: "No information currently available."

"What do you mean no information currently available?"

"No information currently available," the emotionless voice repeated.

"All right. What information was previously available?"

"Previous to update J-33LBY, Comprehensive Personnel Data Matrix listed Lomad Chase as married, children deceased. Saturn Section domiciled, *missing presumed dead*."

I had never heard of someone's data being completely removed. And for a miner? No institution in the Primacy gave a Mirandan dungworm for the life of a miner. Why wouldn't Paladin simply list Chase as missing or dead?

"Who was responsible for update J-33LBY?"

"Unknown."

"Infomech, what authority would someone need for a J-33LBY update?"

"All J-strata updates require minimum security level 15, red key access."

"Who in Paladin's Saturn Section is listed with minimum security level 15, red key access?"

"Paladin's Sectional Leadership Facilitator, Saturn Section, Jadd Conree."

3.

I WAS FINISHING broth and tarzha in the galley when Navmech whistled. "Approaching Saturn Section. Approaching Saturn

Section..."

Up the short ladder to the bridge deck, the videoscope showed a distant pale disk with its telltale white transverse. On the port side we were passing Saturn's moon, Titan, a bustling hub of swarming ships.

Origin had implanted soma-beacons in each of the six of us, so soon Hamilcar would know I was near. There had a been entanglement between Hamilcar, myself, and Altinus. A *love triangle* as the Earthlings say or a *trigon of shame* as the Venusians call it. Hamilcar felt betrayed that I chose the less ethical male. I tried to explain that such things are not choices. I both dreaded and longed to see Hamilcar—all the tumid chemistry to which Origin had condemned us.

Tripping the cowling levers I drew back the armor plates from the ship's cupola. The full panorama of Saturn shone, vast and luminous, through the lucetine bow windows. For interplanetary travel the armor was necessary but I preferred an unobstructed view to pilot in close.

"Navmech release controls."

"Navmech obeys."

I raked the gyrogrips to pull in the starboard sails a bit, which brought the sloop one-quarter windward, and descended toward the rings. Soon I was racing across the curving, glistening ice ribbons. Fifty meters below a few plasma sleds skated on the translucent plane.

The *Antigone* crossed the ring gap, and sped across the inner rings. To starboard a barge shuttle was taking off from a hexagonal platform fixed to the rings by energy pontoons.

Another hexagonal platform six kilometers further on to port was covered by a large hangar, with a dozen parafoils coming and going. Beyond the lustrous edge of the final ring, Saturn's billowing clouds engulfed the horizon. I banked the sloop starboard and scouted along the inside of the rings.

There was still no sign of Hamilcar's beacon.

"Navmech. Identify location of Hamilcar."

"Navmech obeys."

A short pause of whirrs and mechanical stutters before the robotic voice returned: "Hamilcar not found."

He must be directly on the far side of the planet. I don't know where else the soma-beacon wouldn't penetrate.

A hailing frequency and an Earthling voice suddenly came over the intraphone. "This is PAC-MIS-1. Please identify yourself. This is PAC-MIS-1. Please identify yourself. Over."

I took in sail, rolled the ship far to port until I could see distant, tiny Mimas, one of Saturn's innermost moons. It emitted a red blinking light, which—with a few magnifications of the videoscope—became a homing tower next to a command station clutching the moon's surface. I retracted more sail and engaged the jets.

The voice returned. "Repeat. This is PAC-MIS-1. Please identify yourself. Over."

"This is the Sloop *Antigone* approaching to dock."

"Sloop *Antigone*. There's no entry in the manifests. Were you expected? Over."

"Negative."

"I'll need to get an authorization. Standby. Over."

To hurry them along I circled back and made another pass across the rings. This time moving beyond the two hexagonal platforms I found a third, a military emplacement with a battery of trebuchets, massive crane-like catapults, flanked by two ray cannons.

The voice from Mimas returned: "Sloop *Antigone*. Proceed to docking bay number 2. Is Captain Dido aboard? Over."

"This is Captain Dido."

"We'll have a delegation meet you on dock. Welcome to Mimas."

4.

Twenty clicks later I'd landed the ship on Mimas and was stepping out into the bay tunnel. I carried only a light satchel and no side arms. If they were peaceful there was no need for weapons; if they were warlike I'd rather be underestimated. The tunnel led into a large domed atrium, the walls adorned with a stylized ancient metal helmet—the Paladin logo—and 'Paladin Cong.' was printed below in the five official Primacy scripts.

Ahead a blue-skinned Venusian female waited for me backed by two Martian RPs—"Risk Preventers" as conglomerate mercenaries were called.

The RPs wore neck-to-toe pressure suits (with a few strategic armor plates, mostly for show), helmets with reflective visors, and standard-issue ray pistols: ST-64s, nicknamed "geypers" after their original manufacturer. ST-64s were light arms, but they brought up bad memories. The wounds I had been recovering from on Vesta came from a geyper. Retreating pirates on Pallas had left behind an ST-64 they'd secretly rigged to explode. An Earthling who was with me found it and fired it, triggering the blast that killed her and injured me.

"So this is the welcome party," I said.

As the RPs stood motionless the Venusian bowed her head. "Captain Dido, I am obligant Falia."

Falia wore the revealing clothing favored by Venusians—and demanded of obligants—so I could see the shade of blue on her neck and down her bare flanks pale and swirl at the sight of me, the famous Venusian blush. But Falia recovered her composure quickly as Venusians do.

"Captain, we are honored to welcome you to Mimas Station. Facil Conree sends regrets that he cannot welcome you himself. He is on his way now. Meanwhile he asked me to see to your comfort. Please."

Falia gestured and I followed with the RPs faling in behind me. So I was to be, if not exactly a prisoner, not a free guest either.

As we walked the length of the clear-domed atrium a pinnace passed overhead, its white garlands of sail retracting while tongues of blue flames whipped from the landing jets. Pinnaces aren't rigged for interplanetary travel and their hulls aren't large enough for cargo, yet the vessel had a Paladin logo. Wasteful, useless—the hallmarks of authority.

"I expect that's Conree now," I said.

"Yes," said Falia.

"That was quick. He must have a lot to hide or a lot to gain."

The blue of Falia's neck and flanks rippled in darker shades, as she quickened her pace. "Facil Conree asked me to get you situated. Please follow me so that we can get you situated."

I looked back at the RPs. Their fingers twitched toward their geypers. I could kill both before they could draw them. Instead I turned forward again.

"How long have you been employed here, Falia?"

"Two annos in Saturn section. Before that I was on Venus."

Origin sent us to observe these fragile beings, but we've become interwoven with them. To hate them is to deny our true situation. Altinus could not understand this. Hamilcar, for all his pity for them exceeding mine, for all this curiosity about them exceeding mine, could not either. I wondered again where he was.

I spoke to Falia again, this time in Venusian, "Tell me of these Orska about which I have heard."

Few non-Venusians master the language, and Falia's surprise registered as pale striations on her body. Then her blue darkened and she pointedly replied in Groupspeak. "We need to respect conglomerate policy about not discussing current mission complications."

"The Orska are a complication?"

"I would not say that."

"You just did."

Falia's blue turned darker still. I thought of the complex emotional vocabulary the Venusians deploy in their tonal glides, the types of affection and attraction, the types of loneliness. They have an untranslatable word for wanting not to be hated by a person whom one does not truly love. Maybe I agreed to help Ondria Chase as an excuse to see Hamilcar. The Martians would simply say that I'm *undetermined*.

We reached an open hatchway. "We have this stateroom ready for you, Captain, while we endeavor to prepare better accommodation. If only you had given us more notice."

If I'd given them more notice I'd have been met by Primacy grenadiers instead of conglomerate RPs, but I say nothing. Falia followed me in as the RPs waited in the hall.

The 'stateroom' was a minimal security chamber, the sort stations keep near their docks for quarantine or house arrest. They'd quickly added a vase of Titian meergelds, changing colors as they slowly twisted, and an automated nutrimote, a motorized tray piled with foods and beverages.

"We ask that you accept these complimentary gifts. There are delicious Siberian oranges and Jovian chanyo. Also at 0900 tomorrow we have scripture study in task room C off the blue atrium, and tomorrow at 1600 live holocast of music festival from Center City on Europa."

"I won't be here that long."

"In the storage slot next to the toilet facilities, we have provided a pleasuremote. It's programmable to six species..."

"That won't be necessary. Falia, have you ever seen one of the Saturnians?"

"Have I?"

I switched to Venusian again. "Orska or any of them, have you seen them?"

She replied in Groupspeak. "You mean alive?"

"Who says the mudjellies are alive?" came a voice from the hatch. "Captain Dido! This is the most exciting moment of my life. Really!"

A grinning corporateer strode in, wearing a blue frock coat of the style then popular, pinsonthread, with qalim weave. He extended his hand. "I'm Jadd Conree." I concentrated to memorize his iris pattern but he was wearing some sort of protective eye lenses.

He took my right hand in both of his and clasped it tightly as he turned to Falia. "Look at this creature! Look at her! I thought you veenies were gorgeous but this is perfection! Fellas," he shouted at the RPs waiting out in the hall, "Is this a body? Is this a face? So what brings you to Saturn, Captain? What can we do for you? What can I do for you?"

"You can release my hand."

Still grinning he let go. "You see that, Falia? That's a *woman!*" He pivoted back: "Has Falia been good? Have you had a drink? Let's have a drink. Can I fix you a drink?"

Conree was tall for an Earthling, nearly my height, well-featured, and healthier than the undercastes, but reeked of cologne. Perhaps *Dalton Bdolenton* or something equally fetid and expensive. His scent and his prurient leer had the effect of curdling his good looks, making him strangely repulsive.

"I don't want you to fix me a drink. I want to know about a missing miner."

"First let's have a drink. Isn't this a terrific spread? We have Lunar brandy, Callisto rum, Pallas whiskey—I heard you were just in the asteroid belt?"

"How did you hear that?"

"Falia, this is a smart dame. Please Captain Dido, I refuse to answer any question until you tell me what you like to drink. Please, please, please."

"Water."

"Tethys mineral water, Enceladas geyser water, handpicked Saturn ring water—?

"Your local Mimas water will do."

"Slice of Venusian sheerka fruit with it? They say it's an aphrodisiac."

"Just water."

"Splash of sweet-calm?"

"Just water."

"Neuropenthe?"

"Water."

"Falia, you heard the lady."

"I want to know about a miner named Lomad Chase..."

"Speaking of names, please call me Jadd. And as for giving out information, at Paladin we give out *profits*, we give out *opportunity*, we give out *potential*, but we do not give out *information*. And no, you can't go to Saturn. We have purchased exclusive access. But I'd be glad to show you our facilities on the ice rings tomorrow. I'm bringing a few investors for a tour. We'll call it a date."

"I already saw your facilities on the rings," I said calmly, "And I'll visit Saturn whenever I choose."

"On what? You can't pilot a sloop into the Saturnian biozone. Besides, we might have to confiscate your sloop to pay your docking fees."

"You will not confiscate my ship."

"That might sound exorbitant, but you should've checked the docking price before you showed up unannounced. We can charge you anything. But maybe—maybe—you and I can work something out."

"You will not confiscate my ship."

"Dido's right about that," came another voice. Familiar but shocking. "I don't recommend trying to take anything from Dido without permission."

And there was Altinus. Altinus, stepping through the hatch like a dagger into my heart. I hadn't seen him in a hundred cycles and there he was, beautiful and deadly.

I could barely breathe. "Altinus?"

"Hello Di," he said smiling, "I've missed you."

He towered over the other humanoids around us in size and power, two-and-a-half meters tall, broad-chested, handsome, the strongest and most agile of us six, an insolent coil of promise and mutiny.

"Altinus, what are you doing here?"

"Sorry I was late to greet you, my love. I was making sure these fools took proper care of your ship."

"Where is *your* ship? Where is your soma-beacon? Why

didn't I sense you?"

I noticed his neck had a tiny gouge in it in. He'd removed his beacon. Even as arrogant, as rebellious, as impulsive as he was, how could he have dared to remove his beacon?

"Dido," he calmly answered, "There's many things we need to talk about."

Conree clapped his hands in ecstasy. "Commander, you told me that you knew each other but you didn't tell me you *knew* each other! You two were a couple?! Falia, can you believe this?! Falia frowned more, the blue of her flanks a roiling storm.

"*Commander?*" I looked from Conree to Altinus for an explanation. "What are you a *commander* of?"

"My love, you've always laughed at how they call us captain simply because we pilot ships. So I made it real and raised the rank. I have an official imprimatur of marquee from the Primacy."

"We gave him a commission as consultant," said Conree. "It's official."

"Hard work pays off," joked Altinus.

"I need to rest," I said weakly.

"Sure. Sure," said Conree. "But we're dragging you out of here in a couple hours. Repast and then a party for the investors. You came at a perfect time. I'll send Falia. Or should Falia stay?"

"I need to rest," I repeated.

Altinus lingered as the others stepped out. "It is good to see you, Di. I know this is a lot to take in but I'm glad you came. We have so much to discuss. I'll see you this evening."

He left and the spiral hatch rolled shut. I walked around the circumference of the room with my fingertips brushing the bulkhead, finding the location of the gazers. Then I flipped the interphone switch next to the door.

"Yes, Captain?" came a voice.

"Tell Conree or *Commander* Altinus or whomever you need to tell, that I don't like being monitored. Turn off the gazers or I'll destroy them and this stateroom with them."

I waited a few clicks. When I put my fingertips against the bulkhead again the micropulses were gone. They'd turned them off. At least for now.

5.

AT 1700 HOURS Falia came to bring me to the meal. The same pair of RPs were waiting in the corridor. I had concealed two miniature, eight-legged micromotes—'spiders' in Earthling slang—one in my palm, one folded up into an earpiece.

As Falia turned ahead of us, I lagged and whispered to the RPs in Martian warcant, "It is a weariness when the heart wishes battle." A quote from one of their mess songs. The RPs stiffened their posture to ignore me, which gave me the chance to drop one spider. Quickly its spindly legs scampered to a dark corner to wait.

We passed through a pressure hatch from the narrow corridor into a larger windowed concourse. Through the clear lucetine behind us to the right my ship was visible about eighty meters away. Ahead to the right was the station's central atrium lit bright yellow and filled with a crowd. The layouts of cong stations are standardized (they're mass produced in segments and transported to sites), so I had a good mental map from previous travels, but I counted steps and approximated distances, and estimated where each concourse led.

Through the window bays to the left the tiny, dim sun was setting now, but the reflected glow of Saturn and her rings are the true illumination of Mimas. The pale white of ghosts, Hamilcar called them. But though he loved for more the rings and the moons, Hamilcar loved the biozone of Saturn with its vantaroots, hurricane winds, and muddy coagulant islands. The tribes lived in the caves of the island where once a great civilization rose and fell. When we last met Hamilcar shared some of his work. He had been slowly translating the ancient Saturnian glyphs carved on altars the tribes still revered but could no longer read.

"I'm sorry that Conree is disrespectful," I whispered to Falia in Venusian. "It is his shame not yours."

"I do not know what you mean," she answered. But for the first time she answered in Venusian.

Reaching the far end of the concourse, the pressure hatch to the atrium wheeled back. Conree and twenty others were waiting. He welcomed us in a gold, sanch-weave suit and his overpowering cologne. Music played in the background. There was a crowd: Venusian males and females in their scanty clothing, high-rank Martians with the manes adorned, Earthlings in their suits and dresses. Even a Jovian towering over the others. All gawked and waited in a semi-circle behind Conree for introductions to me.

"Look at this amazing creature!" bellowed Conree, "Altinus, how did all of you get so damn good looking?"

"Actually at birth we looked more like your cephalopods," said Altinus matter-of-factly, "But we were regrown this way to please and distract you."

"It's working."

Altinus took my hand and led me through the crowd as he whispered in our Origin language. "Disregard him, Dido."

"Tinus, why is your soma-beacon gone?"

"I removed it. You should remove yours."

"That breaks our vows."

"We all break vows, Di," he said pointedly.

I ignored the reference. "How could you accept a commission from Paladin?"

"Technically the commission is from the Primacy, but I suppose Paladin arranged it. Di, I had a run in with some Jovian Cossacks that left me in need of a ship. Paladin was in need of a consultant. Call it a fortuitous exchange."

The meal was offered in the Venusian style. Guests served themselves from nutrimotes, then sat at nearby groups of chairs and tables. The nutrimotes were piled with decorative arrays of meats, vegetables, fruits, and desserts over carved ice. Leftover scraps would then be sterilized and ground into the self-heating nutripacks given to common soldiers, miners, and others not invited to these parties. One tray included a bowl of pills. The pills, however, even leftover, wouldn't be shared with the undercastes.

Altinus casually took a plate and began putting food on it. And not just the simpler fare, the sliced meats and exotic desserts as well.

"You're eating that?"

"Didona, I've done all the things you fear: I've cooperated with Paladin, acted as their consultant, enjoyed their luxuries." He smiled conspiratorially, "I've even made love to Earthling females."

"No Venusians yet?"

"Not yet. Perhaps tonight."

"Where's Hamilcar?"

"I was hoping you could tell me. Try the food."

"There she is!" shouted Conree, worming his way to me carrying a tray heaped with food, followed by the curious mob. "Captain Dido, let me introduce our chief engineer, Bollan Khav. Oh, and this is Petrarch Nyuen, the Doge of Titan. Stlk Tjan our chief RP, and Admiral Grsh of the 5th Defense Armanda. They happen to be in the neighborhood."

The chief RP and the admiral were both Martians, the admiral of the higher clade as shown by the stripe patterns of their faces. It offends Martian courtesy to speak to the RP first as Conree had done. Not that I'm the paragon of courtesy.

"Admiral," I said, "I saw your trebuchets on the rings."

"No you did not," he laughed. "They don't exist."

"Admiral, it is a violation of the Primacy's First Contract to use nuclear canisters on primitive species." Though we both knew there was nothing in the First Contract that hadn't been violated routinely since its passage.

"Beautiful creature," the Admiral smiled, "You did not see trebuchets. We do not use trebuchets. And if in the future you fly anywhere near those non-existent trebuchets we will shoot you down."

"I hear you're going on the tour with us tomorrow," said Bollan Khav.

"Excuse me," I said. I pulled Altinus away from the others.

"What are you doing with these people, Tine?"

He placed a small box in the palm of my hand. "Open it." I lifted the lid. Inside was a clump of what looked like grass seeds, but as I tilted the container, the clump broke apart like dusty graphite.

"Filament."

"Yes Di, this is filament."

"Look, I came to find out about a miner named Lomad Chase. He knew the risks so there's no vendetta; just tell me he's dead and I'll leave you to whatever it is you're doing."

"We don't know if he's dead."

Conree sidled up. "You'd showed her the filament? Amazing, right? We're talking serious wealth, Captain. This stuff could power this station for a year."

"So does methane from Titan."

"But it takes a lot more methane. Just these filaments are potentially worth more than a tanker ship of methane. Hell, one of these filaments is potentially worth more than the tanker ship itself."

"If it's so profitable, why you can't you afford to reroute the lift away from the Orska?"

"Because of those stupid, filthy, lumbering slugs, every mudjelly tribe on Saturn is now in open rebellion, reneging on deals, sabotaging the lift, taking hostages, killing RPs...!"

"Taking hostages? So Lomad Chase is a hostage?"

There was a moment when he realized what he'd divulged. He sighed and put his hand on his hip.

"No, there aren't hostages, Captain, because there are no negotiations. The Orska have engaged in unfair trade behavior. And we're awaiting final authorization for military clearance."

I looked at Altinus. He looked away. I turned back to Conree. "So you're planning to *nuke* the Orska and your own hostages?"

"There are no hostages, Captain," said Conree through gritted teeth, "Because there are no negotiations."

I looked down at the filament in its tiny box. "Can I have one?"

"One what?" said Conree puzzled.

"One filament?"

Altinus smiled. "Sure."

I touched a fingertip to my tongue to wet it and carefully touched it a loose filament near a corner of the box. It stuck to my fingertip like an eyelash. I handed the box back to Altinus. Then I took Conree's open palm and with the nail of my thumb gently scraped the filament into it.

I leaned and whispered into Conree's ear. "That covers my docking fee."

Altinus laughed. I noticed across the room that Falia was watching the three of us. Her neck and bare flanks dappled in the blue of both hatred and jealousy. When she looked away I let my earpiece drop and unfold into its spider form. It crouched in the shadows beneath a chair to follow Conree tonight. The other that I'd dropped earlier would be also searching for him. One of the two should succeed.

"Now that that's settled, Facil Conree," I said, "I'll gladly come on the tour of the ice ring tomorrow. Also if you check the VIMs you might find my ship has been to the biozone of Saturn already. I'm returning to my stateroom now. Altinus will walk me back."

I headed toward the pressure hatch, Altinus following. As I passed Falia, I leaned in and said in Venusian. "I will not betray you."

6.

ALTINUS AND I were met in the concourse by two new RPs. They kept a wary distance behind us as we made our way back to my cell.

"What was that about with Falia," said Altinus as we watched.

"Perhaps we're becoming friends."

"Also, when was your ship ever in Saturn's biozone?"

"You don't know everything about me." I switch to Origin language. "Give me the coordinates to the Orska. I'll free the hostages."

He answered also in Origin. "We've tried to free the hostages. It was a bloodbath. We don't have exact coordinates and the biozone of Saturn is hard to get around."

"Give me whatever coordinates you have."

"How will you get down there? You can't fly your sloop in the biozone."

"Why are you helping Conree?"

"Conree is harmless. From a certain perspective I find him amusing."

"Falia doesn't seem to find him amusing."

"For one who has chastised me for taking a position among these beings, you seem awfully involved in your own right, Didona."

"How many hostages are there?"

"We don't know. Twenty-two miners originally. The temperature and gravity are like Earth's and the atmospheric pressure is only five times more, so the Earthlings might still be alive if they rigged up an oxygen system. Miners are good at that. But all the RPs were Martian."

"Five times Earth's atmospheric pressure is twenty times Mars'."

"Right. They'll be long dead. But as I said, we don't even know where they are. We never had an exact location, and the islands can shift a meter or more every cycle. There's high winds, almost no light, and no way to track anything with precision."

"Hamilcar knows the groups in the biozone and he's navigated it freely."

"Yes, but he's disappeared. I was hoping you would know where he was."

"You've seen him?"

"I have. Thanks to you he would not work with me."

"But his beacon..."

"He removed his beacon before I removed mine. But Di, he knew about the Orska. He said the Orska had some sort of altar with carved glyphs, and the glyphs might give the coordinates for other altars. Did he ever send you any of his notes about the translations?"

"Why, so you can bomb them too?"

Behind us the lights of the atrium were now flashing and swirling. Detectible reverberations could be felt through the flooring, reverberations of what must be deafening music.

"You're missing the party," I said.

"So are you, and I can have parties when I wish, but you, Dido, are alone. Flying about in your lonely ship. Taking notes on everything and dutifully sending packets back to Origin. Do you think they even read your notes?"

"That's beyond my control. I do my job."

We reached my stateroom and stopped. Altinus took my hand. The RPs stopped too, watching us warily from a distance.

"I'm sorry, Di. I don't want to bomb anyone. But sooner or later we both know the Primacy will wipe out the Saturnians as they've done every primitive group. Or maybe miraculously the Primacy will be overthrown by something else. And the something else will wipe out the Saturnians. And why do you care about the miners? They work for Paladin just as Conree does. These creatures are not like us, Di. Martians, Earthlings, Jovians..."

"These are our people now. We're stuck among them."

"We don't have to be stuck among them. You and I don't have to be. Remember what we were?"

Altinus pushed the button and the hatch to my stateroom unscrolled. He led me in.

"Dido, the filament is highly concentrated, high enough energy and low enough mass it could get a ship close to light speed. We could cross the galaxy. We could go home."

"What home, Tine? Even at light speed by the time we got home we would have been gone for millennia. What's there for us? And how would we live there in humanoid bodies?"

"We *could* rule in these bodies. Origin doesn't understand war, death, greed, hate—none of it. They don't have our strength, our speed—they don't regenerate. Or we could rule this system. Venus has a queen, and she is not your equal. The Jovian bands have their warlords, and they are not our equals. Think of Conree; think of all the weak, inept leaders of the Primacy. We could push them aside and take their place."

"Tine, I don't want to be a queen. I don't want to rule. What would that get us? Bigger trays of ridiculous food? Bigger staterooms? More expensive clothing? More of these lecherous, deceitful idiots flattering us every day?"

"We could give them real leadership."

"I've heard your ideas of leadership: dropping nukes on innocents, monopolizing a fuel that does not belong to us, overthrowing what feeble government these creatures have managed to erect..."

"I love you, Dido. I have always loved you and I will never truly love another, but trust me for once. Please. Trust me."

"You have not *always* loved me. Our love is a chemical state that had a beginning even if the functions of humanoid memory obscure it. What have you done with Hamilcar?"

"That's the problem, isn't it? You could never let him go because you're addicted to the pride you take in his sad passion for you."

"With Hamilcar, there was nothing to let go that I did not

let go. The problem for us was not, is not, Hamilcar. And I've brooded about this for a hundred cycles in my lonely ship. Our problem is that neither my love for you, nor your love for me, can ever reconcile you to the world we must live in. We're trapped here in this star system with these unfortunate beings. And we're not that different. Even we will not truly live forever. If we are not suffocated in space, or destroyed by a weapon, or executed by the Primacy, even then in a thousand years or two thousand, our regenerative powers will break down, our immune systems will collapse or our sensory systems will degenerate or our mental facilities will decay. *Even we will die.* So let us show compassion for those who do not get to live nearly as long. If you are still my friend, give me the approximate coordinates to the Orska, and save me a lot of trouble."

"Goodnight, Dido. You argue better than I do, but that doesn't make you right."

He turned abruptly and strode away. For the first time I wondered if Hamilcar was dead. I wondered if Altinus had killed him.

7.

ALTINUS WASN'T THERE in the morning when Falia and her Martian retinue appeared. Falia was wearing an IEVA, a light space suit. Apparently she was coming with us. Stepping out of the hatch I was able to retrieve both spiders from the shadows where they had returned to wait patiently for me as only machines can. As we walked Falia seemed pensive, either afraid for me or of me, I don't know which, but in the IEVA suit her color shifts were harder to read.

At docking station 3 the executive pinnace awaited with Conree inside. Conree and his cologne. He offered wine, neuropenthe, and himself. Falia bristled.

"I'm just kidding, Captain. Sit down. By the way, I checked the VIMs and your ship was never in the Saturn biozone."

"Sometimes people change the manifests," I answer. But my lie had accomplished its goal.

The pinnace's interior was extravagantly stylish with fixtures of platinum and Jupiter-wood, and at the helm a Jovian steerwight—a ridiculously-priced skill level for shuttling corporateers. Bollan Khav and Stlk Tjan were there, as were Falia and two other Venusians—probably two other obligants since Conree didn't introduce them—plus a half dozen others from the atrium previous night. Behind were two octads of Martian RPs, this time with TK-1 laser rifles. Conree, Khav, and Tjan all carried XT ray pistols on their hip belts.

"Facil Conree, are we going to war?" I nodded at all the weapons.

He laughed. "Call me, Jadd. We don't want potential investors to be frightened. Sometimes baby cyclobites get down under and feed on the plasma of the pontoons. Don't worry, we'll protect you."

He smirked to be sure that I knew this was a lie and the RPs were armed to kill me, if necessary, and that in his opinion I couldn't do anything about it.

The docking arm retracted and jets fired lifting the pinnace from the rumbling deck. The topside armor retracted to give the investors a breathtaking view through the lucetine sides and top. At the pilot's expert hand a single lateen netting of energy sail spread above, and we were caught rapidly in the solar eddies of the space tides.

"Does everyone remember Bollan Khav from last night? We sure saw a lot of him, ha ha ha! Bollan is going to tell us a bit about the whole installation. Bollan?"

"Thanks Jadd. Docking station 3 is receding below us. Of course, Mimas has four fully functional docking stations plus..."

Khav droned on about the amount of materials used to build the station, the size of the local transport fleet, the facilities on the ice rings, and so on. It made the short trip seem much longer. The pilot expertly tacked back and forth against the current until approaching the rings she engaged thruster jets.

The ship zigzagged across the rings, still tacking against the planetary motion. We passed the hexagonal platform I'd seen the previous cycle with its covered hangar receiving and dispatching parafoils. About six or seven kilometers further on—I was having difficulty estimating our speed—we approached the hexagonal platform edged by a tower. A few kilometers beyond, the trebuchets that allegedly didn't exist were clearly visible.

"Of course since the ice rings are not solid planes," continued Khav, "And since our platforms work by equipositive suspension, we cannot use single-set gravity plates. The gravity bleed would distort the particulants in the adjacent area of the ring. We need those particulants to hold their dispersal to maintain the pontoons, so our plasma sleds can function."

The pinnace descended onto the Paladin logo at the center of the landing pad. A walk tube extended from the adjacent tower. The tower was an Aelon H-3. I had been in the same model building on Deimos and knew it's general layout, though there it was on a moon not an energy pontoon.

"That's also why we have to keep facilities separated," continued Khav, "You'll see to port side—that's the right—six point four kilometers away, that's the facility where the parafoils unload from the surface. By the way we'll use localized gravity plates to disembark the ship."

We exited down the narrow walk tube with one RP octad leading and the other at the rear. An airlock led into the workroom of the tower. On the far side other short airlock tubes extended like spokes from the tower out to the ring surface. Between the airlock tubes Cargo doors faced outward and others faced inward to the landing platform. Although the gravity was on for our convenience (As Khav explained in great detail), the room was designed to work equally well in zero-g, with guiderails and open gangways accessing a command level above.

As Khav pointed out features I dropped a spider behind a pallet of nutripacks. I noticed that Conree was eyeing me suspiciously. I don't think he saw the spider, but I didn't want to take a chance. I approached him. "Jadd, is there a private room where you and I could talk?"

"A private room, Captain?"

"Call me Dido."

"You're not just trying to get my ray pistol. Because you know you won't."

"I promise I'm not trying to get your ray pistol, Jadd. But I would like to be in a private room with you. Alone."

"Sure."

He seemed momentarily confused, as if he were so used to being rejected that he couldn't remember what to do now. Or maybe for a fleeting instant he was worried about abandoning his job.

"I don't want to wait," I whispered.

That's all it took. Conree hurried us away from the group, and rushed us up a spiral staircase. I noticed Falia watching our departure. The staircase led to a suspended command floor with videoscopes, control panels, and banks of lucetine windows overlooking on one side the launchpad and on the other the ice rings where plasma sleds sped to and from the distant parafoil hangar.

Amid clicks and rattles and jargon the command floor was worked by two engineers and two technicians—according to their shoulder insignia—in helmetless IEVA suits. Three were Earthlings and one a Jovian. The Jovian was a relief since I would need an IEVA suit my own size. On a shelf above the control panels helmets were lined up for emergencies. The four seemed busy and competent, nodding at Conree, but otherwise continuing their work. They spoke into interphones, checked manifests on electofiche readers, adjusted videoscopes, typed cargo information into automech electrocards, and dictated into infomech transceivers.

Suddenly I smelled cologne and felt my skin crawl as an

arm slithered around my waist. Conree's arm. "How do you like the view, Dido?"

"I don't like it here. I don't like being seen. You said there was someplace private we could talk?"

"This way."

Conree led us to a hatch. I knew Aelon H-3s were manufactured with at least one private stateroom off the command level where facilitators could bunk while on site. Conree tapped in a code. The hatch spiraled open.

We stepped into a small stateroom, not luxurious but there was a berth and a desk with a control panel, including a videoscope, a holoboard, and an infomech interface. Security would be tight on Mimas base itself—the very fact that Conree wore iris protectors implied they were careful about infomech access—but here cargo had to move in and out quickly, so navigation coordinates had to be accessible. At least that's what I was counting on.

I felt Conree's pelvis press against me and his hands groping my front. I turned toward him trying not to show my revulsion.

"Wait Jadd, what is that smell?"

"What smell?"

"You have some sort of perfume."

"That's not perfume. It's cologne."

"Whatever it is, please go wash it off." I nodded toward the bathroom.

"It's *Dalton Bdolenton*. That's three hundred credits a bottle!"

"We can't do this unless you wash it off."

He started toward the bathroom, but paused to retrieve the ray pistol he'd set down on a side table to grope me. Smiling as if not to be fooled, he backed into the bathroom.

"Don't cool down while I'm gone."

"I will be equally as hot when you return as I am now."

Like all rooms designed for use in zero-g, when he entered the bathroom the door automatically closed and sealed.

I flipped intomech switches and turned the knob. The spider I had concealed, the one that had followed Conree last night to observe him using his interface on Mimas, crouched on top of the infomech's gazer facing me and broadcast a superimposed holopix of Conree onto my face, as two of its spindly appendages rapidly clicked the six-key code panel it had observed Conree use last night. The infomech's lights began to flash. The system here couldn't have voice recognition since changes in air pressure would affect sound too much and there were too many different users.

"Infomech. Bring up a searchable holomap of Saturn's surface."

"Infomech obeys."

Saturn appeared floating above the plate. My only guess was to start with the quadrant where Hamilcar had found glyphs. I began digging through the spectral image of clouds with movements of my hands—down three layers to the ceiling of the biozone—and there searching through countless floating islands connected by endless vantaroots, expanding, moving, memorizing as best I could. The sound of water stopped. I stepped over to the bathroom and gave the latch one strong downward kick, breaking the lock.

"Hey," said Conree from inside, "What was that?"

The door rattled. "Hey, the door is stuck."

I rush back to the holomap. Digging faster I suddenly found it. There in the Anton quadrant, Petrov subquadrant I found markings. Some sort of radioactive hash marks.

"Hey!" shouted Conree rattling and banging on the door.

"Infomech. What are these marks?"

"Forbidden area. Violent native activity. Do not fly."

"What ships have visited this area?"

The machine whirred and buzzed and began to recite the registration numbers of parafoils and RPs landers. A lot of vessels for an area theoretically off-limits. That was the area. I slipped a datapin in the slot.

"Infomech. Copy Petrov subquadrant map onto datapin."

"Infomech obeys."

The door burst open. Conree emerged pointing the ray pistol. "Step away from that! Altinus said I shouldn't trust you. You're trying to make a fool of me."

"You were a fool before we met, Conree."

"See, that's where you're wrong. You think the joke's on me, maybe the joke's on you. This way. Over here." He pointed toward the berth.

He was still a meter too far away to disarm. I stepped sideways toward the bed to draw his attention from the control panel. He could see the holomap, he knew what I was doing surely, but hopefully the thought of humiliating me would be enticing enough until the copy was complete.

"I'll show you who's the fool," he said through gritted teeth.

Suddenly the light in the room shifted. The spiral hatch had opened. A figure was standing in the room pointing a ray pistol at Conree.

"No, Jadd," said Falia.

The hatch closed behind her.

"Falia?" Conree stammered.

"Put down your gun, Jadd."

"Falia, if you harm me the authorities will have you executed."

"If she harms you," I said, "the authorities will assume it was me who did it."

He stared to me, his eyes flashing confusion, then terror, as he realized the truth of this. He opened his mouth to speak but the flash of Falia's raygun split the back of his skull in a bloody halo. He fell dead.

I took the datapin from the infomech as the spider raced up my arm to perch on my shoulder. Falia was kneeling over Conree's body.

I knelt beside her for a moment and gingerly took her pistol. "Tell them it was me. Pretend you were loyal and they'll free you." There was no other chance for her. She nodded.

Venusians do not weep but the blue of her face was pale and flowing downward like azury sand.

Opening the spiral hatch, I stepped out onto the command deck. They were scrambling. There must have been sensors to detect changes in heat, light, energy. One of the engineers had her own pistol aimed to fire but I fired faster. I wheel-kicked one the technicians, knocking him out too. Another was retreating into barracks, but the final one, the largest, came at me with a cargo rod. She was the Jovian, large and fierce, but for all her bravery she was no warrior. I blocked the rod, knocked it out of her grasp, hammered her with an elbow, and twisted her arm behind her as I held my pistol to her protothorax.

"Get out of that suit."

The Jovian obeyed. Meanwhile an alarm began shrieking in cadence, the facility's lighting shifted to red. The RPs began rattling up the spiral stairs.

I hummed in a supersonic vocal tone to summon the micromote concealed below. It exploded under the steps tangling the RPs in their own falling bodies.

The Jovian engineer was out of her IEVA suit. I pushed her over the railing. Meanwhile at the far end of the platform RPs were climbing up by a ladder. I tossed my last spider. It unspooled, hit the gangway running, and reached the helmet of the lead RP as he was clanging his awkward laser rifle over the top. The micromote exploded sending the RP reeling backward.

With my legs in the IEVA suit I fired a few shots toward stairs, keeping the next wave of RPs at bay.

As I pulled the suit over my arms, I threw the levers on the grav plates. Immediately several RPs flew upward, feet above head, tumbling toward the ceiling. I threw the levers again sending them to the ground. It would be faster to run with gravity on. I grabbed one of the helmets on the shelf above, vaulted over the rail and landed at a run well down the tower passage, dodging from cargo pallet to cargo pallet as ray blasts followed.

I dove into the first open airlock, and hit the emergency button. The airlock door clanged shut. I sealed my helmet and carefully checked the IEVA for tears. These were light space suits, the easiest to put on, but they had no defensive properties. Everything looked secure. I figured when I opened the outside hatch I would have about 12 clicks to reach the hangar platform six kilometers away and steal a parafoil before the military forces could fully scramble.

Now or never. I hit the exterior switch. It didn't open. Someone had gotten to a master locking sequence somewhere. Instantly, I pummeled the small rectangular panel with my pistol handle and pried it off. I'd have to rewire it before the RPs on the inside door could get to me by doing the same. As I tore two wires and cross-connected them, sparks flew, and the outer door unlocked and dislodged a few centimeters. I got my fingers around the edge and pulled as a fusillade of ray blasts showered the inside of the airlock. The opening door revealed a three-meter-wide gangway with a row of parked plasma sleds docked. Another sled was floating out on the ice ring plane with a driver astride it clutching the handlebars, and behind him a passenger with a laser rifle firing at me.

Behind me the inside door was starting to open. I took one long leaping step onto the gangway and jumped out into the ice ring itself, carried out and down into gaps between the ice chunks, but I grabbed hold of a small ice rock only two few meters across that was caught in the equipositive dispersal of the energy pontoon. As the rock started to move, I pushed off it to another and another. I was still beneath the plane of the gunman who could only shoot randomly downward, streaks of liquid light spearing through the ice particles around me. I made my way chunk by chunk back to the gangway's edge, clutching a sled from the underside and reaching a hand up to turn it on. Then I flipped up onto it, and sped out past the surprised pair.

They spun their sled and followed. Behind them I could

see more RPs emerge onto the gangway from the airlock and claim sleds of their own.

Suddenly, a huge blast annihilated part of the ring plane ahead. It was a disruptor bomb. I swerved and regrouped. Looking back the sleds following had no heavier weapons than laser rifles. Another blast appeared this time to my right. Definitely no laser rifle. Then I looked up in shock as a projectile arced high overhead. Even veering away at this distance, the explosion showered me with debris.

They were firing the trebuchets.

How could they have loaded and fired so quickly? Then it got worse. Ahead a gunboat slowly descended into my path, aiming its double pulse sakers. There would be no way to avoid the fusillade. I pressed the power switch and let the sled drop into the ring, as the gunboat lumbered above hurling pulse shafts through the space and ice chunks around me like raindrops into a lake. Before the plasma sled completely fell through the bottom of the ring, I reengaged the power, rose, pivoted and fired my pistol at the tiller-plate hinge of the gunboat's right aft jet nozzle. It didn't disable the gunboat but it sent it shuddering clumsily off course to the right.

But my trick allowed the RPs behind to close in. Instead of fleeing, I accelerated toward them, passing closely enough to yank the laser rifle from one unlucky RPs grips. He lost his balance, and fell down into the ring. Hopefully, he could grab an ice chunk. If not he would spin forever into space.

As I pivoted back toward the parafoil hangar still almost three kilometers away, my remaining pursuers were doing the same to block my way. Again I charged them, but as we closed I again cut power, dropped down, and popped up again behind them, taking out one with two rifle shots.

Now I spun and accelerated toward the distant parafoil hanger, still with three sleds in pursuit, but I had to veer off again as more exploding trebuchet projectiles blocked the direct path. Aiming backward, I shot the driver of one of the remaining sleds, but the rifleman straddling behind kept control somehow. Meanwhile far ahead another gunboat was approaching, and in the distance nearly a dozen sleds were closing in on me from all sides. The alarm hadn't brought reinforcements. They've been ready the whole time.

I tossed away the TK-1 rifle and bent down low behind the handlebars. There was scarcely a kilometer now to the hangar. I could still make it.

Then I felt a burning in my shoulder. The sled bumps. I've been hit. Sparks are bursting along the sled's plenum skirting. Suddenly the sled leaps from the plane of ice and I'm flipping end over end. I'm thrown from the sled. I'm spinning downward reaching desperately for something, anything but there's nothing to hold, nothing to grab, only ice pebbles pelting me, disorienting me. I feel the cold and realize the shoulder of my suit is torn. The visor of my helmet cracks, breaks open. I try to reorient myself. Think. The lack of air is not immediately a problem. I can go five clicks without air, and I can survive the cold and radiation for longer than that, but the lack of pressure will cause swelling that will soon affect my eyesight and cognition.

I am tumbling out below the ring now, spinning helplessly into space. The gunboats and sleds can't reach me. I'm safe here even from the trebuchets. But it is a bitter, hopeless safety. With no way to right my path or change directions, I will spin through space until I die and then gradually my body will drift into Saturn's orbit, tumbling into the atmosphere past the upper gas layer, into the biozone, and if it is not sliced apart by vines or dashed to pieces on a coagulate island, then it will pass through the floor of the biozone, into increasing temperature and pressure, until long before it reaches the surface I'll be incinerated in the hydrogen rain.

Over and over I see Saturn slide by my field of vision, then the rings, then space, then Saturn, then the rings...

But suddenly around me is energy mesh. I'm no longer flipping. I'm in a net. I'm being pulled toward a ship. The ship reminds me of the *Antigone*—my mythological goddess come to bear me to death. I want to see my death but I can't stay conscious. All turns black.

I'm inside a ship's airlock, the *Antigone's* airlock maybe. Black.

I am being held by someone, being lifted. Black.

Someone is leaning over me. It's Altinus.

8.

I REGAINED CONSCIOUSNESS in my berth on the *Antigone*. Altinus was suturing me with a hand-held medipract.

"Where are they?"

"Didona, sleep now. You're safe."

"You're selling me to them?"

"No Di."

"The nukes? My datapin!"

"No nukes for at least a few more cycles and your datapin made it. We're out past Phoebe moored to a centaur-class asteroid. They haven't followed and probably couldn't find us if they tried."

In a shallow pan beside Altinus were scraps of uniform caked in dried blood.

"You rescued me?"

He smiled devilishly, "How could I pass up a chance to pilot your ship? Now hold still, this is going to hurt tremendously."

"It hurts already."

"Shhhh. I need to concentrate. Healing the sick isn't my strong point."

But Altinus's hands were sure and steady. He cut away the bloody uniform bit by bit, sutured the wounds, as I drifted in the semi-consciousness of anesthetic. "Bath time," he said as he lifted me and gently placed me in a tub of warm water.

"I could have done it myself," I mumbled.

"No, you couldn't have."

"No, I couldn't have."

He brought me a cup of warm broth and held it to my lips, his left hand cradling my head. As he washed me afterwards I drifted into sleep.

I awoke back in my berth. The sheets had been changed. I don't know how long I slept but I felt stronger. My body's regenerative capacity was repairing me. The sutures were scars, and bruises were gone. Altinus was sitting in the galley area across the middle deck, staring out the starboard window. I remembered the time when we were together. I would wake in the night and watch him sleep, my heart full with hope and tenderness. How many days now had he been watching me, caring for me? He turned to me. He'd surely heard the rustling of the sheets or the change in my breathing, but I felt he'd been drawn by the sheer intensity of my longing.

"Come," I whispered.

"You should rest."

"Tine, come."

He crossed and sat on the edge of bed. I raised up and pulled him to me and we kissed, and I pulled him and we struggled to get his clothes off. And we were together as we had been long ago. Afterwards I drifted into a half-sleep, and he with me, and then we awoke and started again, and then lay contented for a time.

"Tine, do you ever wonder why Origin gave us an ability to have sex when we can't reproduce?"

"They don't want us to reproduce; if we could reproduce we could mix and change; they want us always like this. Right now, I wouldn't mind us always like this."

"But why then give us sexuality at all?"

"Maybe Origin made a mistake."

"Tine, what do you remember about Origin?"

"Not much. We were only infants."

"I remember a folk tune from my childhood..." I hummed a bit of it, the tune a simple ratio up and down, but with a haunting quality. "I don't remember the words but something beloved dying. Have you ever heard it?"

"It sounds familiar."

"But we couldn't have had a song like that in our childhood, could we? The vocal quality, the rhythm, it's inherently a humanoid song. This body has rewritten my memories to fit what I've become. Maybe even created the memories. I try to remember what we looked like and I don't know if it's a memory or imagination."

"I like what we look like now. And maybe, Didona, my love, you've become a maker of songs. What's wrong with that?"

"Why did you rescue me?"

"I couldn't let them kill you. Do you trust me now?"

"Where is Hamilcar?"

His face clouded. "I don't know."

"You want me to trust you. Tell the truth."

"He disappeared. I saw him. I was trying to get him to talk to me about the Saturnians. To negotiate with them realistically. He knew their language much better than anything in the Primacy's infobanks. But he refused and I didn't see him again and I couldn't find him. Like I said, he removed his beacon before I removed mine. Hamilcar's like you; you both love dividing whole groups of people into good and bad. Saturnians, good. Earthlings, bad. Origin, good. Paladin, bad."

"Paladin did just try to kill me."

"Do you think the Saturnians won't?"

"They're fighting for their territory,"

"Paladin is fighting for what Paladin claims is Paladin's territory."

"What are you fighting for, Tine?"

"Right now, my love, I'm fighting for you."

We started to kiss again, but I pulled away.

"I should tell you. Conree is dead. I know he was your friend."

Altinus nodded thoughtfully, then laughed. "He wasn't my friend. He amused me. But speaking of friends and of Hamilcar, you never answered my question about the glyphs?"

"Why do you care about the glyphs? They're ancient. The Saturnians can't even read them."

"If Conree's dead that means there won't be nukes till a new facilitator is posted. We have time to go down there, rescue the hostages, and get the filament without anyone getting hurt."

"The glyphs won't help. Hamilcar says they're a syllabary of a language ancestral to the current dialects. An advanced civilization that built the altars and probably terraced most of the islands throughout the biozone."

"Did he ever share any of his translations with you?"

I slipped on a Venusian sovya, and went to dig Hamilcar's last dispatch from the rack locker next to my berth. There were canisters of printed rotographs and some sketches on replisheets. We spread them on the bed. I pulled aside the more personal writing, which Altinus noticed, but for once didn't seem jealous of. Maybe he was changing.

One of a replisheets was a diagram of glyphs, three rows of four with notes below:

A1. Famous/Famed/Known [formal epithet]
A2. Making/Made/Having Made/Having Been Made.
A3. Power/Able/Strong (plural?).
A4. Collection/Gathering/Bundle.
B. [Second row = Long count=4000]
C. [Third row = Names]

I pointed to the glyph. "Hamilcar said the first glyph in almost every inscription just meant something like, 'Behold.' The second row, the long count is a dating system, but he hadn't decoded it. How did they tell time in a civilization with no visible sky?" I pointed to the third row. "Hamilcar thought the names were place names and rulers or leaders of some kind."

"This is the same altar he told me about. I'm sure the 'making power' or 'power making' refers to filament. Advanced civilizations must have power sources and they have to store them in central locations, just as primitive agricultural civilizations use granaries. Hamilcar said the Orska literally sing to this altar, it's magic to them. Again, that would make sense for filament. The proper names could be place names, describing where the stores of filament are kept. Look Di, if we can't get the filament, that's fine. We're going to save the hostages."

"We?"

"If any hostages are still alive, but if we find filament, and the Orska are willing to give it to us, we'd be saving a lot of lives in the future. I don't expect that will happen. But in the unlikely event they'll give us filament, Dido, I want you to agree to take it."

"Sure. So you're going with me?"

"Can't keep me away."

Looking at the drawings I couldn't believe Altinus hadn't seen anything similar. "Tine, doesn't Paladin have anyone trying to decipher the glyphs?"

"They don't even have anyone who can speak Saturnian."

"Then how did they negotiate the route for the vortex lift?"

Altinus let out a half laugh at my naivety. Of course, Paladin hadn't even bothered to negotiate. They just left trade goods and came back with rayguns. At best they probably tried to string a few phrases together with a transmech.

"Didn't you at least have Hamilcar's earliest word lists, back when we were still sharing packets?"

"I had it in my ship, but there were some Cossacks, you see."

"We'll need to communicate. We can rig up a transmech with the Primacy glossary for Saturnian, plus Hamilcar's early word lists. By the way how did you manage to lose your ship?"

"It's a long story filled with greed, violence, and deceit. Mostly mine. But you'll be happy to know that I failed utterly."

"Tine, I never want you to fail."

"One other failure you should know about, Di. I led one of the RP expeditions, so the Orska probably know me."

"Then we'll have to keep you in the background. You're not the only one with a black mark. Even if we rescue the hostages, Paladin will never forgive me for Conree's death."

"You forget. I'm officially a Commander now. We just need an infomech hub. I can make all sorts of mistakes go away."

"Can you?"

"The Primacy loves its own."

"Also before we take this ship down there, I'm going to blow up those trebuchets."

Altinus laughed. "Making military attacks go away is a bit more difficult, but maybe we spotted some Jovian Cossacks in a stolen sloop attacking in the vicinity. I know a group of Cossacks who deserve a comeuppance."

He grinned at his scheme and I felt joy in this, then disappointment in his immorality, his forgotten vows. But I had broken vows too.

"Altinus, I'm sorry I didn't keep my promises to you."

"Maybe we'll do a better job this time."

That isn't what I meant, but I let it go. Altinus and I fell into one another's arms again, and afterwards Altinus, exhausted from nursing me for cycle after cycle, fell into a deep sleep. I watched him sleeping, adored him like a primitive god or an innocent child.

We are all territory of one another but how differently we treat our claims. I rose, pulled the sovya back on, and wandered the deck of the Antigone—my territory. Next to the airlock was the equipment storage. Respirators and equipment belts were laid out in the bin. And of course, the ever-present geypers. I felt a sickness seeing them.

I thought of that Martian RP tumbling off his sled helplessly into space, like garbage jettisoned from a spaceship's bilge. "War-Brother, may you taste the black calda with the gods," I recited in Martian war-cant. I pictured Stlk Tjan, his commander, bowing before the graven images on his behalf. But I knew many of the newer commanders no longer did this, feeling it undignified, unprofessional, superstitious.

Commander. The room was spinning. *Commander.* The air was gone. I felt rising panic.

As I rushed up the ladder to the bridge, I felt the helplessness that Altinus always brought to me. The sense of being trapped, out-maneuvered. As I flipped the switches on the Infomech, as the diodes and meters came to life, I pictured menace in Altinus's eyes, cold calculation, betrayal. I felt rage.

"Infomech," I said quietly, "What is the standard security clearance of a Primacy commander appointed by a text of marquee?"

The machine whirred for a click. "The Primacy rank of Commander is security level 15. Red key access."

9.

WHILE ALTINUS SLEPT I prepared. I had a lot of modifications I wanted to make to the ship and to our equipment. I slotted the stolen datapin maps into the navmech, prepared equipment for the landing—transmech, ailerons, modified spectrum goggles, modified oxygen masks, and of course the ST-64 rayguns—and worked on the ship's gazers and other sensory equipment. I wished we had Hamilcar's more recent language research, but I used what we had. As I took a break from the bridge to work on the word lists, I prepared broth and tarzha for Altinus in the galley.

Later when I heard him wake below, I climbed down the cockpit ladder. "There's broth and tarzha on the galley table."

"You're disappointing me," he said.

"By fixing broth and tarzha?"

"By getting dressed."

"We have Orska to visit. Meet me on the bridge."

I wanted to confront him, to prove that he changed Lomad Chase's status, but I knew Altinus was too adept a liar. He'd convince me that Conree had done it. Beside I needed help getting to the Orska.

Unmooring from the asteroid, the *Antigone* extended sails.

Saturn was little more than a dot on the videoscope but soon the ship was past the orbits of Phoebe and Iapetus and Altinus joined me on the bridge.

"Mind if I help?" He strapped into the copilot chair and hit switches to pull up the holomap on the console in front of him. "I assume we're going into the top cloud layer and then finding some of the smaller, less visible flues and vents in case they follow."

"That was my plan."

The flues were vertical openings in the cloud layers; vents ran horizontally. The major flues and vents had some stability—at least over a period of 20-30 cycles—so Paladin parafoils would be using them to navigate to and from the biozone. Parafoils were no military threat to the *Antigone*—we had vastly better weaponry and armor—but they would call down more powerful allies above.

"By the way, Di, what happens if we find the Orska?"

"We negotiate."

"What makes you think you can successfully negotiate?"

"Because I'm willing to give them everything they want."

We passed Titan. Saturn had grown to a plate-like disk on the videoscope.

"We'll take out the trebuchets first."

"The battery has two ray cannons for defense."

"I saw them."

"But if we come in under the rings and flip topside, they won't be on alert."

"You want to handle the sakers?"

"Aye aye, Captain." Altinus unlatched the weapons rig and armed the two smooth-bore sakers. He was always a better shot than I.

I dropped the ship low. The orbits of Dione, Tethys, Enceladus, and Mimas passed above us. I banked the sloop sharply, spun it, and evened keel in a path along the south "under side" of the rings. If Paladin detected us they would have no time to scramble any sort of intercept.

"Approaching," said Altinus. "60 kilometers, 40 kilometers, 20, 10, 5, 2..."

Engaging thrusters and pulling starboard sails all the way in, I spun the sloop, and slipped her over the ring edge, now crossing on the north side at an angle, the trebuchet installation rising ahead.

"A little more altitude," said Altinus.

As the ship rose forty meters, a handful of figures were scrambling to the cannons. But too late. Altinus' calm, rapid thumb clicks released a shower of pulse beams—paving a swath of destruction across the near-side ray cannon, the trebuchets, the far side ray cannon, before we were racing over the ice ring again. We brought the ship around for another pass that obliterated the trebuchets and pitched the energy pontoons into a twisted slant that sank until it fell out of the ring plane, spiraling off into empty space as ice pieces scattered like dust.

"War-Brother, may you taste the black calda," I whispered for the Martians.

"That was fun," said Altinus resetting the gunnery controls.

Of course, my guilt helped the dead no more than Altinus' callousness.

Rapidly extending sail, everything the ship had, we raced for Saturn's clouds before we could be intercepted.

"Navmech. Put up the drop site."

"Navmech obeys."

A target-shaped holomark appeared on videoscope.

"Anyone following, Tine?"

"Negative. We're clear. Drop location in 5, 4, 3, 2..."

I reeled in sail, engaged the jet thrusters, and sank into the roiling clouds. When we were safely hidden, with the energy mesh tightly drawn, I pulled the bow up and reversed polarity on the ship's grav plates. It wouldn't be enough to stop the ship from falling, but it would soften the descent.

"There should be a vent to the northeast, then a flue down through the next cloud layer."

Visibility was getting poorer so we engaged echolocation and thermolocation, supported by cloud density measures and algorithmic modeling. The primary videoscope now showed what we saw beyond the bow, but with grid lines of the echolocation imposed and coloration to mark thermal.

"Flue coming up in 5, 4, 3, 2..."

The flue opened downward through the brown-yellow clouds of ammonia hydrosulfide. The light was dimming further outside but the temperature was rising and the increase in atmospheric pressure meant the ship was burning less fuel in its descent.

Flue by vent by flue we worked downward until the sloop was skirting the top of Saturn's third major cloud layer, the white water clouds—white when the dim brownish light was corrected by the spectrometer.

"We're at the ceiling of the biozone," said Altinus.

That was the easy part. We directed all lights forward as we crept over the billowing mantle lit by lightning flashes below.

"Watch it here, Di, sometimes the vantaroots can grow pretty close to the top of the clouds."

"I think I'll know if..." I started to say, when there was a scraping sound on the ship's hull.

I lifted the ship a few meters. Altinus smirked.

"Flue ahead in about twenty clicks at current speed," said Altinus checking the holomap on his console. "It'll take us sixty meters. Bring her 30 degrees starboard at the bottom."

At a wisp-swirling hole in the denser bed of surrounding cloud cover, I yawed the sloop 24 degees starboard, knowing the centrifugal force would take me the full thirty.

"Here we go."

I cut the jets and let the ship freefall, keeping level with a few bursts of the landing jets.

We sank below the thicker ceiling clouds into the biozone, a darkness of churning mist, pelting rain, and hurricane storms. Each lightning flash revealed crisscrossed vantaroots stretched in all directions, the thick hirsute coils hung with smaller nets of roots. Vantaroots (a thousand species) were colonies of mycelial organisms, the basic foodstuff of Saturn. They siphoned liquid hydrogen from the layer of clouds below the biozone, up through arteries into bulbous sacks that kept the roots afloat. Meanwhile their abscissions, and the wastes of the creatures who feasted on them, formed the soil-like substance—the 'mud'—of the suspended islands wherever the vantaroots crossed, their undersides draping growth like scraggily beards.

Altinus read the gauges: "Temperature outside 10°C. Pressure 2 atmospheres."

"I'm cutting off echolocution." The grid lines were useless, disrupted by the nearly-constant thunder, atmospheric pressure shifts, and the tendency of the island coagulant to absorb sound.

"Temperature 18°C. Pressure 3 atmospheres. Wind gusting at 57kps," said Altinus.

"Time to test my videoscope modification."

I had rigged a system that would take holopix of the exterior during lightning flashes and put them on the scope. Lightning was frequent enough to create a type of stop-motion imaging. At least I hoped so. I'd gotten the idea from Hamilcar; he'd told me that's how the Saturnians' eyes worked.

"23° 4 atmospheres."

I hit the switch and the next flash of lightning left a still image of the islands and vantaroots around us. After another flash of lightning the image skipped forward. After another flash another image. It wouldn't allow quick movement but I wasn't in any hurry.

"That's amazing," said Altinus. "It works."

"Good thing too, because I rigged our specs to do the same."

"Hash mark ahead."

Paladin's parafoils navigated by the flues and vents, then veer off at radioactive hash marks left by the miners.

"Gust coming!" said Altinus.

Suddenly the sloop was slammed sideways by a gale. We tore through a tangled of vantaroots and plowed against a floating island twenty meters across.

"Damage to the forward starboard thruster," reported Altinus. "Wind increasing. 80, 95, 120... You've got to get the ship behind something."

"Or faced directly into it," I gunned the jets and brought the ship around so the bow aimed at the oncoming wind. That would buy us a little time. "Tine, find me a windbreak!"

"It looks like there's a vent to the South. The clouds aren't filling it, so there must be islands acting as breakers."

"Hang on!" I heaved the rudder to yaw the ship. The sloop spun as the wind caught it, and I hit the thruster, propelling us through more tangles until we made it to the vent and protection from the gale.

"Where are we?"

"Working on it," said Tine. He was dead reckoning by the gyroscope, charts, estimated direction and speed. He frowned. "I don't think we're near the Orska yet."

Suddenly, there was a clang, and the *Antigone* lurched as a simultaneous boom shook the underside. Cracks raced across the bow's outer layer of lucetine.

"Then again I could be wrong," said Altinus as he yanked the levers to close the bow armor.

"There!" I pointed to the videoscope. The most recent lightning capture showed some shapes on the island above us.

Another explosion shook the hull. The ship lurched and fell.

"The starboard aft jet is gone," Altinus reported.

"I saw a flat nodule to the right in the last image capture."
"Are you sure?"
"No."

I hit the thrusters and aimed blindly. We slammed into something skidding until snarling in a jumble of vines. Another explosion glanced off the hull.

"What are they shooting?"

"Crude rockets from sections of hollowed-out vantaroot. Ammonia nitrate for the charge and the fuel. Only accurate to twenty meters at best, but they've taken out plenty of our parafoils in close ambush." He switched on the controls to raise the maxim laser turret. "I'll take care of them soon enough."

"No. Aim near them but don't hit them. We need someone to follow."

Altinus shook his head. "Aye aye, Captain."

He deftly fired a few bursts into the mud near where the attacks came and the next lightning capture showed the shadows in flight.

"Nice shooting. Let's suit up."

10.

WE GRABBED SPECTRUM goggles, helmets (with noise cancellation and intraphone), the aileron packs, geypers, and oxygen masks with a vocal-modifier added. I'd memorized a few Saturnian words, and a switch on the mask would amplify the bass and add a piercing treble to emulate Saturnian speech.

Altinus started to take the TK-1 laser rifle from the rack.

"Pistols only," I said.

"Then let's at least take a few grenades to clear out tunnels."

"I'm sure your Martian RPs had grenades, and it didn't help them."

"We aren't Martians."

"The geypers are enough to fight back if we need to fight

back, and maybe with any luck the Orska have never seen them; maybe they'll assume we're carrying mining tools. Besides, heavy equipment won't work with the ailerons."

"What if we need more firepower?"

"Why would we need more firepower? As you said, we aren't Martians."

I pressed the button on the airlock door. Even with the noise cancellation of our helmets, the wind and thunder hit like a wall.

We adjusted transmission frequency until we could hear one another, and switched our spectrum goggles to the still pix system I'd rigged up, a version of what we'd used on the ship. We stepped down on to the island ground, wet and squishy with tiny writhing vermipods.

"I see why they call it mud."

The googles were hard to get used to, the freeze-framed images constantly appearing with each lightning flash, lingering, and then fading into gaudy shapes of the superimposed temperature patterns. Around us, even protected from the main wind, secondary currents sent sheets of water droplets across the roots, mud, and our suits. In the high atmospheric pressure it felt sluggish to move, not heavy, just *thick*.

We found tentacle marks on the ground and capillaries rubbed off the vantaroot stems where the tentacles had grasped. The Orska inflate hydrogen sacs along their thorax to move slowly up and down through the three-dimensional landscape like Venusian gorbors or Earthling sloths. But for us to go up, we'd have to climb. Altinus and I made our way up a steep embankment using a thin vantaroot as a rope. From there we opened the ailerons—our wing packs—waited for the next holopic, and leapt out into the void, flying blindly toward a destination picked by the still image. We landed on the next island thirty meters away and ten meters lower down.

"Wow Di, they worked!" came Altinus' voice over the interphone.

"You say that like you're surprised."

Here were more tracks and possible burn marks from one of the missiles.

Altinus checked his hand-held navmech. "I'm guessing their nest is that way."

"They've seen you, so you stay back. I'll go on ahead and if we lose communication or if I disappear, you can track me by my soma-beacon."

"Di, you can't negotiate with everyone. If you give every group what they want they'll ask for more."

"That's true of the Primacy, and Paladin, and you. And probably me. But primitive tribes, the undercastes, the weak, you can give them what they want. Maybe someday they'll ask for more, but for a while they'll be fine."

"Dido, at least ask about the filament."

"So it's not me you're worried about."

"If we don't deal with the filament, then sooner or later Paladin will be back."

I put a gloved hand against his in a parting gesture, and wondered if my suspicions were wrong. Maybe my suspicions had always been wrong.

"Tine, don't come too soon, and don't come in blasting. But don't forget me either."

"You're not forgettable, Dido."

I put a gloved hand against his in a parting gesture. I wondered if my suspicions were wrong. Maybe my suspicions had always been wrong.

I turned east, and took the aileron's palm size control bars in each hand, rolling them once so the cords wrapped around my wrists.

After the still holopic from the next lightning flash, I took a bearing on an island 30 meters away. The wind had lulled, I pressed the buttons on the end of each bar, and—feeling the lift and as the opening aileron wings met the thick air—I jumped.

Even the lulled wind were a force for the ailerons. I was

pulled far more to the right than I expected. I dipped the left hand bar forward and twisted my body to dip and sweep back on course. Still the gusts were so strong I had to squeeze the aileron's control bars as hard as I could to keep the outer pinions clipped.

I landed on the next island, quickly retracting the wings to keep them from catching in the jumble of roots. I climbed to another ledge, stepped out on a thick vantaroot, and launched again. This time I was able to bank the wings enough to climb on the air currents and land directly on a thick sagging vantaroot like windraven on a Martian branch. But it made me overconfident, and as I launched again, a stronger gust suddenly spun me off course. Retracting the coverts to keep them from tearing, I slammed through curtains of smaller dangling vantaroots until I grabbed a thick root and wrapped around it. There was a voice in the intraphone.

"You all right? My tracker shows you veering off abruptly."

"I was caught by a crosswind. I might be here for a few clicks till it slows."

"Take your time. We're just here to rescue some hostages."

"Also I can't locate my original target destination."

"See? I told you you couldn't do this alone. Head in any direction and I'll use your soma-beacon to figure out which way you're oriented."

"Copy that."

I started to crawl along the vantaroot in the direction of the largest island I could make out through the sheets of rolling mist and rain. A large anguillipod was creeping toward me, hoping I was food. At the next lightning flash I kicked the poor creature off the root.

"Sorry lady."

When the wind ebbed I was still twenty meters from an island, so I rose up, opened the ailerons, and leapt, landing on a canopy of vantaroots and scrub above a muddy ravine.

"How are you doing?" came Altinus' voice.

I retracted the aileron wings and worked my way down from root to root as the lightning flashes revealed each foothold.

"I think I'm getting the hang of this."

Suddenly, my boots hit a spot of slick exolichen. I tumbled, grabbing roots that came loose in my gloves, and land on my back in thick mud. A moment passes. I try to roll over. Then the mud gives way and I'm sliding off a precipice, a terrifying instant of open air—maybe falling off the island altogether—until I pitch with a splattering thud into more mud. The next lightning flash shows sheer sides of a ravine broken by pitch-black caves and shadows.

Tentacles grab me from all directions.

"Is everything okay?" said Altinus on the intraphone.

The tentacles were lifting me. "Bvostjshun!" I called out, but it was inaudible with my mask, plus the wind and thunder. If I could just reach the vocalizer switch. I struggled to free my wrists.

"Bvostjshun!" I yelled again futilely.

In the next lightning flash I saw that the left side aileron grip was dangling loose but still wrapped around my wrist. I turned my hand to pull it into my palm and pushed the button. The wing extended as I rolled sideways, which dislodged enough of the creatures' grasp that I reached the switch.

"BVOSTJSHUN. MEYTIAMYU ZSHRAYKOST!" came a booming voice, my voice now converted into a slow reverberating rumble of consonants and high pitched squealing vowels.

The next lightning flash showed the Saturnians. They were floating hulks three meters tall, of tentacles, feelers, stalks, and rows of bulbous hydrogen sacs. Hamilcar had written that he found them beautiful, but they were monsters. They were momentarily as motionless in life as in the still image. They weren't moving because they had comprehended me. They didn't let go, but they slackened their grip.

"Bvostjshun. Meytiamyu Zshraykost," I repeated. "Bvostjshun. Bvostjshun." *Peace, peace.*

I wanted to say something more complicated but I knew so little of the language. I held out my palms to show no weapons, and motioned that I wanted to take off the straps of the aileron pack. They released me as I did. I motioned to say I wanted to reach for something in my carrypack—the transmech—but there was a sudden commotion among the lumbering creatures, a sonic interchange, and then they lifted me and dragged me into a tunnel. I didn't fight them, but moved with them in the pitch black.

"Altinus, I've made contact. Heading into tunnels."

"Di, where..." but then Altinus' voice cut out, signals blocked by the mud. He could get a general direction with my beacon, then hopefully find my discarded aileron pack outside (assuming the Orska had left it), but how would he find the right tunnel? The soma-beacons weren't that precise.

The Orska pulled me around a corner. With no lightning the spectrum goggles no longer worked. I pulled them off. There was dim light ahead.

We turned another corner and pushed through a sort of hanging curtain of vines, and we were in a large cave, about fifteen meters square and nearly ten meters high. In the center was an altar, built of coagulant blocks with some sort of polished top. The front had carved glyphs. Around the walls were other tunnel openings, and in a hollowed-out corner was a huddle of humanoids clustered around a dim fosfolamp.

Tentacles pulled my respirator off before I could stop them, and I realized the air was breathable. The Orska released me and backed away. For the first time I saw them not in a still picture but as moving beings—oozing wet heaps of primordial formlessness, topped by jerking eye stalks, hung with quivering, and serpentine coils—as the gill-like filigree along their sides shuddered in waves to rake water droplets toward their respiratory slots.

"Are you friends with Hamilcar?" said one of the emaciated humanoids.

I carefully backed away from the Orska toward the humanoids and knelt. "I am."

The humanoids were Earthlings, filthy, weak, sickly wretches huddled around the fosfolamp, some leaning on one arm, a few trying to sit up, most lying unconscious. Next to them was a pile of packs and gear, and I wondered that the Orska had let them keep so many sources of improvised war or escape.

"I am Dido. Is Lomad Chase here?"

"I'm Lomad," said a skeletal figure on an improvised cot, the face in Ondria's holopic now covered in blotchy fungus.

I approached Chase and pulled out a mediprac. "Your wife sent me. Is this all that's left?"

"This is it."

"How have you survived? This chamber..."

"They let us rig up some oxygen rebreathers."

"You can talk to them?" The mediprac scan registered dysentery, malnourishment, and infection by anaerobic fungus.

One of the Orska emitted a loud noise, pointed tentacles at a machine in the center of the room. "VRISHKEEMEE-DO," the creature bellowed.

"That means they want to speak to us. Hamilcar left this..."

"You knew Hamilcar?"

"He tried to get us home."

The machine was a boosted transmech, something like I had tried to rig up, but better, with a speaker, a dish receptor, and an infomote—all wired to a battery. I turned on the switch.

"VRISHJYAMJO," said the Orska again.

"Ugly Word Asker?" said the machine.

"VRISHJYAMJO," repeated the Orska.

"Ugly Word Asker?"

"That's their name for Hamilcar," said Lomad.

I directed my voice toward the receptor. "Hamilcar? The

one like me? He was my friend but I don't know where he is. I'm looking for him."

The machine simultaneously translated this in the gurgling, thudding bass and the whistling high-pitched squeals. The Orska's eye stalks flitted from one another to me.

"I've come to ask if you will release these Earthlings and how we could compensate you for such a generous act."

"Release us?" sputtered one of the miners. "The Orska are the ones who saved us!"

"Saved you from what?"

"It's true," said Lomad. "Paladin won't let us leave. When our parafoil broke down, the Orska gave us shelter. When Paladin sent RPs to kill us, the Orska protected us."

"Paladin sent the RPs to kill you?"

Outside there was a blast, and a high-pitched shriek. A few of the Orska inside whistled as if in answer, and the beasts began to shuffle out through the tunnels.

"That was their emergency sound," said Lomad. "You must have brought more RPs."

"No. I couldn't have."

A blast shook a tunnel and three Orska backed from it, returning to us in the cave. Behind them Altinus emerged, aiming a laser rifle. He pointed the barrel toward a far wall and the Orska backed into that area.

"Altinus, what are you doing?"

Seeing us without masks, he removed his.

"Dido, my love, I couldn't stay away." He glanced at the wretched creatures huddled beside me. "Earthlings still alive? What is it with your species? As long as you live you mope and complain about your condition, but as soon as you're offered a perfectly good opportunity to die, you hold out till you're walking skeletons."

"Tine, don't do this."

"Di, I'm so glad I brought you to Saturn. You managed what seven octads of Martian RPs couldn't, you got me to this cave. And now, please take out your geyper slowly and toss it this way."

I drew the ST-64 from my holster and pitched it to his feet. He slung the laser carbine over his shoulder, and picked up my pistol in his right hand and drew his own pistol with his left.

"Why Tine?"

"Di, what you refuse to understand is that all these creatures—the Earthlings, the Orska—they're doomed to be what they are, but we are not. It's wrong to be less than we can be. Would you refuse to read because these wretches cannot read? Would you stop piloting your ship, because not everyone has a ship to fly? The filament belongs to us because we can use it and they can't, my dearest Didona. There's enough for us to build a ship and power it home."

"The Orska don't have any more filament," pleaded one of the Earthlings.

"It's true," said Lomad. "There's nothing left. We tried to tell you that."

"Oh there's plenty left," said Tine. "It says so right there." He pointed a pistol at the glyphs. Then he noticed the modified transmech. "Is that Hamilcar's translation device?"

Altinus shouted toward the machine's receptor. "Where is the filament?"

The machine let out bass and squeals but stopped.

"They don't have that word," whispered Lomad to me.

"Stop Tine, they don't know anything about the filament."

The Orska milled and quivered.

"What do these glyphs say?" demanded Altinus. "What's inside?"

The machine thudded and squealed.

One Orska tentatively approached the machine. The creature rumbled and shrieked as the machine translated: "We cannot speak the carved words. The sacred altar is for song."

"Tine, stop this!" I begged.

Lomad was trying to catch my attention. He lifted his ragged blanket to show a concealed mining knife. I reached sideways and took it from him.

"I don't want to hear your song," said Altinus. He stepped up to the altar as the Orska retreated. "We'll see what's inside."

While Altinus faced the altar, his back to me, I lunged, bringing the knife around in an arc. But Altinus was always the strongest and quickest of us six. He sidestepped so the knife only grazed his arm, causing him to drop one of the pistols. I tumbled and rolled until I was in a crouch, and looking up, found Altinus aiming the other ST-64 at me.

"Tine, no!" I pleaded. "Don't do it!"

In that moment, which I had feared and expected for so long, I thought I would see menace in his eyes, cold calculation, proof this was what he'd always planned. But instead there was only rage, as if he were the one betrayed, as if he were the one who was trapped.

He pulled the trigger and the pistol detonated, as I had wired it to do the night before.

The explosion shook the inside of the cavern, knocking us over and showering us with mud and debris. Shards of something ripped into my arms and right shoulder. A cloud of wet dust filled the air and only sulkingly dissipated as the Orska erupted in deafening howls of grief.

They rushed to their altar screeching and shaking. The altar top was broken and shards of the glyph-carved front were strewn across the cave floor. The Orska lifted out torn canisters of stitched vantaroot bark that disintegrated as they were lifted, scattering ripped and rotting bundles of plant-fiber sheets. It was writing. Bundles of shredded writing.

"PASHRAI-KUTRI! PASHRAI!" wailed the Orska, *our songs, our songs*.

Altinus' neck was broken, his skull was split, his face bloody pulp. Injuries far beyond hope of regeneration. I crawled to him. Altinus, thief of my heart. My friend, my joy, my love, my ruin.

11.

ALMOST ALL THE miners survived the explosion. Eventually I was able to get them into the *Antigone* and free.

The Orska in the cave also survived. Since they were on the far side of the altar they had been largely protected, but three had been killed by Altinus outside before he entered the cave. As I was tending to the miners and moving them back to the *Antigone*, I helped the Orska collect and reseal their songs. They didn't want to read them or learn them. They didn't even want to see if the songs in the rolls resembled what they now sang. They only wanted to pack the scraps back into the canisters, and rebuild their altar.

Paladin Conglomerate, at their next Owners Meeting, voted to suspend filament mining. It hadn't been profitable. For the time being they blamed Altinus for the destruction of the trebuchets and the battle on the ice ring—or at least pretended to blame him. But Admiral Grsh of the 5th Defense Armada didn't work for Paladin, and that would have long-term consequences.

The obligant Falia was freed and settled on Europa. We didn't cross paths for a decade but I heard during that time she *lived well*, as the Venusians say.

When I went to Vesta to give Ondria Chase the news, I helplessly watched the effusion of her Earthling tears. She wept and then she thanked me. She thanked me even after I had told her how Lomad Chase had died—died in an explosion I caused.

In my final packet to Origin, I reported Altinus' death and Hamilcar's disappearance, and my growing conflict with the Primacy. And I reported that I would no longer send packets. Then I dug out my soma-beacon and jettisoned it into space.

ACKNOWLEDGEMENTS

We woud like to give a special thanks to the following people for their support as backers through Kickstarter: Y. H. Lee, Christopher Kugler, Duane Warnecke, Dibmoa, Robert Rogers, Thomas Bull, Kim Alek, John Oakes, Thelma McKain McCoy, Jason Kim, Alexander Waletzky, Christopher Jebo, Brian Holder, Ben Wilson, Jess Terrell, Frank Gawryla, Dwight VanTol, David Landry, I. Arreaza, Gryphon Joseph Manion Ludwig, Paul Summitt, Heather Carlson, Briar Chappell, Daniel Tiggemann, Sergi Morraja, Michael Liam Kalk, David Trammel with GreenWizards.com, David Prudhomme, Mary Joe March, Howard Blakeslee, Buddy Hernandez, J. McCallum, Robert C. Flipse, Aaron Emmel, Martin Bernstein, Michael Edwards Carroll, James W. Murphy, Becky Weisgerber, Lorraine Phipps, Aaron Mayfield, Matt Staples, David Geary, Luis Manuel Sánchez García, Cato Vandrare, Mark James Featherston, James Lucas, John Walters, Fred Johnson, Gary K. Woolerton, P. Robert Thorson, Rob Rhodes, A. Miller, Geoff Stratton, Justin Wohlford, Greg Vose, Chris Newell, Darin DuMez, Ruth Duggan, Jonathan Michielsen, Erin Himrod, Lee Turner, Allyssa Andersen, Joel B. Jones, Fenric Cayne, Don Crossman, Clint Spivey, John Mead, Roxanne, Jilian Harker, Matthew Beckham, Wulf Johnson, Mark Newman, Morgan Leigh, Luis Roncayolo, David Paul Guzmán, Sweetkala, Jack Thompson, Marcu Knoesen, Simon Sheridan, Nick Williams, Vincent Kindfuller, Lynne Everett, Mary Gibson, Garrett L. Ward, Riccardo Heald, Darin Thacker, Luke Haugh, Adrián Merino, Matt Forsyth, Gavran, Dagmar Baumann, Benjamin Widmer, Richard Rossi, Dan Mollo, Jen Witsoe, Dylan Tobias Jeninga, SFBook, Grazyna Olszewska, Benjamin Bl., Cliff Allred, Neil Campbell, Tanner Blotter, Daniel Grobani, Tommy Chu, Christiane Henningsen, Eric Priehs, Stephen Ballentine, Robert Gibson, Dr. Greg Conners, John and Sara Jeninga, David England, Kirby Miller, Nikki Jeske, Tim Jordan, William A. Gwaltney Jr, Fred Herman, Jennifer Bullock, Erica Tate, Dark Regions Press, Melanie Mize, Will Oberton, Taylor Bourgeois, Jennifer Priester, Tiago Rodrigues Antao, Ryan Schaap, Jason Miller, Darren Tang, Ydnar Ragenip, Leah Webber, Troy Jones III, Eric Hendrickson, E.M. Middel, Jeffrey Pikul, George Berry, Beverly Clendenen, Elfego Baca, Jaap van Poelgeest, Joy Vernon, Ane-Marte Mortensen, Javier Cruz, Luca De Marini, Tim Stroup, Richard Sands, G.E. Canterbury, Joshua Marin, Emma Varney, Simon Renton, Cat Wyatt, Matt Trepal, Carl Wiseman, Mordaine Barimen, Adam Selby-Martin, Anthony C. Valterra, JP Frantz, Cody Black, August Johnson, Richard Ohnemus, Natasha Liff, Dan "Grimmund" Long, Michael Gonzales, Hiram G Wells, Nick Crounse, Mog, David Zurek, Violet Bertelsen, Ivan Donati, Coop Janitor - NJ0C, Brett Carlson, James Williams, Jean-Pierre Ardoguein, Tuhina Roy, Jeff Hotchkiss, Kabrina Kershaw, Clifton Roberts, Nicolas Huillard, Nicolas Aguirre, Moe Lane, Seung Kang, Howard J. Bampton, T. Vierling, Betsy L., Anya Johanna Jeninga, Joseph Guzzo, Jay Ronald Cumming, Eric Richetti, Jake B., Robert Manio, Russell J. Handelman, Stephen Murrell, Jim Kosmicki, Todd Ellner, Michael Hirtzy, Peter C. Aitken, Jay L. Skiles, Joshua Palmatier, Mike Vermilye, Drew, Heidgerken, Alexander Pyles, Steve Tanner, Lucas Devine, David Greshel, Michael D'Auben, Sean Sherman, Franklin Kuzenski, A Bear, Lukáš

V. F. Novák, Scott Mahoney, Rebecca Moore, Mohammed Azamel, Richard Johnson, Mark Carter, Jeramy Goble, Tom Alaerts, Dennis D'Ooghe, Ryan A. Fleming, Corey T., Edward Delman, Rick Dwyer, Dr. Anita Harlow, Caryn Ojemann, and many others.

Made in the USA
Middletown, DE
06 December 2018